Touches
The
Stars

Lynn Sholes

TOUCHES THE STARS

Published by Stone Creek Books
Oakland Park, Florida

Originally published by Diamond Books

Cover art by Joe Moore

ISBN-13: 978-0692535424
ISBN-10: 069253542X

DEDICATION

This book is dedicated to "Charlie" and all of her people— the People who came before.

———

NOTE: "Charlie" is a skeleton of a young Tequesta Indian maiden who lived about 2,000 years ago. Evidence suggests that she was approximately 17 years old when she died. It is not hard to look at her and see her as she must have been—petite and lovely. "Charlie" was born with spina bifida, a defective closure of the vertebral column, but she had been tenderly cared for. She was well nourished, and there is no evidence of any disease. She was not left to die at birth, nor was she later sent out into the wilderness as a freak and outcast. And when the spirits called her, she was buried with her people, not isolated from the others.

When the Europeans arrived in southern Florida, the Tequestas were described as savages, but "Charlie" shows us that they were a people with a sense of caring and devotion. Their hearts could ache, and their eyes could smile.

ACKNOWLEDGMENTS

I would like to acknowledge and thank some of those who helped make this book possible.

First I would like to express my gratitude to Gypsy Graves for all her expertise and patience.

Juan Leyva, who is perhaps a Tequesta descendant, was gracious enough to relay the lore of his heritage, including herbal remedies practiced by his family and ancestors.

There are many in my other life, my non-writing life, who have given their support in so many ways, and I am grateful to all of them.

Prologue

THE PROPHETIC OLD WOMAN winced as she eased herself down onto the soft, rich, black soil. The ancient-looking gray eyes, set deep within the furrows and folds of her ashen skin, beheld her world. Sweeping the land, as far as she could see, was the brown and green blanket of saw grass, billowing, bending, dancing to the rhythm of the nearly constant southeasterly breeze. The ancient sedge, its edges set with fine saw teeth, so thick and fierce, grew out of the sweet water. It thrust its folded spikes up toward the light and its ropy mat of roots down into the water. Season after season it sprang up in the wetland, living and dying in it, laying down its decaying tissue, actually creating the muck on which it thrived.

Charcoal clouds smeared the sky, bruising the gold and purple blaze of the horizon. If she had had the energy of her youth, she would have let go, floated out of her body, and brushed the grain of the tips of the flowing sedge. She would have let it bristle beneath her thumb, rubbing across it like the stiff hair on the hide of a deer. But she was old and tired. Besides, she was here for another reason.

"Sit, and I will tell you how it came to be," she said, moving a windblown wisp of silver hair from her face.

The child reached out for her hand, feeling the cold, dry, bony fingers of her grandmother.

Shafts of pewter light, rain in the distance, channeled

down from the bloated clouds. A dull rumble echoed far to the west.

"It is time for you to know it all." The old woman's voice coasted on the wind, seeming to be one with it, and the child wasn't even sure she had seen her lips move. Speckles of darting, dark forms flew above them. The black birds, dark shadows, sailed on the same wind. Their shoulders were hunched and their wings spread, coming in to roost for the night, disappearing into the mass of saw-grass prairie.

The child sat by the old woman, joining her in the panorama. She, too, looked to the horizon. The long whips of the saw grass haggled with the breeze, twisting and tangling with one another. At the plum and crimson line of the horizon the sedge softened with the blur of distance. A few splotches of green, other hammocks like the one on which they lived, dotted the glaze of the saw grass. The only other things that broke the monotony were the canoe trails.

Grandmother swept her hand in front of her, indicating the wondrous view. "We are all a part of the same Great Spirit."

"Yes," the young one answered respectfully. "I understand."

"And do you understand that some of us were given a special gift—a gift that passes through our blood? It comes to you through me—through my father."

The child was silent.

The old woman took the child's hand in hers. "I am old, and the time is coming when the spirits will call me to the Other Side."

The child squeezed Grandmother's hand and wrinkled her nose as she held back her tears. She was afraid to speak, because her voice would quaver.

"Do not be afraid. First I will tell you how I learned of the Gift. No one knew that I had the Gift. Not even me."

"But you must have known," the child countered.

"I thought there was something wrong with me, and so did the rest of the People. At first they thought it was evil—that I was evil. I hated the Gift. I did not want it."

"Could they not plainly see that you were special?"

The woman smiled at her grandchild. "It was not so simple."

The two sat quietly for a few moments before the grandmother spoke again.

"Who do you think will take my place when I walk the Other Side? Who will care for the People? Who do you think has been given the Gift by the spirits?"

The child turned quizzically toward her. "Who?"

Grandmother lightly touched the child's cheek. "Close your eyes, little one. Clear everything from your mind."

The girl stared at her grandmother, hoping to deny what was unraveling inside her.

The old woman nodded, telling the child to go ahead and close her eyes. "Tell me when you are ready."

The small one looked straight ahead before closing her eyes. She sat quietly, waiting for the rumbling of the distant thunder, the fluttering of wings, the droning of the insects, and the lashing of the saw grass to fade. Slowly she emptied her thoughts, closing them out, breathing more deeply.

"I am ready, Grandmother," she finally answered softly, suspecting that after this day her whole life would change.

Chapter One

MIAKKA HAD BEEN WITH THIS MAN. She knew that he had been with many women. That was his prerogative as shaman. She studied his face for a moment.

Atula looked at Miakka, a young, small-boned woman. She knelt in front of him, her black hair spilling across her breasts, forming black satiny rivers that hid so much of her.

If he had been just a man, maybe he would have chosen her, Miakka thought. She looked away. The thought was not worth entertaining. He was more than a man. He was the shaman, and she was no more than a woman—a woman swollen with the fruit of his seed. As it should be.

"I am worried," she said. "The child I carry ..." she began, almost whispering, bowing her head in respect.

Being so close to him flooded her with sensations she barely understood. His clear, dark, gentle eyes reached deep inside her. How was she going to tell him? Though she had rehearsed it so many times, now that she knelt before him her mind tangled and her tongue became uncooperative. She would have to put aside those feelings, ignore the effect he had on her. She needed his help to resolve the horrendous thing that was happening to her and to the child that grew inside her.

"What is it that has you so concerned?" he asked, noticing the small tremors in her hands.

Miakka's head was bowed in respect and embarrassment. If she allowed herself to look at him, to realize how close she was to this man, she would lose sight of her mission. She would find herself too snared in emotion.

He could take no one woman to live at his hearth, no wife. Another presence could interfere in his communication with the spirits. Unlike the other men, he could have any woman anytime, and if she conceived she would hold an honored place with the People. The other men had to seek their women from other clans, other villages, not from the small circle of women who were members of their own clan. That was forbidden. The shaman sowed his seed in the bellies of the women of his village. It kept his line pure. One male child would be trained by the father, Atula, and that child would become the next shaman. Which male child it might be, only Atula would know for sure. There would be signs.

Miakka knew she would never live at Atula's hearth. There would never be any more between them than what had already been.

"Do you remember the night that you danced with me at the fire and how you led me to your platform? From that night a child has grown from your seed and has been nourished by my body."

"That is something good," he replied, reassuring her that she had not done anything wrong in the eyes of the clan. She need not worry. He would confirm that the child was his.

It should be something good, she thought. She could have lived with the clan's curiosity, but no one questioned that Atula was the father.

"You do not understand. No one doubts that the child is yours. I am not shunned for conceiving a child without a husband."

"Tell me, then, what has made you come to me? What makes your brow furrow with worry and your lovely mouth turn down?"

As he spoke, his voice conjured up memories of the tender things he had said to her that night. Miakka felt her face flush.

"Do you remember how long ago I was with you?" she asked, unsure that she was beginning correctly. "The night you danced with me and ... and do you see me now?"

Atula did indeed remember. It was after the return of the men from the Big Water. It was a jubilant occasion, and all had had their fill of cassite, an herbal decoction that was a mild intoxicant. From across the central fire he had seen her as she stepped to the music. The reflection of the fire made her hair look like strands of liquid black, charred coals melting down her soft back. Her head was tilted, the moonlight illuminating her delicate face. She swayed to the music like the night air when stirred by a gentle wind.

Atula had slowly walked across the crest of the hardwood hammock that so courageously rose up out of the wetland. He had passed the fire to be closer to her, to watch her as she lost herself in the music. As he had drawn closer, her dance awakened the need in him.

He was also being watched. Amakollee eased herself behind him and then to his side. She smiled as she danced in front of him, tossing her head provocatively and moistening her lips with her tongue. It was a gesture not missed by Atula, but it was Miakka who had his attention.

Atula had smiled kindly at Amakollee, continuing his

walk, but she placed herself squarely in front of him and waited for a response. When he gave none, she took it that he had not read her gestures. She would not touch the shaman without invitation, but she did position herself closer.

"Have you enjoyed the evening?" he asked, hoping to distract her intentions. Through the throng and firelight he could still see Miakka moving alone to the music.

"The celebration is not over, Atula. The night has just begun."

Atula did not want to insult Amakollee. He had been with her before—a few times. The events had produced no child, and Amakollee still belonged to no man. It would not be long before her age would discourage a mate. Without a mate she would become a burden to the clan. Clans often sent young men to other villages to find mates, but no man from any other village had shown an interest in her. She had passed her youth, and the humiliation was becoming intolerable. Atula was her only hope. If she could conceive his child, the clan would always take care of her.

"I am hungry for only one thing this evening. Sleep. Too much cassite has made me groggy," he told her, trying to be polite.

Amakollee flushed with humiliation. Even though he had tried to be congenial, he was not interested. She had made a fool of herself. Her lips paled from their natural deep hue to a pasty gray. The color drained from her face and she was certain he could also see her humiliation. Quietly she moved away from him, realizing that he hardly noticed. She backed away from the fire and the rest of her people and ducked into the brush. When clear of the village and its sounds, she fell to the earth, pounded it with her fists, and screamed into the darkness.

Miakka abandoned herself to the music as Atula approached her. Her movements were fluid and graceful. Earlier, from a distance, she had watched him as she always did, but her shyness made her fear that he might notice. The cassite warmed her insides and unfettered her mind enough that she drifted with the fantasy.

The cassite had not dulled his senses, but it had compromised his inhibitions. He was not usually so forward and blunt. Atula stepped in front of her, began to move his body in unison with hers, and then reached out to wrap his palm and fingers gently around the nape of her neck.

Miakka opened her eyes and slowed her dance, startled by the company.

Though the shadows fell across his face, the sharp lines of his straight nose and strong jaw formed a clean silhouette.

"I like the way you dance. Do not stop," he said.

Miakka's small feet barely moved, losing the rhythm. She tensed. Her knees felt weak, and a shudder ran through her as his hand slid down her neck, brushing the hollow of her throat and then moving out to rest on her shoulder.

"Please continue," he said, pulling her a little closer. He could smell her now, sweet with the light fragrance of flower petals that she had steeped in water and then splashed on her body.

She knew immediately where this encounter would lead. She could not have refused him even if she had wanted to. He was the shaman, and he had the right to any woman of the tribe.

Atula took her to his platform. She was a maiden, never taken by a man before. She trembled at his touch, and her naïveté aroused him. In the protection of his platform, he brushed back her long black hair, exposing her body to his full view, his eyes reflecting his pleasure in what he saw. Slowly he slid her moss skirt to the floor, holding her hand as she stepped out of it. She had responded innocently to him, waiting for each touch, surprised at each new sensation. But she had not let out a sound, nor had she shuddered with the gift of joining. He regretted that. The ceremonial tea must have made him too impatient

Afterward he lay next to her, breathing deeply while she lay curled up next to him in a tiny frightened ball. He had not been proud of himself. Obviously she was a maiden; he had known that, and he had not taken time with her. Then, as he chastised himself, the cassite made him sleep.

Since then she had seen him at a distance a few times, and always she turned timidly away from him. Now she knelt in front of him, her belly enlarged with his child.

Atula's face showed his confusion. The evening he had spent with her had not been that long ago. Again it was about time for the men to make the journey to the Big Water, as they did on each fourth full moon. It was important that the moon be full. Without the light, they could lose sight of the other canoes and their direction. His memory must be tricking him, he thought. Either it had been longer ago that he had been with her or she had not been a maiden at all. Look at how large she was with the child.

Miakka looked up, registering his perplexed expression. Tenderly she touched her abdomen. "It is so large, and I have so much time left to go."

Atula continued to stare in amazement. "Does it cause you pain?"

"No, I would not call it pain. But it is so difficult for

me to do many things. I fear that the child grows too fast, that I cannot carry it, that I cannot bring it into the world, that the child is deformed." Miakka looked down, hiding her face so that he could not see that at any moment she might cry.

Atula read her emotions well. He heard the anguish and fear in her voice and saw it in her eyes as she spoke. He got to his knees and rubbed the palms of his sensitive hands across her tight-skinned belly and then put his ear to it. With his head bent across her, Miakka leaned down to breathe in deeply, taking in the scent of his hair and skin. She closed her eyes, imagining his head turning, his lips falling on her stomach and then slowly making their way up to her lips, leaving a damp trail of warmth along the way.

"Miakka, I cannot feel or hear anything. It is too early. This is just a large child and your first. It will be a fine boy," he said, hoping to relieve her anxiety. "A strong boy that you will be proud of."

"I hope to honor you," she said softly, with worry still in her voice.

The honor was his, he thought. "Go then and speak with Wagahi. She has watched over many women during this time and has aided in the births. Certainly she will reassure you."

Miakka rose slowly to her feet, taking his strong hand for balance. As soon as she stood, she tried to release his hand, but he held it a moment longer.

"May I come again if Wagahi does not satisfy me?" she asked, breaking the heavy silence. "Will you consult the spirits?"

"If Wagahi does not relieve you satisfactorily, come to me again. But I predict only a strong, healthy hunter, a child of whom you will be proud," he said, letting go of her hand.

Though she was truly large for her time, she still moved with grace. After the child was born, perhaps he would entertain the thoughts she always stirred in him.

As she disappeared, he sucked in a heavy breath. She was right. There was something different about this pregnancy. Maybe Wagahi would provide the answer. He would ask for her opinion after Miakka had seen her.

It troubled him that neither his hands nor his ear had perceived the normal vibrations, sensations. And indeed the child was large. Grotesquely large. He would not wait. In the private shelter of his platform, he would consult the spirits.

In the still darkness he searched his pouches for the stems, leaves, and bits of plant that would purify him so that he might call the spirits to bring him a vision. Alone by his fire, he ground the ingredients in his wooden mortar, poured the mixture into a ceramic bowl with a small amount of water, and then suspended it above the coals. As the tea came to a boil, he sprinkled the yellow flower petals of a spiny herb, the prickly pear, atop it. Gently he stirred the potion with a stick, taking care not to bruise the delicate brew. His father had taught him the motion of the wrist, the measurements of the herbs. He had gone with him on his first flight into the spirit world. Atula missed him.

Soon after sipping the elixir he began to feel its warmth spread through his arteries. His nostrils flared as he concentrated, letting an abundance of clean but warm, humid air into his lungs. There was a tingling at every hair shaft on his body. The fragmented long bones of an extinct beast, handed down from father to gifted son, lay at his side. He began with a barely audible humming noise, and as his voice lifted against the chorus of crickets and night animals, it became fuller. After taking three deep breaths through his nose and letting them out of his mouth, he reached for the bones. They were cool and smooth in his hands. Their history and significance flowed through him, connecting him to all the memories, all the magic, of those who had come before.

Lightly at first he tapped the floor of his platform, increasing the intensity of the percussion and hum of his voice until they rang out in harmony. The magic words, the holy words, rode on the night air, passing the leaves and grass that fluttered at the sound. Soon his voice could not be distinguished from the sudden breeze. A quick burst of wind crossed the mound, stirring debris and then letting it settle. The drumming hammered through the dimensions, opening the doors to the spirit world. The incantations completed, the spirit man's head rolled back, his eyes twitched, and he dropped the bone instruments. With a slow roll his head slumped forward, and the vision began.

Chapter Two

ATULA NO LONGER NEEDED his eyes to see. His Spirit eye left his body, hovered above for a moment, and then with incredible speed traveled through the dark tunnel. The brilliant light at the other end pulled him through the air, stretching him into a long, thin wisp of vapor. As he approached the light, it burst with colors, spraying him with warmth. At the exit all movement and sound stopped.

He stood near the edge of a river that teemed with fish. On the bank across from him, three deer came to drink. Turtles were collecting the warmth of the sun that would hold them through the cool night. The sky was clear and azure blue, crisp with the chill of the winter that blanketed the land to the north, the land of the A-po-la-chee, the people from the other side.

Suddenly the black noses of the deer sniffed the air. There was a different scent in the air. Their skin tingled, and they could smell something burning, but it was not fire. At the same instant they were blinded by a brilliant flash of light and deafened by a crack of thunder. They stood stunned, afraid to run. A sudden brisk breeze rustled the leaves, and the deer backed away from the water.

A thin layer of ash-gray smoke slid across the horizon

and then into the blue sky, smudging it. Silently the turtles slipped below the surface of the water, and the deer disappeared into the saw grass. The great blue heron took flight, and the water stilled as if it knew something.

Quickly the light faded as rolling black clouds blotted out the sun. A fork of lightning ruptured the air, sending brilliant blue veins across the sky. It lit the landscape, and the earth shook with the roar of the colliding force of the heavens slamming back together, closing the fracture line. The wind thrashed the saw grass, an infinite landscape of slashing, whipping scored blades that sung the song of the wind. The rain fell in sheets, gushing out of the underbelly of the dark clouds, obscuring and smearing the view.

The river frothed, spilling over, cutting a trench through the labyrinths of gray, black, and yellow limestone, widening into a channel, gouging through the shell-fossil beds, carving its own cradle until it reached the ridge of rock that held back the tidal salt of the Big Water. The new river crashed through the rim of the limestone dam, breaking into a flash of small falls and rapids, finally emptying into the Big Water where it found its peace.

Atula witnessed the sudden clearing of the sky, the darkness rolling backward, sliding the cover off the bed of the sky. The wind stilled, and the clamor ceased. As it all cleared, he saw the dramatic change that had taken place. Before him were two rivers, new and old. The old river had become nothing but a dry bed, a cracked mosaic of sediment and clay. But the new river was filled with all those things on which the clan depended.

Fishermen in a canoe paddled to the fork and began to argue over what they should do.

"We must wait for the old river to fill again," the first

man said decidedly.

"Yes," another agreed. "The old river has always provided for us. It sustained our fathers and their fathers before them. We and the animals we hunt have taken the water to satisfy our thirst. The river spirit has given us fish, turtles, and freshwater mussels. It is the water of life."

"But are you blind, my friend?" another asked. "Do you not see that this is the end of the old river? The river spirit has not deserted us but has come in another form."

"It is a trick. We should not take anything from the new river. It was not meant to be. An evil spirit has tricked you. We should dam it, destroy it before it destroys us."

Another man interjected, "If you walk the dry bed, your thirst will paralyze your throat, and your hunger will pain your belly. You will watch those who have the courage to voyage on the new river, and your hearts will become hardened and jealous. You will watch us fill our stomachs with the treasures of the water and cool our throats with the clear water. When you realize you have made a mistake, your pride will not allow you to take your boat to the water. Instead you will wither like a dead leaf in the shadow of the river."

"Why have the spirits let us become confused? Why do they demand that such important decisions be made?"

The men sat silent, undecided. The division among them had caused the canoe to remain at rest.

The distant buzzing sound became louder and louder, and the vision became covered with a haze.

"There will be a new river. It will be the same water but of a different channel," echoed a distant voice. "The new river is filled with food for the People. It is the provider. Do not hide your face in fear."

Atula took a deep breath and let it out slowly. His spirit eye was rapidly transported back through the tunnel and into his body, making him jump with the jolt of its return.

Such visionary journeys exhausted him. He moved to the mat of soft grasses that was his bed. He wished the vision had been clearer in its meaning. The spirits often spoke in ambiguous ways. Tomorrow he would fast and cleanse himself so that he could enter a holy state to concentrate and interpret the vision. But first he needed to rest so that he would be strong.

He was young to be a shaman and knew he probably withstood the stresses more heartily than many before him had. The bite of the coral snake had sent his father to the Other Side very early in his life.

Atula pictured the colorful snake in his mind. It was deceptive-looking. It was a small snake with small fangs, and only if it bit deep did it kill. But if it pierced some soft, vulnerable part and had time to deposit its venom, it was deadly.

Ochassee, Atula's father, had gone in search of a special plant, the verbena, which bloomed all year in the pinelands. Its small clusters of pink, yellow, orange, and red blossoms made it easy to spot. To get it, he needed to follow the canoe trails through the nearly endless monotonous mass of saw grass. Following the small shallow channels, he traveled through the saw-toothed spikes. The brown- and green-creased blades stretched as far as he could see, an unchanging panorama interrupted only by the tree-island hammocks that grew atop humps of limestone. There the tightly packed muck, the layers of dead, rotting saw grass, was not so thick and had been eroded away. In the open spaces, where they were not in competition with the fierce saw grass, other plants seized the island with their roots, creating tiny jungles that were home to many of the animals and the men of the region. The tree islands grew thick with oak, cabbage palm, wax myrtle, sweet bay, and gumbo-limbo. The tangled mass of strangler figs grew out of depressions and crooks in the host trees. They sprouted from pouches and pockets where birds dropped their seed. Their leather-leafed heads peeked out and sent down their complicated roots to wrap themselves around their host. Eventually the Sabal palm and the cypress toppled and gave in, leaving the strangler standing alone, healthy, tall, and victorious.

Ochassee moved to the east, to the sandier soil of the pine flatlands. He had gone alone in his canoe, traveling the same trails he had traveled hundreds of times before. Quietly, in deep thought, he poled his small boat.

The land to the east was drier and supported the tall pines and scrub palmettos. When the canoe could take him no closer, he walked, watching for the colorful flowers that would be perched on top of square stems.

Finally he spotted what he sought. It had taken him much too long today, and he mumbled to himself and sighed. There was no path here, only the wire grass and the fans of the palmettos. In a few spaces, a myriad of colors erupted from the sun-ravaged earth.

Ochassee sped up, eager to gather the verbena, carelessly neglecting the cautious footwork that one needed in this land. To live in this environment was to be forever aware and alert, cautious and vigilant. A rotting log lay between him and the verbena. He knew that he should go around it or step broadly over it, watching his step, looking before he stepped. But he was in a hurry.

Hidden and safe, resting comfortably in the nest of loam and rotting wood, the beautiful coral snake heard the approaching steps. His black forked tongue darted at the air. Slowly it withdrew farther under the log.

Ochassee stepped on the top of the decaying log. His weight caused the rotting wood to cave in, falling to pieces beneath his foot. He felt a quick jab, no more painful than a sting or the prick of a sandspur, on the side of his small toe. To his horror, the brightly ringed snake tenaciously clung to him. He could almost see the pumping action of the venom gland as it injected him with liquid death.

Ochassee took his knife and slashed off the head of the snake. The headless body wriggled on the ground while the fangs sewed the head to his toe. In terror, Ochassee ripped the head away, tearing small slits in his skin.

The moment he saw the bite, he knew there was no hope. He slowly lowered himself to the ground and tried to prepare himself for death. But the beheaded snake still kept his attention, odd as it seemed, and he studied it.

Unlike the other poisonous snakes of the region, such as the rattlesnake and the moccasin, it did not have the characteristic pit on the side of the head between the nostril and the eye. The fangs were small and weren't movable like those of the other snakes. It chewed on its victim, compensating for the small size of its fangs.

Actually it was quite beautiful, with its bands of black and red and yellow, he thought. It wasn't even an irritable snake. Ochassee surmised that he must have stepped squarely on it, for this snake was usually shy, unlike the aggressive moccasin. As a shaman, he knew about the potions, soaks, and dressings used to save a man from the poison of the rattler and the moccasin. He also knew that there was no cure for the bite of the coral.

He looked at his toe. The holes were tiny, except for the rips where he had pulled the snake's head loose. The wound didn't even hurt; the area was numb. Rattler and moccasin bites quickly swelled and caused much pain. The irony in the lack of pain and the final outcome of the coral snake bite intrigued Ochassee.

He decided to go back to the canoe and travel as far as he could. There was no rush; the venom was circulating inside him, and he was going to die no matter what he did. He wanted his son, Atula, to be with him and to guide him across to the Other Side, but he wasn't sure he would make it back to the village.

The walking accelerated the poisoning process, and he began to notice a weakness in the leg that had been bitten. By the time he reached the canoe, he was stumbling, off balance, and he was extremely tired. He felt as if his body was weighted with stones, and his mouth kept filling with saliva.

Ochassee lifted one leg into the canoe and then let himself fall forward so that he landed inside, the force pushing the canoe off the bank. He rolled to his back and tried to sit up. But his body was suddenly too heavy, and so he lay watching the clouds as the boat drifted.

The canoe came to rest against a clump of reeds. Peripherally he saw flashes of light that he knew were not actually there. His mouth continued to fill with saliva, and some of it drooled from the corner of his mouth. It was hard to swallow, and there was an uncomfortable weight on his chest. In the bottom of his boat, under the blazing sun, he shivered with cold.

Slowly he touched the medicine bag that he wore around his neck. He could feel the symbols of his life inside and hoped that everything was there so that the spirits would know him when he crossed over.

Some members of a hunting party from another clan had found Ochassee and brought him home, and Atula had prepared his father for burial. Alone in the shaman's platform he sliced open his father's scalp, removed a small triangular piece of the skull, and washed it clean of blood and flesh. He carefully drilled a hole in it and strung it on a leather thong. It was the spirit man's amulet, the visual and concrete claim to the Gift, given to him by his father. Slowly he had lowered it over his head as he spoke the secret words. Atula had become shaman.

That night the clan gathered. Atula had wrapped Ochassee's body with medicine leaves, herbs, and roots. His body was put into the central hearth. The moist plant wrap crackled as it touched the flames. Sometimes it made loud popping noises, spraying out a shower of sparks. The air was filled with the sickly sweet scent of burning flesh. The People listened to the words of Atula, their new shaman. They heard his voice call out the prayers of the ritual. When he had finished, they turned the event into a festivity of chanting and feasting. The man of the spirits had gone home.

The young Atula walked away from the fire, his face strained with pain.

———

ATULA REMEMBERED THE DEATH of his father as if it were yesterday. It still tore at his heart, and sometimes he doubted that he had had enough time to learn from him. There were so many things he still questioned and wished that he could ask Ochassee.

How his father must have hated it when the visions were unclear, he thought, thinking of the two rivers he had seen. Why did the visions have to be so difficult to interpret? Was he not supposed to understand the meaning until a later time? He had the same thoughts and questions after each undefined vision, but he had a special interest in this vision. What had the spirits planned for Miakka and the child she carried? Sooner or later the meaning of the two rivers would become clear, and the veil of mystery would lift. It was up to the spirits, not him. With that thought he drifted into sleep.

In the morning the aroma from the cook fires saturated the air. There was the fresh smell of bread made from the thick and starchy root of the coontie plant. Just by sniffing the air one could almost taste the fresh berries and the teas made from them and other tasty herbs as they brewed and steeped over the fire.

Miakka brought a bowl of fresh water from the cenote, the place where the cavernous limestone collapsed in on itself, leaving a sinkhole filled with fresh water. It was probably because of this feature that the spot had been chosen for habitation generations ago.

It felt good to her to kneel by the fire and relieve the stress in her lower back. Across the fire she saw him. Atula was standing off to one side. He seemed to be fasting, she noticed, since he showed no interest in the food that was being prepared. How marvelous he looked standing alone, looking over the people he served. She wondered if he fasted because he had taken her concerns to the spirits.

"Shakia," she called to her friend. "Come and have your morning meal with me."

Shakia looked across the fire at Miakka. After the death of Miakka's parents, Shakia's mother, Tabisha, and Shakia's father, Acopa, had taken her in. Miakka had been present at Shakia's birth, and though they were not real sisters, there was a special bond between the two. When Miakka became a woman, she moved to her own platform, alone.

"I see you still cannot stop watching him," Shakia said

as she sat next to Miakka.

"Does it show that much?"

"Only to me because I know you so well."

Miakka's face turned sullen. "I think the spirits punish me. I always think of him."

"Miakka, you cannot. Turn your head toward some other man. Look to the men who come to visit from other villages. I have seen many pay you attention, and you turn them all away. There is no future for you if you continue to grieve for what you can never have."

"I know. That is why I say the spirits are angry with me, though I do not understand what I could have done to cause it. Why would they want me to suffer all my life? First my mother and father, and now ... I think they mean for my heart always to be empty."

"The spirits are not angry with you, but you must forget Atula. He is the shaman and cannot take a woman as his bride. Perhaps that is the attraction. Maybe you are infatuated with him because you cannot have him. Put him out of your mind. Forget this fanciful dream you have."

Miakka touched her abdomen gently, lovingly. "Do you not see that the spirits will never let me forget? Here, inside, I carry a part of him—a part of me."

"And you are honored," Shakia said, hugging Miakka. "Let it go, sweet friend."

"I know you are right. Perhaps after the child is born it will be easier—that is, if ..." She was too frightened to speak the words, as if voicing her fears would make them come true. She would put the problem out of her mind and talk to Shakia about something more reasonable than her feelings for the shaman and less frightening than her fear for the child she carried.

"And I see the way you watch Wakulla."

"Miakka!" Shakia protested and blushed.

Miakka smiled. "He is quite handsome, and I think he keeps his eye on you rather than on the young women he could choose from the other villages."

"But the cacique may insist that he choose a bride from outside our clan. That is the way most of the time."

"But not every time," Miakka corrected. "There are special situations, and there is no common blood between you and Wakulla. If he wants you, I think Jegatua will approve. And I think Wakulla entertains that thought."

Shakia looked about for him and found Wakulla not too far away. "Do you really think so?" she asked, but Miakka did not answer.

Shakia looked back at her friend and then followed the track of Miakka's eyes. Shakia shook her head. Miakka was looking across the mound to the man she could never have.

Atula surveyed the clan, taking special note of his offspring. There were three sons. Micco was small-boned like his mother, Shani, but his eyes were definitely Atula's. So far he had shown no signs of the Gift, but he was very young.

Wakulla was the oldest. He had been conceived by Kita, an older woman whose responsibility was to teach the adolescent Atula the pleasures of joining. It was the joint duty of the shaman and the clan leader, the cacique, to select the woman. They had agreed that Kita would be Atula's teacher.

A north wind had blown that night, chilling everyone to the bone. Beneath the covers of hides and fur, Kita had guided Atula into manhood. She had not only pleased him, but had also taught him how to please a woman. She stayed with him, fed him, pleased him and slept with him for many frigid days. His memory of that first experience had stayed with him for many winters, and Kita held a special place in his heart.

Wakulla was more than old enough to show the signs. He was a fine young man. The entire clan was proud of Wakulla, and they knew he was destined to be a leader of the People. He had a sense of fairness and a manner that was well appreciated. Even with all his wonderful qualities, he was not going to be the one with the Gift. He was already much too old. This grieved Atula a little. He would have liked for his successor to be Wakulla, especially for the sake of his mother, Kita.

Cacema's son, Cherok, seemed the most likely. He was at the prime age. He had lived through five summers. He had a full head of blue-black hair and healthy olive skin. His temperament and disposition were pleasant and mellow. Cherok even showed a special affection for Atula.

Atula understood the burden of being the shaman. It was not a destiny a man chose of his own will. The shaman possessed a curious inner quality, a special instinct, a knowledge that was a blood gift. The ordinary man could not understand. Even while he was young the child would know certain things instinctively, and Atula would recognize the signs. He would teach his son.

Some tribes had long ago lost that pure strain of shaman, and they knew only the new knowledge that was handed down through teaching. Atula was pure. He had the memories of the generations that had come before him, though much of it had been diluted through the thousands of years. One of his sons would also have the Gift. The mother would have to be of a pure line, not the descendant of a mixing of tribes. Everyone in this clan was pure. Atula could sire many boy children, but only one would receive the Gift. Because there could never be a permanent relationship, joining was strictly for the purpose of procreating or simply to satisfy a biological need. To which child had the spirits passed the Gift through his seed? Atula wondered.

Cherok sat next to his mother as she filled her bowl and his. Atula approached the boy.

Miakka smiled at him from across the central hearth. She liked Cacema, and everyone liked Cherok. She watched the little fellow as he looked up at his father. He was the image of Atula. Cacema was a fortunate woman. Her son would probably be the next shaman. She was raising a very special child.

"Here," Atula told the child, handing him a piece of deer meat. "Finish your morning meal and come with me. We have a lot to do this day."

Cacema listened and then nodded to Cherok, confirming her approval. She tried hard not to smile, but it pleased her that Atula was going to spend time with her son. It was time. Since his birth she had been certain that he was the one. Atula could see something in him, she thought. He was a special child.

Chapter Three

THE BOY CHEWED the piece of tender meat, taking Atula by the hand. His father led him onto the path to the cenote. The small one eagerly walked next to his father.

Atula stopped where the brush cleared, sat down with his legs crossed, and patted the ground next to him. The little one plopped down.

"Look into the water, Cherok, and tell me what you see."

The boy crawled to the edge and peered in. "I see water, Father."

"And what else do you see?"

Cherok looked again. There was not the faintest breeze, so the water was still and smooth, the surface a perfect reflection.

"The clouds. I can see the clouds," he said, jumping up with delight at his discovery.

Atula took the boy's hand to settle him. "Look again, Cherok. Tell me, what do they look like? Be my eyes, Cherok. Pretend that I am blind. Help me feel what you see. Paint a picture with your words."

Cherok looked at the water, fascinated by the reflection.

"Clouds, Father. White clouds."

"More, my son," Atula almost whispered so as not to

disturb the boy's concentration. The sky was dappled with great pearly clouds, puffed heaps of vapor towering against the blinding blue. "Touch the clouds with your heart. Feel them. Become part of them. Go to them and soar above the earth. Look down on me and tell me how it feels to touch the sky."

Cherok wrinkled his nose in puzzlement before he gazed again at the reflection.

Atula continued to guide him, to push him, to make him stretch. "Concentrate. Breathe in. Feel the air and know it. Let yourself out of your body. Feel yourself lighter than the air, rising up above the earth. Reach out to the clouds. Ride the wind, my son."

The small boy looked hard into the water. "I am trying, Father. The clouds are like giant puffs of smoke floating in the sky."

"Good, little one. Let go now. Be free. Do not be afraid. See yourself rising up. Feel the warm, fretful wind touch your face. Let it carry you."

For a few minutes there was silence. The boy stared into the water, concentrating, trying to follow his father's directions. Then abruptly he turned to the shaman. "I cannot tell you how they feel. I cannot touch them. But, Father, I am trying. I want to touch them."

Cherok's small face twisted into an expression of disappointment. Atula fingered his son's black hair. "Yes, I know you do. In time. You did well this first time."

Atula realized that the child was still too young. He had gotten very close, but his concentration was limited. He needed to practice, to learn to focus. And even if he had gone to the clouds, his vocabulary was too inadequate to describe the experience. But Atula saw that he had promise. There was something there.

"Come," he said, "to my hearth." Cherok reached for

his father's hand. Atula held it firmly so that his son would know the difference between a woman's hand and a man's grip.

When they reached the fire Atula closed his eyes and hummed while Cherok drew in the dirt with a stick. When would he know his son? There should be no investment in a relationship with any other child, only the one with the Gift.

Perhaps the Gift would become more difficult to detect, he thought, because with each successive generation it was weakened, spread thinner in the blood. He would need to be patient. The memories and instinct were being constantly compromised through time. It was like a very strong tea to which had been added small amounts of water over and over again. Such strong power wasn't needed now as it had been in generations past. The tribes depended more on communal decision-making and on the leadership and guidance of those who were wise with age.

The shaman remained a powerful bridge to the world of the spirits. Whenever the darkness of trouble fell over the clan, the shaman was asked to consult the spirits and then guide the clan through the darkness with his light. While other men could dream, only the shaman could have visions. Only the holy man, with his medicines and his songs, could leave his body and join the spirits. Only the man of the spirits could understand the symbols and tongues, speak with the giant animal spirits that had once hunted men. That was the realm of the pure shaman, the real holy man. Those were the places that he went and the things that he did. That domain was his alone.

Atula sipped clear broth, not taking any solid food during his fast. He offered a small bowl of it to Cherok. The two sat quietly watching the movements of the rest of the clan as they finished their morning meals and chores.

Atula's attention left Cherok, caught by something else. Miakka stood conversing with Wagahi. Her face was serious. The two finally walked to the place of Wagahi, following a path acceptable for all members of the clan.

The space behind the camp, behind the place of the men's medicine bundles that hung at the head of their sleeping mats, was different from the space in the front of the village. In front of the thatched platforms were trails connecting all parts of the village. The paths led to other platforms, the cenote, the hide-working area, the central hearth, the basket and weaving area, the tool-making place, and the area to relieve oneself. But behind the platforms, on the north side, the trails were for men only, for they led to the hunting ground. The three-sided platforms were aligned from northeast to southwest. No man's platform came between another's and the place of the sunrise, the creation of a new day. All of the openings faced the south, out of fear of the winter when a frigid northeasterly wind might blow through and cause great sickness to sweep the clan.

The People believed that the wind from the northeast was the breath of the giant beasts that used to roam the earth and hunt men. It kept man humble to be reminded of his precarious existence and made him give thanks to the Great Spirit for choosing the People over the animals. In return, the People had an obligation to respect the animals.

Carefully Miakka and Wagahi climbed the ladder up to the platform. Atula watched them disappear inside. She was quite lovely with child. He wished to dance with her again.

The rest of the day he spent with Cherok. He walked

him through the trails for men and into the brush where the child had never been before.

He showed his son how to stalk quietly, carefully. "There are many reasons to be silent," he explained. "You may hear a bird call a sudden alarm or perhaps the snapping of a twig or the rustling of brush. You must always be alert."

As his father demonstrated, Cherok watched, his eyes riveted on the man who knew so much.

"Look around you. Your body should blend with the landscape. If you are in the brush and grass, you will crouch or crawl. In the hammocks, on the river's edge, or in the pine-lands, you must stand tall and still like the trees. Become part of the landscape. Become a tree. If you feel it from the inside, you will be a tree on the outside."

Cherok hunched over in the midst of the saw-grass prairie, disappearing from sight. Atula moved next to him.

"Keep your balance; that is most important," Atula told him.

"I want to be a tree," Cherok said.

Atula laughed. "Then I will show you how to stalk in the woods."

The two of them boarded a small canoe, and Atula guided it through the canoe trails to the east. A few times they had to portage the canoe through shallow water, but most of the time Atula could use his paddle or a pole. The water finally led to a river tributary that flowed through the palmetto scrub and pine flatland.

Atula bound the canoe to a nearby tree and helped Cherok out. "Touch the earth," he told his son. It was different here. They walked deeper into the pinewoods. The smell was different—dry and hot, not moist and steamy like the village.

Cherok scraped up a handful of the sandy gray dirt and let it trickle through his small fingers.

"Shh," Atula whispered. "There, through the trees."

Cherok froze and looked in the direction that his father was gazing.

"Where?" he whispered.

"A deer. There," his father told him.

Cherok saw nothing but squinted to look even harder.

"Keep looking at him," Atula said. "Do not take your eyes off of him and be still. Stand like the trees."

Cherok braced his spine, afraid even to blink his eyes. He could hear his own breathing and was certain that the deer his father saw could also hear him breathing.

Atula whispered again. "Keep your hands and arms next to your body until we begin to move. Do what I do, exactly."

Atula slowly moved his hands in front of his body so that they dangled over his knees and then bent his knees slowly and slightly. Cherok copied his father, who was only a step or two in front of him and off to one side a little.

The boy's eyes quickly returned to the place where he thought he should see the deer, remembering that his father had told him to keep looking at the animal. He still could not see it.

Atula raised one foot alongside his other leg until it was level with his knee. He pointed his toes downward so that he would not snag his foot on anything. He balanced there for a moment. Cherok mimicked him, but found it difficult to keep his balance. Smoothly the man lowered his foot. Just before touching the ground, he turned his toes upward and slightly bent his ankle so that he touched the earth with the outside of his foot. Lightly he rolled across the ball of his foot, testing the ground beneath him. Since it was free of twigs and other obstacles, he slowly lowered his heel to the ground and at last his toes. When his foot was safely planted, he shifted his weight.

Cherok followed Atula's example, though not quite as smoothly. He watched as his father began to move again. Atula swung his upper body forward, reminding Cherok of the way some of the large wading birds moved. His father lifted his back heel and then finally his whole foot. He was repeating the first step bringing his foot up to knee level.

They walked that way, slowly, carefully, skillfully, until Cherok's small muscles trembled with the strain. And he still had not seen the deer.

Finally Atula lowered himself to the ground and sat.

"The deer?" Cherok frowned.

Atula smiled as his son sat across from him. "It was practice."

"You mean there was not a real deer?"

"Not this time. But when there is a deer, you will know what to do."

"How close can we get?" the child asked.

"You can get as close as you are good. Of course, you must remember the wind."

Atula spotted a ground oak. He pulled some of the white fruit from the small patch of shrubs and offered one to his son. The pulp was sweet in Cherok's mouth.

On the way back, Atula took Cherok to some land that had burned during a wildfire set by lightning.

"The deer will soon be here." Atula bent over and pointed to the new succulent shoots of saw grass, urging his son to take note.

On the rest of the return journey, the shaman told Cherok other things, like how to disguise his smell by standing in front of the smoke from the fire. At twilight they reached the village, and Atula returned Cherok to his mother.

After the evening meal Atula walked back to his platform, which was set apart from the rest and somewhat isolated. As he got close, he felt that he was being followed. He let his feet fall lightly on the ground so that he could hear other noises. A small cracking of a twig and the crushing of the grasses told him that someone was definitely close by. Atula stopped, faced the brush, and called out, "Who follows and hides in the brush?"

He could hear the rustling of the plants and grasses as a figure disengaged itself from cover and stepped onto the trail.

"Amakollee, it is unwise to track a man and not let yourself be known. I might have thought you were an A-po-la-chee."

"I would have revealed myself in a moment. You are truly a great hunter, for you heard me," she said, trying to inflate his ego and improve her position with him.

"What is it that you need?"

"Please, Atula," she began, hearing the aloofness in his question. "I have made myself clear in the past. There was a time when you did not turn me away. Have I become so old and unattractive?"

Atula felt himself soften. How humiliating it must be for her. "Where is your pride, Amakollee?"

"How can I continue to have pride? I am one of the few who have lived this long and still have no mate. It is too late for me to go to another village. I would be laughed at. You know that, Atula, and you know that you are the only one who can save me. I can give you pleasure in exchange. I will do anything you ask of me."

Atula felt embarrassed for her and tried to quiet her. "Do not say things that you may later regret. Keep your pride and your dignity."

Amakollee walked a little closer. "Are you still a man, Atula? Do you not still have needs—needs that I can satisfy? I know those things that please you," she said, running her finger across his lips and then his chest. "I know how you ache inside when I let my hands wander over your body."

The sun rapidly disappeared in the west, leaving only a spray of orange low in the sky.

Atula felt a tingling current travel through him as she continued her caresses. He parted his lips to speak.

"Do not say anything," she said before touching her mouth to his nipples: "Answer me with your body."

Atula bent his head forward and pressed his face into her hair.

"Yes," she murmured. "Let your body answer. It cries for a woman."

She kissed his chest and then his neck, letting her hand touch his thigh and trail teasingly upward.

His arms went around her. His body did need to be satisfied, and she was expert in knowing how to do that. He led her up the ladder and onto his mat. He let her undress him, let her be the aggressor, and he enjoyed this reversal of the traditional roles. As she lay upon him, nipping and kissing those intimate parts of him, he closed his eyes. To his surprise he saw Miakka's face. He found himself lost in his imagination. It was Miakka's hair that swept across his belly as her mouth took him in. It was Miakka's hand that held his to her breasts as she lowered her body onto him, leading him into her valley.

Amakollee sighed, almost crying out as he filled her. Atula rolled her onto her back and with his passion made her tremble beneath him. She clutched at his back, pulling him closer, meeting his rhythm until she finally convulsed with the release of pleasure. Atula stiffened and then fell onto her, his breathing deep and rapid, hungry for air to fill his lungs.

"Let me stay a little longer," she whispered. "Do not make me leave too soon."

Atula turned onto his side, pulled her head to his shoulder, and stroked her hair, letting her know that she did not have to leave. He was not so cruel.

Joining always complicated things, except with Cacema and of course Kita. In his heart he knew that joining should involve more than the act. That was why he had avoided Amakollee. Afterward he always felt like an animal. He knew how difficult joining could make relationships.

He had had a painful experience with Micco's mother, Shani. She had been a romantic adventure that had not lasted long. Shani had ended it, though she told Atula she loved him. He had been willing to have Shani as his only woman. But she wanted more than he could give. She wanted a man who could lie next to her all night. She wanted to curl up in his warm arms on cold mornings. She wanted to live at the hearth of the man she loved. She wanted a husband, not the clan, to provide for her.

Atula could not promise her those things that she wanted for a lifetime. He was forbidden to take a wife to live at his hearth. As much as Shani loved him, she knew that her demands would eventually breed ill feelings between them. She chose to let him go. She never wanted him to regret his special place with the People. And she did have the child of his seed, Micco.

If not Cherok, then perhaps Micco, he thought as Amakollee slept at his side. And what of this night? Had his seed begun to grow inside her? Had it found a welcome bed that would nourish it?

He looked at Amakollee's face, and his heart ached for her. She was not the most beautiful, but she was not unpleasant to look at. She was right: She did know how to please him.

Atula began to wonder about his place in the clan. Did he have two purposes, one of which he had just now realized? Was the man of the spirits less than a man or more than a man? Was he an instrument to spread the seed of the Gift, never being allowed the experience of being just a man? He had come close with Shani, but the spirits had moved her heart. Though Amakollee was at his side, he found himself very much alone. He had one purpose—to perpetuate the line.

He gently shook Amakollee's shoulder to wake her. She looked up at him, almost gratefully. He watched her as she made her way to the doorway and then disappeared down the ladder. He turned onto his side and closed his eyes. Tonight he would not talk to the spirits before sleeping. He was too tired, and he had nothing to say.

———

MIAKKA CONTINUED TO SWELL. Always from a distance she watched Atula. She listened and stayed silent as Amakollee boasted to the other women of how the shaman had found favor in her. Miakka felt uneasy, flustered, and though she tried to deny it, a little jealous. She wanted to walk away, but something made her stay and listen.

She watched for signs of Atula's interest in Amakollee. Whenever she could, she followed him with her eyes. She managed to be near him many times but never allowed herself to get close. As much as she watched, she saw no sign of a relationship between Amakollee and him. Instead she saw the bond growing between the shaman and Cacema's son, Cherok.

Atula spent many days with Cherok, now and again noticing a flicker of what might indicate the surfacing of the Gift—a flash in the boy's eyes, a perception, or an observation that seemed beyond his years. There was nothing definite. It seemed that Cherok always stood at the brink, so close, needing the smallest tap to push him over. With time, Atula thought. It was going to take time. Finally Atula seemed satisfied that it was Cherok, and the clan began to look upon the boy with special interest and favor.

Cacema carried on with her usual domestic tasks, also watching from a distance, over time seeing the bond begin to form between Cherok and Atula. Her heart was filled with pride.

Just after Cherok's birth, Okapi had taken Cacema to be his wife, and she was devoted to him. Cacema had consented to joining with Atula, but no romantic entanglement had ever developed. The shaman was strikingly handsome, and it was an honor to have been chosen, but she knew that she could have no emotional future with him and so she had kept that part of her separate from the joining. Atula had found that particularly attractive in her. She expected no commitments, no restrictions, no promises or profound statements of love. He had chosen her on quite a few occasions before she became Okapi's wife.

The relationship between Atula, Cacema, and Okapi was comfortable, and Okapi was privileged to help raise the son of the shaman. Okapi's family would be favored because of Cherok. An additional portion of the clan's food would always be given to his family. Cacema was pregnant again, this time with Okapi's child. If Okapi were to die, the clan would always provide for Cacema and all her children.

———

MIAKKA TOUCHED HER ABDOMEN, feeling the strong kicks and rolls of her unborn child. She was sore and felt bruised. Exhaustion often swept over her like some dark and ominous cloud.

She lay down on her back, resting her hands on her large belly, closing her eyes tightly, feeling the pain in her throat as she fought back tears. She was so frightened.

Chapter Four

MIAKKA STOOD AT THE BASE of the ladder that led up to Atula's platform. To call for him might be too informal, she thought, and so she stood silently, hoping that he would soon detect her presence. She had waited a few more moon cycles, and the child inside her had continued to grow at an alarming rate. She found it difficult to do most daily tasks and even to sleep.

Somehow, she believed, an evil spirit had seen Atula's seed within her and had vengefully turned the child into a gruesome monster. Or maybe it was her fault. Maybe in her cooking she had mixed the flesh of some sea animal with that of a land animal without noticing. That was a definite taboo, and maybe the spirits were punishing her.

She had seen such babies born. She shuddered at the thought of them. Sometimes their spines were not closed or their eyes were not properly spaced. Some even had a split face, their mouths opening into their noses. Usually such recipients of the evil spirits' vengeance died shortly after birth. Sometimes a deformed baby might live for a whole moon cycle or two. The child was innocent, but if it lived, it humbled its mother. The mother would serve the child all its life, and she would cry in the night, asking the spirits why they had allowed such evil to hurt her child. This was a hideous trick that the evil spirits played just to remind the People of their power.

Miakka was certain that she carried such a child, and her emotions were torn between love and terror. Her heart jumped between fear and anger. She would make Atula answer her today. He was the only one who could see inside her, the only one who could talk to the spirits.

And she had an even worse fear, which she forbade herself to think about. She was afraid that if she dared to think of this fear, it might come true—she might make it happen.

Some children were born neither male nor female, but both. They were strange outcasts of the tribe, but they were strong, and when one of these pitiful creatures did live, it was given heavy, burdensome jobs.

"No," Miakka. Whatever the deformity, the possibility frightened her. She touched the tightly stretched skin of her belly.

While she was deep in thought, Atula had seen her, sensed her, and had come down the ladder.

"Miakka," he said, putting his hand on her shoulder.

Startled, she turned sharply.

"I did not hear you descend."

"It is not a noisy task. I thought you awaited me."

"I do," she said, turning to face him. "Wagahi can give me no advice. The other women turn away from me. They are afraid. Look at me. I am filled with a child that I love, and yet I know something is wrong. It is time for you to help me. Do something. You are the shaman. You are the father."

"Yes," he answered, "It is my seed that blooms within you. Come with me," he coaxed as he started up the ladder.

Miakka followed, watching him disappear in the shadows of his platform. He reached for her hand as she climbed to the top. Firmly but gently he helped her inside.

"Lie down and put your heels on this mark," he directed, drawing a line across the floor with a burned stick. Atula rolled up the end of his sleeping mat for use as a cushion. "Rest your head on my mat."

Miakka lowered herself to the rough cypress floor, extended her legs so that her heels touched the mark, then reclined and rested her head on the mat. Atula crouched and then knelt. From a pouch he removed a dried plant mixture and sprinkled some at each corner of an imaginary square around her body.

"Do not say a word. Be very still and wait for me to tell you that I am finished," he said.

Miakka tensed as Atula closed his eyes, tilted his head back, and began to chant, repeating the same syllables over and over. Soon the platform seemed filled with the sound, reverberating with the chant. She could feel his voice leaching something primal from her, over which she had no control, that she had never known was there, a piece of her that had been hidden deep inside, only to be brought out by the man of the spirits.

Louder and louder, his voice rang out. The air seemed alive and filled with tension. His voice, his words, sated the air, assimilating all other sounds. And a part of her slipped away, hearing his voice only in sweet whispers. Feeling as though she'd been separated from her body, she looked down and saw them both, wrapped in the grayness that seeped through the cracks in the floor and thatch.

Suddenly Atula stopped chanting. He opened his eyes and held his hands above her exposed abdomen. His strong hands seemed to rest on an invisible force that hovered over her belly. He moved his open hands in circles, as if gradually wearing away the layer of still air between his palms and her flesh.

Miakka closed her eyes. She no longer felt suspended above her body. Her skin tingled beneath his hands even before he touched her. Lightly his palms and fingers slipped across her. Slowly he added more pressure until she felt the weight of his hands.

The child moved inside her at the touch of its father. Atula swayed and began another chant directed to the child, the spirit that grew inside Miakka. She could feel the child tumble and stretch, hearing its father's words.

Atula rested his hands on her abdomen. Then he plucked two long strands of Miakka's hair and held them up above him while he spoke the magic tongue. Carefully he twisted the hairs together, weaving them into one strong strand.

From one of the many baskets that lined the side of his platform he withdrew a small piece of fire-polished deer bone. He wrapped the woven strand around the bone and tied it on at one end. Holding it in the palm of his hand and cupping that hand with the other, he held it up toward the sky.

His voice rang out again, but Miakka did not understand his words. Atula lowered his hands and stuffed the woven strands of hair and bone into the medicine bag that she wore around her neck.

He spoke a few quiet words of gratitude and sat quietly. The haze inside the platform cleared. The air thinned, and the power that had filled the platform dissipated. Miakka felt her muscles relax. The energy inside the room faded. There was a smell of something scorching in the air, but it quickly vanished.

"It is over," he said softly.

The fire was gone from his eyes. He looked tired, as if

the energy he had brought to the air had been tapped from his body. His voice was close to a whisper when he spoke.

"There were two," he told her. "Now they will become one. There is nothing to fear."

She had seen the shaman work his magic before. She had seen him heal. But she had never been this close to his power, and her body still trembled with the experience. He was extremely powerful, and there was a new depth to her respect for him.

Quietly she stood, realizing that he was too exhausted to escort her down the ladder.

"Thank you, Shaman," she whispered.

He heard her soft footsteps as she left. The air inside still carried the fragrance of her skin, and it was easy with his eyes closed to think that she was still here.

Strange, he thought. He had not had to deal with twins before. In his lifetime no one in this clan had ever carried them. He had heard that the phenomenon occurred, but he had never witnessed it. In the time of his father, a woman had carried two infants. They had fought inside and been born too early, killing themselves and also the mother with their tempers. Atula had saved Miakka and both of her children. As he twisted the two strands of her hair, he had blended the two tiny spirits inside her, uniting them so that they became one strong spirit.

Atula stood up and wondered where he had learned how to do this magic. Had his father taught him long ago, or had the ability come from inside, from the part of him that was shaman? Gripping the amulet that hung around his neck, he walked to the doorway and watched Miakka walk away. Perhaps he would invite Amakollee to his bed this night.

MORE CYCLES OF THE MOON PASSED, and Miakka's size gradually became more appropriate. The time of the birth would be soon.

———

THE MEN OF THE VILLAGE PREPARED for a hunt. It was winter and the proper time for spirit visitation. The shaman would play an important role in the preparations for a successful hunt. There had been an unusual amount of rain throughout the seasons. Even the winter, which was usually dry in the southern end of the peninsula, had been wet.

The edges of the mound had been swallowed by the rising water level. The clan excavated the borrow pit and poured the spoil onto the mound.

The deer, an important animal to the survival of the clan, had sought the limited high ground of the hammocks and ridges. They fed on the tender new shoots of saw grass until it was all gone or covered by the water. They were starving for lack of dry land.

The clan knew that if they overhunted, causing a disharmony in nature, the Great Spirit would punish them. The men sought a delicate balance. If too many were killed in addition to those that died of starvation, the deer could become extinct. But if they did not hunt, all of the deer would die of starvation. If the men had the guidance of the spirits, they would kill the right number of deer so that those who remained could graze and live. They knew how closely woven was the basket of creation. Every animal, including man, depended on the survival of all others.

The fire in the center of the ceremonial platform blazed high into the black night sky. The melodic voices of the People rang out along with the sound of rattles.

Atula, having donned a wooden mask carved in the image of the deer, danced in front of the fire, inviting the animal spirit. His dancing cloak, made from the hide of the deer and colored with vegetable dye, swooped through the air. He carried a rattle of deer hooves, which he shook rhythmically in cadence with his voice. His body was bent over, swinging toward each of the four directions.

The crowd also helped call a spirit. They solicited the rain spirit through their dance of uniform small steps. They hoped the rain spirit would see them and know their dilemma. The clan could not speak with the spirit, but they could please and honor it.

Miakka stood behind a group of women. She looked beyond the crowd, entranced by the handsomeness and power of Atula.

Suddenly Atula groaned, announcing the invasion of his body by the animal spirit. He removed the mask, exposing his painted face. He raised his head, opening his jet eyes. The crowd fell silent. Then he began his prophesies.

"The excessive rain has come to bring us back to the spirits. The spirits feel we have forgotten them, and so we must be humbled. Our hunt will be successful. We will take only what we need. The deer spirit cooperates. The rains will end, and all will return to normal. We will be forgiven when those who have ignored the spirits confess."

Amakollee stepped from the crowd and wound her way toward Atula. She had kept to herself lately. She carried herself proudly and spoke loud enough for all to hear. "Perhaps it was I," she cried, coming closer. She waited a moment before continuing, making certain that she had the attention of everyone. She used those

49

moments to wind her way through the people until she was in the light of the fire.

"I have been blessed," she said, looking at Atula. "The spirits have heard my cry and have answered me. It could be that I have not properly thanked them," she said.

Atula noticed her curved abdomen as she stood before him. She carried a child. Shani also noticed and flinched. She still had no mate and had lain with no man since Atula. Even though she had ended the relationship two winters ago, it still caused her pain to see that he had joined with another. The same pang had pierced her when she first learned of Miakka's pregnancy. He still wove himself through her dreams, and every time she looked into the eyes of her son, Micco, she saw Atula. Perhaps Micco would have the Gift. That would give her some consolation. Nevertheless she would live with her decision. Though she did not have a mate, she did have suitors. She would answer one of them and move away to be properly courted. Bearing the son of the shaman was not enough. She would have a husband.

Amakollee glanced at Shani and then at Miakka, curling her lips into the faintest smile. "I have much to be thankful for," she said, gently touching her belly. "I, too, carry the child of the shaman. And already there have been signs," she said, turning to the crowd. "I have felt his movement from the earliest time, and he has come to me in my dreams. He will be the one with the Gift."

Amakollee knelt in front of Atula. He was glad that she had conceived, but she should not have been so bold as to say that she carried the child with the Gift. It was not for her to say, and her declaration was certainly premature. Even as she knelt at his feet, he perceived trouble. He touched the crown of her head, giving his approval.

Amakollee eased away from him, the back of her hand pressed to her forehead in respect for the mighty shaman who had sown his seed inside her. He would not be sorry. She would give him his heir.

Others came to him for many different reasons, offering their thanks to the spirits. But after Amakollee, Miakka's ears seemed to go deaf, and she felt the sting of tears in her eyes. Quietly she retreated to her platform. From its edge she could see but could not hear. The firelight cast just the right shadows across Atula's face. Again she caught a glimpse of Amakollee. As she watched, she suddenly realized that her feelings of awe for the shaman were mixed with feelings for the man. As much as she wanted to go inside, into the darkness of her shelter, she could not leave, could not stop watching him.

Atula made other prophesies. He shivered as each new spirit entered his body. He spoke in a strange tongue. He proclaimed a forthcoming death and then used his powers to intercede, sparing that clansman's life. He healed some of the sick, and he brought the spirits to bless the People, finding special favor with his clan.

At the clan's request he displayed his power. He reached into the flames of the fire and lifted a coal. He held it before them, charismatically capturing them, pulling their spirits to him. He stood in silhouette against the blaze, looking even taller than usual. Again he reached into the flames and replaced the coal.

"Ayee!" they cried, touching the backs of their hands to their foreheads in awe and reverence. He walked away, disappearing like smoke into the night.

As the fire died in the late hours, the men retired to their sleeping place, a series of slings on the men's side, the north side, of the village. Their medicine bundles hung on sticks at their heads. The night before a hunt they slept away from the women and children.

The men cleaned and checked their weapons before sleeping. The weapons had been protected from the touch of a woman. If by accident a menstruating woman touched a weapon, it would become ineffective. A menstruant was not even allowed to cook the food for the hunters, for her touch would contaminate it, making both the man and the weapon impotent hunters.

When the first haze of light spread across the eastern horizon, the hunters pushed the canoes into one of the water trails. The early morning mist rose from the water, bathing the village in a cloud.

Amakollee stood alone at the water's edge, shrouded in the morning haze.

Chapter Five

THE HUNT HAD BEEN SUCCESSFUL. The village was replenished with the meat of small game and deer. The fleshing process would begin as soon as the hides were stripped from the carcasses. One of the men, Omo-ko, bent over a deer that had been killed in the hunt. He turned the animal on its back and began to make an incision from the base of its neck all the way to the vent. Pachu, his sister's son, watched in amazement as Omo-ko cut with precision, careful not to cut any deeper than it took to free the skin. When he was finished, he took the skin on either side of the incision and began to pull it away from the rest of the body. Carefully he worked it all around to the back of the deer. Occasionally he had to stop and work with his knife, keeping the blade against the underside of the skin, sweeping the knife between the skin and the flesh until it was loose enough so that he could work with his fingers.

He worked from the center backward until he reached the back legs. Omo-ko put down his knife and positioned one of the back legs. At the knee he bent the leg sharply upward. Working with his fingertips, he stripped the skin over the knee joint and down the lower leg, severing it at the ankle. He did the same with the other leg and then began to free the skin from the rear end of the body to

53

the root of the tail. With his knife he split the skin from the underside.

"Watch this," he told Pachu. Between his thumb and forefinger he grasped the tailbone, popped it out and slipped the skin free.

The hunter stood up, inspecting his work. When satisfied, he bound the back legs with sinew and strung the partly skinned deer over a branch, then asked Pachu to help him hoist it to a comfortable working height. He began to pull the skin downward and peel it off. Again he used his knife dexterously until he was stopped by the front legs. Omo-ko followed the same procedure as he had for the hind legs, and then drew the skin to the skull. Skillfully he cut through the ear cartilage as close to the skull as possible. Pleased that the skin had come away clean, he continued to take no chances. He pressed a fingertip against one of the eyeballs, cutting against it until the eyelid was set free. He finished the head, pulling the skin to the ground. His wife would take care of the hide. He moved it aside, and he and Pachu finished dressing the deer.

Over the open fires wooden grates rested on stakes. Strips of meat from the butchered game were smoking there, so that they could be stored. There would be plenty to eat for many days.

The women of the village waited on the men. They served them food and drink and immediately answered their bidding. Men were the heroes, the providers, and women needed to be thankful and show their gratitude.

Atula took a large swallow of his cassite. He watched the women serving their men, the families enjoying the celebration, and he felt emptiness inside.

Amakollee suddenly bowed as she offered him some more drink. Atula accepted but without giving her the attention she desired from him. Disappointed, she moved away, her head still lowered, the back of her hand respectfully pressed to her forehead.

Miakka moved slowly around the fire, obviously encumbered. But the light of the fire made her skin glow, and her hair came alive with the reflection. Atula was tantalized. She was more beautiful now than ever before.

Miakka also watched Atula. The child inside her turned, and she smiled to herself. The night she had joined with Atula was much like this night. The noises, smells, and mood were the same. She could almost catch the scent of his skin on the air.

The sounds of the festivity grew softer as the night unfolded. Some of the people had begun to go to their platforms, some for sleep and some with other thoughts. The adolescent males retired alone after an evening of trying to impress the girls of the clan.

By the time the moon had spent half of its night life, the village was asleep. The snoring of the old ones occasionally broke the silence. Even the purrs and cries of joining had ceased. The wind was still and the sky clear. Atula was the lone figure against a frozen background. He softly chanted near his fire. Something had shaken him from his short sleep. He felt anxiety tense his body at the impending event. Whatever was about to happen was important, and Atula prayed to the spirits to understand it.

Miakka also was not sleeping. At first sleep had come quickly, but then she, too, had been awakened. She clutched a handful of her moss skirt as she took a deep breath. It was time to get Wagahi. From a distance Atula saw her step carefully down the ladder, then pause at the bottom as another pain coursed through her.

In the darkness she crossed the mound and stood at

the base of Wagahi's platform.

"Wagahi," she called softly, not wanting to disturb everyone.

Again she called out, but a little louder, and in a moment, Wagahi's face appeared at the entrance.

"It is your time?" Wagahi asked.

"Yes," Miakka answered. "I believe so. All through the night I have had the pains."

Wagahi disappeared inside, gathering the things she might need to help in the delivery.

"Come with me," Wagahi said, stopping to take a coal from her dying fire and then leading Miakka to the birthing hut, which was isolated across the mound. Miakka hurried until stopped by the peak of a contraction. She rested her head against the trunk of a Sabal palm, closing her eyes, waiting it out until she could move again. At first the pain had come in waves, moments of discomfort that had made Miakka hold her breath and dig her nails into the palms of her hands. They had lasted for only a few seconds and then abated. She had welcomed the pains because they heralded the end of the long wait and the beginning of a new life. But as the time passed, the pains had intensified, blacking out reality while they lasted.

Wagahi motioned for her to enter the small hut. Unlike the other platforms, this shelter was not elevated. A woman about to bring a child into the world would find negotiating a ladder too difficult.

The midwife started a small fire with the coal she had brought. It provided enough light so that they could see. She stood and opened the roof flap, letting the smoke spiral out.

Wagahi brushed the ground with her hands, scattering small insects and debris. "Lie down until it is time. You will know when," she said, pointing to the pole in the center of the hut.

Miakka lay on her side next to the pole. She drew her knees up and swallowed as she felt the tightening begin in her back.

"Save your strength," Wagahi told her as she sorted through her things. "Keep your eyes open, or the pain will sweep over you. Do not let it. Stay above it."

As the pain rolled over her, trying to bury her, drown her, Miakka stared at a small piece of old peeling bark on one of the strips of cypress that supported the thatch of the western wall. She wanted to close her eyes and give in to the pain, but Wagahi kept reminding her not to do so.

The midwife placed one hand on Miakka's abdomen. She could feel Miakka's belly begin to tighten even before the pain really started. As soon as she felt the tension, she would start talking Miakka through it.

"Keep your eyes open. Breathe with it. Try to relax. Stay with me. Stay with me. Do not let the pain win. Good. Good," she would encourage her at the crest of the pain. "It is leaving. It is over. Relax. Let your body relax."

Miakka listened to Wagahi and did what she said, although she wanted to be left alone, to close her eyes. The pain was getting too hard to fight.

She groaned with the next stab, but as soon as she fell silent, she and Wagahi were startled by a shattering noise in the village. Loud cries rang out, followed by the din of people screaming.

"The A-po-la-chee!" Miakka screamed.

Wagahi clamped her hand over Miakka's mouth. "Silence—do not make a sound," she whispered. Miakka began to cry as Wagahi peered through the opening of the hut. She could not see anything, but could only hear the horrible sounds of the A-po-la-chee raiding the village. The war cries and the cries of the injured blended into one piercing shriek. Twice in her lifetime Wagahi had seen such raids. The last one had taken all of Miakka's family and Wagahi's family as well. Wagahi remembered the tragedy clearly.

The A-po-la-chee had come without warning, screeching in the dim light of dawn, waving clubs made from busycon shells bound to the ends of heavy sticks. Some had thrown lances of fire-tempered wood, and some had sliced with knives made from the macrocallista shells. They had used fire-tipped arrows to set the platforms on fire.

Blood of the clan had flowed across the mound, soaking the soil. Bodies had slumped to the ground with their heads bashed in. Wagahi had seen her brother in the throes of death after being clubbed. He had fallen to the ground, face down, exposing to her the hole in the side of his head, from which oozed watery blood and thick gray tissue. His body had jerked with convulsions as their mother turned him over and threw herself across his body.

"Why?" Wagahi's mother had screamed at the A-po-la-chee, lifting her head, which was soaked with her son's blood. None of the clan had ever understood the A-po-la-chee. They were a fierce and warring people, always trying to seize the land of others. So far the People had been strong enough to resist their attacks.

The way of the tribe from the other side was mysterious. This time they had come in darkness. Never had she heard of any tribe attacking another in darkness. Wagahi's stomach turned over.

Miakka lay on her side, digging into the dirt floor with her nails as another pain racked her body. She bit her bottom lip, drawing blood. Wagahi knew that she had to forget the horror that was going on in the village and concentrate on Miakka. It was important now that the woman giving birth work with the pain.

"Get up," she told her. "It is time. The baby comes soon, and you must help it."

Wagahi showed her how to hold the pole in the center of the hut. Miakka looked at it closely as the new pain began. It was polished and worn smooth from the many hands that had come before hers. Holding it tightly, Miakka bent her knees, squatted, and pushed down.

"Good," said Wagahi, wiping Miakka's forehead, which now dripped with perspiration, flinching at the sounds of terror that continued in the distance. She could only hope no one would hear and discover them.

Another searing pain reached around Miakka, bursting into fire in the small of her back, taking away her breath. Again and again it assaulted her, robbing her of strength. It started small and built to a fury, squeezing everything but consciousness from her. She not only felt the pain, but now she could see it. It was a piercing yellow that stabbed through her closed eyelids.

"Push," ordered Wagahi.

She couldn't. There was no strength. She knew that she would be swallowed by the next pain, that it would engulf her. She wanted it to, because then she could slip away and not feel anything anymore. Her stomach churned, and nausea overtook her. "I am going to be sick," she said.

Miakka sank to her knees. She balanced herself with her hands, her head falling between her shoulders, hair dragging in the dirt.

Wagahi reached inside Miakka, feeling for the baby's head. Her fingers probed, and a sudden gush of birth water splattered the earth. Miakka was ready, but the baby would not come down. It was locked inside.

Wagahi withdrew her hand, washed it in a bowl of water, and then helped Miakka to squat upright again. She watched Miakka's face contort as a new contraction began.

"Listen to me. Concentrate on my face," Wagahi said, lifting Miakka's head with her hand. "Take a deep breath and push hard. Let me see your face turn red."

Wagahi placed her hands on Miakka's abdomen, feeling for the height of the contraction. "Now," she demanded. "Push!"

Instead of pushing, Miakka went limp and slumped forward.

"No," Wagahi ordered, straightening her. "Who are you to give up and let this child die inside you? All that it asks is to be born. Birthing is never easy. Listen to the horror that is striking the People. Do you still hear it? Can you hear the cries of death? How dare you give in to the pain. You will kill your own child."

Miakka screamed with the pain and then bore down, grunting at the end of the contraction, releasing the air she had held in her lungs.

"Please, Wagahi, get it out," she yelled. "Help me! Please, help me!"

Wagahi could feel Miakka's belly tighten again. "Watch me. Look at me, Miakka. Breathe deeply now while you can. Be ready; it is coming again."

"No," she screamed. "Make it end! Help—" She was cut off by the intensity of the pain.

"Deep breath. Deep breath. Like this." Wagahi opened her mouth and sucked in air.

Miakka drew in her breath, watching and mimicking the midwife. She was sure she would split in two. She wanted the pain to stop, and she hated the man who had planted his seed in her.

Again her knuckles turned white as she clutched the pole. Her knees shook as she bore down, forcing the infant's head into the birth canal.

Explosively she let out her breath. "Is it coming? Tell me, Wagahi."

The midwife reached inside. Her fingertips touched the wet mass of the baby's full head of hair.

"Yes! Yes! I feel the head." Tears ran down her face.

Wagahi had assisted at many births. She had been trained from childhood by her mother, who was also a midwife. She was now training her daughter, Sima, but tonight she had let her sleep. She wished now that she had made her get up and come with her to the safety of the birthing hut. Quietly she asked the spirits to be with Sima and to protect her. Wagai could do nothing to help her daughter. As lives were being taken, another was coming into the world.

Miakka managed a smile. "Are you sure the baby is coming? You feel the head?" she asked before the smile changed to a grimace. This time at the end of the contraction she screamed. There was no time now for any more questions as the pain rapidly overtook her. Miakka's eyes bulged with the pressure.

Wagahi's hands cradled the small head as it emerged from the mother. "Just the shoulders now," she said in support of the exhausted mother.

One more time Miakka pushed until she thought she was turning inside out. There was a sudden explosion as the child entered the world, followed by a small gush.

Miakka looked down as Wagahi lifted the infant, still covered in the white, pasty covering that had protected it while it was inside its mother. Gently she wiped the baby's eyes and cleaned its nostrils. The infant drew in its first air and let out a healthy cry.

Miakka's eyes filled with tears. Carefully she lay down, and Wagahi handed her the infant.

Wagahi measured a hand's length down the cord and tied it off with a piece of sinew. Three fingers' length from that she tied it again and then cut it between the ties with her birthing knife.

Miakka curled her arm around the baby, stroking its damp hair. This was no monster. Carefully she inspected the baby. The spine was intact. The eyes were spaced properly, and the mouth and nose were separate. The child had all its limbs, fingers, and toes. Miakka stroked her baby's cheek, and the newborn struggled to turn to the touch.

The infant was perfect. Atula's seed and magic were potent. The shape of the face was the father's, but the nose and the mouth were Miakka's. The long slender fingers were also those of the mother. The wonderful golden skin was Atula's more than hers. The child was a remarkable blend of the two.

As the newborn began to suckle at its mother's breast, Wagahi waited for the afterbirth. At its delivery the birth was complete. She scooped up the earth that had absorbed the other products of birth and wrapped it, with the placenta, in a hide made especially for such a thing. She would bury it in a sacred place away from the village and known only to the women.

That would have to wait. Wagahi sat against the wall of the hut, her shoulders shaking with her tears. The awful noise of battle still filled her ears. Suddenly a brilliant light streaked across the sky, a light so luminous that it lit up the inside of the hut. Miakka looked up, and Wagahi stood.

In the village both the A-po-la-chee and the People were stunned, in awe of the blinding light. All eyes froze on the streaking fireball. The A-po-la-chee dropped their weapons, certain that it was a sign of power from the spirits of the tribe they had assaulted. They had won this battle, but they would not war with spirits.

They tracked the light until it disappeared. By then the momentum of the battle was lost, and the A-po-la-chee began to withdraw. Atula stood in the center of the mound until only the light from the moon fell across the village.

The hammock was littered with the debris of war. Broken lances, bloody knives, and the bodies of members of both tribes speckled the rich black dirt.

From the corner of his eyes Atula saw the last A-po-la-chee retreat. He started to sit down in the middle of all the disorder but quickly straightened. The A-po-la-chee warrior was headed toward the birthing hut—and Atula had seen Miakka get Wagahi and go in that direction earlier. It had to be her time, and the two women were alone and vulnerable in the hut.

Wagahi stiffened as she heard the rustle of the brush outside. Someone was near. It was A-po-la-chee, she was sure. Carefully she crept to the door.

"What is it?" Miakka asked in a quiet voice. "Is someone there?"

Wagahi motioned her to be silent as she eased herself through the doorway. The new mother drew her newborn child closer to her. The touch of the delicate tender skin sent a warm flush through her. The baby had stopped nursing, and Miakka pressed her lips to the top of the baby's head, listening closely.

The silence of the night ignited her nerves, and at the chirp of a cricket Miakka jumped. That sound was followed by a muffled groan and then a thud.

"Wagahi?" she whispered, but there was no answer. "Wagahi?" she called again and then bit her bottom lip. There was a noise just outside the door, but it wasn't the footsteps of the midwife.

In the doorway appeared a tall warrior. He was not of the People. He was A-po-la-chee. She was paralyzed with fear as she watched him enter the hut and move among the shadows.

Miakka's people were small but robust. She had never seen a man so tall before. He looked drawn out, like an animal hide that had been stretched out between two trees to cure. The bizarre-looking man walked close to her and spoke, but she had no idea what he said. She stared at his eyes, looking deep inside him. He was someone she should fear.

Again he spoke nonsense words, then let out a deep chuckle, throwing his head back. The warrior brushed her hair out of the way and looked at the infant. He held his knife to Miakka's throat, cupped one of her breasts with his free hand, and let his eyes wander over the rest of her body.

Could he not tell that she had just given birth? What did he want from her?

When the intruder reached for the infant, Miakka lurched upward, pushing his arm away and impaling her shoulder on the knife.

In the doorway another A-po-la-chee appeared, but this one had a look of surprise on his face. He spoke sharply. The warrior inside the hut, apparently stunned, turned his head toward the A-po-la-chee in the doorway.

The warrior carefully withdrew his knife from Miakka's shoulder, and the child began to cry as if it felt its mother's pain. In defiance, as though saving face, the warrior again held the knife to her throat.

Behind the second A-po-la-chee, Atula arrived, calling out to the stranger in the doorway. Although the invader did not understand the words, he turned and raised his open hand, gesturing for Atula to be still.

The A-po-la-chee lifted his spear and turned toward the intruder inside. Atula watched stiffly as the warrior obeyed his apparent superior. The man released his grip on Miakka, lowered his knife, and left the hut.

Atula still held his lance shoulder high. The stranger who had ordered the warrior away lowered his spear and stared at Atula. The shaman lowered his lance and nodded, then moved to one side to let the A-po-la-chee pass. Atula stood in the doorway until both warriors were out of sight.

Miakka looked up at Atula, feeling an unexpected oneness with him. "Come," she said. Her shoulder spouted blood, but she was surprised at how little pain she felt.

Atula edged his way into the birthing hut. The air was filled with the aroma of creation, and he was moved by the sight and smell of the miracle of life. He felt a slight choking in his throat and a burning sensation in his eyes. He was glad that Miakka could not clearly see his face.

"Closer," she urged.

"Wagahi is dead. She has crossed over," he said, bending down next to her. He pressed the heel of his hand over her wound and concentrated on her injury.

Miakka was not surprised. She had heard Wagahi groan and hit the ground. Although she felt saddened, she was thankful to have been spared.

The bleeding was subsiding. "Be still and quiet. Rest, and I will be right back."

She was so tired. Yes, she would rest with the precious

baby nuzzled against her. In moments she was asleep, weakened by the birth and the knife wound.

Atula went to his platform, searched his baskets and pouches for just the right things, and rushed back to her, zigzagging around the bodies and surviving villagers as they began to clean up and to grieve.

Quietly he entered the hut. The wound had continued to bleed while he was gone, forming a small pool of blood. She lay so still that at first it frightened him.

"Miakka?"

She opened her eyes sleepily.

"Did you see the sign?" he asked her as he began to pack the wound with medicine that would control infection and bleeding. Then he took a piece of softened hide and some sinew and bound the wound tightly.

When he was finished, he looked into her lovely face. "Your child was given a very special sign."

"Mmm," she agreed, closing her eyes again.

Atula clutched the amulet about his neck. "Let it be a good sign, Father," he whispered aloud.

The spirits always showed some sign at an infant's birth or within one moon cycle of the birth. This one was clearly meant for this child, and it was a strong sign.

The sun was beginning to rise, and the dim light entered the doorway. The birthing hut faced the east, the creating place of the new day and new life.

Through the shadows of the fading night he marveled at the sight of mother and child just a short time after birth. His giant hand enveloped the child's, and the tiny fist wrapped itself around his finger.

"His grip is already strong," he said and smiled, filled with the pride of a new father.

Miakka turned the baby toward him, removing the wrap, offering the infant to its father. Atula's eyes widened at what he saw.

Chapter Six

BEHOLD, YOUR DAUGHTER," Miakka whispered as Atula's large hands slid beneath the tiny infant.

He was suddenly filled with emotion. "A daughter," he repeated.

Miakka watched as the man held his newborn. His big hands touched her black hair.

"I am sorry that I have not delivered you a son," Miakka said, breaking the silence.

Atula stroked the baby's soft cheek, unhappy that he would not know her well, as he would one of his sons. He slid his finger into the tiny fist and delighted again in the child's response. For a moment the child opened her sleepy eyes and looked into the face of her father.

He had never held one of his children right after birth. The wonder of it caught him off guard, overwhelming the mighty and powerful spirit man with the realization of the miracle. He suddenly felt like a tiny speck of dust in the realm of all that was holy and mystic.

"The Great Spirit honors us each time there is a birth," he finally said.

"And the star?" Miakka said.

"Even the A-po-la-chee were in wonder of the streaking star. It turned the darkness into light. It has declared the child's name. She must be called Mi-sa, Light in the Darkness."

"That is such a strong name for a girl. I hope it is not difficult for her to live with."

"The sign was for her alone. The spirits do not often give such strong signs. It cannot be ignored."

"Mi-sa," she whispered, "so strong and so fragile all at the same time."

"The spirits have named her," he said.

Miakka's forehead furrowed with concern. "How badly have the A-po-la-chee injured the People? I am afraid to know whom we have lost."

"We have suffered. I will know it all soon enough. Brush the painful sounds from your head and hear only the sighs of the spirits as they see Mi-sa."

Atula held the child close, breathing in the sweet breath of his daughter. He then looked at Miakka, her hair tangled and disheveled. The perspiration had begun to evaporate as she cooled, leaving her skin dusted with white salt. He was suddenly thankful that it was the women who gave birth, even though he felt the slightest pang of jealousy.

Gently he returned the baby to her mother. The light from the sun now streamed into the hut. The noise of the village buzzed in the air. There was much to do this day. He had to attend to the wounded and the dead. One by one the families would come to him for spiritual healing. He would officiate and help guide the dead so that they would cross over. This was going to be his last peaceful interlude for a long time. He sat quietly for another moment. Miakka and Mi-sa closed their eyes.

Jegatua, the cacique, the leader of his people, gathered the clan onto the ceremonial dais, an earthen plaza. Generations ago the People had hauled marl to the center of the village to build it up. Here the Council of Men met to make decisions, and the People gathered here for ceremonies or at special times. This raised plot formed an arc in front of the central hearth. The people of the clan sat quietly, their faces inscribed with lines of pain.

They listened as their leader spoke. Jegatua praised the warriors for their courage and the women for their steadfast resistance.

"The attack is over now. As we have done before, and as our ancestors did, we will treat our wounded and find the strength of the spirits of those who were taken from us. The A-po-la-chee will not crush us. Women, you will weep alone, in privacy. Comfort your children and fill them with pride. Men, grieve silently. Feed on your heritage. Let the strength of our ancestors fortify you. We will not let the A-po-la-chee steal one moment more than they have already taken from us. Put this behind you, but never forget it. Go and do what you must, and then be as you always were."

The People stood and left the gathering plaza. They made efforts to begin their day in defiance of the A-po-la-chee.

Atula's stomach growled with hunger as he smelled the turtle, rabbit, and bird roasting over the cook fires. Even in the face of tragedy the clan would carry on. They would eat and hunt. They would laugh and cry. The women prepared the morning meal even though many grieved for their husbands or their sons. Some women, too, had been lost to the savages from the other side.

The smell of berries and coontie bread pervaded the village as the women in their mossy air plant skirts tended the fires and the men performed their grisly chores. In a short time, the People were carrying on with their familiar lives.

They were a strong nation, Atula realized as he looked

about. They would not allow the A-po-la-chee to destroy them, either in body or in mind.

Amakollee, bringing fresh water from the cenote, approached Atula.

"Miakka's child was born just before dawn?" she asked.

"Yes. Miakka has given life to a beautiful girl child."

"The child is female?" Amakollee seemed surprised by that fact. Her lips turned up in a smile. The child born last night would not be competition for the one she carried.

"The spirits have already named her," he said.

"You mean the star that crossed the heavens? How could that be? The night sky was brilliant with its light. Everyone saw the star. It was from the spirits. It defeated the A-po-la-chee. How can a girl have such a powerful sign?"

"I do not question the spirits. The sign was meant for this child," he replied, becoming a little annoyed with Amakollee's questioning. "As always, they have their reasons."

"Atula, do you hear yourself? Your father never would have been fooled like this. The star must have been a sign for something else, and you have missed it, thinking it was meant for the child."

Atula stopped and faced her squarely. "Are you the shaman? Do you talk with the spirits?"

"No," she continued to argue, "but I will not be the only one to question your judgment. No one of this clan or even of the tribe will believe that such a sign was meant for a girl. As soon as the others know, they will begin to talk."

"And they will know her name at the time of the naming ceremony. If they wish to question my power, my judgment, let them. No one knows the ways of the spirits better than I."

"You will name her for the star?"

"I will call her by the name the spirits gave her."

Amakollee shook her head in disbelief. How could Atula believe that such a powerful sign was for that child? At least it was a girl and no threat. Surely the child she carried would be a boy and have a strong sign, but what could be stronger than the sign that was given last night?

Atula remembered twisting the strands of Miakka's hair into one strong thread, weaving the twins inside her into one. Perhaps that was why there had been such a mighty sign; it needed to be strong enough for two.

Amakollee was right. The clan would have a difficult time accepting his interpretation of the star, particularly while they suffered in the aftermath of the attack. Such signs were few and reserved for a child destined to lead or to have some very special quality. Most signs were simple, like the earth.

Wakulla came and stood by Atula. "We have lost many loved ones, and some still live in the pain of their injuries."

Atula put his hand on his eldest son's shoulder. "You have never seen an attack before. Keep the image in your mind and carry it with you all your life. We must all carry the memory so that the horror of it will never permit us to become like the A-po-la-chee. Watch the older ones. See how they go on, not letting the desire for vengeance overtake them."

Wakulla kicked at the dirt. "But we have young, strong, and courageous warriors. We could take the A-po-la-chee by surprise, and that would end the conflicts."

"Yes," Atula agreed, "you and Talasee and the others fought bravely. Without the official ceremony, you achieved the right of manhood. I watched you whip up the strength of many, and I saw your courage as you stood toe to toe with the enemy. But we cannot become the A-po-la-chee. Hate and vengeance are not our way. They are the way of the wicked and despised. Do you understand?"

"Some warriors my age were frightened, and now they feel humiliated. Shame is a slow death—another way of cutting out the heart of the People. I struggle with the idea of allowing it."

"You speak of your friend Pachu. He has nothing to be ashamed of. He fought bravely."

"But now he shakes and hides in his platform."

"He will recover. Be patient. He has yet to become a man."

Jegatua was coming toward them. He carried something in his old bony arms. When he got closer, Atula fell to his knees, raised his hands to the sky, and called out.

Jegatua held Micco, his tiny arms hanging lifelessly, swaying with the cacique's steps.

The cacique laid the boy before his father.

"And Shani?" Atula asked in a gravelly voice.

"She was killed while struggling against one of the savages. The last thing she did was throw herself over her son to protect him, but the weight of her death also took Micco's breath from him. There is not even a small scratch on him."

Wakulla stood by Atula, wide-eyed. He admired his father for his control. As his throat tightened, he watched his father pick up the child and proudly carry him away. His back was straight and his head high. The A-po-la-chee would not break him.

The following days were filled with sorrow and the ceremonies of death. The dead were placed on the elevated floor of the charnel house, a platform erected over a small slough that separated the village from the burial place. The scavenger birds would clean the flesh away. Later the bones would be gathered, bundled, and interred in the burial area to the south. The use of a charnel house helped prevent animals from digging into the burial mound. The bodies decomposed on the platform surrounded by water. When the remains were collected, they would be brittle white bones, bleached by the burning sun.

And as those first long, wrenching days passed, the People let go of their visible grief. No spirit, no tribe, would see them weakened. They would deal with their pain inside.

Miakka's pain was from the wound in her shoulder, but she also suffered inside. The birth of her daughter had been tainted with the attack, and so she could not enjoy telling other women of the birth nor could she speak much of her good fortune. Mi-sa was a reminder of the horrible night when the A-po-la-chee had come.

Atula appeared in the doorway of her shelter as she folded one of Mi-sa's wraps.

"I have come to examine your shoulder."

"The wound is nearly healed," she answered. "Your medicine is good."

Atula watched her as she busied herself about the platform. "Have you regained all motion in your arm?"

"Almost."

"Let me see," he said, moving closer and taking her wrist in his hand. "Straighten your arm all the way out," he told her. "Now," he said, sliding his hand up her arm, gently helping her lift it, "lift it high over your head."

Miakka raised her arm slowly, letting Atula guide Her, feeling his breath against her cheek.

"Good," he said as he delicately moved her arm in an arc.

Miakka grimaced at the stiffness and soreness that still remained in her shoulder. Atula watched her face and returned her arm to her side.

"Can you swing it across in front of you?"

"A little way," she answered.

"Let me help." He took her hand and supported her upper arm with his other palm.

Her skin was warm and soft, and the scent she wore flooded him with memories of their night together.

Atula wore no scent, but Miakka did recognize something in the air that was his. His hand was gentle and firm, just as it had been when he took her. For an instant her knees weakened.

"My arm is fine," she said, unable to look at him. She was certain that he had seen her wobble.

"Why do you look away? Have I offended you?" he asked, noticing that she deliberately looked away from him.

"No," she said awkwardly. "I think Mi-sa is awakening."

"The naming ceremony will be soon. Are you prepared for that?"

Both knew there would be grumblings about the child's name, and Atula hoped Miakka was ready to deal with it.

"The spirits gave her that name," she said, letting out a deep breath. "I know it will be difficult. Already her birth reminds people of the night of the A-po-la-chee. Her name will cause conflict. I know that. But I do not doubt it or challenge it. It is the will of the spirits."

"Good. Mi-sa," he said softly, looking at the infant. "It is a good name."

For the next few days Atula thought of almost nothing but Mi-sa. He consulted the spirits but got no answer. The star sign was firm and not to be challenged. He hoped that he could convince the clan that the powerful sign was meant for a girl child, and from that sign she would be given her name, Mi-sa.

The moon turned in its regular cycles, giving more time for the People to put the night of the A-po-la-chee behind them. Atula would wait as long as he could before he announced the child's name. He wanted to make certain that the People had put behind them the association of the birth with the attack. He knew they would not forget, but with more time the memory of that night would not be so raw.

Amakollee's belly continued to grow large with the child who would save her. She dwelt on the impending birth excessively, more than first-time mothers, thinking and talking of nothing else. Her friends tired of her relentless preoccupation. The child would be born very soon, and they hoped that when she was busy caring for the baby, the obsession would end.

———

WHEN THE DAY OF THE NAMING CEREMONY CAME, the village was filled with activity. The last two days had been fasting days. The children of Cherok's age, six summers and older, were also asked to fast. This temporary starvation brought on a holy state. The body became free of impurities that bogged down the mind and spirit. Fasting set the spirit free and unclogged the portals, allowing spirits to enter.

Children began informal fasting at an early age. During ceremonies, the children who had never fasted before were given their first fasting stick. The sticks were carefully measured for width and length against a scarred and notched stick that only the medicine man used. All the sticks started out the same size. They were charred in the fire that perpetually burned in the central hearth. Atula said prayers over the sticks and then distributed them to the children who were experiencing their first fast. The eager children quickly painted their faces with the charcoal sticks. The older children held sticks of varying lengths, depending on how often they had chosen to fast. The parents were delighted if their child's stick was used up quickly, proving the worthiness and nobleness of their offspring. As the children drew black lines across their faces, the parents swelled with pride.

In the evening by the light of the fire the men danced small sacred steps to the rhythm of animal-skin drums and Atula's turtle-shell rattle. The carapace and the plastron of the shell were tied together, encasing hard red poison beans. Where the head of the turtle had once extended out of the shell was a slash pine handle, intricately carved like the neck and head of the turtle.

The men dripped with shell necklaces and anklets, clinking against one another, bumping against their warm brown skin. Their chests and faces were painted with the red stain of the pokeberry and the yellow stain of decomposing iron-rich limestone. The bodies of the women were coated with oil so that they gleamed in the light.

Atula circled the fire, looking at the children's fasting sticks. He separated the girls from the boys and then motioned the young men closer to the fire.

The man of the spirits shivered and groaned, announcing that a spirit had entered his body. The crowd hushed and waited for him to talk. He mumbled and chanted softly until finally he opened his eyes and stared blankly across the throng.

The music-making men began to tap their drums lightly and hum as Atula touched the head of a tall boy, Pachu. Atula continued to swoon as he made his way through the group of boys, concentrating deeply.

He stopped again to touch Talasee and then Wakulla, his eldest son. As soon as Atula's hand touched their heads, the boys fell to the ground as if thrown there by an invisible force. The parents of those he touched were filled with excitement. Their sons were coming of age. The spirits recognized them as soon-to-be men.

Tomorrow with the first pink of daylight, the chosen young men would go out alone, naked and weaponless, along the trails for men.

The shaman gave all of the children an animal totem sometime during their first four seasons of life. In their medicine bags the shaman placed tangible evidence of the animal totems that would take care of them until they found their own totems.

It was time for Wakulla, Pachu, and Talasee to find their own totems, their animal protectors. Tomorrow they would be sent alone into the wilderness. They would sing the songs of the animal spirits that had been taught to them since birth. Naked, as they had come into the world, they would entrust their destiny to the animal spirits. In the marsh and muck they would intuit what to do. During the ordeal, a special animal would make itself known to each.

Amakollee rubbed her protruding belly as if she could pass on the scene and her thoughts to her unborn child. Cherok, too, watched carefully, knowing that one day he also would become a man.

The chosen young men soon recovered from their trancelike state and rejoined the crowd, accepting congratulations from all of the men. If the mother of the boy had a brother, it would be his duty to stay with the boy throughout the night, telling him the story of his own totem quest and the one that had been told to him by his uncle. The stories passed from generation to generation. If there was no mother's brother, a volunteer, related matrilineally, would gladly take on the task.

The crowd finally quieted. Atula returned to the central hearth and fed it more fuel. He withdrew a handful of powder from a leather pouch and tossed it into the flames. It suddenly blazed and crackled, alerting the crowd that another ritual was about to begin.

The clan quieted as Atula stood with his back to the fire. Clusters of white breeding plumes from the great egret were banded to his upper arms. He wore a cape made of the white feathers of the wood ibis, the great egret, and the snowy egret. A carved shell medallion hung around his neck as did the shaman's amulet, which dangled and danced in the firelight. Across his cheeks and forehead were sharp white lines, a shocking contrast to his olive skin. The rest of his body had been washed with lime, making it a ghostly chalk white. He wore the symbols of new beginnings. It was time to give the new child its name.

Everyone drew close as Atula began his songs, calling the spirits to witness.

Suddenly Cherok began to sway to his father's song, and his small feet stepped lightly, turning him in circles. He was the image of his father, and his spirit had heard his father's song.

Cacema saw it first, and then Atula. The rest of the People fell silent as they watched. Atula at first slowed his song but soon returned to the natural rhythm. But then Cherok stopped, smiled at his mother, and took her by the hand. Amakollee blanched, and the baby kicked inside her.

Atula called Miakka from the crowd. She carried the child at her breast until she stood in front of Atula. The shaman took the child and held her above his head and again sang into the night. Then slowly he lowered her and held her out toward the crowd.

"The night this female child was born, the spirits sent an unmistakable sign. No other child was born that night, and so it could not have been meant for any other. It was a strong sign, a powerful sign, and her name will be the same. She is called Mi-sa, Light in the Darkness."

"Ayee!" the crowd screeched, not believing that Atula had given such a name to a female child.

"Atula," called out one of the clan, "how do you dare?"

"Did not everyone see the star that streaked the heavens just moments after the birth? Such a sign cannot be ignored."

"Perhaps it was a sign for something else," another retorted. "It was the night of the A-po-la-chee, an evil night. And now you give a female this name? Perhaps you have misread it. A star is the most powerful sign. How could it be for a female child?"

"Do you doubt the omnipotence of the spirits? Do you question their decisions?"

The crowd again grew silent. Atula was the shaman, and he knew the spirits better than anyone. The People would not challenge him, but they remained skeptical about his interpretation of the sign. They had never before had cause to doubt anything Atula said or did, and to do so was almost sacrilege. But this was nearly too much.

A scene from the vision he had had flashed before

Atula. He had asked the spirits about the child even before it was born. He remembered the fork in the river; the new river and the old. He remembered the division between the men.

Amakollee grimaced with disgust. How could her child have a more powerful sign and name than the one given by a star? This was a hideous error on Atula's part. She was carrying the child with the Gift! Was she the only one who realized that?

Atula felt something tug at his leg. It was Cherok. He had silently woven his way through the crowd almost unnoticed, finding his way to his father's knee. His eyes were filled with wonder and curiosity. Small smiles found their way across many lips even in the middle of the solemn ceremony as the clan watched the small boy ask for his father's attention.

"What is it that you want, Cherok?" Atula softly questioned the boy.

"The child with the star sign—I wish to see her, Father."

Cradling the baby, Atula squatted down so that Cherok could see, forgetting the intensity of the naming ceremony. It had taken Cherok, as if by magic, to soften the crowd with his innocence.

The small brown eyes glittered with the light of the fire as he looked upon the infant. "Mi-sa, Light in the Darkness—that is a nice name." Cherok looked up at his father. "I saw her naming sign. It was the night of the A-po-la-chee."

The boy looked again at the tiny face. The baby stared into the night sky, her eyes fixed on the white and blue fires that twinkled above. The stars were the hearths of those who had crossed to the Other Side, and they were also the hearths of many spirits that watched over the

People.

Cherok stared, in awe of the miniature life held by his father. He touched her hair with his small hand and then lowered his head and breathed in the scent of the baby's skin. His dark eyes sparkled as he watched her gaze so intently.

For an instant he met her on the plane where all children communicate with one another. He remembered the time when he had stared into the cenote, looking at the clouds with Atula. How hard he had tried to feel them, to touch them as his father had urged. For a moment he knew what it was like—what his father had tried to get him to do. For a moment he was with Mi-sa. And then he knew what it was he saw in the baby's eyes.

"I think she touches the stars, Father."

Chapter Seven

CHEROK'S INNOCENCE HAD CALMED the crowd, and the questions stopped. In his small voice they had heard the spirits. Even though some harbored doubts about the child who had been born during the evil attack of the A-po-la-chee, they would trust their shaman.

Atula stood silhouetted by the glow of the coals of the fire, the feathers of his costume moving in the southeasterly breeze. That nearly constant wind blew across the warm Gulf Stream, preventing most of the northern cold fronts from reaching them.

Atula waited until most of the People had disappeared into the darkness. They were tired, and so was he.

As Cherok started to leave, he turned back to look at the awesome figure of his father, the magnificent full moon above his head, the dying embers at his feet.

Miakka also turned to take a last glimpse. Atula stood tall against the night sky, filled with the supernatural and yet tempered with the heart of man. She clutched Mi-sa tightly when she saw Amakollee standing in the shadows near her platform. Miakka pretended not to notice and hurried along to her home.

Finally she rested on her mat, holding Mi-sa to her breast, looking out through the opening. The white feathers of Atula's costume caught the silver of the moonlight, making him barely visible, a ghost of a figure floating through the night air. She closed her eyes, wishing she could hear his footsteps fall on the earth beneath her platform and then climb the short ladder. With her fantasy she drifted into sleep.

Wakulla could not sleep. Hamet, Kita's brother, had filled his ears and mind with so many stories that he had them all confused into a jumbled mass like the moss that hung from the live oaks. At first Wakulla had listened attentively, thrilled with each new story of a quest made by some distant relative, but the threads of the stories became intertwined until he heard one common story of all his ancestors. Finally Hamet had finished and fallen asleep.

But to Wakulla it seemed the night would never pass. Tomorrow he would begin the quest for his totem spirit. He would end his journey through boyhood. The crickets roared loudly in his ears, and the insects incessantly buzzed around his face and nostrils. Even the night noises of other men sleeping seemed to echo across the land. The stars that had shone so brightly earlier in the evening had been covered by dull gray and shapeless clouds. The air temperature was mild but humid with the dampness of spring showers. Even though it wasn't hot, the humidity sucked perspiration from all the clan. At least there was a breeze to evaporate the thin film of sweat and keep him cool.

He was glad to see the eastern sky lighten with the birth of the new day. Quietly he walked to the cenote and bathed the night odors from him. The cool water cleared his eyes of the grit that came from lack of sleep. He did not linger long in the water, aware that alligators often cruised the banks in search of deer.

Had the other two boys been able to sleep? he

wondered. No sooner had the thought entered his head than they both appeared on their way to the sinkhole. Each nodded with respect, but there was to be no conversation with anyone from this day until they returned with their spirit totems.

Wakulla climbed the bank and walked back up the trail to the village. Kita, his mother, was awake and stood at the base of the platform. Though her heart ached to, she could neither speak to her son nor provide nourishment for him on this morning. Today he would begin the journey into manhood alone and at the mercy of the spirits.

Miakka also stirred as Mi-sa began to whimper. The mother pulled her infant to her breast. As the baby nursed, Miakka thought of mothers who were watching their sons leave to go alone into the hostile wilderness unclothed, unarmed, vulnerable. She cradled Mi-sa closer, glad that she had given birth to a daughter.

Wakulla laid all his belongings along the north side of the platform, the masculine side. If he did not return alive, his possessions would be distributed among the people of the clan. If his body was found, no grave goods would be buried with a boy who could not become a man.

The fast had ended for everyone but the three chosen boys. The smell of the food on the morning fires wafted through the platform, but Wakulla did not weaken. He was no longer hungry for the food of this world. He was amazed at how the fasting had worked. He truly realized for the first time that earthly things did not matter. The quest was for the spiritual.

When he had finished laying out his things, he climbed down and walked to the central hearth so that all might see him leave on his venture. It was important that as many eyes fall on him as possible. He would take with him small pieces of those who looked upon him, and that would give him added strength. He saw Talasee and Pachu also walking through the village.

Finally Atula and the cacique, Jegatua, came to the hearth. Jegatua planted a painted staff, as tall as a man and then half again, in the muck. Osprey feathers hung from the top. The osprey, a large hawk, was a symbol of strength and free flight. It could see for long distances as it soared high above the earth, and the shaman often flew on its wings during visions.

Wakulla, Pachu, and Talasee stood before the two most powerful men of the clan.

Jegatua spoke. "Go into the wilderness. Go into the land of the man, the hunter, the provider, the warrior. Humble yourself. Prove your faith in the spirits, and they will answer. Find your animal totem. Let him reveal himself to you. Whoever he might be—bird, turtle, deer, or other—he will give you his special power and will represent and counsel you. It is a special bond between man and animal. Keep safe."

After Jegatua spoke, the boys went along the trails walked by men until they reached the water. Each took a small pirogue and poled down the shallow canoe trail.

After a while the three separated, each following his call along a different trail. Wakulla stood in his dugout and looked across the vast river of grass. In the far distance he could barely make out the trees against the sky that marked his home. He hoped he would return soon with a good totem.

Suddenly he felt very much alone. He had never been alone before, and now he was so far from home. A small shudder ran through him. It was fear, and Wakulla balked at it. He could not be afraid or he would not become a man. His totem spirit would not reveal itself to him, for the spirit would choose only a strong and brave man, not a whimpering boy.

Wakulla dug the pole in and pushed off again, turning toward unknown territory. Slowly the village behind him grew smaller and smaller until it was merely a dot, and then it disappeared, absorbed by the distance.

A red-shouldered hawk swooped overhead, catching Wakulla's attention. It roosted on a bay tree that grew along the edge of a hammock. The hawk turned its head and stared at Wakulla.

It was a sign, the first of the adventure. Wakulla recognized it and quickly adjusted the course of his pirogue toward the hammock. This is where he would stop. This was the place where he would wait.

He tugged at the bow, grounding his canoe. The sun streamed down in hot ribbons, drenching his brow with sweat. The shade of the trees was welcome, and Wakulla ventured deeper under the canopy. When he reached a place that looked friendly, he cleared away some of the debris and made camp. He gathered stones for a hearth. He would build a fire later after he had fashioned some tools. The pointed sticks weren't much, but he could use them if an A-po-la-chee came by surprise. He made the weapons with that in mind as well as their common use. When his quest was over, and not before, he would hunt and fill his belly for the first time as a man.

Darkness arrived by the time he finished. Over the fire he charred and tempered the sticks that he had sharpened. The fire-tempered wood was strong.

He hunkered low near the coals and stared into the flames, letting them work their magic on him. In the flames he could see scenes that were buried in his memory. He caught flashes of himself as a child, glimpses of his mother's face, and visions of the shaman. The smoke swirled up into his nostrils, filling him with the breath of the fire. Finally, exhausted from the day, he stretched out and slept.

The next day Wakulla sang to the spirits and bathed in the water of the earth. He tortured himself, purging all impurities, feeding the fire in the daytime and leaning near it, drawing all the fluids from his body. He hallucinated and dreamed. His muscles cramped, and his lips cracked and bled.

For days he left himself exposed and vulnerable as he waited for his animal totem to present itself. Each day he pushed himself further, fearing that he had not proved himself.

On the night of the fourth day Wakulla again brought the fire to a blaze and sat next to it. His naked body was smeared with black muck, and his hair clung to his scalp. His bones stuck out at angles, and his once supple skin was stretched across his cheekbones. Dark circles, like half-moons, appeared under his dull eyes. He tried but failed to moisten his lips with his swollen tongue. He swayed as he watched the flames that seemed to pull him into the fire.

At first he poked a stick in and out of the yellow tops of the flames. He worked closer and closer, his concentration deeper and deeper until the stick fell into the fire, and Wakulla's hands danced through the lapping flames.

The silence crackled with the quick rustling of the brush as a small animal darted away from a predator. Wakulla responded, grabbing one of the spears he had made. He stood and backed away from the fire. Was it the A-po-la-chee? Would they kill him for sport? He did not understand the A-po-la-chee. Would they torture him?

Acutely aware of every sound, he could sense the nearness of another warm-blooded hunter. The normal night sounds intensified, ringing in his ears. He could hear his blood circulating, whooshing through the veins and arteries of his body. His heart pounded in his ears, and the air rushed into his lungs like the wind in the trees. The blinking of his eyelids sounded like the cracking of a twig. How could he clearly hear the sounds of the intruder?

But he could. The noises came closer and closer. It was not man. It walked on four feet—four padded feet. The animal slinked closer.

Wakulla was frightened, and his hands trembled, but he knew he should show no fear. He was being tested, challenged by the animal spirits. It could be his totem that awaited him, checking his worthiness before it agreed to share its spirit. But what if it was just an annoyed animal or a hungry beast? He would have to trust the spirits.

Wakulla walked back to the fire, making himself clearly visible, demonstrating his faith and courage. Suddenly he noticed that the cricket and frog sounds quieted. Another shadow slipped through the brush, and he strained to make a shape from it. A dark form crouched in the shadows, creeping almost on its belly, stalking him.

"Show yourself," he finally spoke, trying to sound sure of himself.

Twigs and dead leaves crackled under the animal's feet as it revealed itself in the light, paused with a front paw raised, and then moved in smooth, long, confident strides. Like a sleek ghost, the large cat walked into camp. The fire should have scared it, not drawn it, Wakulla thought.

The panther stared at the boy through the flames. Its amber-green eyes reflected the colors of the fire, and

Wakulla suddenly felt as if he had dived into the two pools that watched him. The panther remained still, letting the boy in.

The world faded into blackness around Wakulla as he left his body and became one with the panther. The feeling was incredible. The air filled with odors he had never smelled before, and the night filled with light, letting him see in the blackness. He could feel the muscle fibers in the panther's strong limbs and the sharpness of its canine teeth. He could sense the power, agility, and stealth that made the cat a good hunter. As he gathered the cunning and strength of the animal, gratitude overwhelmed him until tears filled his eyes.

The boy was suddenly free and back on the other side of the fire. The panther remained motionless for a few more moments, staring as if to make certain that Wakulla had recognized him, and then walked into the brush. Wakulla stood breathless, still in awe. The panther had come to him, found him, and offered his spirit. He had found his animal totem. Wakulla sank to his knees and wept.

In the morning Wakulla ended his fast. For the first time in days his belly ached to be filled. A rabbit scurried by as he sat hidden in the grasses. Wakulla offered a quick prayer to be thankfulness. With a swift thrust of his arm, he felled the rabbit. Not until now had he truly felt and understood the relationship between man and animal. He knew the story as it had been told to him, but he had never felt it before.

The hunter approached the dead rabbit. The shadow of the animal would return to the sky to be born again in the flesh of another animal, thus completing the cycle of creation.

With respect, Wakulla lifted the rabbit. Because he accepted its meat, the animal's spirit was allowed to continue its journey. Wakulla dressed the rabbit at the kill site, said a prayer, and properly disposed of the remains, even turning the enriched earth that caught the animal's blood. The relationship between man and animal was an ancient and sacred one. And now Wakulla not only knew of it but had become part of it.

After filling himself with roasted rabbit, he covered the bones and the fire with dirt, making certain that all coals were extinguished. He took a last look around and left his camp. Wakulla stood tall in the dugout, a single spire against the blue sky.

He was a man.

Chapter Eight

WAKULLA APPROACHED the village. The mound was straight ahead, a small green island the earth had heaved out of the flat land. Slender spirals of smoke from the fires coiled into the air. The sun hung in the blue sky, a blinding yellow-white sphere. He dug his pole into the shallow water and pushed the canoe forward, riding on the shallow sheet of fresh water. Wakulla was filled with the excitement of a boy and the dignity of a man. Suddenly he propped the pole against the canoe, thrust both arms toward the sky, and whooped.

Closer to home he took one last look at the wide, shallow river. It stretched as far as he could see in all directions. Now it was his world. He was an extension of it, an integral part of the elaborate creation chain. Such an exalted feeling of glory rippled through him that he thought he might explode. The sun glinted off the water and glazed the grasses with golden light, turning what was left of the morning dew into tiny dazzling jewels along the blades of grass. He would miss the boy in himself, but he appreciated his new wisdom. The boy felt the sun beat down on his back like a spiritual playmate, but the boy felt no obligation to give anything back. The man was overwhelmed by the beauty and complexity of the earth. He wished to be a boy a little longer, to feel no responsibility, to revel in that freedom, to scream loud with joy, and to cry for mercy without shame.

He was closer to the village now, and Wakulla could smell the morning meals. In a moment he would pull his dugout onto the land and touch the soil of his childhood as a man. He would enter the village by way of men's trails. His feet would tread the path that his ancestors had walked before him. His grandfather's feet had stepped this way on the day he became a man.

One last time, after he beached the pirogue and tugged at the bow, dragging it onto dry land, he closed his eyes tightly, tensed his entire body, and let the boy grin.

When Wakulla turned toward the village, his face was somber and appeared miraculously older. A few people noticed his arrival. The women offered the new man, the new warrior, some food, and the young women turned their heads toward him. Wakulla obliged them by eating small portions of everything offered. It would have been rude not to accept, even though his stomach was still full and warm with the rabbit, whose pelt dangled from his hand.

Kita saw her son as she stood by her fire. She wanted to rush to him, brush his hair back from his face, and kiss his cheeks. Instead she grasped her medicine bag and silently thanked the spirits for watching over him and returning him safely. Holding back her tears, she watched him come closer.

He was wonderful to look at, she thought with pride. His black hair framed a broad face with sharp cheekbones under smooth, dark skin. He would always be her son, her child, no matter how old.

Wakulla held his arms out and firmly embraced his mother.

"I have brought you something," he said, turning her

loose.

Kita stepped back. "A marsh rabbit fur. It is special—the first from my son as a man. I will start a new blanket with it, as you have started a new life."

Jegatua, the aging cacique, came up to Wakulla and placed a hand on his shoulder. "It is good that you have returned safely. You are the first."

Wakulla suddenly realized that he had not seen the other two. How inconsiderate he had been not to inquire.

"When all have returned," Jegatua continued, "we will hear your stories and learn about your totems."

"I am anxious to tell it," Wakulla responded.

Near Kita was Tabisha's fire. She tended to the meal with her daughter Shakia. Wakulla watched Shakia as she knelt near the bed of hot coals, her long hair falling over her shoulders and almost touching the ground.

"Wakulla? Did you hear me?" Atula asked. He and Hamet had joined the group, and Atula had invited his son to his hearth to eat and talk, but Wakulla had not heard, his full attention focused on Shakia.

Atula called once more.

"I am sorry, Father. I am thinking of so many things."

"Mmm," Atula responded, noticing Shakia's sideward glance. "She looks at you, too," he said with a deep chuckle.

"Yes, she is lovely," Jegatua agreed.

"You really have become a man," Hamet agreed.

By late afternoon Talasee had also returned and was properly greeted by all, especially Wakulla. The two young men rested their hands on each other's shoulders and looked at each other, thinking how exciting it would be when they revealed their totems and told their stories.

"Ahh," Wakulla said, "you do indeed look like a man, Talasee."

"And you," Talasee responded.

"I looked like you when I first returned," Wakulla replied, drawing a finger through a patch of caked dirt on Talasee's chest. "Believe it or not, you will feel better after bathing."

"Where is Pachu?" Talasee asked, surveying the village.

"He has not yet returned. Only the two of us."

Talasee's face revealed concern and disappointment. "I hope he is safe."

"He will be here tomorrow, surely."

The two young men walked down to the cenote. Talasee went to the edge and onto a shallow ledge, where he sat and allowed the water to cover him up to his neck as Wakulla waited on shore, watching for alligators.

"I feel wonderful," Talasee said. "Did you realize how hungry you were?" he asked, lying back and floating out in the dark water.

"When I awoke this morning, I did. I had not noticed until then. What about you?"

"My hunger came later in the day. I was still awaiting my totem revelation when the sun came up."

"What did you hunt?" Wakulla asked.

"Turtle. What else would be so quick and easy?"

"I hunted a rabbit and brought back the pelt to my mother."

"We will sleep soundly this night," Talasee commented, pulling himself out of the water, shaking his head and sending a wet shower out in a halo around him.

Shadows began to blanket the village, and the People began to ready themselves for the darkness. The central hearth was banked with wood to keep the fire through the night. The People shook their grass mats to rid them of creatures that might have found refuge inside the weave.

Atula sat in the doorway of his platform. The sky was radiant, glittering with stars, and the moon was full. He watched Miakka climb her ladder. She turned and looked through the distance toward him. She was too far away for him to be sure, but he was certain that she smiled. *She is beautiful,* he thought. Of all the things he had done with his life, he wished he could have that one night with her over again. But relationships for him were not like those for other men. The sting of his affair with Shani had made him realize that. He heeded to stay away from this woman. She touched him too deeply. Inside he felt a warmth gush through him. Summer's heat had begun, but this he knew was a heat of a different kind.

Atula went inside his home and lay down on his mat. He closed his eyes, his thoughts reeling. Almost dreaming, he remembered his first time—the first time the fire was quenched through joining.

Kita had begun by touching his face softly, drawing the backs of her fingers across his lips and down his throat. Though in the eyes of the clan he was a man, he knew at that instant that he was still a boy, a floundering child in the new world of men.

Although Kita was older than he, she was beautiful. Her exotic eyes were slightly slanted, like those of the ancient ones in the legends.

He had lain still on his back as she worked miracles with his body. He could hear himself breathing as she undressed and slid her body next to his beneath the cover of hide and fur. When she raised the covers, a rush of cold air stunned him, making even greater the contrast between the chill of the night and the warmth of her body. She had nuzzled his neck, then covered his chest with kisses. Slowly and teasingly she'd trailed her mouth over his tight abdomen, feeling the tense muscles beneath, drawing lines and circles with her tongue.

Kita had taunted and aroused him, impassioned and inflamed him. It was unbearable torture; it was incomparable pleasure. He had tried to respond, to wet her with his mouth, his kisses, to return some of that pleasure, but she refused, finding some new way to please him. He fumbled with his hands, clutching frantically and clumsily at her.

Atula's heart had pounded in his chest, and he could hardly get his breath. He heard sounds come from him that he did not even recognize. He was in agony—no, ecstasy. He ached and burned deep inside, cramping with the pleasure of a wonderful, urgent throbbing that was nearly pain.

But she had the experience, not he. Tonight she was taking him, giving to him the reward and pleasure of joining. Tonight he was only the recipient. She had been honored with that charge. Tomorrow she would train him to bring pleasure to a woman. But tonight belonged to the young man who trembled beneath her.

Slowly she covered her body with his and then gently guided him into her. She wrapped her legs around him, setting the tempo until he could no longer be patient. He drove into her, groaning and gasping. The pleasure was sudden and explosive, blacking out everything but the gratification of his most primal need.

Afterward he had said nothing. He was wonderfully exhausted, and as he tried to catch his breath, he fell asleep atop her. Kita had let him stay for a while before she slid out from under him, rolled onto her side, and fell into a peaceful sleep.

Now, remembering that first time, Atula shifted on his

mat and let out a deep, satisfied breath. The memory was vivid and pleasant. His eyes became heavy with sleep, and finally his head filled with fantasies and dreams.

With no one to see it, the sky blackened and churned, whipping the wind that bent saplings and tore old branches from the trees. Angry that no one could witness its wrath, the storm spirit loaded its atlatl with a shaft of lightning and launched it at the earth. The brilliant light was followed by a crash of thunder, waking most of the People. The posts of the platforms vibrated from the thunder. The children crawled next to the parents, compounding the heat of their bodies with the warmth and humidity. The discomfort and the noise kept them awake.

When the storm waned, those who still could not sleep moved their children back to their mats and fanned themselves. When they finally got back to sleep, a shriek split the air, a woman's scream, high and filled with pain. The women recognized the sound: A child was being born.

In the birthing hut, Wagahi's daughter, Sima, held a cool compress to Amakollee's forehead. Her skin was as gray as clay. Her lips were stretched thin and tight, her jaw muscles clenched.

"One more push and it will be over," Sima told her.

Amakollee's face contorted as she grunted, and Sima caught the child as it slid out. The young midwife wiped the baby's face as it lay still in her arms. She looked at the cord. It still pulsed.

"Breathe, little one," she said, clearing its nostrils and hearing the thunder rumble in the distance.

Amakollee let go of the pole and eased herself down, looking at her baby. "A boy. I knew it was a boy," she said as she lay down. "He is the one."

Sima was not smiling like the mother. The child still did not breathe. She turned the baby over her thigh and slapped his back, hoping to dislodge any mucus that might have been blocking the airways.

The baby did not respond, and Sima quickly stood, holding the baby upside down by his feet.

"Breathe, baby," she shouted as she struck his back more soundly. This was her first delivery alone, and she was nearly as frightened as Amakollee. Something was wrong with the child, and Sima squinted to keep back the tears. Wagahi would have known what to do, she thought. If only the A-po-la-chee had never come.

Stunned, Amakollee sat up, "What is the matter?"

"I cannot get the baby to breathe."

"No!" Amakollee screamed, pulling at Sima. "Give him to me!"

Sima handed the still baby to his mother. "No! You will breathe!" Amakollee shook the newborn and then blew her breath into him. "Take mine," she cried. "Take mine!"

Suddenly the child sucked in and gurgled a weak whimper. Sima praised the spirits, and Amakollee wept.

"He is breathing. He is alive," she cried, cradling her son to her.

Amakollee studied the face and body of her newborn son. His nose was small and somewhat flattened compared to the sharp, straight noses of the People. His tiny hands were short and broad, which she thought meant he would have strong, muscular hands. His mouth was slightly open, but he did not cry.

The eyes were his most interesting feature, sealing her suspicion that he was the one with the Gift. His eyes carried the sign. They were slanted, not like Kita's, but more severely, uniquely. Around the colored irises were gray flecks, as though his eyes had been sprinkled with the sand of the Big Water. It was a sure sign. And how quiet he was. Another sign.

"Look into his face, Sima," Amakollee said to the midwife. "Do you see all the signs? He has the Gift. Even at his birth the spirits speak. He is the People's next shaman."

Amakollee put the infant to her breast, but he did not suckle or cry. "He has the peace of the spirits," she whispered to Sima.

But it was a good sign for a newborn to cry, thought Sima, and yet perhaps Amakollee was right. He did look odd. As she stared at the newborn, somehow Sima was not convinced that the child possessed the Gift.

The passing storm released a bolt of lightning, instantly followed by the crack and roll of thunder.

The clan waited for the strong wail of the new baby, but it did not come, and many mothers turned fitfully on their mats.

Chapter Nine

WAKULLA'S MOTHER FLESHED the rabbit pelt her son had brought to her. It was the first kill Wakulla had made since he became a man, and it deserved special attention. Miakka sat with her, holding Mi-sa, helping when she could. Sometimes she found herself staring at Kita. What had it been like to teach Atula, to guide him into the realm of manhood? Suddenly Miakka was flooded with warmth. Her face felt hot, and her limbs tingled.

Kita had staked the rabbit skin to the ground, flesh side up. She scraped off the flesh and fat with the serrated leg bone of a deer, and then soaked the pelt in clear water. Next she spread it over a log and scraped the inner surface to get rid of all remaining particles of flesh. Into a pouch of water suspended over the fire she dropped some hot stones and the brains and liver of the rabbit. To that she added some fat. After it blended she thoroughly rubbed the inside of the skin with the warm mixture, being careful not to let it seep onto the fur side. Kita then set the pelt aside. When it was completely dry, she would work it back and forth over a smooth, round-topped stake. When she finished, the hide would be soft and pliable, a nice beginning for her blanket.

She was lucky, she thought. A boy's search for his

totem was dangerous. She was thankful that the spirits had smiled on her son.

"Tonight I will be filled with pride," Kita said.

"You should be," Miakka answered. "There is even talk that Wakulla will be the next cacique."

"But tonight there will be sadness mixed with our joy," Kita reminded her.

"Pachu?"

"Yes. It is sad that he never returned."

"Kita," Miakka interrupted, "it is the way of the spirits. It is sad, but do not let it diminish the happiness and pride that you feel."

"I suppose. After tonight my son will be a man in all ways."

"Who do you think will be his teacher?" Miakka asked.

"It would be too brazen for me even to think about that," Kita answered.

Again Miakka looked at the woman who had first joined with Atula. "It is a privilege to be the teacher."

"Yes," she answered, looking at Miakka with her gentle and curious smile.

Miakka wondered if Kita knew what she was thinking. Was her infatuation with Atula written on her face, in her eyes?

―――――

THAT NIGHT WAKULLA and Talasee told the stories of their totem quests. The young boys paid special attention and envied them. Talasee's totem spirit was the moccasin. As he told the story, every person listened intently. He stood in front of the fire, his voice full of the excitement he'd felt throughout his ordeal.

"My mouth was dry, and my lips cracked from thirst and hunger. I had begun to think the spirits had rejected me. They brought me visions at first, but then they stopped. Another day and night passed without a sign. I lay on the ground under the hot sun, waiting, always waiting. I closed my eyes and lived in my dreams."

"What did you dream?" someone in the crowd asked.

"In the dream, like the earth and the water, I baked under the sun as I lay adrift in the bottom of a canoe. It had not rained, and the earth was dry and parched like me. I stood in the dugout and called to the spirits to hear me. I cried for rain—for relief. The spirits answered, and I could feel each droplet as it touched me, quenching the need for moisture on my skin. I turned my face to the sky and stuck my tongue out to catch the rain. Mist rose from the river and the earth."

The crowd sensed the climax of the story, and they leaned toward Talasee, straining to hear each word, to catch each inflection of his voice.

"I pulled the boat onto the land and then stretched out on the ground, reveling in the wonderful rain the spirits had sent me. A cold rivulet of water streamed across my chest. I reached out to dip my fingers into the lifesaving water. To my surprise it had form. Shocked into wakefulness, I realized that my hand clutched a serpent, a cold, living death. Then a voice told me to be still. This was the work of the spirits. The voice told me to prove my trust and my courage. And so I released the water moccasin and lay perfectly still, feeling each belly scale move across my chest."

Talasee smiled inside as he heard the oohs and aahs of the clan. Indeed he had been brave and worthy.

"The spirits clearly spoke to me. My totem is the water moccasin. My spirit will mingle with his."

The crowd was thrilled with the story. The sign had been definitive and strong.

Wakulla stood as Talasee sat. He waited for the crowd to quiet. When the settled, Jegatua nodded to Wakulla, letting him know that he could begin his story.

Wakulla's description was so vivid that everyone's mouth went dry, just as his had done. They could feel his famine, his thirst, his desperation. His body moved into the firelight as if to music, taking advantage of the streaks of light and shadow to add drama. He almost sang his story to the rhythm of some ancient liturgy. With his words, his movements, he took them all with him.

"I was drawn into the deep amber-green pools of the panther's eyes. I looked out and saw the earth as the cat. I could feel his hunger and his strength. The earth smelled sweet with grasses and moist black soil. My feet stepped quietly, and I stopped to sniff the air. In the distance I smelled man. I recognized my own scent. I was one with the panther. Then the great cat released me and let me sink back into my body. When he saw that I had returned safely and that I recognized him for what he was, he turned and left. But my spirit will always be with him, and I gratefully accept his favor."

Shakia watched and listened, intrigued by the young man. His strong voice entranced her. When he looked across the crowd at her, she felt warm and weak, and her knees nearly buckled. What was this strange and wonderful influence he had on her?

When the two young men completed their tales, Atula stood. As he walked to the center of the ceremonial plaza, those he passed lowered their heads and pressed the backs of their hands to their foreheads, offering him their deep respect.

Jegatua came and stood next to him. Together they had decided who would teach the young men in their last quest—joining. After this night, all the secrets of manhood would be known to Talasee and Wakulla. Joining was rightly reserved for the last ritual.

Talasee and Wakulla stood nervously before the People. Jegatua walked to Talasee's teacher and motioned for Talasee to leave with her.

Atula delighted in the selection he and Jegatua had made for his eldest son. Antahala had a husband but no children. She was experienced but still young, and she was especially beautiful.

Wakulla watched as his father approached her. The teachers had been told of the honor ahead of time and had kept the secret well.

Antahala smiled as Atula gestured for his son to come to his teacher.

The crowd felt exhilaration as they watched the young men leave with the two women. Older men basked in memories. Young women felt the rush of romance, and the young men enjoyed their own fantasies.

Antahala took Wakulla to the shallow shelf of the cenote and bathed him. The moon was full, allowing Wakulla to see her hands clearly as they splashed the warm water across his chest and danced across his belly, which fluttered with her touch.

Wakulla's head fell forward as her lips and tongue touched thousands of sensitive spots on his torso. His mouth opened, and he bit at her hair, trying to maintain enough strength to remain standing.

She found every sensitive part of his flesh and set it afire. He breathed in grunts and groans and did not care that she heard.

Gently she guided the young man to the edge of the water and coaxed him to the ground, kissing his thighs and sides. Once he was stretched out, she began at his feet, then touched, kissed, and nipped her way up his body until she lay across him.

Wakulla was lost inside a place where she had taken him, and the rest of the world did not exist. As she guided him into her, he was certain that he loved this woman. When he heard her soft moans, his body instinctively responded, jarring and quivering with the explosive pleasure.

Antahala continued her lessons for one moon cycle, teaching him how to give and receive the gift of joining. In the hours not occupied by lessons, Antahala talked softly, convincing Wakulla that he was not in love with her. She helped him recognize the difference between the pleasure of joining and real love.

"When you have both, that is the special and sacred gift," she told him.

MANY THINGS HAPPENED as the moon went through its cycles. Summers and winters came and went. Amakollee's child was given the name Kachumpka, Silent Thunder, for he had been born during the storm but had not cried. The name was peculiar and ambiguous—but so was the child.

At first he had not suckled at his mother's breast. Amakollee would offer it to the baby who tried desperately, pursing his lips and drawing in his cheeks; smacking his lips and thrusting out his tongue. Even though he was frustrated, he did not cry.

His mother thought it was a mark of total control, the type of control that made a man a shaman. She rewarded his attempts by expressing small streams of milk into his mouth. It was an endless effort to provide Kachumpka with nourishment, and it exhausted her. Sometimes he choked and sputtered, gurgled and strangled, but finally he would be fed. Though the child rested and slept without complaint, Amakollee sensed when it was time to start again, rousing the baby, dripping her milk, helping him swallow.

Dark circles ringed her eyes, and her cheeks had sunk into the cavern of her mouth. Even her voice was weak. She was tired and appeared unkempt, but there was no time for vanity. She devoted herself to the child, almost constantly expressing her milk into his mouth.

Kachumpka's eating difficulties caused him to grow slowly and he was slight in build, but he did live through that time of needing mother's milk. He was a placid child who seemed forever content. He demanded little and did not seem to need entertainment.

Amakollee bragged to the other mothers, who did notice Kachumpka's easy temperament. As he grew, he gathered even more notice. By his second summer he still was not walking. The other women began to talk, but Amakollee held fast to the belief that this, too, was a sign of the Gift.

She believed that Kachumpka had to be different from the others so that the clan would recognize him. Kachumpka did not need or desire the things that ordinary youngsters wanted. He was in no rush to run and play the games of children. Amakollee said he was conversing with the spirits—another reason he did not need to speak the language of man.

Amakollee's arguments made sense, and the other mothers buried their suspicion that the child was incomplete somehow, for if Amakollee was correct, their thoughts would anger the spirits.

Wakulla had developed into a respected hunter and leader. He was level-headed and knew how to talk to others. He was often the peacekeeper or at least an effective arbitrator. He had taken Shakia as his wife, realizing what Antahala had meant when she said that having both love and passion was the sacred gift.

As Jegatua had grown even older, his skin had thinned to a translucent and fragile covering. Deep lines creased his mouth and forehead. His once fiery eyes were clouded and had sunk, now peeping through layers of sagging skin. He moved about the village with the aid of a walking stick, but most of the time he sat huddled near his fire when it was cool and breathing heavily in the shade during the heat.

He had outlived his wife and all of his children. There was nothing left for him in this world.

Jegatua would have enough time to observe the clan for a few more summers, not much more. His intuitions would need to be keen. Before he crossed over to the Other Side, he would need to decide which young man would become the next cacique. He watched daily, scrutinizing the young men for qualities that would make a good leader.

Atula sat with the old chief on many evenings discussing the possibilities. Both had drawn the same conclusion.

Wakulla.

Atula had also begun to train his son Cherok in the ways of a shaman. It was not yet time to tell all the secrets. There had been many signs that Cherok was the chosen child, but an official appointment still had to be made, and though the clan seemed convinced, and though Atula wished it to be so, he still harbored a thin thread of doubt. Cherok was a marvelous boy, and he felt a certain pride that he was his son. The boy was quickly approaching adolescence and the time of apprenticeship.

Cherok often helped Miakka look after Mi-sa. The

child was delightful, and they got along well. On this day, Cherok sat with Mi-sa, helping her count berries from the saw palmetto. The fruit was usually used for a tea, but Mi-sa was arranging the hard black berries in heaps and groups. Cherok helped her match a berry for each finger and taught her the word for those five numbers.

Mi-sa mixed up the piles and then redistributed them, counting a berry for each of her fingers. She was quick to learn, and her curiosity was endless.

"Leave the berries, Mi-sa. Do you not ever tire?" Cherok asked as he tousled her hair.

"Teach me more," she said, looking at her friend who opened the doors to her mind.

"Not now, Mi-sa. Come with me."

Cherok took her small hand and led her to the cenote.

"Sit by the edge of the water."

He looked at the delicate little girl. She had intrigued him since her birth. He knew the star sign had been right. Looking at her cherubic face was like looking upon light in the darkness.

Cherok had sensed something special about her from the very beginning. He didn't understand why others did not see it.

Mi-sa looked into the still pool. "I see you, Cherok," she said, giggling and making a face at the boy's reflection as though it were alive.

Cherok stood behind her. "Look through the water to the sky, Mi-sa," he said, placing his hand on her shoulder.

Mi-sa's face grew serious. "Are you going to teach me something, Cherok?"

"Maybe. Look into the water. Tell me what you see."

Cherok wondered what she would see. He remembered sitting there with his father, trying so hard to touch the clouds. He could not, but he knew inside that

Mi-sa would be able to do it, and he would see and feel it through her. Somehow he and Mi-sa were linked. He had known it from the first time he had seen her, when his father had held her and she had looked to the heavens. He had briefly been with her then, and as she had grown, it had happened more frequently.

"Can you go to the clouds and take me with you, Mi-sa?"

Mi-sa's eyelids fluttered, and she shivered. The water was suddenly the air, and the clouds rushed past her face. The air was cool and the sun bright. Now when she looked down she saw the village below, a verdant dot in the vast expanse of dull and drab, dun and brown.

"Close your eyes, Cherok. Listen to my song."

Mi-sa began to chant softly. Cherok didn't understand the words, but the chant was soothing. Slowly he sank to his knees and sucked in a deep breath. His hand still rested on Mi-sa's shoulder, but it was becoming difficult to tell where he ended and she began. Her words called to his spirit, letting it flow freely from his body.

Cherok could feel the coolness before he opened his eyes. Now he touched the clouds and stood in the air, looking at Mi-sa, his half sister. She smiled at him.

"Do you like it here?" she asked, hoping he was pleased.

"Yes, Mi-sa. I have always wanted to touch the clouds."

Suspended above the earth, they looked in all directions.

"There," he said, pointing to the east. "See the river that winds and spills itself out into the Big Water?"

"Oh, yes, Cherok. You show me such wondrous things."

"And there," he said, "to the north is the land of the

A-po-la-chee. Do you know what 'A-po-la-chee' means?" He did not wait for her response. "It means 'people from the other side.' "

Mi-sa held his hand, squeezing tightly with the excitement. "I wish we could stay here," she said.

"Take us back, Mi-sa. Back to the earth. Back inside ourselves."

Mi-sa closed her eyes. A cool wind blew her hair back, and Cherok later remembered seeing the sunshine on her small, calm face.

Amakollee came to the cenote for some water. She saw the two sitting on the edge. Kachumpka rested on her back, his arms about her neck and his legs wrapped around her. He could walk now, but he was so slow and clumsy that Amakollee often carried him. He was almost too large for her to lift, but her determination, devotion, and obsession gave her added strength.

"Do not worry, little one. Neither is a threat to you," she said, looking at Cherok and Mi-sa. "You are the one," she said, twisting toward Kachumpka and kissing his forehead.

Cherok's eyes were still closed when Amakollee got close.

"Why do you close your eyes and feign a trance for me, Cherok? You know that you will not be the next shaman. Kachumpka is the one with the Gift"

Mi-sa touched Cherok, and he opened his eyes. He had not heard a word that Amakollee had said, but Mi-sa had, though she didn't understand.

Why was this woman so bitter? she wondered. Kachumpka gurgled something, and Mi-sa smiled and walked over to them.

"Mi-sa," Cherok said. "Come. Let us go."

Mi-sa reached up and touched the toes of the child.

He was very close in age to her, according to the seasons, but inside she knew he was much younger. Inside he had not grown.

She started to speak to the little boy, but she suddenly shook with a tremor. Her eyes clouded with tears.

The girl unnerved Amakollee. Why had she shuddered like that? And that blank look on her face—now she was going to cry. What was wrong with her? The child of the star sign was strange.

"Get away," Amakollee said, pushing Mi-sa's hand off Kachumpka's foot.

"I am sorry," Mi-sa whispered through her tears.

"Sorry? For what? What is the matter with you? Cherok, take her away."

Mi-sa reached out again and stroked Kachumpka's leg. "He ..." she started but couldn't finish. She didn't know the words to describe what she knew about Amakollee's child.

"Cherok, tell me the words."

"What words? Come, Mi-sa, let us leave."

Again she touched the boy, and a tear rolled down her cheek. "I am sorry," she said again before taking Cherok's hand and walking away.

Amakollee watched the strange child leave. She was glad she was gone. Mi-sa made her feel uneasy and apprehensive. Near the water she put Kachumpka down. He sat watching the wind blow the grass blades and leaves of the cypress. Amakollee filled a pouch with water, put it over her shoulder, and went back for her son.

The pouch slid from her arm as she jolted with what she saw. Kachumpka was lying stiff on the ground. His back was arched, and his whole body shook violently. Amakollee tried to pick him up. He was rigid, and white foam seeped from the corners of his mouth. His lips were turning blue. He wasn't breathing. She threw herself on top of him, trying to still him.

"Help," she screamed. "Help me!"

A few villagers heard her cry and hurried to her. Just as they drew close, Kachumpka went limp and too a deep breath. He whimpered slightly. Amakollee clutched him to her.

"An evil spirit entered my son. It was horrible," she cried, rocking him at her breast. "It tried to take him from me, but Kachumpka has won. Did anyone see? He was stiff and unable to move. He was not breathing. His breath was taken from him. It was terrible," she sobbed.

One of the women knelt beside her and brushed her face. "It is over, Amakollee."

Sima knelt next to the overwrought mother. "Let me see him," she said, touching Amakollee's arm. "Let me hold him," she urged, speaking softly and reassuringly.

The mother stopped wailing but still suffered from the spasms caused by her hysteria, making her gasp unexpectedly. Reluctantly she moved aside.

Sima looked the boy over carefully, speaking to him in a calm and soothing voice. She could see that Kachumpka was very tired.

"He is fine now, Amakollee," she said, handing him back to his mother.

"Did you see him, Sima? Did you see how the evil spirit racked his body? Why did this happen? He has angered no one."

Suddenly Amakollee's face flushed with color and her eyes filled with fury. "It was Mi-sa. She did this to him!"

Chapter Ten

MI-SA RAN AHEAD OF CHEROK. Amakollee had frightened her. All she wanted to do was tell Amakollee she was sorry that her child was not whole. There was something missing. Something was wrong with the boy, and that had made her sad.

"What did I see? What makes me see, Cherok?" she asked, sobbing as she turned to him.

Cherok could not explain to her because he wasn't sure either. He did know that she had powers—special powers that others looked for in him. Those things came so easily to Mi-sa. And she was the only one who did not press him.

"You are special, Mi-sa," he said, lifting her chin with his hand. "In the darkness, where others cannot see, there in that blackness your eyes can see. You are Light in the Darkness."

"I hate it. I hate my name, and so does everyone else. Whenever they speak it, they think of the night of the A-po-la-chee. Why, Cherok? Why did the spirits do this to me?"

As she ran from the scene, she heard Amakollee screaming and then the horrible accusation. She didn't know what had happened to Kachumpka, but it had to have been awful, and she was to blame. What had she done? she wondered. Perhaps she really was a bad spirit. This hatred and suspicion had begun the very night of her birth.

"Clear your head, little one," Cherok said comfortingly. "They just do not understand. You have not done anything wrong. What happened to Kachumpka had nothing to do with you."

Mi-sa wrapped her arms around Cherok. "If it were not for you, I would not have a friend in this world," she whispered. "I love you, Cherok."

Cherok stroked her hair tenderly. "Shh," he whispered.

He walked her back to the village. Amakollee and others had already arrived, and there was quite a stir among the villagers. Every eye seemed fastened on Mi-sa as she walked through. When she looked at them, they turned away as if they were afraid.

Miakka stood at her fire and noticed the sudden hush that fell across the village. She saw her daughter crossing the crest with Cherok, her small face stained with tears.

When she saw her mother, Mi-sa started to run, and the sobbing began again. Miakka quickly ushered her up the ladder into the privacy of their platform.

"What is it, Little Light?"

Mi-sa continued to cry too hard to explain.

"Cherok?" Miakka called. But when she looked around, she saw that he had not come up the ladder.

Instead Cherok trekked to the platform of his mother. He huddled quietly in a dark corner of inside. He needed to talk to his father. He needed to tell him the things he knew. But if he did, would he be confirming the whispered rumor that Mi-sa was a witch, a bad spirit, born under a warning sign? That would be bad not only for Mi-sa but for his father as well. How could his father have misread the star sign? And Mi-sa?—he could not believe she was evil. She was just different—special. He was confused.

He could hear the women outside, whispering. His mother, Cacema, was also listening.

"She is a bad spirit. She touched the boy, and then he was taken by an evil spirit," a woman's voice said.

When the black shroud of night covered the village, Cacema sat next to Cherok and gently pushed the hair back from his face.

"The People talk, Cherok."

"Of Mi-sa?"

"Yes, they speak about Mi-sa. They feel that she has a harmful spirit."

"But she does not," Cherok said, pushing his mother's hand away.

"It is important for you to stay away from her."

"Just because she was born on the night of the A-po-la-chee?"

"No," his mother continued. "It is not that alone. There is more. And you saw what happened to Kachumpka today."

"Mi-sa is special. She knows things, but she is not evil."

"Do you not see what you are saying? That is the same thing that people whisper about. How could she know things unless she has the help of some evil spirit?"

"No. No. If she knows things, it is because she has help from a *good* spirit. She is special."

"Cherok, you are the one who is special. Only the shaman communicates with spirits unless you befriend a spirit from the Darkside."

"Amakollee is jealous of Mi-sa. That is why she says those things. Mi-sa has a strong star sign. Amakollee wishes it belonged to Kachumpka."

"Yes, Mi-sa's sign is strong—perhaps too strong, our people say. But if Amakollee is jealous, it is of you. You will be the chosen one, not Kachumpka. That is why it is best if none of the bad things spill over onto you."

"Mi-sa and I are friends. She is part my sister. We share the same father."

"Be careful, Cherok. Mi-sa may be a spirit that you must battle. Do not let her weaken your objectivity. Evil spirits are deceitful."

Cacema left Cherok's side when he pretended to sleep. When all was quiet, he climbed down from the shelter and slipped through the darkness of the night toward Mi-sa's platform.

When he was almost there, he saw a dim fire burning. The small, nearly spent orange coals glowed in the darkness. Beside it sat Mi-sa, gently tapping two stones together.

He started to call out to her, but then decided not to, for fear of awakening someone. He walked closer, thinking she would notice his approach and look up. When he came near her, he heard her chanting softly. Her voice was soothing, but he could not catch the words.

Out of the stillness an icy breeze blew her hair, whirling it back, and Cherok could see that her eyes were closed and her face serene.

When the quick burst of wind stopped, Mi-sa rocked her head back and began to sway.

"Mi-sa," he whispered. "Mi-sa?"

She didn't seem to hear him. Her small body moved to the music of her gentle voice. He knelt next to her, listening, trying to make out her words. It was no use; the sounds made no sense.

"Mi-sa," he said, shaking her shoulders.

Slowly she opened her eyes and seemed to try to focus. Then she shivered and dropped the stones.

Shocks of blue light, like dwarfed bolts of lightning, shot out of her shoulders, through his hands, and up his arms, jolting him backward to the ground.

Chapter Eleven

"CHEROK," MI-SA CRIED, seeing him sprawled on the ground. "What happened?"

Cherok sat upright. "What were you doing?"

"What do you mean?" she asked, still confounded by the situation.

"Here, by the fire. You were chanting and tapping these together," he said, picking up the stones and showing them to her.

"I do not remember," she answered.

"Mi-sa!" he said accusingly.

"I really do not remember, Cherok," she said, her voice quavering with the threat of tears. "I could not sleep, and so I came down here by the last of the fire. I asked the spirits to help me and protect me. That is all. And then I saw you lying on the ground. What happened?"

She appeared frightened. It was enough that she had to suffer because of Amakollee's evil tongue. He could not bring himself to tell her what he had seen or about the shock she had given him. "Nothing else. I could not sleep, either.

When I saw you, I hurried over and stumbled. I think you were more tired than you thought. You had fallen asleep sitting up. When I fell, it awakened you. I was quite a sight, was I not?" He laughed, trying not to frighten her.

"I do seem to be very tired now," she conceded, apparently accepting his explanation. "But something is haunting me. I had a dream. I did not even know that I slept, and yet I had a dream."

"What was it?" Cherok inquired, hoping to get some insight into what had just happened.

"I felt frightened. It was something bad. I do not want to remember."

"Maybe if you remember we can talk about it. It was just a dream, Mi-sa. Dreams are not real."

"Then it was not a dream. Not like when you are sleeping. This was different."

"How? What did you dream?"

Mi-sa rubbed her upper arms. "I am cold," she said, avoiding further questions.

"It is warm tonight," he remarked.

"I am afraid of something. Something bad is going to happen."

"You just had a bad dream. Go back to your bed and sleep. You have nothing to be afraid of."

Mi-sa turned to him as she started up her ladder.

"Do you believe what the People say, Cherok?" she asked.

"Do not listen to what they say. It is only the waggle of a troublemaker's tongue."

Mi-sa climbed down and threw her arms around him. If Cherok believed them, she would be all alone.

A sudden image flashed before her, and she remembered the dream. No, it was not a dream. It was a vision. A look into the future. Mi-sa's stomach churned, and its contents backed up into her throat. She had good reason to be afraid, and the worst was that she could tell no one.

"Good night," she whispered before letting go of Cherok and climbing the ladder.

———

AMAKOLLEE TOSSED IN HER SLEEP. Buried deep in a dream, her thoughts wandered in darkness. Out of the bleak shadows she heard screeching and screaming. It became louder and louder, almost deafening. Suddenly there was a bright light, and the darkness retreated. Before her was the dream image of Mi-sa bent over her Kachumpka, sucking the air from him.

He struggled, coughing and sputtering. As if suspended from the night sky, Mi-sa seemed to hang over him, siphoning all the air out his nostrils.

Amakollee saw herself approaching them from behind. Out of nowhere her vision field turned to crimson. Blood dripped like a saturated curtain in front of her eyes, covering Mi-sa. Slowly it soaked her hair and then her moss skirt. Kachumpka's chest heaved with relief.

Amakollee watched and believed all that she saw in her dream. In the still of the night she sat upright, enlightened. Her son was the chosen one, and she was his guardian. The spirits would work through her to protect him.

The message was clear, sent to her from the spirits. Mi-sa was a threat to Kachumpka, just as she had thought, and it was up to her to free her son of the evil threat. The evil ones did not want the clan to have a shaman, a holy man who knew their ways. The evil spirits would be hard to stop. But the good spirits were just as determined. They had not forgotten Amakollee. Had they not chosen her to be the holy receptacle of Atula's seed?

The night also spoke to Atula. In his dream there was a

terrible thunderstorm as he watched the same two rivers he had seen in his earlier vision. They forked, and the People stood helpless before them. He looked at the dry and cracked bed of the old river. The rainwater skirted it, draining into the new river. Many of his tribe walked in the dry river bottom, afraid to leave.

When he looked into the water of the new river, he saw a face disguised by the distortions of the wind on the water. The face did not surface; it was not ready to be seen. It waited for the storm to subside. It waited for the People to be ready.

———

AMAKOLLEE DID NOT SLEEP the rest of the night. She was too energized. Her direction was so clear.

At dawn she walked to the sinkhole, dragging a sleepy Kachumpka behind her. In the water she washed her face and then her son's. She had finished and was attending her morning fire before anyone else emerged.

First she would need an instrument. Women did not fashion weapons, nor did they receive any instruction in making or using them. But she had thought of a way.

Carrying Kachumpka on her back, Amakollee walked off the mound, away from the village.

She felt the pouch at her side, making sure her secret was still there. Every few minutes she obsessively touched it again, not trusting her last touch.

Finally, at the base of a tall pond cypress, she put her son down and handed him a stick with which to scribble in the compost and dirt.

She sat also, slightly out of breath. Age was beginning to tell on her, and she thanked the spirits for Kachumpka; without him she would have been doomed. The humiliation would have been intolerable. Yes, she was thankful for Kachumpka, and she would see to it that no one ever threatened this son who had saved her.

She leaned her head back against the thick trunk of the tree allowing herself time to catch her breath and recover from the burdensome walk.

Again she checked on Kachumpka. He was still stirring the leaves with the stick, stopping only to pick up exposed insects.

From her pouch she brought out her prize, an awl made from split deer bone. With it she had sewn fishing nets and had put together animal skins to make blankets and cloaks that kept her and Kachumpka warm in the winter.

Amakollee rubbed her thumb down the side of the awl, enjoying the feel of its cool, smooth surface, polished from years of use.

It was her favorite. When it was first fashioned, she'd had no idea of its fate. Strange how the spirits had designed her destiny, she thought.

Kachumpka swirled the stick through the layer of compost. Repeatedly he whisked it through the debris, around and around, making a background sound so monotonous that it was almost hypnotic.

Amakollee withdrew a sharp-edged stone from her pouch and slowly began to shave away the sides of the awl, working it to a keen point.

For hours she worked while Kachumpka played with the stick and rocked. Blisters formed on her thumb, filled with fluid, broke, and then blistered again before she had finished with it.

An awl was a woman's tool, not a weapon, and unless someone saw the tip, no one would suspect its purpose.

The light that pricked through the green canopy of leaves seemed to halo her son's head. It also brought out the deep hues and tones of the bone, as if still nourished by the animal of which it had once been a part.

Indeed the spirits had guided her well. Mi-sa was an evil spirit, bent on hurting and discrediting Kachumpka. She was an obstacle, a test, and Amakollee had found her out.

Yes, it was all coming together, she thought. By the light of day tomorrow, Mi-sa would be out of the way. Then the People would see that Cherok had no powers. It was Mi-sa's evil that made them see Cherok as the one with the Gift. Mi-sa wanted it that way because she favored Cherok. It was the bad spirit's way of keeping the rightful one from the People. Amakollee would fix that. Then the way would be clear for Kachumpka. The People would be free of Mi-sa's evil. Their vision would clear, and they would see the rightful one—Kachumpka.

At dusk the villagers began their evening meals. Amakollee visited with the other women, stopping at each hearth and spreading her bitterness.

"Look at her," she directed Sassacha and nodded toward Mi-sa, who sat near her mother. "You would think an evil spirit would be ugly to look at. It does a good job hiding inside her."

"Mmm," Sassacha agreed, looking at the child.

"They gave themselves away by sending her into the world the night of the A-po-la-chee. Everyone still whispers about her sign. Now that she is known—since I have found her out and exposed her—the spirits will call her back as a failure. You will see." Amakollee smiled.

"Perhaps," Sassacha said. "Or maybe they will continue the fight. An evil spirit does not give up easily."

Both looked again at the child.

As if she had heard the women, Mi-sa stared through

the smoke from the fire, her gaze piercing it, penetrating the smoke and the distance between them.

Sassacha shuddered and looked away quickly. "She has heard you, Amakollee," she said, filled with an icy chill.

Amakollee continued to glare back, and from her pouch she withdrew the awl, discretely flashing it at the child across the camp. Amakollee's lips curled into a sneer, and Mi-sa finally looked away.

The little one wrapped her arms around her mother's waist. She wanted to tell but knew she couldn't. If she revealed her premonition, Miakka would want to know how she could see the future.

"What is it?" Miakka asked, feeling her daughter's arms tighten around her.

"Nothing," Mi-sa answered with a shaking whisper.

Guided by a mother's instinct, Miakka lifted Mi-sa's face so that she could look at her child's eyes. At the same time she felt her forehead. There was no heat. Mi-sa's eyes were clear and not glassy. But she did see something in her eyes.

"What frightens you?" she asked her daughter.

Mi-sa looked at the ground. Nothing was going to stop it, even if she told. And if she spoke out, she would only create more problems. There would be questions, disbelief, and distrust.

"Do you love me?" she asked her mother.

"Of course I love you. What would make you ask?"

"Will you always love me, no matter what?"

Miakka turned Mi-sa toward her, hugging her close. "Always, Mi-sa. Always."

"What if it turned out that there was something wrong with me?" she asked, pulling away and looking up at her mother's face.

"But there is nothing wrong with you. And even if you

had the most terrible, terrible thing wrong, I would always take care of you and love you. I would never desert you."

"But what if there was something wrong—inside me—something that you cannot see—something bad?"

The conversation made Miakka feel sick. What was Mi-sa thinking? What horrible fear did she have? Had Amakollee's miserable talk begun to trouble her precious daughter?

"Stop all this nonsense," she said, hugging her again. "Whatever you are worried about is nonsense. No one listens to Amakollee. Pay no attention."

"Yes, they do, Mother. And they believe her."

"Shh," she whispered in her daughter's ear. "Let us get ready for the night."

"Can I go and see Cherok?"

"Why do you want to do that now?" Miakka questioned.

"He is my friend, and he thinks I am good.I do not frighten him."

"Before the dark, then. Watch the sinking sun."

Mi-sa kissed her mother's cheek and ran off looking for her friend. When she drew close to Cherok's platform, she saw him. He was with Atula, and they seemed to be having an important conversation.

She decided not to bother him. Cherok had important things to learn from Atula. Instead Mi-sa hid behind a clump of brush and cried.

The horizon was ablaze with the setting sun. Mi-sa wiped her eyes and stood up straight. There was nothing that she could do about her fate. She could not change the destiny the spirits had designed for her. Slowly she returned to her platform.

Miakka heard the light footsteps as Mi-sa ascended the ladder. It was too dark inside the platform for Miakka to see her daughter's swollen eyes, but she knew Mi-sa had been crying. She could tell by the heaviness of her steps and the slope of her small shoulders.

"Come," Miakka said, patting Mi-sa's mat.

Mi-sa lay down on the mat, and Miakka began to hum softly, lightly scratching the child's back. Though she thought she would not be able to sleep, Mi-sa soon drifted off.

The hearths of the spirits and the deceased twinkled in the night sky. The crickets and frogs sang their night songs, and peace fell over the village.

Except Amakollee.

Amokalee sat straight up and looked over at Kachumpka. Satisfied that he was sleeping, she padded to the side of the platform and reached deep inside a basket, beneath some berries and roots. She fingered the weave at the bottom of the basket until she felt the hard, cold object wedged between the reeds.

Carefully she grasped it between her index finger and her thumb. She withdrew the sharp awl like a magic splinter. She tapped her fingertip against its point. Each time she was assured of its sharpness, but she had to do it again and again to be certain it was sharp.

Finally convinced, she wrapped it in a small piece of leather and then descended the ladder.

Staying in the shadows, she made her way through the village, winding around the platforms.

At the base of Mi-sa's platform Amakollee paused, listening. She clamped the leather-wrapped awl between her teeth. Hearing nothing but silence, she quietly ascended the steps.

Her palms were soaked with nervous perspiration, and she feared that they might slip from a rung, giving her away. She wiped her right hand on her moss skirt, but that did not dry it. She would just have to be very careful and not let her nervousness cause her to hurt herself or keep her from carrying out her plan.

At last she peered over the edge of the platform. She would have to move past Miakka, her mat being closer to the entrance.

Her hands trembled as she pulled herself onto the floor and began to crawl toward Mi-sa.

Near Miakka's face she stopped and listened to her slow and easy breathing, attesting to her deep sleep.

Amakollee moved closer to Mi-sa, whose back was turned to her. When she was directly by the child's side, a sudden noise startled her.

Miakka mumbled and turned onto her side. Amakollee froze, holding her breath in fear. She had no argument with Miakka, but if she interfered, Amakollee was certain that the spirits would order her to stop Miakka, too. She had to fulfill her mission.

Miakka drifted back to sleep, never opening her eyes.

Assured that she was safe, Amakollee unwrapped the instrument. She wadded the leather into a ball and held it and the awl straight overhead, as if awaiting some supernatural blessing.

Amakollee crouched over her target, a spindle of saliva dangling out of the corner of her mouth.

Mi-sa felt the hot breath on her neck, and her eyes flew open as she twisted to look at her attacker.

At the same instant Amakollee jammed the leather wad into Mi-sa's mouth, silencing her. Mi-sa looked into Amakollee's wild eyes as she gagged on the hide. She lurched as Amakollee thrust the point of the awl into her back.

When Amakollee withdrew it, a quick spurt of the

girl's blood gushed over her hand. Again she shoved the deer bone into Mi-sa, feeling her warm blood stream from her.

Mi-sa's stiff body suddenly went limp, and her jaw slackened.

Chapter Twelve

JEGATUA'S BONES ACHED. No matter how he lay, within a short time he began to ache. The pain was nothing new. He had been suffering for quite some time. He never slept through the night anymore. Instead he napped for short periods and then needed to move around.

His left hip ached, and so did his back. Slowly he pushed himself up on his elbow and finally into a sitting position. The hardest part was getting to his feet. His body seemed to work against him, and then there was always the pain.

Jegatua coughed and he reached for his walking stick. The spasms choked him, battering his lungs and making his head throb. The cough finally subsided, and again Jegatua tried to pull himself up.

He needed to walk a bit and work the stiffness out of his body so that he could sleep again. Carefully he made his way down the ladder.

When one foot finally touched the soil, he heaved out a gust of air, cautiously planted his other foot, then bent forward to pick up his walking stick, which he had thrown down. He needed some of the medicinal leaves Atula had given him before. He had let his supply dwindle. Slowly he made his way into the brush, searching for the plant by the light of the moon.

He was short of breath, and no matter how hard he tried to breathe, he could not seem to fill his lungs or satisfy his need for air. The tightness in his chest increased to a crushing sensation, and the slow ache now shot like fire down his arm.

The old cacique saw a shadow moving close by. He needed help.

He focused as best he could, looking deep into the night at the figure that turned to face him.

Jegatua extended his arm, beckoning the only person who could help him.

"Help me," he called.

The figure stood fast, seemingly paralyzed.

"Amakollee?" he whispered as he slumped to the ground, disappearing behind the tall grass.

She took a few steps toward him, and then stood still, wiping her tangled hair from her face, smearing blood on her cheek.

The old man's eyes bulged out as he looked at her with terror. At first he had not understood why she did not try to help. But then he saw the wild look in her eyes and the blood on her hands. What had she done?

His breathing became raspy, shallow, and irregular and then finally stopped. His eyes remained fixed upon her streaked face as his chest tightened into a fireball.

Amakollee turned and walked away toward the cenote. There she walked into the water to rinse the blood from her body and toss the awl out into the deep water.

Dripping with water, she returned to her platform, climbed the ladder, stripped off her wet moss skirt, and stretched out nude. Immediately she fell into deep peaceful sleep. The spirits were proud of her.

———

MI-SA'S BODY LAY MOTIONLESS in a pool of blood. A thin wisp of a cloud darted toward her, encircled her, and then entered her nostrils. A tiny flicker of life was fanned, and Mi-sa groaned.

She lay face down, her long dark hair matted with blood, one small arm reaching out toward Miakka. One leg was drawn up, the other extended.

Again she groaned, unable to open her eyes or to move.

Miakka turned in her sleep and then recognized the noise as real, not from a dream. She opened her eyes, trying to see in the darkness.

Nothing seemed amiss. They were alone.

"Mi-sa?" she whispered, thinking that her daughter had been having a nightmare.

Mi-sa did not answer. Miakka adjusted herself on her mat, satisfied and ready to go back to sleep.

She lowered her head and placed one of her arms beneath her cheek as she lay on her side. She was somewhere between being awake and being asleep, her mind wandering in that limbo when she felt it.

A warmth seeped through her mat, past the hand beneath her head, and then along her ear. Miakka shifted, but the trickle continued past her ear, following the dam that was her neck. She opened her eyes and held her hand in front of her face. It was too dark to see, and her eyes were slow to adjust.

She rubbed her fingers together. They were covered with a tacky wetness.

Quickly she sat up, looking beneath her head. The dark liquid dripped down her neck and down her arm and chest.

At last her eyes began to adjust to the darkness. She

traced the fluid across the wooden floor to the pool that surrounded her daughter. Rivulets of blood oozed into dark streams, dipping into the crevices between the lashed-together logs, rising again to flow over the curves, spilling out in a foul red web.

Miakka screamed, now seeing the source of all the blood.

"Mi-sa!" She turned the child into her lap and pulled the gag from her mouth.

Mi-sa did not move. Her eyelids were slightly open, but a cloudy film covered her eyes.

"Help!"

Her shrill cry punctured the stillness.

Miakka began to rock, holding her daughter close, trying to spread the life from her body into Mi-sa's. She called out again, her voice quavering. Did anyone hear? Why did they not hurry? "No! Mi-sa! Oh, Mi-sa," she cried over and over. "Someone! Please!"

Wakulla was the first to appear. He was shocked and sickened at the sight.

Mi-sa was a small mass of blood in her mother's lap. Her arms hung limp at her sides as Miakka held her, kissing her face.

"Get Atula," she cried. "Get him now."

Wakulla started toward the ladder but Atula was already at the base.

"It is Mi-sa," Wakulla said, moving out of the way for the shaman.

A crowd began to gather at the foot of Miakka's platform. They waited for Atula or Wakulla to tell them what had happened.

The shaman moved to Miakka's side..

He felt Mi-sa's throat and chest for signs of life. He put his cheek to her nose. Just as he was about to sit up, he felt the faint movement of air that was her breath.

"She is alive," he said, moving the small child to the floor.

"Go," he told Miakka. "Help Wakulla bring the baskets of medicines and my healing rattle."

Miakka could not move, still stunned.

"Go now," he ordered.

Miakka finally stood. Her chest and legs were covered with her daughter's blood. She edged her way down the ladder and then followed Wakulla to Atula's platform.

Her head was spinning. She could not think on her own. She stood inside Atula's platform waiting for Wakulla to give her directions. She felt numb and deaf.

"Take these," Wakulla told her, filling her arms with pouches, bowls, and baskets. He poured the contents of several small baskets into two larger ones, handing one to Miakka. He careeid the other. On the north wall he found the rattle. Wakulla grabbed it, then gently pushed Miakka, encouraging her to move.

"Follow me," he said as he directed her.

While they made their way back through the village, Atula huddled over Mi-sa, drawing circles in the air. His voice was low as he began to utter the secret words that the spirits knew was a holy man's call.

The mumbling of the gathering below hushed when they heard the shaman's voice. There was urgency in his chants and prayers. His voice rose as he repeated and repeated the words, calling the spirits. "Come this way. Come this way and heal this child."

The sky deepened in darkness as a thick cloud covered the moon. The leaves and small branches grew still as the gentle breeze halted. The animal noises were absent, and the night was tense with the quiet.

The only sound was Atula's echoing voice. The

villagers bent low to the ground. Everything on the earth would bow to the man of the spirits.

Wakulla pushed people aside, making a passage for himself and Miakka.

Miakka was covered in blood, and they both carried the things of the medicine man. It was a bad thing that had happened. Of that the villagers were certain. But what could it be? they wondered.

Perhaps they should not be so curious, they thought. It was rude to intrude. After a while most left.

Atula steeped some of his leaves, roots, and stems over a fire below the platform. When the medicine was ready, he poured it into a cool bowl and carried it up the ladder.

He motioned for Miakka and Wakulla to move aside. Slowly he poured the hot liquid into Mi-sa's wounds, irrigating them. When he had finished, he packed them with pieces of hide soaked in the warmed juice of the pilosa plant. The tiny spines of the plant were often a nuisance because they adhered to almost anything they touched. But the juice extracted from it, when warmed and applied to wounds, stopped the bleeding. It was a good medicine, but Mi-sa's wounds were serious. He would need to do more.

"Bring me a stick heated until the tip glows red," he told Wakulla.

Miakka sat on her heels, looking down at Mi-sa. "Who would do this?" she whispered.

Atula had no answer. He wished he did. Mi-sa looked so small and fragile. His heart was pained.

Gingerly he laid some pulp from the joint of a prickly pear on each wound. Over her he chanted and sang his spirit songs. The inside of the platform resonated with his calls. He was interrupted by Wakulla who carried a burning live oak stick. The shaman took it and blew gently on the end, bringing it aglow.

The bleeding nearly stopped after he touched each stab wound with the glowing stick. There was a sizzling noise and the smell of burning flesh.

Mi-sa did not flinch.

Atula ordered that more juice from the pilosa plant and other medicines be prepared. When they were ready, the shaman bent over them, saying the holy words that gave the magic to the medicine. He sang the words that empowered his potions with the medicine of the spirits. Using a reed, he sucked in the steam from one bowl and then blew it forcefully into Mi-sa's nostrils.

He followed each puff with a short song. Just before the sun rose, he sat back from the small child. He walked up behind Miakka and massaged her neck and shoulders.

"Rest for a while," he gently urged her. "I will watch over Mi-sa."

His magic hands untwisted nerves and muscles that had tied themselves into painful knots.

Wakulla sat propped against one wall, his head finally lolling forward as he fell off to sleep.

"Will she live?" Miakka asked, taking Atula's strong hand in hers, turning her head to look up at him.

"The spirits will decide," he told her.

"Then I will wait," she said, denying herself sleep.

"Let me fix you some tea, then," he said. "Sit by Mi-sa until I return. If anything changes, call out."

By the fire Atula prepared Miakka's tea, lacing it with syrup made from the seeds and flowers of a special plant.

rWhen Miakka swallowed half the liquid she felt a warm rush, and drowsiness set in.

"You have made me drink a sleeping potion," she said almost without emotion.

"Yes." He smiled. "You can do nothing for Mi-sa now. Save your strength."

She was determined to fight the weariness, but her eyelids became heavy. She found it nearly impossible to focus; her eyes crossed as her head nodded. Mi-sa's face blurred and faded.

Miakka's mat was saturated with Mi-sa's blood. He would dispose of it. From a peg in one of the supports of the platform hung a blanket for the winter. He spread it out on the splintered floor and then gently moved Miakka onto it. She looked so tragic and vulnerable. Even in sleep her lovely face was etched with lines of worry.

Atula sat at Mi-sa's side, packing and repacking her wounds, chanting and shaking his rattle. He dusted a circle of yellow powder around her and laid certain leaves and stalks inside it next to her body. His medicine suddenly seemed so impotent.

In a quiet moment he began to wonder who might have done this. Until then he had not allowed his concentration to be interrupted with irrelevant curiosity. His objective had been to focus all his strength and power on healing Mi-sa.

Now in the quiet, after he had done all that he could do, he searched for answers. This had never happened in the clan before. Only the A-po-la-chee were capable of such an act. Life was too precious to the People.

There had been harsh talk about Mi-sa ever since her birth. Her sign had angered some, and of course there was Amakollee. But Amakollee was just a poor woman who had lost touch with what was real. She could not face the truth about her son, Kachumpka, and her mind had slipped away, sparing her the reality.

No, Atula thought. Amakollee could not have done this. Besides, only men were trained in the use of weapons for the purpose of killing.

It had to be someone, though, he thought, and that thought sent waves of nausea through him.

If Mi-sa ever awakened, the truth would be known.

As the eastern sky began to lighten, another crowd assembled, shouting and crying. Those who were already awake roused the others. Only the night of the A-po-la-chee had been worse than this.

The cries drew Atula and Wakulla into the doorway.

"There is more horrible news," Talasee shouted, his face reflecting his disbelief.

Chapter Thirteen

WAKULLA PUT HIS HAND on Atula's shoulder, as if telling him to stay.

"I will go down," he said.

Lethargically, anticipating more bad news, Wakulla descended the ladder.

Atula braced himself. Below, Talasee talked softly. Atula watched as Wakulla's head dropped. Atula knew that Talasee's news was grim.

Talasee walked away, obviously burdened with the bad news.

"Jegatua is dead," Wakulla muttered as returned to a dark corner of the platform.

"How?" Atula inquired, nearly afraid to hear the answer.

"It was his time," Wakulla answered.

Atula breathed a sigh of relief. "Coincidental," he remarked, walking closer to Wakulla. "Are you ready?" he asked.

Wakulla sat on the rough floor near the side.

"You will be the next cacique," Atula said. "Jegatua and I have discussed it many times. I am certain the Council of Men will agree."

"I know," he said. "Jegatua also spoke to me. He tried to tell me all that he knew about the People and how to lead them. Even though I have watched his failing health, his death still comes as a surprise."

"The clan will mourn him, but in time you must encourage them to bury their grief and let the sorrow go. You and I are charged with that responsibility. No matter what you feel inside, no matter how weak and weary you are, you may show only your strength."

"With the help of the spirits."

Miakka finally stirred from her drugged sleep. Atula sat next to her.

"Mi-sa?" she asked even before she opened her eyes.

"She is the same," he answered, brushing his hand across Miakka's cheek.

The tiny fragile child lay still. Her lips were washed of color, and her cheeks were gray.

Miakka stood unsteadily and made her way to her daughter's side. She took Mi-sa's small hand in hers and rubbed it as she sat next to her.

"She is so cold," she said, looking at Atula. "Why is she so cold? Is she dead?" Miakka cried.

Atula grabbed her shoulders. "No, Miakka. Here," he said, guiding her hand to the throat of her daughter, feeling for a pulse.

Beneath her fingers she felt the flickering beat of life. Miakka turned her head into Atula's chest and sobbed with relief.

"I need to go and tell Shakia," Wakulla remarked, "though she has probably already heard. She will want to be with Miakka," he said before leaving.

Softly Atula stroked Miakka's hair, comforting her as best he could. "Trust in the spirits," he whispered to her. "Mi-sa means something special to them. That is why they sent the star the night she was born."

"The People remember only the A-po-la-chee. They

never see Mi-sa's birth as something good. They associate her with that horrible attack. But she was not responsible. She has never hurt anyone."

Tenderly he embraced her. "No, she does not deserve this. I do not understand, but we are not always meant to understand the spirit ways."

Miakka pulled away and stood up. "The spirits have never protected Mi-sa. Even before her birth, if it had not been for your intervention, what do you think would have happened to her? Do not talk to me about spirits." She wept with anger.

Miakka jerked at the medicine bag around her neck. The leather was strong, and it bruised the back of her neck as she pulled at it. Finally she ripped it over her head and threw it across the platform, expelling the contents across the floor.

"All of these things mean nothing," she shouted. "No good spirit would make a child suffer like this. Mi-sa has been tortured all her life. What good has any spirit done for any of us? The People are stupid. Do they question why the spirits allowed the A-po-la-chee to come? No. They only question Mi-sa. There are no spirits. No one watches over us," she sobbed. .

Atula let her go on. She needed to rid herself of the frustration and anger. He went to her and again allowed her to cry in his arms.

"Miakka," he whispered in her ear, "we must be strong for Mi-sa. Reach inside yourself for your strength."

Miakka's sobs lessened to whimpers. She wiped the tears from her face. On her hands and knees she picked up the totems she had strewn about,placed them in her pouch, threaded it, and then hung it around her neck.

Atula watched quietly, letting her compose herself.

When she was calm, she sat by her daughter's side and

kissed her forehead. Atula treated Mi-sa's wounds with more medicine.

Shakia entered the platform and embraced Miakka, saying nothing.

Cherok arrived later, stunned by what had happened. Cacema had not wanted him to go, but he told her it was his responsibility to assist his father.

Cherok paled when he saw Mi-sa. The sight of her took his breath away. No man cried, he kept reminding himself. Male children were taught from infancy not to cry. Each time a male baby cried, the mother would pinch it. It did not take the baby long to find ways to express its needs, and crying was not one of them.

In earlier generations, when the People were hunters and gatherers who wandered in search of food, even the girl babies had been taught not to cry. If the clan was sneaking up on a food animal and a baby began to cry, it would scare off the animal, and the clan would starve. That had also been a time of many wars between tribes struggling to claim land that would support them, and a crying baby would give away their location.

As the way of the People had changed, only the males were raised not to cry. It somehow seemed that it increased their endurance and made them emotionally strong. After all, they were the ones who made the important decisions for all the clan, and they could not be influenced by emotion. Their decisions needed to be based on clear, unencumbered thinking processes. Personal fear could not play a part. They needed to be able to control all emotions; they experienced emotions, but they held them in check.

Cherok closed his eyes and focused on a pleasant imaginary scene, pulling back the loosed emotions. Within an instant he was able to look at Mi-sa again.

"Has she spoken?" Cherok asked.

"No, she has not awakened at all," Atula answered. "She lost a lot of blood." He nodded toward the red-brown bloodstain on the floor. "She will sleep."

Miakka cleaned her face and hands, but her hair was still matted.

"Go and wash away the blood," Atula suggested.

"I cannot leave her. What if she wakes and I am not here?"

"I will send Cherok for you immediately."

"You will feel fresher," Cherok added. "And if you go now, no one will be there. If you wait until near dusk, you will run into too many."

"I do not want to answer questions or be stared at. Do you promise that Cherok will come right away for me if Mi-sa wakes up?"

"Did I not say I would send him?"

———

ON HER WAY TO THE CENOTE Miakka walked around the perimeter of the village where she would not encounter any of the insensitive or curious members of the village. She wasn't ready to answer questions. She didn't want to talk to anyone.

She scanned the surface and then stepped into the tepid water, the breeze quickly evaporating it from her exposed skin. Slowly she lowered herself into the water and then leaned her head back, letting the spirit of the water sap the dried blood from her hair.

On her way back, she realized that the village was operating as it always did. Smoke from cook fires wormed its way into the air, and the aroma of freshly brewed tea and warm bread wafted to her nose. It seemed a betrayal almost—a profanation. Didn't the others realize what had happened to her Mi-sa? To Jegatua? How could others just go on as always when her life was crumbling?

She saw Amakollee talking with Antahala, Sassacha, and others at Sima's fire. Kachumpka sat on the ground alone near Amakollee's hearth. Miakka's stomach tensed as she became nearly overwhelmed with anger. If only Amakollee would stop all this. Mi-sa was no threat to Kachumpka. She was no threat to anyone. Amakollee's mind had become so twisted, and her poison had ... Had Amakollee done this to Mi-sa?

She began to trot toward home, breathing hard, trying to use up her anger.

Chapter Fourteen

THE TERRIBLE THOUGHT festered in Miakka's mind like an infected sore. As the next few days passed, she found it difficult to concentrate on anything except Amakollee and the possibility that she was responsible for this atrocity.

Miakka perched where she could look out from her platform. The sky was darkening, though it was not quite twilight. The tops of the cypress trees moved briskly in the intensifying wind. The moisture in the air amplified all the smells—the muskiness of the decaying leaves, the rich heaviness of the black earth, the acridity of corrosive smoke that came from some fire started by the lightning, the pungent bite of mildew. The sky grumbled in the distance but reached far across the land with its tentacles of reverberation. The welkin grew heavy with rain that hadn't fallen. It stretched and swelled, at first staining and tarnishing the golden glow of sunlight with a dull gray and then bloating, blotting out the last speckle of fair sky.

The rain was fitting, Miakka thought. Behind her Mi-sa rested, near death. The child did not sleep through all the pain and Miakka could see her little face twist with the agony. She almost wished the spirits would call her daughter to the Other Side to end the suffering. Mi-sa lay still most of the time, moaning now and again, shaking as if chilled at other times, crying out for her mother, begging Miakka to make the pain stop. Miakka cradled her, held her, cried over her when she slept, and sang the soft, sweet songs she had sung to her as a baby. When Mi-sa cried for the hurt to go away and called to her, Miakka felt helpless. If the spirits were going to take her, then they should just let it end, not let her baby suffer anymore. Yet when she thought that way, she hated herself for giving in, for being so weak. But when she begged the spirits to spare Mi-sa, she felt selfish.

Atula stayed by Mi-sa's side. He tended her wounds and comforted her mother, encouraging Miakka to trust the spirits.

Miakka looked at the gloomy sky. The rain would stop the curious stares from the other villagers. It would drown out the sound of Mi-sa's shallow wheezes, her desperate attempts at breathing. And when the rain did finally start, Miakka stepped down the ladder and stood with her face to the sky. The water sliding over her skin and pelting her back felt clean and good. She turned beneath the shower and pulled the hair back from her face.

As Miakka walked away, Atula looked out and watched her. It was good for her to leave the platform for a while, even if it was raining. He, too, wondered why the spirits were so unpredictable.

Shakia, watching from her shelter, also saw Miakka make her way across the village.

Miakka stood in front of the cenote, watching the rain stipple the water, hearing it smack the surface. She let loose her moss skirt and tossed it onto the soggy bank, then stepped into the dark water. She let it creep to her neck before she turned over onto her back and floated in the deep pool.

When she had finished, she stepped onto the bank, twisted her hair into a thick black cord, and wrung the water out of it. She didn't want to be gone long, but the fresh air doused with the clear rain made her feel much better. She squeezed some of the water from her skirt and tied it around her waist. Tomorrow she would get Shakia to bring her some fresh moss.

The downpour began to let up, the lightning and thunder never coming any closer. She began walking back but stopped suddenly.

"What?" she said, answering what sounded like someone calling her.

"Here," the voice summoned. "Under the tree."

Miakka followed the voice with her eyes, squinting in the rain. It was Shakia, hunkered beneath the low branches of a cypress.

"What are you doing out in this storm?" she asked Shakia, coming closer.

"I should ask you the same thing."

"You know I cannot come to the cenote without enduring stares and whispers," Miakka said, taking shelter under the tree with Shakia.

"That is why I have come out in this rain. I wanted to see you alone. I think you should know what Amakollee is saying."

"No," Miakka nearly screamed, standing to leave. "I do not want to hear anything she says. I do not even want to hear her name."

"Do not leave, Miakka. You need to know so you can protect Mi-sa."

Miakka bristled. "Do you want to know what I think, Shakia?" she asked without waiting for a reply. "I believe that Amakollee has done all that she is going to do to hurt Mi-sa. I believe that it was Amakollee and no one else

147

who stabbed Mi-sa. I do not even pretend to know why she harbors so much hatred, but I believe that in her twisted, mad mind, she feels that Mi-sa is a threat to Kachumpka. She has been hostile to me since Mi-sa's birth. So when you say I need to know so that I can protect Mi-sa, I think it is a little too late. Amakollee has done her damage."

"Those are serious charges you make."

"I do not understand why nothing is being done."

"Sit, Miakka. Let me tell you what I have come to say."

Miakka looked at the rain that still fell.

"Please," Shakia pleaded.

Miakka's eyes filled with tears. "Tell me," she said as she knelt next to her friend and rocked back on her heels. She scanned the scene in front of her. The big raindrops had shrunk to tiny, nearly invisible sprinklings, thickening the air, making it touchable, giving it form and tint. It drifted through the lacy leaves of the cypress, a moving, dripping silver fog.

"Amakollee has been talking as she did before all this, but much more openly now. Do not say anything," she said, noticing that Miakka was ready to speak. "Just listen. She is talking to people, leading them to believe that the suspicion that Mi-sa is evil has come from their own heads. She insinuates, hints, acts dumbfounded by what has happened, but plants enough seeds so that her efforts are rewarded. The end result is that there is talk that Mi-sa's injuries were caused by the spirits themselves. People say the spirits are taking revenge on Mi-sa. They believe she has brought bad spirits to the clan. When the night of Mi-sa's birth is brought up, many become so emotional that they begin to believe Amakollee's lies. Even Mi-sa's name conjures up bad memories. You need to be prepared to counter these ridiculous accusations. Wakulla and I have both been trying to still this talk."

Miakka shook her head. "I suppose the spirits do not intend for me to understand. Atula should be able to stop the rumors."

"Perhaps they would listen to Atula," Shakia agreed, "but he spends most of his time at Mi-sa's side."

"I do not know what to do," Miakka said in a shaky voice. "Right now all I want is for Mi-sa to get well."

"She will, Miakka. I know she will."

"I must believe that," Miakka answered, putting her arms around her friend and then rising and turning away.

"Miakka?" Shakia called, stopping her before she left. "What you said about Amakollee—that she actually stabbed Mi-sa—I do not think it would be wise to say to anyone else. Not now, anyway. That is a serious accusation and may cause even more dissension. I know it is hard, but perhaps you should keep that conviction to yourself for a while." Shakia paused for a moment before speaking again. "Do you understand what I mean?"

"Yes," Miakka responded. "I do understand." Her voice sounded far off, nearly broken with exhaustion.

Shakia watched her friend leave. She knew that if Miakka made such harsh charges against Amakollee, she would not find much support. Besides, how could Amakollee have done such a thing? Murder was unheard of among the People, and women did not even handle weapons. It was ludicrous. But if Amakollee didn't do it, then who did?

Miakka disappeared into the translucent veil of rain.

Atula saw her coming and stepped back into the shadows of the platform, closer to Mi-sa. Miakka had needed some privacy, some time alone, away from the depressing interior of the platform. He heard her climbing the ladder.

"Do you feel better?" he asked when she appeared on the platform.

"Fresher, but not better," she responded as she bent over her daughter and kissed her pasty cheek.

Atula stroked Miakka's wet hair as it spilled over her shoulders and slid across her back. His hand cupped her shoulder, gently turning her toward him.

"You would give your own life for hers, would you not?" he said.

"Without hesitation," she quickly answered.

Mi-sa suddenly made a gurgling sound, coughing, fighting for a breath. Miakka grabbed Atula's arm. "She is choking."

Atula reached for the child, who was now silent and rapidly draining of all color. Her lips and eyelids turned blue.

"Do something. Help her," Miakka cried, covering her mouth with her hands as soon as she had spoken.

Atula lifted the child's head and torso into his lap. He turned Mi-sa to her side and hit her squarely between the shoulder blades, hoping to miss the wounds and not cause them to open again.

Mi-sa gurgled, spit up some blood, and finally drew in a deep, hungry breath. Miakka slumped.

Atula laid the child on her side and placed a rolled-up hide under her head and shoulder. Mi-sa drew up into a ball and whimpered, calling to her mother. "Please make it stop." She sighed painfully.

Miakka regained her composure, sounding confident. "Yes, my Little Light, the pain will stop. I promise you. Now rest and sleep. I am here by your side."

Mi-sa whimpered again, and Miakka stroked her face. "Sleep, Little Light. Sleep."

In moments Mi-sa had drifted into that grayness of

sick sleep. Her mother began to sing tenderly to her sleeping child. Her voice was mellow and soothing, but soon cracked as she started to cry. The song ended, and Miakka walked into a dark corner of the platform before letting herself weep.

Atula went to her and took her by the shoulders. "You deserve to cry."

"I am so full of anger," she said. "Why has this happened? I want to hit something, to strike out and hurt someone," she sobbed, raising her clenched fists.

Atula pulled her closer, wrapping his arms around her as she laid her head on his chest. He held her close until she stopped sobbing.

"Now," he said, "you listen to what I have to tell you. The spirits will not let Mi-sa die."

"But you do not know what Amakollee is saying."

He held her away from him so that he could see her face. "Look at me," he told her.

Miakka looked into his black eyes as he started to speak. "It does not matter what Amakollee or anyone else says. The spirits favor your child. They even sent a special star sign for her. We cannot understand how or why things happen, but the spirits would not desert a child to whom they have given such a powerful sign."

Miakka looked over at Mi-sa. "Then explain this," she said, nodding toward her child.

Atula cupped her chin and turned her head back toward him. Her face was a breath away from his. Gently his lips touched her forehead before he tilted her head and touched her lips with his. Miakka stiffened as his arms went around her. One of his hands clutched a handful of her still wet hair as the other gently pressed her even closer. He tasted the saltiness of the tears that clung to her lips. Atula wanted to ease her pain with his tenderness. He could feel her small body relax as he enfolded her.

Miakka yielded. For an instant she hid in his arms, withdrawing from wretchedness and anguish, drowning in the solace she found in his embrace.

From behind her, she heard Mi-sa's whispered moan. Abruptly she pulled away from Atula.

"How can you do this to me?" Miakka asked sharply.

"What do you mean?" he asked, sounding confused. He had wanted to comfort her, not inflame her.

"You take advantage of my grief. You wait until I am weak and vulnerable. You can have me anytime—that is your privilege. But you have no conscience."

"I—"

"Please do not say anything. Do not encourage me to believe that you have special feelings for me."

"Miakka," he said, coming closer, reaching for her again.

"Please." She stepped away and turned her back. "Just make Mi-sa well. Make my child well again."

———

IN THE MORNING, Amakollee and many of the other women climbed into canoes and set off with the men to gather coontie roots. Most left their children with the older women of the village, but Amakollee dragged Kachumpka by her side. No one would look after him as she would. She carried him in her lap in the canoe so that he did not take up space and she could avoid objections by other women.

With them they carried large baskets that they could tote on their backs. They left early to avoid the white-hot sun's rays that glinted and radiated off the water. In the dry pinelands, where they were headed, the temperature would scorch the sandy soil, and the rust, brown, and gray bark of the pines would grow parched. The heat would suck the evergreen breath from the slash pines, and at midday the small leaves and blades of the ground cover would turn gray-green as they curled and shriveled.

The men escorted the women into the pinewoods, then watched as they grubbed in the thin layer of dirt over the coral rock and limestone. They dug through the gritty soil with pointed sticks, extracting the large, rough, brown-skinned root of the coontie, swollen with starchy pulp.

When they returned to the village with their bounty, the women emptied their baskets and sat with groups of friends as they pared and diced the roots. The gathering and preparation of coontie was a community affair. Amakollee worked with several women of the village while Kachumpka sat near the brush behind her, slapping at lizards and drawing in the dirt with broken twigs.

The women worked in small teams, sharing the responsibility. Into a stout hollowed-out log that served as a mortar, they poured the diced coontie. Amakollee took the first turn with the large wooden pestle. Even in the shade, the sweltering heat drew perspiration.

She lifted the pestle as she spoke. With her other wrist she wiped away the sweat that had beaded on her forehead. "The child has not said that anyone did this to her. If she knew, do you not think that she would say?"

"I suppose," answered a particularly and peculiarly tall woman in the group. Her face was thin and bony.

"Suppose? Why would the child keep the name of her attacker to herself?" Amakollee asked.

"Well," said another, picking up on Amakollee's direction, "she may not be able to tell because it was not a man. Perhaps it was a spirit."

"I think you are right," Amakollee interjected, supporting the conclusion of the woman. "The People do not attack one another. And certainly if one did, the victim would be quick to tell the name. Yes, I think you are correct. Mi-sa does not tell a name because there is no name."

Another of the women bit down on her bottom lip and took the pestle from Amakollee. More of the coontie was emptied into the mortar as the women began to grind. "But why would spirits want to hurt a child? That does not make sense either."

Amakollee's nose twitched, and her eyes darted toward the doubtful woman. "The spirits must know something about her that we do not. Oh, of course we have always suspected, but no one would want to hurt Miakka and speak it aloud."

"You mean the night of the A-po-la-chee?"

"And do you remember what she did to my Kachumpka?" Amakollee reminded them.

"I think the good spirits, the spirits that dwell with the Breath Giver, are angry with her. I think she harbors evil," Sassacha said, pushing her hair out of her eyes. "I think that we should stop being quiet about it. The child is dangerous. If she does not die, she is a danger to our people."

"Those are strong words," Amakollee said.

"They should be strong words," Sassacha replied.

"Wakulla does not believe it," said the woman who was grinding.

"Of course not," Amakollee quickly responded. "He is Atula's firstborn son, and have you not noticed Atula and Miakka?"

The women fell silent for a moment, and the pestle was passed to the next in the circle.

"Do you really believe that Atula is influenced by Miakka?" asked one of the women.

The bony woman had been silent through the whole conversation, but now she spoke. "I think that what we are saying is dangerous and cruel. Mi-sa is a child—an injured child—and do not forget she is his child. Of course Atula would spend time with her and her mother."

Amakollee smiled patronizingly at the woman. "Yes, his child. Precisely. Do you not remember how children are begotten? And maybe there will be another. He has spent days and nights inside that platform with Miakka."

"With Mi-sa," the argumentative woman countered.

"From what I understand, Mi-sa sleeps most of the time," Sassacha added.

"I agree with Amakollee," another said. "The child would tell if she could, and Wakulla protests because of his father. Atula is blinded by Miakka."

The disagreeing woman shook her head.

Amokallee suddenly turned her head toward the brush. She felt that she was being watched, listened to, but she saw no one. She poured a bowl of water into the mortar with the ground coontie. Like thin blood, the water turned red. The women would let it sit and separate into red water and a sediment of fine white starch. They would drain off the water and then add more, continuing the process, washing and rewashing until the water ran clear. Only then would the coontie be safe. Then they would allow the starch to dry in the sun.

"Did you see anyone lurking behind me, hidden by the brush?" Amakollee asked, looking behind her again.

The women shook their heads. "Why? What did you hear?"

Amakollee didn't know how to explain. She could feel the stare, the intrusion, cold and slick and real. The presence was not friendly or merely curious. The eyes were a meddling menace. Someone had listened and eavesdropped, and her words would be used against her in some way. Mi-sa was out there—or some protective spirit of hers.

Amakollee shivered at the horrible thought. She turned again, looking and searching, disbelieving the empty view. There was nothing but a small open space and the spindly scrub. She had felt the same compulsion when she touched the awl over and over again to make sure it was sharp. She kept turning and looking, expecting to see something squatting, hiding, sneaking.

"Amakollee," the thin woman said again, "what did you hear?"

Amakollee held her hand up as if asking the woman to be quiet. She strained, tilting her head slightly as if it would improve her hearing. Something was there. She knew it. Suddenly she realized that something was missing. Her eyes widened, and she turned her pale face back to the women, terror inscribed in the lines that cut through her forehead and around her eyes.

"She wants Kachumpka," she hissed, stumbling to her feet, searching in panic. "Where is he?"

Chapter Fifteen

AMAKOLLEE PIVOTED in every direction, screaming her son's name, breathing hard.

"Kachumpka!" she shrieked, both hands tugging at her hair.

The other women also looked for him. "There," Sassacha said, standing and pointing.

Amakollee grabbed her, shaking her arm. "Where? I do not see him."

"There," Sassacha said again.

Amakollee tracked her eyes and spotted Kachumpka. He had wandered off and stood in the middle of a group of children. His smile was wide but empty.

Amakollee ran to him, calling his name. Kachumpka stood still as if he hadn't even heard her. He appeared intrigued by the other children, enchanted by all the activity—arms flailing, voices shouting, laughing, taunting. It was the closest contact he had ever had with them. As they ran around and past him, he bounced with excitement, standing on his toes, squealing and making odd sounds.

Amakollee swooped her arms around him, pressing his face into the cushion of her ample breasts. She lifted his gangly body, and he wrapped his legs around her waist as she carried him away. He cooed and giggled, still apparently impressed and reacting to the lively motions and noises of the children at play.

———

CHEROK SLIPPED THROUGH the brush wondering why Amakollee never let it rest. She had initiated the conversation and set its direction. She had led the other women to their conclusions. She was determined to destroy Mi-sa.

He hadn't set out to overhear the conversation. He had been stalking a rabbit in the wild, seeing how close he could get, how good he had gotten. He had come close to his prey, but a careless movement alerted the rabbit, sending it skittering away. Cherok was hiding, waiting for that rabbit or some other to come by again when the women had arrived. Once the conversation started, he was afraid to leave. The women would think that he had been there just to eavesdrop. So he had sat very still, becoming one with the landscape as his father had taught him to do when hunting. Amakollee had suspected something, though he wondered how. He had not moved, almost not even blinking. He was relieved when Kachumpka had wandered off. It broke up the group and gave him an opportunity to escape.

Cherok ran to Mi-sa's platform and called up.

Atula appeared and climbed down. "Mi-sa cannot speak, Cherok. When she is awake, she is delirious."

"But I want to be with her."

"Then go up and sit quietly. Shakia has taken Miakka for a walk and to encourage her to eat. I am going to stretch and get some fresh air. I will stay here. Call down to me if Mi-sa shows any changes."

Cherok was coming of age. His concern for Mi-sa was more than a display of friendship; it was evidence of maturation. His time was coming.

Cherok stepped inside and sat next to Mi-sa. His mother would be happy if he stayed away from the child, he thought. But look at her. There was no way he could desert her. He would not tell Cacema he had been here.

"Mi-sa," he whispered, "can you hear me?"

Cherok closed his eyes, emptying his cluttered mind, settling his body to a smooth, slow hum. He let the air flow through his flesh, through his bones, becoming lighter and lighter inside, releasing the fetters that tethered his spirit to his heavy body until he had collected all of himself in a special place near the crown of his head. From here he could reach out to Mi-sa. His father had taught him how to get there, but he had never been able to leave his body without Mi-sa.

Without using his voice, he called to her. He waited for her to come to him in this silent, unconventional world. He called to her again. She had come to him many times through the cool white haze, drifting on the air, her hair blowing back from her face. He waited and then called again, but no small girl cloaked in clouds came to lead him.

She was not coming this time. He would have to go on his own, outside himself without a guide, to look for her. Frightened, he took two deep breaths and blew them out, sending his apprehension out and away. Mustering all the strength he had, he focused himself, looking out, seeing without his eyes. At first there was blackness and an annoying buzzing in his ears. He found it hard not to be distracted and started over again and again, sinking deeper into the darkness, waiting for it to swallow him. At last the blackness covered him. In the stillness he waited, holding fast to his concentration. The darkness faded into a haze. He looked down and saw his body next to Mi-sa's.

He had done it! He was free.

Suddenly a white mist blanketed everything. "Help me find you," he called to her with his spirit voice. A small breeze blew the mist away like smoke, clearing it enough so that he saw Mi-sa's face.

"You came, Cherok. I knew you would," she said softly.

"Of course I came. We are special to each other, are we not?"

The fog began to grow thick again, obscuring her face.

"Do not go," he pleaded. "Wait, Mi-sa."

He heard her whisper her answer. "I am too weak. Help me, Cherok. I am afraid."

"Mi-sa," he called. The mist thinned again, and he saw her small sad face.

"Tell me who did this to you."

Mi-sa's face wrinkled, and she started to cry.

"Please, Mi-sa, tell me who it was."

The white haze grew thick and opaque. "Tell me," he pleaded a last time before she completely disappeared. Far away he could hear her pitiful cry.

"Cherok, please help me."

"I will, Mi-sa. I will," he answered her, hoping that she heard him.

Without a warning, he was drawn into a black cyclone, and a loud roar filled his ears. It was over. Silence. His eyes flew open. Mi-sa lay still in front of him. He touched her cheek.

"Do not be afraid, Little Light. I am with you."

Cherok felt drained of all his energy. He could not let her die, he thought. The idea of living the rest of his life without her, without the things she helped him do, was a paralyzing thought. Without Mi-sa he could never be what Atula and the People wanted. And she did not even realize that. She thought that Cherok was teaching her.

Cherok felt anxious and alone. He wanted to please his father and his mother, but they expected so much from him. Atula had told him that as he got older, his tasks would become easier, but they had not. Those wonderful things that his father wanted him to do, he had never been able to do alone. Mi-sa was his wings above the earth, his eyes in other worlds. "No," he said aloud. "She cannot die."

Miakka's hand touched his shoulder and made him jump.

"Miakka, there is something ..." he started but then noticed Shakia and Sima. He wanted to tell Miakka how special Mi-sa was, how he was linked to her in some powerful and extraordinary way. He wanted her and Atula to know. He wanted to confess how impotent he was without her. He had carried that burden too long. But he couldn't tell her with Shakia and Sima here.

"What is it, Cherok? Is something wrong?" Miakka began when Cherok halted. "Is it Mi-sa? Did something happen?" She knelt next to her daughter, touching, feeling, looking for any sign.

Cherok sat silently.

"Cherok, what is wrong? What happened?" she said, louder, sounding alarmed this time.

The boy just looked at her and then at the other two women. "Nothing," he finally answered as he hurried to the ladder.

Miakka looked up, puzzled.

Cherok scrambled down to the ground. At the bottom, while backing away, he tripped over something.

"Cherok?" Atula called as the boy stumbled and then ran off.

Atula quickly ascended the ladder. Had something

happened to Mi-sa? When he entered the platform, he was relieved to see the three women at ease.

"What was wrong with Cherok?" he asked.

"He started to say something and then decided not to. At first we thought something was wrong with Mi-sa, but she is the same," Sima said.

Miakka still gazed at her daughter. As soon as she heard Atula's voice, she felt awkward. She did not want to look at him or talk to him. She was grateful that he spent so much time with Mi-sa, but her feelings were confused. She wanted him near, and yet she wished he would leave.

Atula bent down next to her and touched Mi-sa's face. The little one's eyes opened, glazed and blank.

"Hello, Little Light," Miakka whispered, smiling.

"It hurts, Mother."

"Sima, go and get me a coal to start a fire," Atula said. "I will prepare something to ease the pain."

He moved to the ladder and climbed down behind Sima. He stirred the hearth with a stick. There was no flicker, and the bowl that held the fresh water was empty.

"Miakka," he called up, "bring some fresh water. I will need it to prepare the elixir."

Miakka and Shakia climbed down, took the bowl, and hurried to the cenote.

"This way," Miakka indicated, changing the route, leading her friend into the jungle of trees, vines, wiry underbrush, and flowering plants. "Do you mind?" she asked Shakia, brushing a spiderweb out of her face.

"I understand. Would you rather I went alone?"

"No, I feel the need to be useful, to do something. Most of the time I feel so helpless," Miakka said, stopping to look at Shakia and judge her understanding.

They skirted the perimeter of the mound, winding through the trees that dripped with air plants and orchids and rookeries. Above them, stealing a ride on the thermal currents, rode a pair of glossy white birds, soaring, then sinking and flashing, turning to find the channel of warm air rising from the earth. Brilliant green and blue dragonflies fluttered through the maze on iridescent wings, lighting on the tips of stiff stems. Hurries of yellow-and-black-striped butterflies darted in and out of the pillars of sunlight.

At the edge of the cenote, which was crowded with lilies, a raccoon batted a crayfish, toying with her dinner. Shakia pointed the animal out to Miakka, saying, "She must have babies or she would not be out so openly this time of day."

No one else visited this part of the sinkhole to bathe or collect water. Miakka bent with the bowl, reaching down through the clustered water plants and then coming up with water. She poured a small amount into the palm of her hand, the clarity being difficult to judge inside the dark pot. The water was clear.

Miakka looked into her hand as the water slowly ebbed away. Her eyes started to sting.

"She will be all right," Shakia said, putting her arm around her friend's shoulder.

"I have to believe she will," Miakka responded, straightening, stopping the tears. "We will go back by the common path," Miakka said bravely. "It is time I faced the People."

"Are you sure?" Shakia asked. "Make certain you are strong enough. There will be stares and whispers."

"I know that," she answered, lifting her head higher. "Perhaps mumbling unkind speculations about Mi-sa will be more difficult for the People if I confront them. I will not hide anymore. Mi-sa deserves more than that."

The two women began their trek along the edge of the

cenote, making their way to the clearing and the path that led back to the village. Miakka stopped at the rim of the pool. Here the water was not clogged with lilies. She splashed some of the water on her face. Before she crossed the village she wanted to be sure that there were no tearstains on her face.

"How do I look?" she asked Shakia.

"Wonderful." Shakia plucked a long-stemmed pink flower and wove it into Miakka's hair. "Delightful and lovely. Beautiful,"

"Shakia," Miakka protested with a smile, "I appreciate your efforts, but do not make your compliment less credible by exaggerating. I saw my reflection."

Shakia rolled her eyes. "Presentable, then."

"I will settle for presentable." Miakka laughed and started to leave with her friend. As she turned and took her first step, she bumped squarely into something.

"Miakka," a deep voice said softly, "trust your friend. 'Delightful and lovely' is a good description."

It was Tican, a man from another village. He had come before with other men, looking for women to court and eventually take back as brides. He had always paid special attention to Miakka, though she was surprised that he had not yet taken another woman.

Miakka blushed, lowering her head, looking down. "You always flatter me," she told him.

"No, I do not flatter. I tell the truth. This is not the first time you have heard a compliment from my lips."

Miakka stepped forward, moving past him. "It is nice to see you again, Tican."

Tican looked at Shakia. "She never hears my words," he said, shaking his head in disappointment.

He walked over to where Shakia had picked the flower and took a handful of them, cutting the stems with his knife. Miakka had continued up the path. He caught up with her, calling her name.

"Take these with you, and when you look at them, think of me thinking of how lovely you are. I do not give up so easily."

"When you find the right woman, she will be fortunate to have a man who expresses his feelings so beautifully."

"But I have found the right woman. She just does not know it yet."

Miakka touched the petals of the flowers. "I will think of you," she said, then turned and proceeded up the path. Tican stood watching her leave.

Shakia trotted until she caught up. "I do not understand why you never return his affection. He is so handsome and a leader of the Men's Council in his village."

"Do not make me explain to you," Miakka snapped.

Shakia ignored her. "One day he will find a woman who appreciates his ways. You should take him more seriously."

"Enough, Shakia. I cannot even think about it now, not with Mi-sa and everything that has happened."

"Then when Mi-sa is well—the next time that Tican comes, at least encourage him to come back again."

Miakka stopped. "Tican is a nice man. Any woman would be lucky. But not me."

"You cannot forget Atula, can you? You know you have no future with him. He is Shaman. Give Tican a chance. Do not push him away with your indifference."

"I do not mean to hurt him," she said sadly, turning to look back at her suitor. She smiled at him and then turned back around. "When Mi-sa is healed, I will think about it," she said.

Shakia dropped a step behind Miakka, twisting her

head around to see Tican coming up the path behind them. She smiled and nodded at him.

Tican grinned, flashing his straight white teeth, and stretching one strongly muscled brown arm toward the sky.

Chapter Sixteen

THE MOON WAS FULL, a bright night sun, polishing the village with its gossamer sheen. Wakulla sat next to Shakia inside his platform. This was the night he would be made cacique. The hammock's live oaks and strangler figs caught the light, played with it, fanning it and tossing it so that it fell on the earth in lively, frolicsome patches of animated glimmers.

"You should have a smile on your face instead of a frown," Shakia said to him, touching the back of her hand to his thick black hair.

The shadows and light made gay games of dancing in and out the shelter. Wakulla watched and listened, hearing the chirping music of the crickets, the bellow of the proud male alligator attracting his mate. The tops of the tall Sabal palms were standing in the light, hovering above the canopy of the other foliage, like sentinels overlooking their charge. The night was beautiful, and Shakia was right; he should be smiling, but deep inside he felt restless and fearful. Not the kind of fear he had felt the night of the A-po-la-chee. This was different. It was like the disquietude he had felt when he was out alone, searching for his totem spirit, becoming a man. It was a gnawing, subtle doubt that came from within. He was about to become the leader of his people, and he wondered if he was worthy. He was only a man, like all the men, no different, no better, no worse. He had done nothing extraordinary in his life to prove his worthiness or superior judgment. And yet all of the villagers had placed their unequivocal trust in him. Whatever he said, the decisions he made and the advice he gave from this night on would carry the weight of all the wisdom of Jegatua and his predecessor and the other caciques before them. This was an honor and a responsibility like none he had ever borne before.

Talasee was banking the hearth in the center of the plaza, and the flames suddenly lapped at the air with orange tongues, spraying the air with tiny flickers of light, filling the night air with the crackle of the fire's spirit. Shakia stood, and Wakulla reached for her hand, pulling it across his shoulder to his mouth, kissing the back of her hand.

"You are good for me, Shakia," he said.

Shakia placed herself behind him, wrapping her free hand over the tight muscles of his shoulder. She kneaded them, loosening the knots of tension that coiled and twisted there. She said nothing. He needed to know that she understood, and she could best show him she did by just being near.

He turned his head and kissed the arch of her hip.

"These are troubled times," she murmured, feeling the damp night breeze cool the small patch of skin that was still moist from his kiss.

They could hear the crowd beginning to gather. Many things would happen tonight during the gathering. Atula would fulfill many obligations—talk to the animal spirits, intervene in illnesses, orate, and convey the wisdom of the spirits on matters concerning the clan. The highlight of the evening would be the ritual and the final proclamation that would make Wakulla the cacique.

———

ATULA SAT ALONE in his platform. He had spent much of the day at Mi-sa's side, dripping the medicine through the corner of her mouth, slowly, methodically until she had taken the entire dose. Finally her moaning had ceased, and she had slept undisturbed by the terrible pain. Miakka had slept then, too.

Atula held the triangular amulet in his hand and thought of Ochassee, recalling many of the things that his father had told him. Now he wished he had listened more intently, learned all that he could before his father was called to the Other Side. His father had been a patient sage and teacher, issuing simple adages that the boy could understand. As Atula grew older, Ochassee offered him more complicated, more powerful information. But Ochassee had been taken to the Other Side early in his life. Had his father finished with him? Atula wondered. Were there small gaps or even great chasms in his knowledge? All this talk about Mi-sa worried him and some of it filtered deep into his gut. Had he been right? Did he have all the wisdom that Ochassee could have imparted? Had he correctly read the star sign?

He hated it when these uncertainties crept into him. He rubbed the medallion, hoping to absorb some more of his father's wisdom through his fingertips.

His voice sounded like a soft hum as he began his prayers. Today had been a day of fasting for him. It had been a day of cleansing, preparing his body to be a receptacle of the spirits. Early in the morning, before the sun rose, he had prepared his emetic tea, purging his body of the remains of earthborn needs. Then he had bent over the fire, forcing his body to give up the unclean

169

poisons and fluids. It made him dizzy and nauseated, a sign that the cleansing was nearly complete. He had walked to the cenote and dipped his sweaty body in the water, washing away the uncleanliness that the fire had drawn from him. He rinsed his mouth and his straight black hair. Then he began the day. When he arrived to medicate Mi-sa and to check on her, Miakka went below and prepared her morning meal.

In late afternoon he had returned to his platform to gather some leaves and stems from baskets, knowing each by its color, shape, texture, and smell. He tore them into bits and dropped them in a pot suspended over the fire. Atula waited for the water to begin to bubble, then covered the pot with a black clay slab. He brushed a clear spot near him and set the pot down on it. Over it he sang softly, chanting the prayers, sending the words on his breath into the wind, the invisible courier. His canticle, which matched the singing wind, would make the medicine effective. Just before the ceremony tonight he would drink it.

Now as darkness dropped and the sun gave way to the moon, Atula could hear the people gathering. It was time. The spirit man picked up a leather-wrapped bundle and climbed out of his platform and sat next to his hearth. He removed the slab from the pot and swirled the tea with his finger. He scooped the herbal debris from the surface and discarded it. He had one last thing to do.

Atula began to chant softly, almost inaudibly, calling the spirits, inviting them. As he sang, his strong hands delicately unfolded the pale hide. Inside was a special tool. Wedged into a carved antler handle was the sharp blade of an obsidian knife. The handle was etched with a serpent that began to coil at the base, then wound around the shaft and ended with its mouth open to the blade, becoming an extension of the hand that held it. It had been polished, first in fire and then with oil from the generations of human hands that had held it. This holy instrument was used only during the ritual that gave the clan a new leader. Atula had never even held it before. Deftly and steadily he drew the blade through the skin on the inside of his forearm. Then, perpendicular to that he sliced through his arm again, forming a cross, a point for each of the directions. It filled with blood, which oozed down his arm. Atula held his arm over the fire, letting the blood drip and sizzle in the flames. He sang with his eyes closed, waiting for the spirits to stop the bleeding.

When it was done, the spirit man raised the pot to his lips and drank its contents.

The medicine worked quickly. He closed his eyes, letting the elixir do its work with no interference. It opened his mind to things the ordinary man could not see—things Atula could not envision without it. Now he could see and hear the spirits, speak and understand their tongue, receive and interpret their messages.

This was his reward for the fast and the misery with which he tortured himself. The medicine brought on a mystical, incredible feeling of well-being. It stirred a depth in him he could never reach any other way.

The fire keeper, Talasee, stirred the logs and embers. All of the villagers had now gathered and sat waiting. Atula wrapped his black bear cloak around his shoulders, the soft underhide caressing his skin. It fell from his chest almost to the floor. He twisted his hair into a knot in the back and drove two long bone pins through it to hold the knot of hair in place.

He dipped three fingers into some wet clay dyed with the magenta pokeberry. Lazily he drew his fingertips across his cheeks, leaving three red lines on each.

Atula could already hear the spirit voices and see the colors they brought with them. Glowing whorls, spinning eddies of red, blue, and yellow, some colors he could not even define, swirled before his eyes, and the sounds of this world became distant echoes, leaving him free to hear the closer voices of the spirits.

Suddenly he saw before him the rolling, grumbling, roaring head of a black bear, angrily upright on its hind legs, baring its long meat-tearing teeth. Atula blinked, and the bear disappeared. It had been a brief vision, just a flash. He was ready.

———

WAKULLA WAITED IN HIS SHELTER for Talasee to come for him. Shakia touched her hand to his lips and left him.

"I will wait to kiss the cacique," she said with a promise in her smile.

Indeed she was good for him, he thought. She always knew just the right things to say and when to say them. She left him with something else to think about, to look forward to. He could tell by the glint in her eyes and the way her lips curled into that teasing smile that she meant more than a kiss. In her quiet, discreet way, she never failed to arouse him with the smallest hint. If there had been time, he thought, he would have called her back up to him, inside the darkness of the platform. But she was right. The joining would be later tonight, when he was the cacique.

Kita sat near the fire. She did not want to miss anything this special night. Her son, flesh born of her flesh, blood of her blood, was going to be proclaimed the new leader. She held in her lap a blanket of rabbit fur. Her leathery hand probed at the soft fur, the ropes of blue veins showing beneath her translucent skin. This was the blanket she had begun with the pelt Wakulla brought back from his totem quest. Tonight she would present it to her son, to the cacique.

Shakia came and sat next to her. Tabisha also took a seat near Kita.

"Does Miakka come?" Tabisha asked Shakia.

"She will not leave Mi-sa," Shakia answered.

Tabisha had raised Miakka after her parents' death, and in her heart thought of her as her daughter. It anguished her to see how Miakka suffered. She sat quietly for a moment, watching the crowd grow, but then stole away.

She found Miakka sitting in the dark moonshadow of her platform.

"I can hear Mi-sa from here," she said, feeling it necessary to explain why she was not inside.

"Of course you can," Tabisha told her.

"You are going to miss all the—"

"And so are you," Tabisha interrupted. "But I have seen it before. I remember the ceremony for Jegatua. But you were not yet born. You have never seen such a ceremony."

"No, never. But my place is here with my daughter."

"Everyone should see the making of a new cacique. The ceremony will live in the memory of everyone."

"I am certain that it will," Miakka agreed.

"Though I was not your mother, did I take good care of you?" Tabisha asked.

"You were my mother in all ways. You were wonderful to me. Why would you ask? Surely you have no doubts."

"Then you will let me stay with Mi-sa while you go tonight."

"I—I cannot go. I should be here."

"You just told me that I was a good mother, though I did not give birth to you. I can do the same for Mi-sa for such a short time. It would please me if you showed me that much trust."

"Oh, Tabisha, you know I trust you with my life. But—"

"It would please me. I am unable to do anything else. I cannot relieve your suffering or Mi-sa's pain. I cannot make her well again. Let me do this small thing. It will make me feel better in my heart."

The manner in which Tabisha had worded her request left Miakka with no option. She could not refuse her without insulting her. Tabisha had planned it just so.

"Will you come for me if Mi-sa asks for me?"

"I will come right away."

"Would you mind sitting inside with her?"

"I had planned to. Now go so that you can see all of the ritual."

"Are you sure?" Miakka asked.

"I want to do this. And I want you to go. It fulfills my motherly needs."

Miakka smiled at her.

"Go, then. Let yourself enjoy it."

Miakka started to walk away. "Thank you."

"Go," Tabisha commanded.

Miakka walked up behind the gathered villagers. Talasee had fed the fire, and it blazed into the night sky. Atula already stood in front of the fire. He appeared to be more than a man, majestic in stature, the way he moved, the way he stood. With his penetrating eyes and resounding voice he captured his audience, holding them spellbound with his displays of power. He amazed them with the strength and height of his body when he reached toward the sky—sleek, defined with muscles, strong.

Miakka watched. Cherok sat in the front of the crowd, studying his father, watching, sometimes mimicking every move in some discreet way. She saw Kita and Shakia next to each other. She looked about, and her stomach turned over. Amakollee was in the middle of the crowd. Sassacha and other friends crowded around her. She held Kachumpka on her hip, leaning to one side to help support him. She whispered as Atula danced and sang. Miakka did not need to hear the words; she knew the kinds of things that Amakollee whispered.

Miakka turned away. She would not watch Amakollee.

Shakia had spotted Miakka and approached her.

"Come and sit with Kita and me. Come," she said, taking Miakka's hand and leading her. As they made their way through the crowd, a hush met them along their path. Even Atula paused when he saw Miakka.

Bowls of cassite were passed from person to person, each taking a sip. Kita handed a bowl to Miakka, who did not drink but handed it on to Shakia.

"I do not feel like a celebration," she said as she passed it.

Shakia did not take it. "Celebrate with me. With Sima. Share in our joy for Wakulla."

Miakka could not refuse and put the bowl to her lips, taking a gulp. "For Wakulla," she said after swallowing.

"For Wakulla," Shakia repeated, taking a drink.

Suddenly the rhythm of the shaman's rattle broke through the noise, and a hush fell over the crowd again. They stood. The spirit man was ready.

An older man stepped forward.

"I am ill, Shaman," he said, pressing the back of his hand to his forehead and looking down to show his respect. "Rid me of this evil and fill me with good. Ask the spirits to come this way."

Atula stretched his arm out straight, put his hand in front of the man's face, and rotated it from side to side while mediating on the causes of the illness.

In a moment he led the man closer to the fire until the proximity became uncomfortable. If the man took a step closer, might burn, but he trusted the shaman. There he stood until the sweat poured from him.

Atula handed the man a bundle of herbs. "For four mornings brew yourself a tea from these. When you vomit, take the spoiled soil north, to the direction of evil, and bury it there. When you return, sit before your hearth until no more poison exudes from your skin. Wash it away and then sleep."

Before the man took the herbs, Atula said magic words over them. The man thanked Atula as he faded back into the crowd.

Others also came forward, wanting to be healed. For each there was a different recipe and different words.

When the sick and ailing had been taken care of, the bowls of cassite were circulated again. Atula rested and prepared himself for his next obligation.

Again his rattle and voice silenced the people. This time they watched as Atula called the spirits, speaking unknown words. They sank to their knees in wonder as the wind picked up, swirling the leaves, making them dart and turn, then twirl and settle. The leaves were brown and green phantoms, flirting with the flickering light of the fire and the shadows in the moonlight. When the stillness came, Atula shuddered with the entry of a spirit. His voice changed pitch, ringing out into the night, eerily blending with the natural sounds of the fire, the insects, the nocturnal sounds.

From the voice of the spirit came the predictions through Atula's mouth. The people listened intently. He spoke of common things—the animals, the weather. Suddenly the wind blew again, stirring everything that had settled before. And then came a message that no one understood, not even Atula.

"The water of the new river is for the People. It is a good thing and there is nothing to fear."

Atula shuddered again, nearly collapsing as the spirit left his body, a misty apparition curling into the night.

Chapter Seventeen

THE CROWD WAITED as Atula prepared for the most important event of the evening. More cassite was passed, lightening the heads of all those who partook.

Miakka blinked, refocusing her tired eyes. This time she took the bowl of cassite as it was passed to her, wrapping her hand around the black and gritty surface. The first sip had been bitter, a stinging bite that trickled hotly down her throat. But now it was friendlier, a warm tea that slid down to her stomach where it created a comforting flush. She closed her eyes as she put her lips to the rim of the bowl. She filled her mouth, taking more than just a sip this time. She held the bowl out to someone, then tilted her head back and swallowed.

Atula attracted her attention. In the firelight he stripped off the bear cloak, swinging it around in the air, then spun and wrapped the fur about him. His voice had grown louder and louder. Wakulla approached, walking through the crowd as it separated for him.

Shakia was filled with love, and her eyes glossed with tears as she watched him come closer. Kita clutched at the blanket in her lap, feeling the downy softness of the rabbit fur. They watched the man they loved humbly present himself to the People and to the shaman. The firelight and moonlight created an aura about him as he walked closer to Atula.

Miakka's eyes remained on Atula. She watched him, not Wakulla, as he called to the spirits and presented Wakulla with the staff that belonged only to the cacique. The young ones of the village had only seen Jegatua's gnarled hands holding the staff. Now a younger, smoother hand grasped the rod. But in time it, too, would wrinkle and grow crooked. Aging came not only with time but also with responsibility.

The people were enthralled. At times it was so quiet that the very breath of the shaman could be heard as it left him. At other moments, as Wakulla was endowed with rights, obligations, and duties, there was a buzzing, a thrum of noise as the People murmured their approval.

When it was over, the solemn and intense faces of the crowd loosened to smiles. Now was a time of exultant celebration. It was a time of dancing and singing, the People showing their acceptance and gratefulness. With one another they were bonded anew, tightening the ties of the clan.

Miakka felt sluggish. Her feet tamped the soil in a dance, but she lacked the energy the others felt. She was tired. Since Mi-sa had been hurt she had slept little and at odd times. Though Shakia had encouraged her to eat, she had not wanted much. To appease her friend, she had prepared the meals, but she had a difficult time getting any of the food down.

She swallowed some more cassite, feeling it rush through her. Her fingertips felt numb, and her head grew muddled as if filled with cobwebs. She stopped to get her balance, looking out across the festive group.

Their feet were trampling, making a swelling, booming thud on the moist black earth. The sound pounded inside Miakka's swooning head, louder than it really was, echoing, resounding, deafening. She pressed her hands to her ears, blocking the relentless sound. She felt dizzy and off balance.

Miakka stood away from the rest, unsure of herself, unsteady on her feet. But she needed to say something to Wakulla. It would only be polite. The others had spoken to him to extend their congratulations and to show their respect.

Wobbly, she pushed through the crowd. She still heard the voices as distant echoes, and the faces of those who were close were distorted, pulled and drawn into warped, misshapen countenances. She finally saw the new cacique a few steps ahead, talking with Atula. Her peripheral vision began to blacken, leaving her with a bizarre tunnel through which she could see.

"Wakul—" she managed to say before crumpling onto the ground at his feet.

————

IN THE BLACKNESS she was moving, bumping along but wrapped in warmth. Miakka struggled to open her eyes. Where was she? What was happening? Above her was the black sky with the twinkling fires that burned eternally, the glittering hearths of the spirits and ancestors of the People. Her eyelids were so heavy. Slowly they closed again, weighted with fatigue, emotional exhaustion, and cassite. She drifted, losing her weak grasp on what was real.

Atula carried her across the mound, one of her arms dangling. Draping her over his shoulder, he carried her up the ladder to his platform. She would not be able to care for Mi-sa tonight. Gently he laid her on his mat. For an instant she opened her eyes and looked up, but those deep jet pools were quickly covered again, her long dark lashes feathering across her cheeks.

Wakulla sat cross-legged next to her. The medicine tea had worn off, and the spirits had left him. But the warmth of the cassite spread through him. He sat watching her, listening to the background sound of voices in song and chatter. She would sleep for a while, he thought to himself and smiled. He would sleep little tonight. First he would check on Mi-sa and ask Tabisha to stay the night with her.

He went to the fire beneath Miakka's platform and brewed a medicinal tea. As it simmered, he instructed Tabisha. "Wake Mi-sa several times during the night. Make her drink this. That is important. If she can only drink a little, then wake her more often. It is not so important that she drinks large amounts at one time as it is that she keeps drinking until the medicine is gone. By morning she should have finished it all."

Tabisha nodded as she listened and watched. "I will see that she takes it all. Reassure Miakka that I will watch Mi-sa carefully and that I will call for you if the girl needs you."

Atula thanked her and left. He meandered through the village, noting that the celebration was beginning to quiet down. He stopped and drank some more cassite with Wakulla, who asked about Miakka.

"She needs rest," Atula told him. "These past days have been excruciating for her. Her body could stand no more. Tabisha will stay with Mi-sa for the night."

Atula left Wakulla reminiscing with Talasee about the day they had become men. The voices Atula heard were comforting, affirming that the clan was stable and healthy. For the night at least they had put away the idle destructive talk that Amakollee loved to invite. He hoped they would focus on something else.

Atula climbed up to his platform. The full moon bathed the inside of the shelter in gray light that splashed in through the opening. He looked at the lovely body curled up on his mat. Miakka had misunderstood his kiss that last time. It had seemed such a natural act. It was his way of showing her ... What was it that he felt? he asked himself, knowing the answer before the question was finished. He knew what made him ache inside for her, to see her again, to touch her. He knew what made him find such delight in the simple things about her: the way she tilted her head in question, the way she moistened her lips, the way she brushed a breeze-blown strand of hair from her face. He recognized the way she evoked a low burn inside him, deep and intense.

So long he had stayed away, protecting himself from those very feelings.

Atula sat in a corner of the platform. He would sleep for a little while and then go back and check on Mi-sa and Tabisha.

His eyes closed, and sleep swept over him.

———

ATULA HAD NOT BEEN ASLEEP long when he heard Miakka whimper.

"No. No. Mi-sa." she cried in dream whispers.

Atula moved to her side and brushed her cheek with his hand. "Shh," he whispered to her. "It is all right."

Miakka seemed to drift off, but then she suddenly lurched up and screamed Mi-sa's name.

"It is all right, Miakka. You are dreaming."

Miakka threw her arms around his neck. "Every time I sleep it comes back to me. I feel her blood seep beneath my fingers, and then I see her. Over and over I see the blood. Again and again."

Atula held her close, swaying gently.

"Where is she?" Miakka suddenly wailed. "What has happened? Why have you taken me from her?" she cried, pulling away from him. "I need to be with Mi-sa."

"Not tonight. You need a night to sleep. Tabisha is with Mi-sa. I have already checked on her and will do so throughout the night."

"But I should be with her." She started to get to her feet. "Why did you not take me there? Why am I here?"

Miakka staggered as she stood, feeling weak and woozy.

Atula stood and supported her, easing her back to the mat. "You would not sleep if you were with Mi-sa. If you do not get some sleep, you will not be any good to her at all."

Miakka's head spun. She put her handa to her temples as if to stop it. "But I cannot sleep. I dream. I see her floating on a sea of blood." Miakka started to cry. "When will it end? When?"

Atula wrapped his arms around her and pulled her head to his chest. "Miakka," he started but could not find the words to comfort her. Instead he leaned his head into her neck and kissed the soft flesh at the curve of her neck and shoulder. His hand held the back of her head, stroking her silken hair, which emitted the fresh floral scent he always associated with her.

Miakka's cries faded to whimpers as she felt his hot lips burn into her neck. His strength around her sheltered her, protected her from her nightmares, from the rest of the world. She sighed as his hand traced smooth lines down her back.

"No," she barely whispered, satisfying her need to protest.

"Shh," he murmured into her ear as he stretched her

out alongside him. His mouth nipped at her chin, and his lips touched her eyelids. His hand wandered over the profile of her body, exploring the curve of her waist and the union of her thigh and her hip.

Miakka could feel the tenseness of his muscles as they strained against her. She wanted to disappear beneath him as he moved her to her back, his arms cradling her. Her breath caught as his mouth moved to the hollow of her throat and then onto the fullness of her breast. Her hands frantically reached for him, driving her fingers through his hair as he left a trail of kisses to the crest of her hip and then across her stomach.

An urgent moan escaped her when he touched her teasingly with his tongue. He was the only man she had ever been with and only that one time. It had not been like this. She had never felt these sensations before. She raised her shoulders, reaching for him, crying for him. But Atula would give her the gift he had robbed her of before, and Miakka fell back onto the mat, a victim of his expertise. He stayed with her as she twisted in pleasure, finally crying out with the incredible explosion of pleasure he gave her.

Atula raised up, looking down into her face. Miakka's eyes were closed. A lock of hair crossed her face. He brushed it aside and smiled, then touched his lips tenderly to hers.

Miakka breathed out a deep sigh. "Sleep now," he said, moving off her and stretching out next to her. His arm went around her, and she nestled against him.

Now her sleep was peaceful. Later he slid away from her and went to check on Mi-sa. He stopped at the cenote for some fresh water and to sit in the quiet peace. There he shook his medicine rattle, which dripped with feathers and deer hooves. Tonight he had many words to say alone.

———

IN THE MORNING MIAKKA SHIFTED on the mat before opening her eyes. Lazily she finally awakened. At first she did not remember the night before, but it slowly became clear. Immediately she looked for Atula. She expected to see him next to her when she turned, but he was not there. Miakka sat up. He was nowhere. Mi-sa, she suddenly thought. Was something wrong with Mi-sa?

She scrambled down the ladder of Atula's platform and ran across the mound. She never should have stayed. She never should have ... She did not want to think about that now. What kind of woman was she? What kind of mother was she?

She ran past those who were sitting at their morning fires, making them gawk with curiosity. She finally reached her platform. Atula was on his way down.

"I was coming to get you," he said as he touched the ground.

"Mi-sa," she cried, clambering up the ladder.

Chapter Eighteen

MIAKKA'S EYES WERE SLOW to adjust from the bright morning sun to the shadows of the platform. In the pit of her stomach she felt the grip of fear. She clutched her midriff, trying to stay calm as she looked at her daughter.

When she got closer and could see, she fell to her knees and reached out to Mi-sa as she wept.

Mi-sa's eyes were open, and there was a delicate and fragile smile on her face. Miakka had been afraid that she would see her daughter cold and stiff, her spirit gone.

"Do not cry, Mother," the child whispered.

"Oh, Mi-sa," she said. "I cry because I am so happy."

Atula stood behind Miakka. "I think the spirits have answered." He sat next to the child and took Miakka's hand in his.

Mi-sa smiled and closed her eyes.

"Let her sleep," Atula advised. "The spirits will heal her body while she sleeps."

Miakka looked into his face. The flood of emotion she felt was overwhelming. She worshiped this man whose touch was so tender and whose medicine was so powerful. She remembered the night before, his gentle touch and his lips on hers. He had saved her child.

Atula kissed her forehead. As if he could reach inside

her, see inside her, feel her heartbeat, he answered her unspoken question. "Last night I was with you as a man, not as a shaman. It was not my right but my desire."

Miakka tried to lower her head in embarrassment, but Atula lifted her chin. Last night she had been no more than a wilted petal, but with his magic she had sweetly flowered beneath him.

"You are not sorry, are you?" he asked.

She did not know what to say. In the daylight things were different somehow. He had taken advantage of her again. She had been so vulnerable—susceptible and accessible and uninhibited. She had been compliant, and now she was embarrassed. He had clearly seen how she felt about him, how easily he could make her tremble.

"I hope you have no regrets," he continued.

"Joining with me is your privilege," she commented, unwilling to accept his continued openness.

"Miakka, did you not hear what I told you? I was with you as a man, a man who wanted to touch you, to bring you pleasure. A man who still wants to be near you often, to see and smell you, touch you, taste you, hear your voice. A man whose feelings are so strong that he risks your rejection, your refusal."

His lips fell gently on hers. Slowly she yielded, her questions and fears dissolving, vanishing at the moist warm touch of his mouth.

He wanted to be with her again, now, only this time he wished to quench the fire that burned within him. Yes, he wanted to fill her, saturate her with his passion, but he ached for the fulfillment that would come to him so easily when her flesh touched his.

"I want you to be my woman," he barely whispered in her ear. "I want no other."

Miakka choked. This was the man she had watched

from afar, had wanted for so long. Was she dreaming? Was this some chimera, some illusion, that would vanish if she opened her eyes?

"Tell me that you are mine. Tell me that you want to be my woman." He sighed, pressing his nose into the bouquet of her hair.

"Yes," she answered, her voice filled with emotion.

Atula bit into the tender flesh of her neck. There was a noise at the base of the ladder, announcing that someone was ascending. Miakka straightened herself, pulling away from him.

"It must be Tabisha," she said.

"No, I sent her home before the sun rose."

Miakka looked to the top of the ladder. It was Wakulla.

"Look, Wakulla," Miakka said, indicating Mi-sa. "She opened her eyes and smiled for me. See her color. And her lips are not so dry and cracked. Atula has made her well." Miakka hoped Wakulla could not tell that she was flustered.

"I came to see about Mi-sa, but also about you," Wakulla said to Miakka. "You have been through so much."

"I am fine," she answered him. "I am sorry I did not get to finish my congratulations."

"Please," he said sincerely, "you do not need to offer an apology." He paused a moment before adding, "Now let me look at Mi-sa." Wakulla stood next to them. "She does look better. We have a potent shaman."

"The spirits find grace in Mi-sa," Atula told him. "They would not forsake a child to whom they gave a star sign."

Wakulla nodded, a look of concern on his face, as if Atula had struck a nerve.

"What is it, Wakulla?" the shaman asked.

"Nothing," he answered. "I am just happy to see that Mi-sa is showing signs of recovery. Shakia will come later," he noted before leaving.

"Why did you question Wakulla?" Miakka asked when he was out of sight.

"There was something in his face. He does not hide his feelings very well. He never has. It is what makes people believe him so easily."

"What did you see? What was it?"

"Something I said troubled him. I do not know what it could be other than Mi-sa's sign. I thought the discontent over that had long since passed. Perhaps it was nothing, just as he said."

Mi-sa again opened her eyes. "I am thirsty," she said.

Miakka raised her daughter's head and put the bowl of water to her lips.

"Make her drink a little of that also," Atula told her, pointing to the bowl of medicinal tea that he had brewed while he watched the sunrise. "We do not want to stop it too early."

Miakka put the water aside and offered Mi-sa a sip of Atula's medicine. When it seeped through her lips, Mi-sa wrinkled her nose and shuddered.

Atula chuckled. "I apologize that it does not taste very good."

"Atula's medicine may not taste good, but it is strong, and it is making you well."

"The spirits are healing you," Atula corrected.

"Where is Cherok?" Mi-sa asked.

"He is not here," Miakka answered.

"But he has been here," Mi-sa said.

"Yes," Miakka answered, a little confounded. "But you were not awake. How do you know that he was here?"

"Cherok talked to me," the little girl said.

Atula and Miakka looked at each other. It must have been a dream, they both thought.

"Turn so that I can check your wounds," Atula told her.

"Mi-sa," her mother said, "do you remember what happened? Do you know who did this?"

Mi-sa was silent, turning to her side. She stared at the thatched wall, turning her face away so they could not see her expression.

"Do you remember?" Miakka probed.

Atula touched a finger to Miakka's lips. "Perhaps she can have some nourishing broth. Why do you not warm some for her?"

Miakka understood. Atula was suggesting that Mi-sa should not be pushed to remember yet. And he was right. She would go and warm some turtle broth. It would be the first nourishment Mi-sa had taken in days—another good sign.

As the steam from the pot of broth swirled into the air, Shakia came and sat next to Miakka.

"You are smiling today. What makes you so happy?" she asked.

"Mi-sa is awake and alert. She is going to be well. Of course she is still very tired, but Atula says that the spirits heal her while she sleeps."

Shakia hugged her friend. "That is wonderful."

"Yes, it is," Miakka agreed. "It was Atula who made her well. He has been with her much of the time."

"Mm," Shakia acknowledged without enthusiasm.

Miakka's eyes reflected the extent of her happiness. But it was not Mi-sa's health alone that made her glow with elation.

Shakia recognized the same coals she always saw

burning in Miakka's dark eyes when she spoke of Atula.

"Now you will have time to think of Tican," Shakia said, wanting to see Miakka's response.

"I do not have time to think of Tican. I have too much to think about now."

"But you said that when Mi-sa was well—"

"But Mi-sa is not well."

"She is getting well. Her wounds will be healed soon."

"Well, then, I will think about him at that time, but not now."

"I do not think so. You will never let go of Atula. Miakka, there is no future with him. I have told you before, but you knew that already."

"Perhaps my future will just be different from yours," Miakka argued.

"You really love him, do you not?"

Miakka was reluctant to be so forthright, but she was bursting with the happiness that he had brought her.

"Yes," she finally answered. "And he makes me believe he feels the same."

"Miakka, you can never be his bride. And now is the worst time of all to—"

Shakia did not have a chance to finish. "Why do you argue with me about this?" Miakka asked. "I want to be with him even if I can never live at his hearth. I do not care."

"You need to care, Miakka. Your relationship with Atula is important because of Mi-sa. The people question Atula's judgment because they suspect you influence him."

"They only talk. Once Mi-sa is well, they will find something else to grumble about."

"The doubts and fear have gone deep into the hearts of the People. The wariness and mistrust grow every day."

"We have spoken of this before, Shakia. I am aware, but all this agitation and gossip will end."

"The People are certain that the spirits did this to Mi-sa."

"That is absurd," Miakka said. "You know that. Do you not say anything?"

"Of course I do, as does Wakulla. They do not listen."

"How can they not listen to Wakulla? He is Cacique."

"And he is Atula's son. There is talk that you and Atula—"

"Stop," Miakka said sharply. "No one will listen to Wakulla because they think that I influence Atula, and he in turn influences Wakulla?"

"I am afraid that is true, Miakka. So you see, you cannot give yourself to this man. When Tican comes again, hear him. He would take you away to be his wife if you would go with him. Mi-sa has no future here, and neither do you."

"But this is the clan of my mother. I belong here. Mi-sa is the child of the shaman. These are her people."

"Too much has happened. That is not your fault and not Mi-sa's fault, but many things have led the People to think terrible things. They still discuss the events that occurred on the night she was born, and this horrible deed especially frightens everyone."

"Mi-sa is getting well. Soon she will tell us who did this to her, and that will put an end to the gossip. The person who did this will be exposed. Amakollee will be held accountable."

"Who will believe the child? Amakollee has many friends."

"I will believe what Mi-sa tells me. Atula will believe."

"That will not be enough, as I have explained. The

best thing for you to do is keep your distance from Atula so that people's suspicions will die down. Perhaps he can eventually turn their ears, and so can Wakulla, but that will never happen if you become Atula's woman. And I seriously wonder if even then it will happen. So much damage has been done."

Miakka was silent. Mi-sa was the beautiful fruit of her father, the shaman of the People. Both she and her daughter should hold an honored place within the clan. The thing that ate at her, that ripped at her gut, was that she was not certain this would have evolved if Mi-sa had been born a male child on the night of the star—the night of the A-po-la-chee. If she had delivered a boy child, the clan would stand in awe of the infant born under the star that crossed the sky. They would believe that the star sent away the A-po-la-chee when it lit the sky. But because Mi-sa was a girl, the star sign, the glorious light that had shown Mi-sa's newborn face to her mother, was believed to be a burning marker of an evil event. Mi-sa might as well have been an A-po-la-chee.

Miakka poured some broth into a bowl and took it into the platform, leaving Shakia sitting by the fire. When she came down the ladder she had felt so full of happiness but in the time it had taken to prepare the broth, all of that had changed. What had she done in her life to deserve this? What had she done to anger the spirits?

Atula was dressing Mi-sa's wounds. They were less angry-looking, less red, less ragged. He had heard Miakka enter.

"She is healing quickly now. She is proof of the spirits' miracles."

He gently rolled Mi-sa over on her back. He lifted her head as Miakka held out the broth to her.

"Drink this, Little Light," Miakka urged. "It tastes much better than the medicine."

Mi-sa sipped at the broth but soon tired. Atula made her take a few sips of another tea that would help her rest easily. "It will not be long now, Mi-sa. Soon you will be playing and will forget all about this."

Miakka wanted to ask her again if she knew who had attacked her. The sooner she had an answer, the sooner she could still the maddening talk. But Atula had discouraged her from pressing too soon. She did not want to risk a setback in Mi-sa's recovery.

Before leaving, Atula held Miakka by the shoulders. "My woman," he said softly. When she heard his words, she felt weak. She could not tell him what the People were saying now.

———

ATULA WENT TO GET CHEROK. He had neglected Cherok while tending to Mi-sa. The attack on Mi-sa had driven a spike into Cherok's heart. He needed some time with his father, away from the cruel talk, away from the village.

Cherok was grateful that today Atula came to take him and follow the canoe trails alone with him.

Standing in the dugout, Atula poled away from the bulge in the earth that was home to the village. As the distance grew, the smell of the soil, the oiled bodies, and the fires dissipated. Cherok was silent, taking in all the sights and sounds.

The thin sheet of water glittered beneath the rays of the sun as it slowly flowed over the flat land. Atula pushed his pole in, feeling it plunge through the mud that swallowed it, setting the bottom into a roiling, churning brown storm. He followed the familiar trails, winding through the prairie until the water deepened into a channel and then snaked through drier land. Here the banks dripped with moving green tendrils, fronds, fans, and pads. Atula guided the dugout through water congested with lilies, then jumped onto the shore and wrapped his arm around the vine-covered trunk of a cabbage palm. Cherok took his hand and hopped out onto the bank before Atula pulled the dugout ashore, scraping its nearly flat bottom onto the land.

"Know where you are. Smell the earth, feel it, taste it if you need. Wait until the wind carries the fragrances of the plants to you. Use all your senses. Always know what to expect. Know where you go, where you tread."

Cherok lifted a handful of the soil as Atula did, sniffing it, recognizing the clues it gave him. The soil was dark and heavy with the mustiness of decaying leaves, like the soil of his village. Without looking, he knew what he would see. There would be no pines and little palmetto scrub. He would see the floor of the land erupting with uncurling ferns. Moonvines would cascade over stumps and branches, heart-shaped leaves spilling across the land like green waterfalls, fragrant white flowers waiting for nightfall before opening. Sabal palms would reach into the sky, seeking the warm southern sun, pricking the blue with their heads, peeping above the other plants. Their trunks near the top would support more ferns and hanging dead brown fronds ready to drop to the ground. Strangler figs, with their gray bark flaking away in spots to a black inner bark, would wrap themselves around the trunks of the Sabal palms, not strangling them as they did other hosts, but only asking that they die back far enough so they could claim their rightful piece of the sun. They would provide ripe red berries, more food for the birds and animals than any other tree in this tropical forest. Probably there would be cypresses, wide at the base and slender at the crest, rich with light green feathery leaves.

Atula dropped his handful of dirt, and Cherok followed his direction, brushing his hand against his thigh to clean it. The two of them stepped quietly under cover of the canopy. They scouted about, noting the sounds of the animals moving and using their voices, indexing the fauna onto whose territory they had intruded. In the distance the sound of a panther rang out. It began with a low pitch that built to a crescendo, shrill and much like the cry of a woman. It was an unusual sound. The panther was most often quiet, invisible and silent as it slinked through the brush.

An otter, somewhere downstream, let out a satisfied grunt, obviously enjoying his meal. Closer, a deer that had probably been resting in the shade blatted a warning after sniffing the air and catching the scent of man. Suddenly the deer scuttled through the brush, cracking the dry and fallen branches underfoot. Lizards rattled the brown dead leaves as they scurried from place to place, stopped, then jerkily turned their heads to survey the area before skittishly scurrying away again.

All the animal sounds were accompanied by the orchestra of buzzing and droning insects that infested this part of the peninsula.

Atula led Cherok through the woodland, pointing out those things he thought he should know—testing him, probing, teaching. There was still so much more to teach him, to give to him. Had Ochassee felt the same way? Again he wondered if Ochassee had finished with him. Was it always this way? Were bits of knowledge lost with each generation? He knew that the gift of his birthright diminished with each descendant, but not until recently had he wondered about the taught knowledge.

They gathered heavy ironwood and lugged it to the

bank where the stream was narrow and not too deep. They stacked it atop a pile that had been started by someone else. Whenever people visited this place, they gathered the heavy wood. Atula cleared away the debris from a spot near the water and stretched out on the patch of ground. Cherok sat next to him, pitching small sticks into the water. Across the narrow neck of the stream, old branches had been driven into the bed. Cherok knew that this was the skeleton of the dam the men had built for use during special fishing expeditions.

"Tell me how it is done," Cherok asked, loving to hear the details again and again.

"This place was chosen long ago. The branches have to be replaced sometimes, but they serve as the base for the dam. In front of those braces, the men throw other logs. They lash them to the ironwood so that they do not float away. That is why we have gathered some ironwood. It will be used the next time. When the dam is complete and the flow of water is slowed nearly to a stop, we sprinkle poison on top of the water. The spirits reward us for our hard work, and the fish float to the top—small bream, large bass, gar. The surface is covered with them. We rush into the water and gather them to take back to the village. When our work is done, we dismantle the dam."

"But why does the poison not hurt us when we eat the fish?"

"The poison is made from the vines we bring back from the beach. It is very special. It stops the fish from breathing—that is what kills them—but it does not hurt us. You know that we cannot eat all the berries that the birds eat. Some birds can eat things that would poison us. It is the same sort of thing."

"I wish I were old enough to go to the Big Water with

197

you. I would like to fish and gather the poison vines."

"When you are a man, you will go. That time is not too far away. Be patient; there is still much for you to learn."

"Father," Cherok began, having wanted to ask this question many times before, "is Mi-sa going to be well?"

Atula watched the boy's face as he spoke. It had contorted into tortured lines. He moved closer to his son and wrapped a reassuring arm around his shoulders. "Yes, Cherok. The spirits have answered my calls. They have spared her."

Cherok looked up with relief. "Are you certain?"

"I have seen the signs this very day." Atula paused a moment and then asked, "She is special to you, is she not?"

"Very," Cherok said in a low voice before continuing. "Father, she helps me ..." He stumbled, not knowing how to explain or even if he should try. Would his father also think that Mi-sa was evil if he knew the ways that Mi-sa helped him—the things she could do that he could not? And what would Atula think of him?

"What do you mean?" Atula inquired curiously.

"I practice those things you have taught me, and sometimes I cannot do them, but with Mi-sa ... sometimes she helps me do things."

Atula thought he understood. He thought perhaps that Cherok was close to Mi-sa and that it was easy for him to be with her. She did not intimidate Cherok, and so of course he would find it easy to practice his skills with her nearby, whereas with adults and others he might feel awkward.

"The two of you have a close relationship, as if you lived at the same hearth with the same mother."

Cherok knew that his father had not perceived his

meaning. He had hoped that Atula would understand and tell him that it was normal, that he was the one in control, that it was he who led Mi-sa, that someday he would be able to do the things Atula wanted him to do without Mi-sa.

But Atula did not tell him.

Chapter Nineteen

ATULA WAS ANXIOUS TO RETURN to the village. The sun had begun to hide behind the horizon, splattering the sky with pink, gold, and tangerine. He pushed the pole into the water, heaving the dugout forward. He handed the paddle to Cherok.

"Take us home, Cherok."

The boy grinned with pleasure as he took on this new responsibility. He dipped the paddle into the water, making it swirl as he directed the canoe. The smell of the interior of the cypress dugout rose to his nose. The smell was imprinted deep in his memory. From it he conjured up the memory of his first canoe trip with his father. He could remember watching a giant of a man plunge the long pole into the water and with little effort guide the canoe wherever he wished. Many times Cherok had spent all morning with Atula in the small canoe, never hearing him speak, just experiencing his world.

As the stream grew shallow, breaking down into a flooded marsh, Cherok put the paddle inside the boat, stood, and took the pole. Atula nodded his approval. Cherok was filled with pride, standing tall against the skyline, feeling the wind at his back, the pole piercing the emptiness above him as he lifted it. His father was giving him all the skills he would need for the day he would be sent out into the wilderness in search of his totem spirit, and he longed for it. He wanted to be a man like his father.

When they arrived at the village, he watched to see who might notice him. As the bow of the canoe bruised the edge of the hammock, Cherok hopped out. Atula followed, watching his son struggle with the weight of the dugout as he pulled it ashore. He was tempted to help, to make the task easy, but he resisted, letting the boy complete the job. Cherok looked up and grinned at Atula, who put his hand on his son's shoulder.

"You are a fine oarsman," he said loudly so that those nearby could hear.

"You are a fine teacher, Father," Cherok responded.

Amakollee watched the show of pride, growing angry, feeling her stomach tighten and her head begin to pound. Several men had gathered around Atula and Cherok.

Kachumpka sat propped against the trunk of a tree. Did they not see him? Amakollee wondered. Why did they still look to Cherok? The spirits had shown that Mi-sa was filled with evil spirits that wished to deny Kachumpka his heritage. Mi-sa was the one who made the People think that Cherok had the Gift. She was the one with the magic. Evil magic!

Amakollee began to breathe hard, fiercely forcing the air in and out loudly. She stood next to her son, stroking his hair, gently at first and then more firmly until she was pushing down on his head, making him lean forward. She knew what she had to do. She had heard that Mi-sa was going to live. The spirits were too kind. But that was their decision. She would not question it. The spirits were going to use her once again as their instrument. She— Amakollee—would show the People what Mi-sa was and what Cherok was not. And she would have to get Atula's attention.

She waited for the small gathering to disperse so that Atula and Cherok were alone.

"Come, Kachumpka," she said, helping him to his feet. "Come with me to see your father."

Amakollee led the boy to Atula and Cherok. "Cacema is waiting for you," she told Cherok. "She waits to eat until you return."

Cherok looked at his father.

"Go eat your evening meal and tell your mother about your journey this day," Atula said. "Tell her how you brought us home."

Cherok ran off, eager to relate the story to his mother.

Atula tried to ignore Amakollee by walking away behind Cherok, but she had come to speak with him.

Her mouth was dry, her tongue sticking in her mouth. She made an effort not to breathe so hard. She wanted to appear calm and coherent. "This is also your son. Kachumpka, look at your father."

Kachumpka followed his mother's direction, looking blankly at Atula. Atula stooped so that he was the boy's height. "Such a handsome fellow," Atula said, smiling into his face. Kachumpka returned the smile and held his hand out, offering a stick he had been playing with to Atula.

"That is a good stick for drawing in the dirt. You keep it," Atula answered.

"You see how filled with good he is? He knows who he is, and he is patient. He spends all his time with the spirits. He does not run and play, wasting time like the other children. He meditates. He knows."

Atula sighed. "I am certain that you are proud of your son, Amakollee."

"Our son," she corrected. "He is the fruit of your seed, or have you forgotten? He is the product of your pleasure, the pleasure that I brought to you. Or does the shaman not recall? Does he lose his memory so soon?"

Amakollee's voice was tinged with the anger. Her words were bitter.

"I do recall," Atula responded to her charges.

Amakollee remembered when she would not have touched him without an invitation. "Then do you also remember how you dug into my flesh with your passionate hands and how I fulfilled your every desire?" she asked, touching her finger to his chest and sliding it toward his belly.

Atula moved her hand away. "You are bold, woman. And that was a long time ago."

Amakollee would not let the conversation end. She stepped a little closer, cocking her head to one side. "Here," she said, "put your face to my neck and see if the touch of my skin and the scent of my body make that time disappear."

Barely touching him, she feathered her fingers up his sides. "But you are right. It was a long time ago. Too long ago."

"Amakollee," he said carefully. He did not want to hurt her, but she was so persistent. "You have a son from my seed. You hold an honored place in the clan."

"But I want more. Kachumpka deserves more," she continued, her voice starting soft but getting louder and less in control.

Atula stepped to one side and moved around her, but Amakollee placed herself in front of him again.

"How can you walk away when I humble myself in front of you? How can you let me humiliate myself? And your son—you ignore him. Can you not see that he carries the Gift?"

Her voice vacillated between a near scream and a whisper, sounding mad and deranged.

"Let me pass," he told her softly but firmly. Amakollee held her ground. "You gather an audience, Amakollee. Let me pass."

Amakollee looked around. Some of the villagers had stopped what they were doing and stared, straining to listen. They quickly returned to their tasks, moving about when Amakollee looked their way.

She stepped aside, whispering to him as he walked past, "The spirits will have their revenge."

Amakollee walked away—toward Miakka's hearth, pulling Kachumpka by his upper arm. Miakka looked up at the woman's whisper.

"The spirits have decided that Mi-sa should live. I will abide by that decision."

Miakka dropped the bowl she held. Black shards scattered as the bowl smashed.

———

ATULA WAS GLAD that Amakollee had finally ended the confrontation with him. He was sure she was mad. Perhaps Miakka was right. Perhaps Amakollee had done it.

The appetite that he had worked up while he was out with Cherok quickly dwindled. The encounter with Amakollee left his stomach unsettled. On the way to his platform he decided to ask the spirits to help her and Kachumpka. He was not certain what was different about the boy, but he certainly did not have the Gift. He had deficits, holes in his mind. Atula had heard about children like that, and the problem seemed to occur when the women who bore them were older. Amakollee was fortunate that her son had lived. Children like that often died at birth or shortly thereafter.

Inside his shelter he gathered some stored herbs and plant parts to make a new medicinal tea for Mi-sa. First he would talk to the spirits.

Atula picked up a ball of resin wrapped in leaves that had been greased with fat. He had collected the copal resin from the gumbo-limbo tree. It was a fine incense, which he used sometimes when he communicated with the spirits.

When he was finished gathering, he went to his hearth and laid the entire collection out on a piece of hide. He left the plants there while he went to the central hearth to fetch a coal.

Atula returned to his hearth and dropped small portions of dried moss and grass onto the coal. He blew on it until it caught, then added more moss and, at last, the wood and the incense. With his knife Atula cut the plant stems into smaller pieces and placed them in his wooden medicine bowl. He tore the leaves and sprinkled them into the bowl, and then he ground them with his small pestle.

Satisfied, he poured water over the mixture, swirled it with his finger, and began his prayers, his holy words. The medicine was no good without the spirits' help. The spirits, not the plants, gave the potion its power.

When he was done, he also asked the spirits to keep him strong, to help him see clearly the path they had chosen for him. He asked for a sign if he had strayed, something that would tell him he was wrong. Finished, he poured the contents of the bowl into a clay pot, which he hung over the fire. He let it heat so the water would effectively leach the medicine from the ingredients.

He had completed his chores and was about to leave.

The sky had grown dark, and the blanket of night spread over the village. Wakulla approached and sat near the small fire. Atula stirred the coals with a stick, bringing it ablaze again.

"You prepare to see Mi-sa?" Wakulla asked, but he already knew the answer. It was just a way to begin.

"I have made her a new medicine. As she heals, the ingredients in her medicine will change. This one will help her sleep more soundly and will encourage rapid healing," he said, agitating the elixir by shaking the cooled-down bowl. "But it is not as potent as the medicine she has been taking."

"You will also see Miakka?"

Atula looked at Wakulla. What a strange question. "Of course."

Wakulla shifted, obviously uncomfortable. "You have spent so much time with Mi-sa that you have not heard the talk of the village."

"I have heard," Atula said. "Why do you bring this to my attention?"

Wakulla stood up to leave. "Because you are my father and the shaman. Because I know Miakka has a place in your heart."

Atula watched Wakulla disappear into the night. He knew there was more on Wakulla's mind, but he must not have thought this the right time to discuss it. He would come again.

Atula crossed the mound as the villagers began to settle in for the evening. Reaching Miakka's platform, he called to her to come down. Her fire still burned, and Atula sat next to it, watching her come down the ladder.

"She has been awake most of the day. She finds it difficult to sleep." She sat next to him.

"That is a good sign. I have prepared something that

will help her sleep. It will be stronger than the discomfort."

"She has eaten some more food, even a little bread."

Miakka wanted to reach out and touch him, and she would have if Shakia had not spoken to her earlier. She wanted to lean against him, rest against him, but now she knew that she could not.

Atula watched her as she looked into the fire. "You look so beautiful in the firelight," he told her, taking her hand.

Miakka pulled it away. "Give me the medicine. I will take it to Mi-sa."

"What is wrong?" he asked, handing her the bowl, not understanding the change in her. "What happened while I was gone? The last I was with you—"

Miakka did not permit Atula to finish. "There is no future in this. It cannot be," she said, stepping onto the ladder.

"Miakka, wait. Please explain."

"Go, Atula. We started something that is no good. It is too complicated, too selfish," she said as she disappeared inside.

He started to go after her, to question her, but decided not to. The argument would not be good for Mi-sa. Tomorrow he would see Miakka again. For the first time in a long time he had allowed himself to speak from the heart, let himself feel from the heart. Miakka had somehow opened all the closed-off spaces inside him. He had allowed her. Perhaps it had not been wise.

Miakka came back to the opening of her platform as she heard him leave. Her only happiness was to be Mi-sa. She watched Atula walk away. She had come so close to living her dream, but as always happiness was ripped away from her. If she was selfish, Mi-sa's life would be forever ruined. Maybe one day things would change.

Miakka sat next to Mi-sa. "Sip the tea the shaman has made for you," she said, holding the bowl to Mi-sa's lips. "Drink it."

Mi-sa held her hand over her mother's, helping to guide the bowl. This tea was not so bitter. When Mi-sa was finished, Miakka lay down near her. Mi-sa seemed to drift off quickly; the medicine was effective. But Miakka could not sleep. Her mind spun in all directions, but all her thoughts led back to Atula. He was the only man she had ever wanted. She did not care that she could not have him as a husband. The conventions did not matter. He had chosen her, and she had sent him away with no explanation, turning him away with coldness in her voice.

Miakka turned to her side and closed her eyes. What would their time together have been like? she wondered, playing with images created in her mind. She could see Atula pressing his lips to hers and gently wrapping his arm around her waist. Then suddenly she saw Amakollee standing and watching, holding Kachumpka against her leg. Amakollee was stealing her life. She was sure that Amakollee had attacked Mi-sa, no matter what anyone else thought. And now she continued to steal from her with her wicked tongue. And that peculiar message from Amakollee had implied that Amakollee thought she was permitting Mi-sa to live. She had said that she would— what was the word?—*abide,* that was it. At least there was some comfort in knowing that Amakollee would not come for Mi-sa again.

Miakka sat up and reached out to touch Mi-sa. "Are you sleeping?" she whispered. There was no answer. Miakka slipped down the ladder and crossed the mound, staying in the shadows. Quietly she climbed Atula's ladder. Never before had she entered his platform without solicitation.

"Atula," she said as she stood inside.

Atula had nearly dropped off to sleep when he heard her call his name. "Miakka?"

"I sent you away, and I was wrong. I need to explain."

Atula stood, looking at her silhouette in the doorway. "Come to me," he said softly.

Miakka walked closer until their bodies almost touched. "Let me explain."

Atula pressed his index finger to her lips. "No explanations." He took her hand and placed it on his chest. "Hear only the beating of my heart."

Miakka started to speak again, but he stopped her with his mouth, exploring with his tongue, begging for entry. Miakka opened her lips, welcoming him. Suddenly the explanation did not matter. His arms went around her, and his hands loosened the band that held her skirt. It fell to the floor, and Atula cupped her buttocks in his hands.

Suddenly he stepped back and brushed her hair over her shoulder, uncovering her breasts. "This way," he said, leading her into a shaft of moonlight that streaked the inside of the platform.

"Stay there," he said, backing away from her. "Stand there so that I can look at you."

Miakka stood still, bathed in moonglow. A moment later he held his hands out to her, beckoning her back into the darkness. Gently he placed his hands on her shoulders and then slid them down, pausing at the outer swell of her breasts and then venturing on, feeling the indentation of her waist, following the curve of her hips.

Miakka's hands sought his body, caressing the muscles that rippled beneath his skin. He was made of the night, of the shaman's magic, and wrapped in the body of a man. She pressed her forehead against his chest as he removed the small leather flap that was draped in front of and behind him.

Slowly he urged her down onto the mat on the floor, then lay on top of her, touching his flesh to hers. He touched her lightly, almost afraid that she would disappear beneath him. She pulled him closer, pressing down on his shoulders and back, wanting to feel the pressure of his body on hers. As he gave in to her, a soft moan escaped her lips. Atula nibbled at her ear, moving down the side of her neck and out to her shoulder. He took both her hands and locked his fingers in hers, stretching her arms out to the side, feeling his chest move against her breasts.

Atula rolled, turning onto his back, lifting her so that one breast fell into his open mouth and her hair spilled across his face. Slowly he lowered her weight onto him, groaning as she moved against him.

His arms surrounded her, crushing her as his teeth bit into her lips and neck. Again he moved her mouth to his, running his hands up through her hair. Miakka's hand wandered along his side, slipping between them, reaching for that part of him that throbbed against her. At her touch his legs shook, and his stomach jerked. A deep sigh gushed from him.

He turned her to her side, desperately reaching for her, touching those hidden places that swept her away like a feather in the wind. Again he moved her to her back and pinned her arms out to the sides, moving his mouth across her, down her, until he had to release her hands.

Miakka arched her neck, turning her head from side to side as he tasted her sweet nectar. She opened to him, unfolding, offering all of herself to this man who knew her body better than she did. She grabbed a handful of his hair, bending her knees, begging him with her body to give himself to her.

Atula slid forward, guiding himself into her, feeling her warmth embrace him and shroud him with her passion. He rocked her slowly, watching for her rhythm to be in harmony with his. In a moment she matched him, driving him deeper, filling her, becoming one with him. She clutched at his back, heaving for air, answering his need with her own, abandoning everything except the burning desperation.

He pressed his lips to hers, hungry for her, almost brutal. He held back, wanting to satisfy the incredible consuming desire, the ravenous plea of his body. But he waited for her, rising to the peak as he felt her raise her head and shoulders and then fall back, shuddering beneath him. Never again would he leave her without the Gift.

As she shook beneath him, he lost control of the rhythm, his passion driving him to his own convulsive pleasure. A few moments later he lay heavily upon her, covered in a sheath of perspiration, unable to move.

Miakka sighed, a satisfied fullness deep in her throat. She was Atula's woman.

Chapter Twenty

AMAKOLLEE GRUMBLED while dragging, pulling, and lifting Kachumpka up the ladder. Her encounter with Atula had left her frustrated, fixed on going over and over it in her mind. He had rebuffed his heir, refused to acknowledge him. He also pretended not to remember the many times he had satisfied his need with her body, how she had unselfishly offered herself to him, how the spirits had chosen her to nurture his seed and give birth to his rightful heir.

At the top of the ladder she tugged on the boy, who stumbled inside. This night would be no different from the rest. Earlier she had taken Kachumpka to the cenote and carried him around her waist into the water, cajoling and humoring him to keep his crying to a minimum. It was unusual for Kachumpka to cry, except when she bathed him, but every evening as Amakollee placed him in the water, he whimpered, cried, and sometimes wailed, bellowing deep, hoarse protests. Once she had him in the water for a few moments, he actually seemed to enjoy it. But every time it was the same: He began crying when they stepped in; his complaint grew louder as the water crept up their legs; panic seized him as she set him on the shallow ledge; then she finally heard his gurgling laughter.

The days were often long for her, Kachumpka always

requiring her supervision. By evening she was tired. Her back ached, and her legs cramped. She never questioned her responsibility, never resented her son. He deserved her constant attention. After all, he had saved her from disgrace. He was a child born to the spirits; it was her duty to take care of his earthly needs. It was her duty, as guided by the spirits, to intervene if anyone obstructed or interfered with his destiny.

Amakollee had not especially enjoyed hurting Mi-sa, but doing so had been a virtuous deed. She had no right to refuse. She had been surprised that Mi-sa did not die, but the spirits had their reasons. Amakollee had fulfilled her obligation. The people of her clan now knew for certain what Mi-sa was, a child born under the totem of an evil spirit, a child who would mislead the People, use the bad magic, trick the People. One day she would tell them that she had attacked Mi-sa. Then the People would know how closely she had worked with the spirits, and they would thank her.

Tonight she continued her ritual. She prepared Kachumpka's bed, shaking his grass mat to make certain that it was clean and safe. She brushed his feet clean, and then pulled out from its hiding spot the large ceramic bowl that he sometimes used in the night. It was a simple idea that kept him from soiling himself. Amakollee awakened every night and led him to the bowl. When he finished she would put him back on his mat and sneak down the ladder to dispose of the contents in the brush, sometimes scratching a shallow latrine to take the waste and then covering it up. When she returned, she could sleep the rest of the night uninterrupted.

Amakollee sat next to her son as he lay down, put his head in her lap, and held his face close to her. She rocked, singing her usual song, waiting for him to sleep, waiting for her time alone.

At last Kachumpka's mouth went slack, and he slept. Amakollee eased herself away, carefully placing his head on the mat. One only had to look at him when he slept, she thought, adoring the innocence of his face, to know that he was special. Beside him she said her prayers to the spirits. She thanked them, saying the same words every night. When she stumbled over a word or used a mistaken sequence, she started over from the beginning, thinking the liturgy defiled and powerless.

When she had finished, she lay on her mat, heavy with exhaustion. She closed her eyes, hoping the sleep that sometimes eluded her would come easily. She lay still, clearing her mind in case the spirits had a message to deliver to her. They had come to her before, many times, in just this way. Nothing tonight. No voice. No message. Had she done something wrong? Had she not been thankful enough? The spirits did not talk to her every night, but what if they would have come to her tonight but did not because of something she did or did not do? The thought tormented her. After tossing on her mat for a time, she finally sat up and started the prayers over again. Perhaps she had said them wrong or forgotten something. She had to say them over—from the beginning.

Amakollee moved to the worn spot on the platform floor where she said the prayers every night. She sat with her legs crossed, aligning her tired back into a straight and reverent line. The position of her body was just as important as the words. If she was careless with her posture, then the words meant nothing. Amakollee folded her hands in her lap, closed her eyes, and began again.

Outside the village the daylight breeze diminished to the stillness of night. The flitting butterflies skimming across the open spaces sought asylum in the trees. The swishing of the saw grass, the rustling of windblown leaves, and the singing of the birds fell away. The people of the village slept.

Her supplications completed, Amakollee moved to the open edge of her platform. She gazed out, shoulders slumped, back curved, still able to see much of the village in the luminous moonlight. Small bright baubles of hot coals glowed, dotting the mound like a flippantly tossed basketful of fireflies. In a moment she would try again to sleep.

Something caught her attention. A slim figure, lithe but well curved, definitely a young woman, slipped across the mound in the darkness. Amakollee knew immediately who it was. Inquisitively she leaned farther out for a better look.

It was Miakka. Where could she be going? Ah, she thought as Miakka made her direction clear. Atula. Yes, she was going to see Atula, to be with him because there was something between them. She was right. She had known it all along. How stupid of those who doubted. The shaman was being used by the mother of the evil one. Miakka was under Mi-sa's influence, and she pulled Atula under with her. Why were hers the only eyes that could see?

Amakollee sat down, smirking, pleased with her adroitness. The relationship between Miakka and Atula would become evident to everyone else in a short time, she hoped. But she would be careful not to alienate anyone by pointing out that she had known all along, whereas they had been slow. No, she would be quick to compliment them on how perceptive they had become. If they needed help piecing together the deceptions, she would craftily push in slivers of insinuations, letting the others come to the conclusions on their own.

The spirits never failed Amakollee. She had sensed they would speak to her tonight. It was a good thing that she had said the prayers over. She was worthy, and the spirits knew and appreciated that.

Now she would be able to sleep, to rest, until she awakened to help Kachumpka relieve himself. It would be a peaceful night after all.

———

MIAKKA LAY CURLED in Atula's arms. She turned to face him, kissing his chest and snuggling closer. She lifted her head, straining to see his face.

"I do not think that we should tell the others how we feel about each other."

Atula looked puzzled. "Of course we should. What has happened to us is a wonderful thing. We should share our happiness."

Miakka lowered her head so that he could not look into her eyes and she did not have to look into his. Being with him felt so right, and yet she had to tell him that for now it was wrong.

"There is talk," she started.

"There has been talk for a long time. That is nothing new. It does not change anything."

"The talk has gotten closer, more specific, more harmful. I understand there is the opinion that I influence you, that we are lovers. Wakulla has tried to make them dismiss the notion that Mi-sa is associated with some horrible evil spirit, but because he is your son no one listens. They do not take their own cacique seriously. Some do not heed his word on the subject at all."

"But there was nothing between us until—"

"It does not matter," she said, interrupting him.

"Someone—probably Amakollee—created the story, and now it is true. If we continue this, it will only add validity to everything she has been saying."

"Miakka, I have watched you so long. I have been alone so long. I do not want to give you up now."

Miakka sat up, looking across the platform, staring into the distance. "Atula, I must think of Mi-sa and her future. This is her home. I cannot let her be driven from it through my own self-indulgence. Look what has already happened. I am her mother," she said, turning to look at him. "She is my child, and I would deny myself everything for her."

Atula let her words seep through him. He lay still and silent. He was not going to give her up willingly without exploring all the alternatives.

"I do not want to be without you, Miakka. You are in my heart."

The words were a sweet song that lifted her, blotting away a lifetime of tragedy, and at the same time puncturing a deep hole of pain. These were the words she had dreamed of, the words she had longed to hear him speak, never imagining that he would do so. Why was she allowed so close to happiness only to have it snatched from her?

"Oh, Atula, I do not think you know how much you are in my heart."

"Then stay with me. We do not need to tell anyone. All I want is to be able to touch you, hear you, feel you, tell you of my love for you. We can find time to be alone. We can be careful. I cannot bear to see you about your daily tasks and know that I can never be near you."

"I am afraid," Miakka said, laying her head on his chest.

"There is nothing to be afraid of. I will protect you."

"I am not afraid for me. I fear for Mi-sa. She is so little, and the viciousness is so big. She is just a child. I want her to feel like and live like any other child."

"In time, Miakka. The spirits will never desert her. That was told on the night she was born beneath the star."

Atula realigned her head, raising her face so that he could again place his mouth on hers, again feel the delicate softness of her lips and the tiny quakes of her body when he touched her. His passion for her was complicated, transcending the physical. He was not going to part with this woman.

When Miakka left Atula's platform, she hid in the shadows, being careful not to step on dry twigs that might snap and give her away. She would see him again and again, in the shadows and secretiveness of the night. They would wait out the daylight, going about their routine tasks, but after the sun set, when the rest of the world slept, they would be with each other.

Before stretching out next to Mi-sa, she touched her daughter's forehead. Mi-sa shifted, letting out a sleepy sigh.

Miakka stared out into the darkness, afraid to close her eyes, afraid that if she slept, she might awaken to find this night had been only a dream. Good things were finally starting to happen to her. Mi-sa was getting well quickly, and the man she had always loved also loved her. Her happiness was so deep and so intense that it did not even matter that she could not share it with anyone else. That day would come. For now it would be their secret.

While she stared, hearing the night sounds set to the tempo of her heartbeat, certain that she could not sleep, her eyelids grew heavy.

———

MI-SA CONTINUED TO IMPROVE, each day getting stronger and stronger. Her mother sat next to her, stroking Mi-sa's hair as the child leaned against her. It was pleasant for Mi-sa, too, at long last to feel the sun on her back again, adding its own power to the healing. Above her, gray splotches—birds on the wing, too many to count—soared across the sky silently, gliding forms that gracefully pumped their outstretched wings, pushed out their proud chests and let their long legs drag behind them. But because she was watching, without effort her attention focused, and she sped through the wind, sharing the spirit of one of the birds as it worked the air, pushing against it, feeling it rush through its feathers and lift it.

They flew to the south where the Big Water conquered the land, carving saltwater channels and where the saw grass gave way to thick clusters of mangroves. The sea breeze was laden with sticky white salt that adhered to everything. The last of the fresh water broke into small falls and rapids, quickly turned brackish, and then disappeared. Coming from farther north, fresh water secretively seeped through underground solution channels, straits, necks, narrows, and depths, wearing smooth the rough limestone edges of the course, only to surface again as a freshwater spring, bubbling up in the middle of the great sunlit expanse of salt water.

"Mi-sa?" Miakka said nervously, noticing the child's distraction.

At first there was no answer, but Miakka pushed her daughter forward, touched her cheek and called to her again. Mi-sa's eyelids fluttered, and her eyes focused on her mother.

"Are you all right?" Miakka asked with forced calmness, not wanting to worry her unnecessarily.

Mi-sa looked at her mother and smiled. "I was with

the birds, flying to the Big Water. It is beautiful there."

"You are fanciful, Little Light. Your imagination is as healthy as ever."

"No, Mother. I really did see the Big Water."

Mi-sa began to describe what she had seen, and Miakka looked puzzled.

"How do you know all this? You have never been to the Big Water. Have you listened intently each time the men have returned and told about their journey?"

Mi-sa began to feel frightened. Bizarre things often happened to her. She had seen the infinite blue water, felt the ocean breeze and tasted the salt. She would not say any more about it. She troubled her mother. The only one who understood was Cherok.

Miakka watched as a group of men began to congregate around the central hearth. The Council was about to meet to discuss the needs and concerns of the clan. Talasee checked the hearth. The coals were still live, as always. The fire in the central hearth was never allowed to go out. It burned beneath a high rectangular thatch roof supported by tree-trunk posts. The smoke could easily find its way through the thatch or out the open sides. The fire was built on a raised earthen hearth of packed dirt that protected it from high water. Even after downpours Talasee could break open some of the larger hardwood logs and find the glowing heat of hidden fire clinging to life. With proper nurturing the fire would stay alive.

It was too warm to bring the fire ablaze, though Talasee loved to watch the flames leap into the air. That, he supposed, was the only reason he liked it when the weather turned cold. That did not happen often, and for the health of everyone, warm weather was best

The Council was meeting early in the morning to

avoid the midday and late afternoon heat. Still, the warmth from the hearth would bleed them of fluids. No man would speak too long, and decisions would be made seriously. Besides, it showed respect for the People for a man to inflict himself with discomfort while discussing the well-being of all. It demonstrated the soberness of the occasion.

The women performed their chores and tasks quietly, so as not to distract the men. Though they carried on, they listened, catching words and phrases that gave them clues to the issues being discussed. Amakollee found many trivial things to keep her lingering near the hearth, close to the men so she could hear them.

She had talked to many of the women, pleased when they lifted their eyebrows at the possibility of Atula and Miakka being lovers. That small bit of innuendo undermined the most respected man of the village, Wakulla. Amakollee liked Wakulla, but like Miakka, he had to be dealt with. She did not think that it would affect the respect anyone had for Wakulla other than on that one subject—Mi-sa. And if perchance it did, it was justifiable.

Amakollee flexed her neck, shifting her head to hear better. It was Atula's voice. Strange, she thought, how angry she could be with him sometimes and at other times feel so grateful. Sometimes she hated him because he had rejected her, rejected his son. She hated him because in those intimate moments they had shared, he had been tender and passionate. She had been certain—by the way he touched her, the way he moaned when she let him enter her, the way he held her when he had satisfied himself—that he loved her. But then he had rejected her, turned her away, as though she meant nothing to him.

Suddenly her head began to pound, and she found herself breathing hard, loud enough to make Sima look at her as she passed by. Thoughts of Atula's rejection were confusing. Those thoughts always made her head ache, always made her agitated. She pressed her hands to her forehead, trying to still the thoughts.

Kachumpka pulled at her leg, mumbling, babbling. He had been sitting near a cluster of dead brown leaves, picking up handfuls and tossing them into the air. Amakollee shook her head, clearing it, and looked at her son, who had crawled over to her and now sat at her feet. In the palm of his hand he held a scorpion set to strike, its tail curled.

In one swift sweeping motion, Amakollee lowered her hand from her head, swung it quickly around and beneath Kachumpka's hand, slapping upward, sending the scorpion flying into the air. She captured Kachumpka in her arms and lifted his deadweight, placing his arms around her neck, kissing his face, and crying.

Amakollee looked toward the men, clenching her teeth. "Did you not see, Atula? Your son carried a scorpion and was not stung. He is a part of the spirits. What does it take for you to see? For all of you to see?" she angrily cried, her mouth and nose full of saliva and mucus, spraying spittle as she screamed.

The men stopped at the outburst. Amakollee turned, still carrying Kachumpka, her steps awkward as she struggled to support his weight.

Miakka watched, as did everyone. In a way she felt sorry for the woman. She put her arm around Mi-sa.

"I am afraid of her," Mi-sa said softly so that no one but her mother could hear.

Miakka pulled her a little closer. Now that Mi-sa was well, the time seemed right to ask about her attack.

"Mi-sa," she began, "let us sit down." Miakka brushed the earth next to her before she sat. Mi-sa quickly sat next to her mother, cuddling up, feeling more secure as she snuggled against her.

"You seem completely well now. You do not need any medicine. Do you also think that you are well?"

Mi-sa looked up. "I think so, but my back is sore, and it hurts a little sometimes when I move."

"It will probably be sore for a while yet. You had a terrible wound."

Mi-sa did not say anything, but she did look down.

"Do you remember when this happened to you?" her mother asked quietly.

Mi-sa shifted. "I remember you giving me medicine. I remember Cherok."

"Good," Miakka said encouragingly. "Now think back a little farther. You were sleeping. Do you remember?"

Miakka tried to lift her daughter's head so that she could look into her eyes, but Mi-sa resisted.

"Someone came into our platform and hurt you. We were sleeping. Do you remember when it happened?"

"Can we go for a walk?" Mi-sa asked.

"Not yet, Mi-sa. I want you to remember. Who did this to you? Who hurt you? Try, Mi-sa. Try very hard to remember. I know you do not want to, but you must. Please. Think back. You can do it."

Mi-sa frowned. "I do not know who it was," she answered too quickly.

"Keep trying. I have to know. You must have seen someone."

Mi-sa swallowed hard and kneaded her mother's skirt nervously.

"You remember, do you not?" Miakka said.

Mi-sa looked up, her eyes filled with tears, ready to speak.

Chapter Twenty-one

MI-SA'S THROAT TIGHTENED, as if she were being strangled. Her face contorted. She could see herself lying on her mat. She could feel the sharp, cool, smooth bone awl as it plunged into her back, the hot pain as it drove into her again, the warm flood of blood as it poured from her.

The scene tumbled before her. She was there again, and she could see it and feel it. She looked back, twisting her head to see who was hurting her.

Suddenly there was blackness and emptiness, and the scene ended. She blinked her eyes, and tears trickled down her cheeks.

"I do not know who it was. No one was there," she said, throwing her arms around her mother and crying.

Miakka held her, comforting her. "All right. All right. Shh."

If only Mi-sa would try a little harder, she thought. If only she could remember.

"Is she all right?" Cherok's voice sounded behind them.

Miakka nodded that she was, still holding Mi-sa against her, kissing the top of her head. Cherok sat, waiting for Mi-sa, wanting to visit and talk.

Cacema had continued to discourage his association

with Mi-sa. Cherok understood what his mother told him, and he wished he could follow her advice and wishes. But Mi-sa was special to him, even though she was a girl and was significantly younger than he. He was, not complete without her. She was an extension of his core, as if a part of his spirit had been born in him but another part, an essential and integral part, was born in her. He had often tried to understand but had finally just accepted the mystery, no longer trying to figure it out.

He had expressed those thoughts to Cacema on several occasions, but she had stilled him each time. He had also made several attempts to discuss it with Atula but had stumbled over his words, not making himself clear. Each time he became anxious, feeling that perhaps his father would be disappointed in him.

Cherok ached to become the man his father anticipated and desired. He practiced the things Atula taught him. He spent mornings and afternoons alone, walking the permissible area around the mound, identifying medicinal plants, practicing the words, the chants and songs, striving to speak in a manly voice. He listened to himself, hearing each intonation, each inflection, until he was either exhausted or satisfied.

Sometimes he sat at the edge of the passage to the trails walked by men, watching, trying to learn all the secrets that special place could teach him. He fasted at every appropriate opportunity, sat closer to the fire than the other boys, sweating, feeling perspiration drip and sting his eyes.

Yet despite his determination he remained just out of touch, never quite reaching his goal. Only when he was with Mi-sa could he cover that extra distance. And when he spoke to her of such things, little as she was, she understood. Sometimes she even seemed to know his feelings before he had a chance to tell her about them. Always she instinctively knew how to help. The things he worked so hard for were incomplete without her.

Now he watched her crying against Miakka, and it made him feel melancholy.

"Mi-sa, would you like to go for a walk?" he asked, hoping to calm and distract her. "We have not walked together in a long time."

Mi-sa looked up, fixing her blurry eyes on his.

Stop your crying, Little Light. Come with me.

Mi-sa sat up, not depending on her mother for support. She wiped the tears off her cheeks and dried her eyes. She smiled, making her mother smile, too, but Miakka's face was traced with a curious look of wonder. Cherok knew just the things to say to Mi-sa, she thought.

"Yes, Cherok," Mi-sa responded, getting to her feet.

Miakka watched them walk away, Cherok holding her small hand in his.

"I am glad that you came, Cherok. I am always glad when you come—even when I was sick," the little girl spoke.

"You remember?"

"I remember being afraid, but you came and made me feel better. You told me that you would be with me."

"And I was with you. Do you know how you always come for me—inside?"

Mi-sa knew what he meant. He would ask her to take him with her, out of his body, and she would come, appearing in the white haze, leading him out, taking him with her.

"That time, Mi-sa, the time when you were so sick, I left my body without your help. I went and found you. I have never been able to do that alone. Only with you. But I did it," Cherok said, his voice filled with excitement.

"Of course he could do that. My mother does not understand how I remember that you came to see me. There are a lot of things she does not understand. Only you can understand these things," she said, spontaneously jumping in front of him and hugging him.

"And you," he said, lifting her up in the air, making her squeal with delight.

When she stopped giggling, Cherok turned serious. "Things are so easy for you to do. You have special gifts. You do things the People expect of me."

Mi-sa looked inquisitively at him. "You do those things too."

"But I cannot do them without you."

"Yes, you can. You came to me when I was sick. You came and found me—inside—by yourself."

"But it was such a struggle, and I do not believe I could do it again."

"Yes, you could," she argued. "Try," she said, running to a shady spot and sitting down. "Try now."

"I cannot, Mi-sa. The spirits helped me when you were ill."

"And they will help you now. Please."

Cherok lowered himself, folding his legs, closing his eyes, taking deep breaths. He tried to clear his mind, but it was a jumbled mess.

"Take me to the clouds," she whispered to him.

So many things distracted him. A bird squawked in the distance, and a quick breeze ruffled the blades of grass. He was afraid to try because if he failed ...

Mi-sa opened one eye, peeking at him. She saw the lines cut into his apprehensive face as he squeezed his eyes even tighter, trying hard to concentrate. She was certain that he could not do it that way.

Gently, quietly, easily, she put her hands on top of his.

She could feel his fingers relax as the tension flowed out of him. She peeked again. Slowly his face was easing as he calmed, gaining confidence through her simple touch.

Cherok felt his spirit collecting, gathering inside near the crown of his head. He could hear the song in his head, softly at first, barely audible, too far away. He sucked the air in through his nose and let it out through his mouth. With each breath he went deeper inside until finally he was ready.

Though they sat in the narrow shade of a Sabal palm, perspiration poured from Cherok's body. Leaving his body was hard work. For an instant that thought flashed through his mind. He quickly cast it out before it intruded too deep and broke his concentration.

From out of nowhere came another distracting thought, bursting through the wall that surrounded him, shattering his concentration. This was a thought about doubting himself.

Cherok tried to focus, but his rampart continued to crumble. Then suddenly out of the confusion he heard Mi-sa's voice.

"Come, Cherok. Come back. Come for me. I am waiting."

Her voice was tranquil and magical. In an instant he was again at the portal, his mind free, ready.

Suddenly he was there, above them, floating, looking down, enveloped in the white haze.

"Mi-sa," he called with his spirit voice. She appeared smiling in front of him. "You did it, Cherok!"

Yes, he had done it, but still it was Mi-sa who moved him, first with her touch and then with her voice.

"Higher," she said. "Above the birds, where the air is cool. Take me there."

Cherok looked below at the humps of teardrop-shaped hammocks strewn haphazardly across the brown-patched earth. He could see the meandering shallow that flowed lazily across the land and the thin strands of white clouds that blanketed it.

He loved it here, outside, where he was able to fly, to see, but he knew he did not belong here. As much as he wanted to be a part of this power, this incredible knowledge, he knew it was not his domain. This was Atula's dominion. This was Mi-sa's realm. He would always be an outsider.

Cherok's shoulders slumped with deep sadness.

"Smile, Cherok," Mi-sa said to him, troubled by his dejected look. "Teach me something new, as you always do."

"I have nothing to teach you. Let us go."

Mi-sa took his hand, and in a blaze of brilliant blue light, they were again beneath the Sabal palm.

"You should be happy, Cherok."

Cherok did not answer. Instead he helped Mi-sa to her feet and led her back to the village.

MIAKKA KNEADED CLAY, making it soft and smoothing out the lumps. She added some sand to temper it. When satisfied, she rolled a small portion into a coil. This would be the base of her pot. After rubbing another portion between her palms, she made a long rope of clay, which she coiled around the base. She kept building the coils, layer upon layer, until she was happy with the depth of the pot. Then she moistened it and smoothed the sides with her fingers and a stone. She looked over her pot, feeling for uniform density, eyeing it for symmetry. Carefully she placed it in the open, in direct sunlight, to harden. After many days of drying, she would lay a hardwood fire, place the pot inside, cover it with more oak, and set it ablaze to fire. If it did not crack, she would have a pot that was sooty black, a wonderful background for the sparkles of the sand temper.

She heard Atula's voice and Wakulla's. There were other loud voices also. She could not understand what they were saying, but she did understand that they were involved in strong discussion. She was suddenly glad that only the men met in Council to make important decisions regarding the clan. She did not want to clutter her mind with any more troubles than she already had.

Mi-sa and Cherok were approaching. Mi-sa looked lighter, happier than she had seen her in a long time. Cherok was the one who looked laden with worry.

Cacema stood with Sima who had just examined Kachumpka to make certain the scorpion had not stung the boy. Amakollee was sure that Kachumpka had not been stung, but Sima insisted on checking. Sima knew that the boy did not always respond to things the way other children did. If he had been stung, she had some leaves to soak and use as a compress. But she found no evidence of any sting.

Cacema saw Cherok walking with Mi-sa. She had told him so many times to break away from his relationship with the strange little girl. She could not ask Atula to speak with him. She was certain the shaman would not support her. But Cacema did have a brother. She would ask him to talk some sense into the boy.

"Cherok," she called loudly when she thought he was close enough to hear. Her voice sounded harsh and scolding, and she immediately regretted the humiliation it must have caused him.

Cherok nodded to Miakka as Mi-sa ran to her mother's side, and then he quickly and respectfully advanced to Cacema.

"Yes, Mother," he answered as if he did not know why she had called to him.

"Cherok," she began, looking into the dark, kind eyes of her son, "we have spoken before. I do not need to say more."

Cherok hung his head. His mother meant well, and he knew that she loved him. He would not argue his point, especially here with Amakollee.

Amakollee smirked. Cacema did not see, but Cherok did. He knew that woman resented him and Mi-sa. She was the source of all the trouble with Mi-sa. He wished his mother would not listen to her.

Cacema excused herself from the others, taking Cherok with her. She passed close to the Council, the argumentative voices still carrying on. She led him to the home of her brother. She made Cherok stand alone while she talked to his uncle, and then she left as her brother put his arm around Cherok's shoulder.

At dusk Cherok returned home. Cacema searched his face for some clue as to how he had received his uncle's advice. She would not bring up the subject. He had had enough for one day. Now as the day closed, she wished for peaceful, pleasant moments with her son.

Miakka helped Mi-sa prepare for bed. Just before going inside the platform, they sat together watching the last of the magnificent sunset. The sun sprayed orange rays, like golden paths, across the sky. Miakka saw the reflections in her daughter's eyes and thanked the spirits aloud that Mi-sa had recovered.

After Mi-sa had fallen asleep, Miakka spoke out to the spirits. She thanked them again, but she also asked them to end the cruel rumors. She asked them to give Mi-sa peace and happiness and to let the meaning of her star sign be known. And she thanked them for her secret happiness.

Miakka moved from her daughter's side, sitting back in the shadows but looking out into the darkness. She watched the coals of the cook fires burn down as the time passed. She had seen Atula earlier. He had reached out to touch her hand, finding that touching her impossible to resist, forgetting that someone might notice. Miakka had quickly withdrawn her hand, scolding him with her eyes.

Atula loved the way she talked with her eyes, even if she was reprimanding him. Her eyes spoke as loud as her voice, so full of expression.

"Later," he had whispered, checking to see that no one was near. His smile was seductive.

"Mmm," she had answered him, moving about as if she had some purpose.

Atula had walked away, but he wanted to look back, to smile at her again, to shout "Later" to her again and watch her response. But even more than that, he wanted to be with her under the cover of the night, where she belonged to him, where he could hold her and be true to his feelings.

Miakka had not looked up to watch him go because Shakia had come to talk to her. Shakia watched Atula leave, and she watched Miakka's response to his departure.

"Peculiar that you find it so easy to keep your eyes away from him now," she had said. "There was a time when you could not. Why is that?"

Miakka swallowed. "Perhaps I have listened to my friend."

"I hope you have. When Tican comes again, I hope

you will let him have a chance at your heart."

Miakka had not responded, appearing busy with some basketry.

"Did you hear what I said or are you ignoring me?"

"I heard," Miakka answered without looking at Shakia.

"I know you so well. After all, we have lived as sisters."

Miakka finally looked at her. "And I know that you love me like a sister. I feel the same way about you. I have heard your advice, and I know it comes from your heart."

Shakia had kissed Miakka's cheek, sat down, and changed the subject.

Miakka listened to the sounds of the village as she remembered. It was growing quiet. When the sounds of the clan died out and the last of the coals vanished in darkness, Miakka kissed her daughter and crept down her ladder.

Atula was waiting. He heard her coming quietly up his ladder. As soon as she entered, he wrapped his arms around her and pulled her close. His mouth was hungry for hers as he bent her down onto the mat that was his bed.

"My woman," he whispered in her ear as she held him close.

This was where she belonged, she thought, and she was certain that she had made the right decision. One day Amakollee would find something else on which to focus. Then Miakka and Atula would share their happiness with the others, but right now all that mattered was that this magnificent, wondrous man held her in his arms, whispered loving, sensual things to her, and returned her love. This man who could have any woman, any time, had chosen her. How long she had watched him, admired him, dreamed of him. Long before he had noticed her, she had seen him choose other women, take them away from the fire, and lead them to his platform, to his bed. She had seen him respond to Amakollee when she provocatively danced before him. She had seen him enamored with Shani. She had even watched the fruit of those affairs grow as children. And now his eyes watched only her, begged her to come to his bed, pleaded with her to touch him, to let him touch her. So none of the past mattered, only the moment.

Atula tasted the soft flesh of her chest as it began to rise into the splendid delicious curve of her breast. She could smell his distinctive scent, as he pressed his ruggedly muscled body against hers. Her tongue savored the salt of his skin as she bit into his arm. Had she awakened in the night, in blackness, she would have known him by taste, touch, and smell.

Her hand trembled as she twisted to remove her skirt. Every move he made tore more away. Any moment now it would be totally destroyed, unmendable. She fumbled beneath the arch of her back. He lifted himself, leaving a small space between them. With his strong hands he began tearing the skirt away in large spidery clumps.

Miakka started to resist, but his lips, his tongue, the urgency that sounded in his throat as she allowed his tongue entry, weakened her, drowned all other thoughts. She slid her hand between them, bumping his hand as she helped him rip away the skirt.

Finally he lowered his weight on to her, making a soft gush of a sigh escape her. She waited for him to ease her legs apart and enter her, but he did not. He wanted to love her longer, make it last, enjoy the passion as it grew.

He had thought of her most of the day, often envisioning what this night would be like. Tonight he would revel in every curve, fold, and crook of her body. Tonight he would explore her and search out any forgotten, untouched places.

So many times he had found himself imagining such an exploration. From a distance he had seen her walk, watched the gentle sway of her hips, the subtle dance of her hair as she moved. Closer he had seen the fullness of her breasts and the indentation of her small waist hiding beneath the black veil of her hair. He had seen the moistness of her lips and the flush in her face as he reached for her hand. He had waited for tonight for what seemed much longer than it really was.

Now at last the night had come, and he could feel her beneath him again. Atula whispered to her. He felt her smooth, supple body aching with desire as he moved against her. He opened his eyes, loving to look at her as she filled with passion, her eyes closed as the heat inside her turned her face warmly ablush. He did not want it to be over too quickly. He did not need to imagine any more. At last they were alone.

Or so they thought.

Chapter Twenty-two

AMAKOLLEE HAD SAID THE PRAYERS over. She was certain she had said them right the last time. She had not stumbled or left anything out. There was nothing she could remember that she had done wrong. Yet she could not sleep. She was lying in the same position she always did. She was on the correct side with one hand under her head. Her knees were flexed. Actually she felt stiff because she had lain there so long. But if she changed positions, she would never sleep. This was the way she always went to sleep.

She sat up a moment, looking through the darkness inside the platform. Her eyes had adjusted to the blackness, and she could see shades of light that outlined objects. Kachumpka was still. Her baskets were neatly lined up on the east side of the platform. Some of her cooking utensils hung from pegs in the support posts. Her ceramic pots, which broke easily, were arranged in the corner.

Amakollee got up and went over to the pots. They were arranged by size, the largest to the smallest. A few of the odd-shaped pots sat alone. By them was a small round pot that belonged at the end of the line of graduated pots. It was out of place. How had she done something so foolish? She quickly rectified her mistake, immediately feeling better about it.

She checked the pots again. If she had made the mistake once, she might have made it more than once. They seemed to be in order, but they must have seemed properly placed before or she never would have left them that way. Again she looked them over. Just to make sure that the dark shadows inside the platform played no tricks, Amakollee leaned closer, touching each bowl with her hands. Finally satisfied, she paced inside the platform, looking at all her belongings. Had she misplaced something else?

It worried her that she had put that pot in the wrong spot and had not noticed it. Those kinds of things were happening more and more often to her. It was a little frightening. The other night she had thought that she needed to add some tender center heart of the cabbage palm to her broth. She looked for it but couldn't find it. She moved everything, grumbling and mumbling to herself as she looked for the section of palm. After finally giving up, she had moved her stew broth off the fire only to find the palm inside the pot. She had already added the ingredient, but she had forgotten.

There were too many things for her to think about lately. They cluttered her mind and frustrated her. Perhaps tonight, since she could not sleep anyway, she would sit quietly and sort things out, reorganize her mind. It seemed like a good idea.

Amakollee went below and stirred the last dying coals of her fire. She rebuilt the fire and added some wet oak leaves to make it smoke and keep the insects away.

Smoke had its own magical powers. The method of smoking food—digging a shallow pit and burning the wood to coals, then layering it with wet oak leaves—kept fish from spoiling rapidly, and an additional benefit of the smoke was that it kept away the mosquitoes, which were a constant source of irritation to all of the People. Only when the cold winds blew or during droughts was there any relief. To protect themselves from bites the People often coated their skin with fish oil or even bear grease, when it was available. To keep the fat from turning rancid, the women rendered it over a warm fire and scooped off the top as it cooled.

Amakollee sat close to the smoke. The night was the worst. She could hear the mosquitoes buzzing in the air, eager to get to some host and fill themselves with blood. She moved even closer to the smoke.

She sat thinking, convinced that if the evil spirits had not come with Mi-sa, her life would be more peaceful. The People would not be blinded. They would realize that Kachumpka, not Cherok, was the child with the Gift. Cherok was getting older. Before long he would become a man. The evil ones would be pleased if the People had an impotent shaman who had no power. If the People continued to be fooled, that was exactly what they would have—Cherok. She was sure that was not Cherok's doing, but Mi-sa's. It was her power that made everyone look to Cherok rather than Kachumpka. Cherok was a victim, just like her boy.

Amakollee stirred the fire again, keeping it alive, adding another handful of wet leaves. The breeze blew the smoke into her face, and she coughed and sputtered. Somehow, she thought after clearing her lungs of the smoke, she had to convince the People that Kachumpka was the chosen one. Atula was as blind as the rest, and she was certain that was so because he was involved with Miakka. Amakollee needed proof.

She stood suddenly and headed toward Sima's shelter. At the base of the platform she did not hesitate but quickly went up the ladder.

"Sima," she called in the darkness.

Startled by the loud voice that called her name, Sima jumped and sat up.

"Who is it?"

"It is Amakollee. You must come with me. I will show you proof."

Sima was confused. What was Amakollee doing inside her platform in the middle of the night, waking her, talking about proof?

"Get up, Sima. Quickly. Come with me and you will see for yourself."

"Amakollee, I do not know what you are talking about. You are not making any sense. Is Kachumpka sick?"

"No, no, no," she said with irritation in her voice. "I am certain that Miakka is with Atula. I know it. I want you to see. I need proof. I need you to see so that no one thinks I invented the story. Come with me, and I will prove it to everyone."

"Amakollee, go back to bed. Everything will work out as it should. Trust the spirits."

"You do not understand," she said almost angrily. "The spirits guide me and work through me because I am the mother of the chosen one. It is my duty. Now let us go."

"I do not think this is a wise thing to do. Think about it. You want to sneak into the platform of the shaman. Does that not sound a little bizarre?"

"You are blind," Amakollee screeched. "Like the rest. The evil spirits tell you what to see, what to know. I will do it myself. I am the only one." She disappeared down the ladder.

Sima, still confused, sat looking in the spot she had last

seen Amakollee. Something was wrong with Amakollee. This kind of behavior was very strange. She had either lost her mind or was indeed in touch with spirits that were guiding and controlling her actions.

Amakollee moved across the mound, not caring if she was seen and heard. Her mission was noble and honorable, and she did not care what others thought. They would be thankful one day, and she was willing to accept the responsibility alone.

When she got closer to the platform of the shaman, however, she did become more discreet so she would not alert Atula or Miakka. For an instant she thought of the possibility that Miakka was not there at all, but she quickly dismissed that idea.

At the base of the ladder she stopped to catch her breath. She would need to be quiet as she climbed up so that she would give them no warning.

One slow step at a time she moved up the ladder until at last she could see over the edge of the floor.

Their shadowed figures moved in unison, undulating to the tempo of their need. Atula enveloped Miakka, cloaked her with his body, making her part of him.

Amakollee noisily emptied her lungs of air. She had expected Miakka to be there. She had even expected to find them entwined, but the sight still took her breath away.

Atula reared up, hearing Amakollee over his heavy moans and sighs. "Who is there?" he said, his voice raspy and hoarse.

Amakollee bolted down the ladder, then scrambled back across the mound and into her shelter. She did not care that she had been caught. What she had just seen had shaken her.

Atula collapsed over Miakka, heaving for air, his body

tangled inside with passion and surprise.

"Was someone there?" Miakka asked softly, afraid to hear the answer.

"I am not sure," he answered.

"Tell me," she whispered.

"Amakollee—I think."

Miakka moved beneath him, encouraging him to move off of her and to her side. "Why does she do this? Why can she not leave me alone—leave Mi-sa alone? What is it that she wants from me?" Miakka's voice broke with tears. She was angry, frightened, and confused.

"She wants Kachumpka to be the next shaman."

"But Mi-sa is no threat to Kachumpka. Cherok is the child with the Gift, the one Amakollee should fear. I do not understand."

"She believes the star sign was an evil sign and that Mi-sa is connected to that evil. She believes that Mi-sa gives Cherok false power."

Miakka blinked back tears. There was some connection between Cherok and Mi-sa. But Amakollee had it all wrong—made everything about Mi-sa seem ugly and frightening.

"She will tell everyone what she saw tonight," Miakka said.

Atula rolled over on his back. Miakka was right, and he knew what was coming next. "You are going to leave me, are you not?" he said, not looking at her. "You are going to tell me that we will never be together again."

"I do not want us to be apart, but you must see that Amakollee will use us to destroy Mi-sa."

Atula did not answer.

"Now, instead of just suspicion, Amakollee has something true to tell everyone. She will turn people against Mi-sa. My daughter will have a terrible life."

"But your leaving me now will not undo anything," Atula said.

"We will have to deny that we were together, or at least say nothing. We cannot afford to have her see us again, and perhaps bring someone else with her."

"But my heart is yous, Miakka. It always will be. I do not want any other woman."

Miakka felt sick inside. She had never wanted any other man. "You will have to have other women. The People will be suspicious if you do not. Amakollee and the others will watch to see if you take women to your bed. That is your right. It is expected of you."

Atula touched his fingers to her lips. "No, Miakka. Shh."

Miakka moved his fingertips from her lips. "People will notice if you do not ..." The thought was too difficult for her to finish. She bit down on her bottom lip. "Perhaps," she started again, choking on her words, "even Amakollee. Giving her your attention may be the only way to silence her, to make her stop."

"Never," he said.

"Do not say that now. Please. How do you think I will feel every time I see you take some woman toward your platform? Do you think it will be easy for me? Do you not think that the sight will gnaw at me from the inside? But you must. And you must take Amakollee. Doing so is the only way to end this."

Miakka stood. Her skirt was in shreds. She had not cared at the moment, but now she had to leave. Atula sat up, and pointed to a blanket. Miakka wrapped herself in the soft coverlet. Atula stood and reached inside the furs. For the last time he slid his hands down her sides and up over her breasts, imprinting on his memory the curves and lines that were hers. His lips fell on hers, filled not with the aggressiveness of desire but with tenderness and pain.

"Someday this will be over," she whispered, pulling away.

"I will count every moon," he told her as he watched her go.

———

AMAKOLLEE SLEPT WELL. Miakka and Atula did not. When the sun came up, Miakka felt her swollen eyes. They burned and felt full. She had cried most of the night. Atula's head ached, and his energy seemed to have left him.

Amakollee was busy about the village. She had wasted no time spreading her new information. When Miakka and Mi-sa went to the cenote, she noticed that the women seemed to go out of their way to ignore her.

As the days continued, the attitudes of the clan became even more obvious. Shakia and Tabisha were the only women who spoke to Miakka. Even Kita had withdrawn. But Miakka understood. Wakulla was Kita's son, and the connections between Miakka, Atula, and Wakulla were dangerous to her son's authority. Kita liked Miakka and Mi-sa, but she felt it best to disassociate herself from them.

Whenever Miakka walked past, the clan members turned their heads or moved away. The children did not come to play, and they excluded Mi-sa from their fun. Cherok, however, continued to defy his mother's wishes even now that they had grown so strong. Openly he visited Mi-sa, making no excuses to anyone.

Mi-sa sat next to her mother, helping her make a pot. It had sat drying for a few days and was firm enough to be stamped with a decorative pattern. Carved on a wooden paddle was a pattern of hatch marks. Miakka took Mi-sa's hand in hers, curled it into a ball, and covered it with her own hand, then placed their fists inside the bowl. Their hands would hold the form while the pot was decorated. She told Mi-sa to pick up the paddle and strike the pot with it. Mi-sa lifted the wooden paddle and grinned at her mother before smacking the bowl, leaving a clean, deep-stamped impression in the plain gray surface.

"Again," Miakka said with a light laugh. "All the way around."

When she had finished, Mi-sa eyed her first attempt at potterymaking and then smiled at her mother.

"You have made a fine bowl," her mother said. Miakka set the pot aside. "It will be ready to fire soon, and then you will have your first pot."

"I hope it does not crack," Mi-sa said to her mother.

"That would be a shame after so much hard work. And the bowl is so pretty," Miakka replied, stroking her daughter's long black hair.

The noise of the children playing nearby caught Mi-sa's attention. She watched them running and tumbling, laughing and tagging one another.

"May I play, too?" she asked her mother.

"Should we start another bowl, a larger one?" Miakka answered, ignoring Mi-sa's question.

Miakka watched her daughter's expression turn sad. She knew that Mi-sa would stay with her if she asked, but she also knew that Mi-sa wanted to join the other children. Maybe the children would let her join in.

She nodded, and Mi-sa ran to join the group. Miakka's stomach rolled into a tight ball as she watched. Before Mi-sa even reached the crowd of children, Miakka regretted her decision. She should not have let her go.

Mi-sa stopped short of the children, waiting for an invitation. The wind was strong, blowing her long hair away from her back. Her small body still looked frail, but the scar on her back was barely noticeable.

The little girl watched as the deep golden skin of the many little ones flashed in the sun as they twisted and darted in front of her. Mi-sa bounced with excitement. She raised her small hands in the air and squealed as two children fell at her feet, giggling, rolling on the ground. She wanted them to ask her to join in, but instead they hopped up and sprinted away, ignoring her as if they had not even seen her.

Mi-sa followed, trotting, restraining the urge to break into an eager run. The children breezed past her, a rush of noise and color, leaving her standing alone.

"May I play?" she shouted as they got farther away.

Two girls turned and looked at her, made a face at each other as if they did not know how to answer. Then they turned away and rejoined the others.

"Please," Mi-sa called.

Miakka felt ill and angry. Running to her, as she wanted to do, would make Mi-sa feel even worse because the children might tease her. Miakka stood firm and watched her Light in the Darkness fill with gloom. All the happy lines of Mi-sa's face turned downward as she watched the playing children continue moving away from her. Mi-sa looked at her mother, who held her arms out. Mi-sa ran to her, letting her mother wrap her arms around her and hide her from the rest of the world.

Miakka closed her eyes, swallowing, trying hard not to cry. She could think of nothing to say that would take her child's hurt away. She would have known what to do for a scratch or a skinned knee, but this pain was deep inside, a gouge in Mi-sa's heart, as well as a stab in Miakka's heart.

Suddenly Mi-sa looked toward the area where the children now played. "Choktulee," she murmured.

"What?" Miakka asked.

There was a sudden high-pitched wail, a child's cry of pain. Mi-sa and Miakka began to run. The children had already formed a circle around a young boy whose head was bleeding profusely.

Miakka quickly bent over him and turned his head to see the injury. Apparently he had fallen while playing and had struck his head on a jagged rock. The wound looked serious.

"Go get some help." Miakka said to the group. A few of the children left to seek help, but others stayed, holding one another in fear.

Mi-sa wandered a few feet away and plucked some fuzzy leaves from a tall, slender plant. She chewed them until they were soft and then spit them out into her palm. She knelt next to her mother and pressed the handful of leaves to the wound, packing the gash with the contents of her hand.

Miakka looked at her, confused. "What are you doing?"

Mi-sa did not answer. Miakka called her name softly. Then she heard her daughter begin a quiet chant, words that she did not understand. The girl closed her eyes and sang words to a rhythm that pulsed somewhere inside her.

Miakka heard the adults as they approached. Choktulee's mother was screeching the boy's name. When she got close enough to him, she screamed at Miakka, "Get away from him! Get Mi-sa away!"

Miakka looked shocked. "Mi-sa," she said softly, taking her daughter's arm, moving her hand away from the wound. She pulled harder when she got no response.

"Mi-sa," she said loudly, grabbing her and lifting her.

Mi-sa stood, and the two of them backed away as Choktulee's mother knelt beside him.

Miakka and Mi-sa retreated from the gathering crowd. Miakka wanted to talk to her daughter where no one else could hear.

"This way," she said, walking away from the village into the jungle of trees and vines. Mi-sa followed but kept looking back. When they had walked far enough away, Miakka sat down with her daughter.

"Mi-sa, what did you put on Choktulee's head wound?"

The child shrugged.

"Mi-sa," her mother scolded, "tell me what you did."

"There is a plant, Mother. It is good for injuries like the one Choktulee had."

"What plant is that?"

"I do not know the name."

"And how do you know that this plant is good for wounds?"

Mi-sa stared into her mother's eyes but gave no answer.

"And the words you said? Where did they come from? What song did you sing?"

Mi-sa still did not answer, and she was beginning to make Miakka angry. She held her daughter by her shoulders. "Where did you learn those things?"

Miakka gently shook her daughter. Mi-sa looked down.

"Look at me, Mi-sa. Tell me what you were doing. You are scaring me."

Mi-sa looked up again, and her tiny face crinkled as she started to cry. "I just knew I had to get the plant and say the words. I do not know how," she answered in sobs.

Miakka reached around her little one and pulled her close, rocking her as she cried with her.

"I am sorry. Shh. Shh."

Miakka was ashamed that she had spoken to Mi-sa so harshly. But how had the child known such things? And had not Mi-sa called out Choktulee's name an instant before the boy screamed?

Chapter Twenty-three

THE SUN BAKED THE LAND, cracking the riverbanks as the water retreated. The lens of water that embosomed the earth thinned and in some places disappeared, leaving the river bottom exposed to sun. On it lay the sun-bleached remains of gar, bass, and colorful flag and killifish that had been trapped in shallow pools, unable to find their way to deeper water. The grasses turned a dreary gray and brown. The newly hatched apple snails dropped from their opened eggs onto dust, where they perished.

The alligators snuggled into the earth, heaving their thick bodies from side to side, digging with their feet and snouts, working their way into the soil, scratching out basins. Here the animals gathered to drink the coveted water. Even the timid were forced to visit the alligator holes. Cautious and frightened, but so thirsty.

The sun was searing, sweltering, scorching, and the People were careful to control their fires. The prairie was dry tinder. Short, fierce thunderstorms brewed in the heat, but not enough rain came to end the drought or to stop the fires started by lightning.

Beneath a crystal-blue sky that burned with the blazing sun, the Council of Men met to discuss the issues again formally. This was a new season, time to reassess. It was also time for atonement.

The morning brought more heat, and the dew quickly evaporated. There was no smell of cook fires on this day of fasting for the men. The women and children ate leaves, berries, and raw plant stalks. For the next four days the clan would carry out a sacred tradition that had been passed from generation to generation.

The men began the day by swallowing a dark tea made from the berries and leaves of the ilex and the button snake-root. The emetic was quick to work, purging them of impurities.

Talasee brought the central hearth ablaze. When the sun was directly overhead, the men gathered by the fire. They chanted prayers led by the shaman and the cacique. They asked the spirits to purify them and make them receptive to their directions. They asked that they be forgiven for any unworthy acts. They proved their worth by torturing themselves with the heat. What their stomachs had not emptied, their skin gave up, pouring and dripping sweat from them.

At last Atula began his song. It was a song of thanks, pleasant and humble. When he stopped, the men stood and walked quickly to the cenote. They dunked themselves in the dark water to cleanse away all the impurities that stuck to their skin. At last they were clean, pure, and able to make clear decisions.

When they emerged, Wakulla led them back. As they sat together, this time away from the dying fire, Atula opened a medicine bundle and spread it before them. Inside were sacred totems, tools, and fetishes. He chose a special tool. The handle was made from a deer antler, shiny and polished, carved with a quatrefoil and other decorative shapes and lines. Inserted in the tip was a stingray spine. Atula held it out so that the men might see as he chanted. He then walked around the circle scratching each man's upper arm with the spine, leaving a fine line that oozed blood. When he had scratched the last man, he drew the spine down the center of his chest, piercing his skin, creating a shallow cut that filled with blood.

They were ready.

For the next four days, one for each of the four directions, they would discuss issues and make decisions for all the clan. Wakulla opened the Council. The first day they were concerned with general matters. The men consulted Atula about the drought. He assured them that his visions had shown him it would end, but there were still many days coming without enough rain.

"Who is responsible for this punishment?" someone asked.

"Someone has broken a custom," Atula answered.

The men shifted looks from one to another.

"If the one who has erred will confess tonight after the White Feather Dance, the drought will end," Atula continued.

While the men proceeded, the women began to bundle white egret feathers and tie them to sticks and staffs that would be carried during the dance. The women washed themselves with lime, coating their bodies with the yellowish-white substance. They strung shell beads around their necks and ankles and made more for the men. They cleaned the area that would be used for the ceremony, quietly sweeping the earth with brooms of bunched palm fronds, removing roots, rocks, and weeds that had grown tall.

The women moved about the village with little or no sound, keeping their children close and quiet. It was not the time to disturb the men.

By dusk everyone was ready and anxiously awaiting the onset of night. The men adjourned as the late afternoon sun shone down at them in hot slanted streams. Again they washed their bodies before readying themselves for the ceremony and dance.

The women presented the men with the sticks of egret feathers and dropped strings of clanking shells over their heads. They wore anklets and armbands made of shells and feathers, and ear buttons made from shark vertebrae. They drew their hair back into a knot and placed large fire-polished bone pins, some with triangular points, some curved bones from the raccoon,through the knot to keep it in place. Wakulla and Atula wore beautifully carved masks. The cacique wore a wooden mask of the cormorant with glaring shell eyes. Atula donned the mask of the great white egret. Others carried small model heads of animals with jaws that moved, painted with dyes and pigments. With every ritual, every ceremony, they paid respect to their animal brothers.

The men embellished their bodies with white chalky lines and swirls. With charcoal they drew black circles around their dark eyes. When they gathered beneath the moon, in the flickering firelight of the hearth and the burning torches, they were a magnificent sight.

Their voices began in a low hum, sounding like a distant rumble, but as the men moved their feet in the pattern of the ancient dance, the hum changed to words—important sacred words.

Amakollee stood next to Sassacha, holding Kachumpka's hand. She waved his fasting stick before her, displaying it for all to see. Her feet stepped to the same rhythm, and a great smile crossed her face.

Miakka stood back, her hands resting on Mi-sa's shoulders. Cherok stood near Cacema, totally engrossed in the performance. He listened to the words, saying them softly to himself, mimicking the dance in miniature. He studied Atula, watching him turn and swoop and step. He listened to the inflections in the shaman's voice, the accents on important words and phrases. He watched Atula's head movements and the expressions on his face, the gestures of his hands, and the posture of his body, as the shaman led the White Feather Dance.

The music of the dance grew louder, accompanied by the percussion of sticks being beaten together, rattles made from turtle shells, reed flutes, and strong masculine voices. Cherok imitated and scrutinized, learning all that he could.

Mi-sa watched also, her eyes glittering with the light and fascinating forms. Miakka felt her little shoulders begin to sway and rock. If she had not held Mi-sa back, she was sure the child would have danced beside the men, making the same steps, feeling the same call of the music and rhythm. She thought she heard Mi-sa whisper and leaned down so that she could hear her. As her ear got closer, she heard a string of whispered words chanted by her daughter. She hoped no one else had noticed.

"Mi-sa," she said in her daughter's ear, "do not sing. This song is for the men. The shaman teaches it to the boys before they become men."

"I like the song," Mi-sa said, turning her face up to her mother with a smile.

"I like it also, but it is only for the men. Listen to it. Enjoy it."

Mi-sa realized she had again done something that was not acceptable and that upset her mother. She was afraid she might do something else inappropriate without knowing. The music had been strong and compelling, the words so comfortable and natural. How would she ever learn what was expected of her? Why did she not know proper responses like the other children? She must be such a burden and an embarrassment to her mother, she thought.

"I am very tired tonight, Mother. Would it offend the spirits if I went to sleep?"

"Do you not feel well?" Miakka asked.

"I am well, Mother. There is nothing to worry about. I am just very tired."

It had been a long and miserable day for Mi-sa. She and Miakka were always alone, tending to daily chores and tasks. The other children ignored Mi-sa and treated her rudely, and so she usually stayed away from them, helping her mother.

"Do you want to go to bed now?" Miakka asked.

"Could I?"

"Are you certain that you are feeling all right? Nothing is hurting or bothering you?"

"No, Mother."

Miakka took Mi-sa's hand and led her away to her platform. Inside she scratched the child's back and sang a lullaby. Outside she could hear the excited crowd as they watched the dance continue. Miakka felt very alone, isolated, and empty.

Mi-sa closed her eyes, enjoying the feel of her mother's nails gently scratching her back. At first she feigned sleep, and then she comfortably drifted off.

Miakka watched the end of the ceremony from the edge of her platform. The dance was complete, and the people mingled, laughing and talking. Though the men were tired and hungry, they acted full of energy and contentment. Atula was easy to spot because of the headdress that only he wore. It abounded with white spiked plumes that pierced the blackness.

Would he take a woman this night? she wondered. It was customary. She scanned the crowd, looking at all the people who had once been her friends. Kita stood talking to Shakia. Tabisha stood quietly, also looking on. Amakollee conversed with Sassacha and some other women. Miakka watched as Amakollee leaned over and spoke to Kachumpka. Then she took his hand and put it in Sassacha's hand. Amakollee's friend looked down and smiled at the boy. Amakollee wandered away.

Miakka followed her with her eyes. The woman slipped through the crowd, stopping to say a few words now and again, but making her way to the other side of the mass—toward the white feathers that stood above the heads of the others. Toward Atula.

Miakka had seen enough. She withdrew inside the platform, curled up on her mat and closed her eyes.

The next morning, the fast ended but not the heat or drought; there had been no confession. The aroma emanating from the cook fires filled the air. The next two days would be filled with feasting and festivity; the last day was always more solemn.

Again the day began with a clear pink and blue sunrise and the hot pale yellow sun. By late morning the wild grasses had folded in, curled over, the deep green sucked out of them by the merciless heat. The gray-green blades became thin and wiry, hiding as much of themselves from the sun as they could, reluctant to transpire precious water.

The People stayed outside in the shade, taking advantage of the breeze. In pockets the black muck dried out and smoldered, trapping the heat inside, eventually bursting into flames that speedily consumed vast expanses of the dry prairie. The relentless searing sun rose straight overhead, beating the land, making it throb in blistering agony. The air filled with humidity as the heat took up the water from the thin fragile veil that remained. Great swollen gray clouds began to grow above. In the distance thunder rumbled, and the people of the village looked to the sky, hoping for rain.

But by dusk the angry underbelly of the sky had dissipated. The earth was still dry and parched, thankful for the small drop in temperature as night approached.

Raccoons grubbed in the mud at the edge of a gator hole, looking for a tasty hiding crayfish. A deer came to drink, stepping, stopping, ears twitching, cautiously checking the area for enemies. Its hoofprints trampled over those of a bobcat that had come the night before. The cat's tracks were round impressions that showed no claw marks. The center pad left its distinctive mark, two lobes on the rear margin and an indentation in the front.

The opossum had also been here, leaving its pointed, overlapping tracks circling the gator hole.

On the last of the four days, the Council gathered again. The men were restless. The most pressing issues had been resolved. Talasee fidgeted. He had been privy to some of the discreet discussions and conversations. He knew what was to come today. This issue had been put off until the end.

Wakulla recognized Omo-ko, Pachu's uncle. Omo-ko had been silent much of the time after Pachu failed to return from his totem quest. He had not spoken in Council for a long time.

Omo-ko had been responsible for teaching the young Pachu hunting and survival skills that he would need through life and especially on his totem search. Though many moons had passed, he still felt the deep pain of guilt. He believed that he had failed. He knew the belief of the clan, that a boy was selected by the spirits to become a man. If the boy was not worthy, he did not come back. There was no blame, no disgrace; it was between the boy and the spirits. But Omo-ko had never accepted that in his heart, and the constant misery his guilt caused him had changed his once pleasant disposition to one that was cynical and critical. His misery made him look for transgressions and weaknesses in others. Somehow he always thought that exposing others' imperfections and misdeeds would relieve his guilt, but it never did.

Omo-ko stood, bowed his head, and then lifted it, showing respect to the young cacique.

"There are many of us," he began, "who need to express some concerns."

The men sat quietly, their tension almost a presence in the air.

Omo-ko continued. "It is about the child, Mi-sa."

There were muffled sounds, mostly of agreement.

"What concerns do you have about such a small child?" Wakulla asked.

Omo-ko glanced at Atula and then looked toward those he thought might support him, and then back to Wakulla. "Mi-sa was born on the night of the A-po-la-chee. It was not a good time for a child to enter the world. And there was a star." Omo-ko swept is arm in an arc, pointing to the sky.

The crowd nodded, and Omo-ko felt braver.

"We have considered that perhaps the star marked the night of the A-po-la-chee and was not the totem of the child."

Atula straightened, ready to object, but he held his tongue.

"It would certainly be an honest error for any

shaman," Omo-ko said, patronizing Atula. "Even before Mi-sa's birth the mother knew something was wrong. Did she not consult Wagahi and you, Atula?"

Omo-ko did not permit time for an answer. "We would like to put this matter before the Council. The child, Mi-sa, is not guided by the right spirits. We do not presume to know her purpose, but we do not want to continue to provide for her. We wish to show the spirits our faith. We do not want to participate in the care of someone we feel is the tool of the Darkside."

Atula stood, having heard enough.

"Atula," Wakulla said, "it is still Omo-ko's turn to speak."

The man of the spirits clenched jaw, holding back his anger.

"I will yield," Omo-ko said, sitting.

Atula argued the issue. His personal anger was difficult to disguise.

Omo-ko responded, hoping to pacify Atula. "I have no argument with you, Shaman. The misreading of the star sign is understandable."

"Arrgh," Atula snarled. "You are misled. What you contemplate is cruel and unfounded."

Omo-ko started to speak again, but Wakulla halted him by raising his hand, palm out. He looked at Atula to respond.

"I will not discuss the star sign again. I am the holy man, and I interpret the signs according to the spirits. I am not obligated to explain to anyone. The sign is Mi-sa's—on the night of the A-po-la-chee was an unfortunate coincidence. Amakollee is at the root of your groundless fear of this child. Do you see what Amakollee has reduced you to? Men who are afraid of a small girl. Amakollee's accusations are unsupported. She is not the shaman. She is not an instrument of the spirits."

Atula sat, disgusted, glaring hard at the men of the Council.

"It is wise to listen to our shaman," Wakulla remarked.

"May I speak again?" Omo-ko asked.

Wakulla gestured that he could, although he had hoped the debate would end.

"With respect for you, Cacique, and you, Atula, I must bring before the Council all our thoughts. Some have noticed that Atula is intimately involved with the child's mother, Miakka. All of us understand the passions of the heart. Sometimes they cloud our perceptions, color our opinions and judgments. And our cacique, wise as he is, is the son of the shaman. A shaman and his son have a special relationship. Wakulla, we honor that relationship." He paused and then continued. "Our cacique's wife is Shakia. Was not Miakka raised as her sister? Though you may think these close associations do not influence you, we are not so sure. On the outside we believe we see things less distorted. We speak in the best interest of our clan. It becomes even clearer why the spirits direct us to choose our mates from other clans and not the clans from which our mothers descend. Only in special cases do we disregard that code. We must resist our emotions and make just and clear decisions."

The men mumbled, mostly expressing their agreement with Omo-ko. Some seemed relieved that at last these facts and suggestions were all in the open.

Omo-ko paused so that Atula and Wakulla could see and hear that these were clan opinions, not just the ideas of one man or two.

"As I have said, we must serve the spirits," Omo-ko continued, "and resist the deceptions of the evil ones. We cannot participate in activities—"

Tabisha's husband, Acopa, interrupted. "Forgive me for my rudeness, Omo-ko, Cacique. I must speak."

"Do you object, Omo-ko?" Wakulla inquired.

"Let him speak," Omo-ko answered as he sat.

Acopa stood, his tall and lanky body an aberration in the smaller, more robust clan. "I will provide for Mi-sa and her mother. I was the provider for Miakka after the death of her family. Her mother was my sister. Miakka is my responsibility. I took care of her before the birth of the shaman's child, and I will resume that responsibility—for both of them. I am not afraid of some old woman's gossip."

The men of the Council sat quietly. Amakollee had indeed spread her poison effectively. And, Atula thought, Miakka had been right. The relationship between Miakka and him would only fuel the heat of dissension. The venomous treatment and talk of Mi-sa would end only if it died like a fire with no fuel left to burn.

Perhaps, Atula thought as the Council dispersed and he walked away, he would never touch her again. But Miakka could never be ripped from his heart.

The People watched the sky grow dark and heavy again with the promise of rain. Maybe a storm would come this night. They prayed the drought would end.

Miakka also looked up as a loud crack of thunder sounded. At first the rain was light as if it needed to be coaxed into falling.

Miakka saw the Council break up and the men walk away. She saw Atula leave unaccompanied, and she believed she understood why. Now and again she had heard certain words, read some expressions, caught Mi-sa's name. The drops of rain washed over her face, mixing with her tears.

Mi-sa hugged her mother's thigh as she, too, looked

into the rain, singing the same soft chant she had sung all day. No one had even noticed. The child smiled as the rain began to fall harder. She could finally stop her song.

Chapter Twenty-four

THE SEASONS CAME AND WENT, winter after winter, summer after summer. Other droughts had come and gone, leaving parts of the People's world scorched by fire, black and leafless until the heavy rains came again, encouraging succulent new green shoots of saw grass to break through. But high water had also come and gone, inundating the land, driving the animals to high ground. On the shorelines the water drove back the coastal inhabitants. Inland the rising water lapped over the edges of the mounds, forcing the residents to dig marl off the shores of the tree islands with their conch picks and pile it on top of their village mounds. Sometimes the level of the water rose and remained in depressions on the hammocks, making their world wet and soggy. The danger from snakes and alligators and disease increased. The high water winked at the sun, rising up, covering all but the tips of the saw grass so that the once keen-edged blades that had blown and rippled in the wind now appeared to be no more than a series of short, trimmed whisks.

Enormous turbulent storms came, born of the heat at sea, tempestuous whorls spinning and churning across the open warm waters and blasting onto the land, ripping away at the coastline and flattening the lush tropical foliage.

The pattern of rising and falling water—of extremes—continued. Water was the life giver, but it was also the element that most often threatened the People. Forever they planned and formed strategies to deal with the storms and the droughts.

Shakia had not yet had a child, and this grieved her as well as Wakulla. Kachumpka had grown into a young man. Though his time had come, Atula had not sent him on his totem search. His body had grown, but Atula did not feel his mind was ready to become a man. Amakollee had not pressed the issue, strange as that seemed. She knew in her heart that her boy would not survive a totem quest. He was so close to the spirits, she believed, that he would too easily cross into their world. She had never accepted that her child was less than whole, that his mind had empty spots that even she could not fill, though over the many seasons that fact had become more apparent to most of the villagers.

Amakollee had grown older and more bitter. She fed on the alienation of Miakka and Mi-sa from the rest of the clan. Other than Kachumpka, her animosity was the only thing that made her keep going. Long ago she had caught Atula and Miakka together and that had been the fatal bit of information that had led to Miakka's and Mi-sa's exclusion. It had kept Atula and Miakka apart. He had even taken Amakollee to his bed again—once—not long after the men had decided to stop providing for the child and mother.

He had frightened her that night. She had offered herself to him in front of others. She held out a bowl of the dark tea to him, interrupting his conversation.

"Perhaps this will help you think of more pleasant things," she had said to him, letting her tongue linger on her lips, wetting them. She teasingly tossed her hair so that brief glimpses of her breasts could be seen through the moving strands.

"Take some," she said, holding the bowl to his lips. "The shaman needs to relax."

The men standing with him had chuckled. Some envied Atula's position and told him so.

Amakollee had placed her fingertip in the center of his chest and slowly slid it outward, pausing to draw circles around his nipple, then ventured on down his center. At his waist she had stopped and looked up at him.

"Do you wish me to go on?" she said in a throaty voice. "You know that I can please you, do you not?"

With a grin on his face, one of the men elbowed Atula. "I think I shall go and find my wife," he said, laughing and walking away.

"My body is yours, Shaman," Amakollee had said, first smiling at him and then the other men.

She knew that Atula would not be able to refuse. Her only regret was that Miakka did not witness her flirtation. She had seen Miakka wander off to her platform earlier. She nodded at those she passed as she walked with Atula, wanting them to notice.

But inside the shadows of his platform, he was not the man she had joined with before. He was rough with her, tearing her skirt from her, yanking her head back by her long hair as he mouthed her breasts. His mouth was hard on her and never touched her lips.

His hands had been crude and savage. He was not gentle when he pulled her down to the floor. He was immediately on her, driving deep into her, fiercely, angrily, grunting with his powerful strokes. She had tried to slow him down, move him off her, not allow him entry, but he had persisted. He offered her no tenderness, only the nearly violent pursuit of his satisfaction, ignoring her until he finally stiffened and let out a loud grunt. He let his full weight fall on her. He was sweaty and heaved for air. Amakollee lay beneath him, feeling ashamed and degraded. He finally moved off of her and slept. She left without speaking.

In the morning she was sore. She had a bruise on her breast, and the insides of her thighs were dotted with small blue and purple spots where he had harshly moved her legs apart as she resisted. Amakollee had not offered herself again.

Miakka had seen him lead other women toward his platform, though he usually waited until Miakka was not able to watch. When he felt the touch of another woman, he always closed his eyes and remembered Miakka's hands, Miakka's lips, Miakka's warmth. He did not take women often, but when he did, he made certain that many saw his intention. As far as the clan could see, all was right with the shaman. He was thankful that no more children had been conceived from his seed.

After a while some people even doubted whether there had ever been anything between Miakka and Atula. But after that fateful Council meeting the rain had returned, a sure sign that the clan had appeased the spirits. The rain was their answer. Their refusal to provide for the child had pleased the spirits.

Men from other clans had come to their village seeking brides. Though others from his clan came often, Tican had not come again. Miakka heard from one of the men of Tican's group that Tican had found a wife from a village to the east. Miakka was happy for him, glad that he had not wasted his youth waiting for her. He was a fine man. She had passed the age of the women who now drew the young men's attention when they came looking for wives. Now it was Mi-sa's turn.

Mi-sa had grown into a young woman. She had entered her first moon cycle and had participated in all the rites and festivities. At the announcement the villagers had gathered at the central hearth for congratulations. No one congratulated Mi-sa directly except Tabisha and Shakia. Sima had also spoken, but she had whispered her congratulations and had looked around nervously. Afterward, as part of the ritual, Mi-sa stayed isolated with her mother for five days. She did not come out of her platform for anything. Now the five days had ended and there was another celebration, welcoming the new woman to the tribe, but the People did not make Mi-sa feel welcome. They showed little enthusiasm and performed the songs and dances without excitement. Even though she was a part of the ceremonies and rituals, she remained alone. What should have been a time of extraordinary happiness was a time of awkwardness. Mi-sa was glad when the ceremonies ended.

Atula watched Miakka across the gathered clan. He could see the pain in her eyes as she felt the humiliation her daughter suffered. The gifts the women brought to Mi-sa were small and reflected their unwillingness to truly accept her. Instead of staying after the ritual for the festivities, the People wandered away as soon as the required songs and dances were done. Mi-sa remained standing alone in the center of the plaza.

Cherok, Wakulla, Shakia, Tabisha, and Acopa remained behind and came to Mi-sa's side. They tried to carry on with the gaiety but failed miserably. Mi-sa thanked them and then asked if they would forgive her if she retired early. She explained that the recent events had exhausted her. The five stood with Miakka and watched the young woman walk away.

The men of the village usually constructed a new platform for the new woman of the village, just as they did for the boys when they became men. They usually did this within a few full moons after the official declaration that the child had become an adult. But there was no talk of building Mi-sa's new home. Cherok brought this problem to Wakulla's attention. He in turn decided that he, Cherok, Acopa, and Atula would build the shelter. Acopa said he would continue to bear the responsibility of providing for her.

Mi-sa was pleased that the new platform was so near Cherok's. Miakka helped move her things inside. How had her Little Light grown to a woman so fast? Where had the time gone? All the wonderful things she had planned for her daughter the night she held her in the birthing hut beneath the brilliant light of the shooting star had somehow been lost. Now she was a woman, and there was no more little girl.

Miakka held her daughter by her shoulders and looked into her eyes. She pulled her close, embracing her.

"You will never be a woman to me. Always my Light in the Darkness, my Little Light." Miakka loosened her hug and looked into Mi-sa's face. "This will be a happy house. You will see. The spirits have something special planned for you. I know they have. If you have any doubts, ask your father. He is a man of the spirits. He knows. Be proud of who you are and be patient, my sweet little one."

"You have so much faith, Mother. I love you."

Miakka held back her tears until she was inside her platform. For the first time since Mi-sa was born, a lifetime ago, she lived alone. The space that Mi-sa filled was more than just the physical space on the floor. The emptiness of that space swept over Miakka. The corner where the baskets of Mi-sa's things had been stored was now empty. She ran her finger over the dark stain in the floor, the place that had soaked up her daughter's blood. Mi-sa had never been able to tell her who had attacked her, though Miakka was sure it was Amakollee. The clan had never pursued the truth, accepting that the attack was the work of the spirits, especially since Mi-sa herself had never accused anyone.

Miakka heard someone call out to her from below. She moved to the edge of the platform and looked down. It was Shakia.

"May I come up and speak with you?" she asked.

"Yes, come," Miakka answered, happy to have the company. It would help to lighten her mood.

Shakia came up and looked about. "Your home looks so empty," she commented.

"Yes, it does," Miakka responded. "I did not realize how empty it would be."

Shakia noticed her sadness. "You should be happy. Your daughter is now entitled to all the rights and responsibilities of a woman. When men come again to look for brides, they will not be able to see anyone but Mi-sa. They will be stricken by her beauty. One day she will present you with a grandchild, old woman," she joked.

"I hope that will happen. Mi-sa deserves that happiness."

"Sit down so that I can talk to you," Shakia told Miakka.

The two women sat, Miakka wondering what Shakia wanted to say.

"Well?" Miakka probed when Shakia did not start right away. "What is this special thing you have to tell me?"

"How do you know that it is so special?" Shakia asked.

"Was I not raised as your sister? Your face, your eyes, your smile, and your voice tell me that you are fighting to keep from exploding with some secret. So tell me."

Shakia grinned. "My moon cycle has not come for a while. Do you think—"

Miakka did not let her finish. "A baby! You carry a child. Oh, Shakia, how wonderful." She quickly hugged her.

"Miakka, I am afraid. What if it is not true?"

"How many cycles have you missed?"

"Three."

"Three?" Miakka said excitedly. "Of course it is a child. Have you spoken with Atula?"

"Not yet. I want you to come with me. I cannot bear to hear that it is not true."

"I will be glad to come with you. What does Wakulla say?"

"He does not know," Shakia said shyly.

"What? You have not told him?"

"Miakka, there have been other times when I thought that perhaps a child grew inside, but I was wrong. I could not put Wakulla through that disappointment yet another time."

"But it has been three moon cycles. Has it ever been that long before?"

"Never. But I do not have other symptoms. My stomach is not upset, though I eat so much. And my breasts are not tender anymore."

"But they do not stay tender. Only at the beginning. At least it was that way for me when I carried Mi-sa. And all women are not sick when they have a child inside them. It is different for everyone. Do not listen to all the tales the women tell. Oh, Shakia, after all this time the spirits smile on you."

Shakia stood. She had a small frame but was still fleshy, with no sharp, jutting points or angles.

Shakia glared at her abdomen, flattening out the moss skirt, pulling it as taut and smooth as she could without tearing it. "Do you think it pouches out? Can you tell?" she asked Miakka.

"Maybe a little. It is hard to tell," Miakka answered.

"This is a miracle of the spirits, Miakka. It really is if it is true. I am not such a young woman any longer. I am so happy and so afraid."

Miakka stood and hugged her again. "Let us go to the shaman right now. Let Atula confirm it, and then you can go and tell your husband."

Miakka escorted Shakia across the village. Atula was not near his platform. They called up, but there was no response. Shakia's face fell.

"We will find him. Be patient."

They wandered through the village, Shakia feeling more discouraged.

"The spirits do not want me to know. They protect me from disappointment."

"Do not be silly," Miakka told her. "Atula is busy. He has many things to do. The spirits are not interfering. Ah, look, he comes with Wakulla."

The cacique and the shaman emerged from a stand of strangler figs and Sabal palms. Shakia stopped.

"I cannot ask him now without my husband knowing."

"Let me take care of it. Stop searching for so many excuses. I feel good about this."

Miakka continued to lead Shakia toward Atula. When they got close, they bent over respectfully as they addressed Atula.

"Shaman, forgive our interruption. We hope we have not intruded," Miakka said. It was always disturbing to her to speak with Atula in such formal terms, ignoring the feelings that he always spawned, speaking to him as if there had never been anything between them. But at least she could be near him, hear his voice, look at him.

Atula gestured for the two women to stand erect. "I have come to seek your help, Shaman," Miakka continued.

Atula excused himself and walked away with the women. Wakulla was curious, but it would have been impolite of him to inquire. He would ask Shakia later if the matter was important.

"This is a private matter, Shaman," Miakka told him at the base of his platform.

Atula went up the ladder. Miakka and Shakia followed. When they all sat, Shakia began. "I seek your help, Shaman. I did not want my husband to know."

Atula's complacent expression changed to one of worry. Was Shakia ill?

"As you know, the spirits have not given me a child," she went on. "My husband has been disappointed many times when I thought that perhaps a baby grew inside me. Again I hope I am carrying a child, but I will wait to tell Wakulla."

"You wish me to confirm your suspicions?"

"That would please me," she answered, lowering her head.

Atula told her to lie down and clear her mind. When she was ready, he began.

Miakka watched the remarkable man prepare himself. She recalled the time she had gone to him, worried about the child she carried—Mi-sa. As Atula began his chant, the song brought back many memories. She had not been this close to him in a long time.

His hands traveled in small circles just above Shakia's belly, polishing away the distance until they finally touched her skin.

With his eyes closed and his voice in song, he could see with his hands, feel the warmth from inside Shakia as it reflected back on his palms and fingers.

Inside Shakia he perceived a small, fragile form. The warm halo that surrounded and outlined the tiny but vibrant life radiated out to the shaman's hands. The ability to feel it, sense it, understand it, was part of the Gift.

From a face so solemn, so tense with concentration, with a puff of a word, a thanks to the spirits, he ended his chant and opened his eyes.

Miakka watched, studying the face she had once touched with trembling hands. It had changed, grown more rugged with time and experience. There seemed to be more depth to the black eyes, those charcoal seas of mystery.

The return of the natural sounds that had been drowned out by the magic inside the platform announced the end of the session.

"You have reason for joy," he said. "Go and tell your husband."

Shakia made sounds of happy laughter mixed with sobs and tears of happiness.

"Thank you, Shaman," she repeated over and over as she left, putting her hand to her head in respect, not noticing that Miakka lagged behind.

"You have made her very happy," Miakka said in the stillness.

"The child makes her happy—a gift from the spirits, not from me."

Miakka wanted to say so many things that she thought some of them would spill out of her. But instead neither of them could say anything as they stood looking at each other. For a moment the air seemed alive, charged with the energy they contained.

Miakka raised the back of her hand to her forehead, head bowed, eyes looking at the floor, as she backed to the ladder.

Atula opened his mouth even as he held his breath, ready to speak, to call to her, to ask her to wait. His body leaned into the air, ready to step toward her, to reach out and touch her.

But Miakka never saw him.

Chapter Twenty-five

THE PEARLY LIGHT OF MORNING crept through the thatch, pricking the inside of Miakka's platform with sharp needles of light. Miakka shifted. A splinter had poked its way through the deer hide that lay under her mat, also working its way through the weave of the mat and finally into the flesh of her hip.

Miakka twitched and then started. She sat up, pulled up her mat and deerskin, and ran her hand carefully over the lashed-log floor, feeling for the sliver. When it poked her palm, she grabbed it and ripped it away, then tossed it out of her bed. She swatted at several mosquitoes that landed on her arms. Was this the way her day was going to be?

She lay back down, her slim body feeling the hardness of her bed, unable to find a comfortable position. It was light anyway. Time to get up. Giving in, she gathered some of her grooming things, put them in a basket she had woven from rushes, and walked to the cenote.

Before entering the water, she removed her skirt and checked the bank. A cantankerous moccasin eyed her. She looked around for a long branch, but the best she could come up with was a stick from the bay tree that stood nearby. She needed to encourage the snake to move away into the brush, not into the water where she was going to bathe. This meant she had to come up on him from behind, from in the water.

Miakka took the stick with her and made a wide circle, ending up in the edge of the water. She was careful not to slosh and give the snake warning. It had not turned to see her. Miakka lunged forward with the stick, jabbing the heavy-bodied nearly black water snake. The moccasin turned, but instead of slithering off, frightened, it stood its ground, opening its mouth to show the white lining as it gaped at her.

Maybe she would have to give the snake its claimed territory. He didn't seem anxious to leave. The woman looked at the length of the stick and comparatively judged the length of the snake if it uncoiled itself. The stick was too short. The snake was long enough so that, if she prodded it and it decided to strike, which a moccasin would probably do, it would be able to reach her.

Miakka suddenly caught a glimpse of something moving in the brush behind the snake. It was a man—Tican, she thought. He motioned to her to keep the snake's attention. Miakka slapped the water with the stick. The serpent opened its mouth again, flaunting its deadliness, as if taunting her. Tican came from the cover of the brush and ran a long stick under the snake, quickly flipping it down the bank into the thick bushes away from the women's bathing place.

"Tican, it is you," she said as she saw him come toward her.

"It has been a long time since I have visited your village. I remember the last time."

"You look wonderful. The passing of so many seasons has been favorable to you," she told him. "I heard that you had found a wife. The news made me happy in my heart. I hope she has been a good wife to you."

"She was," he answered.

Miakka stepped out of the water. "Was?"

"Two summers ago the spirits called her to the Other Side."

"I am sorry, Tican. I hope your grief has eased," she said, lowering her eyes with genuine concern and sympathy.

"It eases but never leaves. The children miss their mother. They live with her sister, but it is not the same."

"Of course not," she said, walking closer.

"But I must continue."

Miakka just listened, unsure of what she should say.

"I have decided to take another wife."

"Are you ready to do that?"

"Yes. I have given it much thought. It is not too soon."

"We should be pleased that you come to our village. Do many come with you?"

"Two canoes."

"There are some very nice young women in our village."

"For the others, perhaps. I am too old, though I like to entertain the idea," he said, chuckling.

"Any woman, young or old, would enjoy your attention."

Tican was mute. He looked as though he wanted to speak but did not.

"And what brought you to the cenote? Why are you not with the others? And," she added curiously as she noted the earliness of the day, "when did you leave your village?"

"We left before the sun rose. We must be anxious."

Miakka smiled at him. "You flatter our women." She slapped at a pesky mosquito and saw that Tican was doing the same. "They seem especially thick lately. Even the oils do not hold them back."

"Come," he said. "I will walk you back."

"But I just got here—for my morning bath. First I had to get rid of the snake, but now that you have done that I can bathe."

"I did not mean to interrupt you. I walked alone by the water, not ready to join the others." Tican paused. "It is difficult for me. I have not looked for a woman in many, many seasons."

"I understand. You do not need to explain."

"I ramble. I apologize." He started again. "I saw you and our unpleasant friend. Now I find that I have interfered with your bath."

"You need not apologize for anything. I told you, I first had to drive off the snake. You did that task for me. I am the one who has been neglectful. I should have thanked you. I am glad that you came. Moccasins," she said with a huff of breath, emphasizing her distaste for the creatures. "I do not trust them. Even though they swim with their heads out of the water so that you can see them, I do not want one near the water where I bathe."

Other women could now be seen coming down the path. "You will have company," he said, looking at them and hearing their chatter.

"Not really," she remarked.

Tican was perplexed by her comment. "I will ask you about that later," he said as he walked away.

Miakka rushed through her bathing routine, eager to get away from the gathering women. She usually came early enough to be finishing up as the others arrived. Bathing alone had made her a little anxious at first—the snakes and alligators always worried her—but it was better than enduring the snubbing she got from the women.

She repacked her basket, wrung out her hair, and walked the path back to the village. She would repeat the routine in the early evening. She found it difficult to sleep if her body was still coated with the residue of the day and the sourness of perspiration. It was a habit she had passed on to her daughter.

She passed Mi-sa on the way back. "You are late this morning," she said.

"Yes, but Shakia is just behind me. I will stay near her."

"Good," her mother said. "Did you see the men who have come?"

"Yes, I saw some of them. Why have they come so early?"

"Tican says it is because they are so anxious."

Mi-sa smiled at her mother's answer. Then she realized fully that Miakka had mentioned Tican.

"Tican?"

"He has lost his wife and feels it is time to seek another."

"He comes for you, Mother."

"That was long ago. I do not think so. We are like old friends. It is your turn now, Mi-sa. The men come to see the young maidens. Wait until they see you."

Shakia caught up. "Can she stay by you?" Miakka asked.

"Do you think you need to ask?"

Miakka looked at Shakia's stomach. "Hmm. I think it does pouch," she said, commenting on Shakia's rounding middle. "In the time of one moon cycle, the child has grown. Is it not the most wonderful feeling?"

Shakia lovingly touched her protruding abdomen. "It is the most incredible feeling." She took Mi-sa's hand and held it against the swell. "He moves inside."

Mi-sa's face lit up. "Yes, I feel it. Little ripples from inside you."

"They might feel little to you, but from the inside they feel much stronger. At first they were just small flutterings, like being brushed with butterfly wings. Wakulla sleeps with his hand on my belly."

"I am so happy for you," Miakka said.

"One day it will be you, Mi-sa," Shakia said, grinning at the young woman. "One day. Take a close look at the men who came today. One of them may be the one for you."

"Maybe," Mi-sa said shyly.

"Maybe," Miakka agreed with a nod. She kissed her daughter's forehead and continued up the path.

————

THE VILLAGE WAS BUZZING. The young women gave special attention to their grooming, fingering the tangles from their long hair, brushing their friends' hair with bound stiff grasses. They spread berry juice on their lips, adding rich color. They made fresh skirts that still had the green hue and velvety texture in the twirls and curling tendrils of the air plant moss. On themselves they splashed water in which aromatic flower petals had been steeped. They painted midnight-black circles around their clear young eyes. They threaded shell beads through their long hair, an occasional feather garnishing the strand, floating on the small currents of air the wearers stirred as they moved.

The visiting men had oiled their bodies so they gleamed and shone in the sunlight. The village became the scene of glistening bodies, flirtatious smiles, and dangling, jingling shells. Necklaces of pink and orange mother-of-pearl, pendants of lustrous columellae of conch, large polished and carved ornaments of shell, tortoiseshell, and bone hung from their necks, their wrists, their ankles, and their belts. The young men paraded around in their plaited palmetto-strip breechclouts, dapper raccoon tails at the back, bobbing and swinging as they strutted.

The young women giggled at the show, whispering to one another and secretly smiling at the man they found most handsome.

Mi-sa kept back, staying near her platform. Cherok encouraged her to move about, to let the young men see her.

"No, Cherok. I do not think I can do that. I am too self-conscious. Look how silly the girls behave. I cannot do that. Besides, I have no one to giggle with."

"But once the men see you, they will not look at the others."

Mi-sa protested, embarrassed. "Cherok, you and Mother and Shakia—"

"Come with me. I will escort you to the plaza. Mi-sa, it is time. You are a woman."

Mi-sa reluctantly followed Cherok. Only the eligible young maidens circulated around the central hearth. The mothers and grandmothers looked on, some remembering their first experiences.

Miakka was inside the platform when Cherok led Mi-sa away. She felt tense and apprehensive as she watched. Her stomach eased as she saw that Mi-sa was laughing with Cherok. Miakka climbed down the ladder and edged her way closer.

Cherok introduced Mi-sa to some young warriors he knew from previous visits. The men listened respectfully to Cherok, knowing that he was to be the next shaman.

But after each introduction the man turned away politely, but definitely uninterested. At first Cherok thought nothing of it and soothed Mi-sa. But as the introductions continued, it became more and more obvious that the young men wanted nothing to do with her.

"They have heard, Cherok," she whispered, tugging on his arm to take her away.

"Wait, Mi-sa. Let me find—"

"No more, Cherok. Please walk away with me. Now."

Miakka had been watching. A weight sat in the pit of her stomach as she watched Cherok and Mi-sa walk toward her.

"Mi-sa?" Miakka asked, wanting to know if she was all right.

"I am fine, Mother. Cherok tried, but they have heard something about me. They are not interested."

Miakka wanted to hold her and rock her as she had done when her daughter was little; but Mi-sa was a woman, not a child. Every muscle inside Miakka ached to hold her, to comfort her, to take away the humiliation and the pain. If only she could suffer it for her.

"Do not look so upset, Mother. Really, I am fine. I must have anticipated the men's reaction." She paused and looked back. "Look, Mother. Tican is calling to you."

Miakka proudly studied her daughter. She was no longer the little girl who cried in her arms when she hurt. She could not kiss away the kind of pain Mi-sa knew as a woman.

Miakka looked where Mi-sa pointed. Without speaking out loud, Tican motioned for her.

"I would be pleased if you went to speak with him. He looks like a sad little boy," Mi-sa said.

Cherok nodded to Miakka.

Miakka did not want to go. She wanted to be with her

daughter, but her presence might call too much attention to the situation, she decided.

Tican smiled when he saw her coming.

"Perhaps we should walk away from the crowd of young people," he said when she got close to him.

Miakka did not object, and the man led her away.

"Mi-sa has grown to be a lovely young woman."

"She is beautiful and a kind and gentle person. She has qualities—qualities that should be admired."

"And they are not?"

"Much has happened since you last came, Tican. I do not know where to start," she said, stopping a moment and looking at him.

"I have heard."

"Mi-sa has never done anything other than be born during an attack by the A-po-la-chee."

Miakka's voice was bitter. She had long ago stopped crying whenever she spoke about her daughter.

Tican's eyes were soft and sympathetic.

"I am sorry, Tican. I do not wish to speak harshly to you. Mi-sa has suffered so much. Did you see what happened today?" she asked but did not wait for an answer. "We have endured so much, and I believe the torment will never end."

Tican silently urged her to walk again, circling the cenote on the less traveled paths. His body and face told her that he did not challenge her, that he accepted her explanation and did not want more. He led her close to the water and brushed away some debris, clearing a spot for them to sit.

Miakka sat next to him as he pitched a twig into the still water. They watched the ripples spread out and disappear.

"I am sorry for all the misery you have suffered. It

hurts me to know of your pain," he said, still not looking at her. Again he tossed a small stick into the water and then turned to look at her and speak. His words were kind and his voice gentle. "All this time there has been a special place in my heart for you. When I was a young man, you were my dream. I took every chance I had to see you, even if from afar—to hear your voice, to watch you. I do not think you ever knew how enchanted I was with you."

Miakka looked down, embarrassed by his words. "But that was long ago, and you found a wife."

"You did not see me because you did not look. Your eyes were only for someone else. It became quite clear to me that I could never have you, that I was wasting my time, my youth. It took a long time for me to finally understand that. Yes, I found a wife, and I loved her. But my heart kept a hidden place saved only for you."

He paused, hoping that she would speak, but she did not. She looked at him with eyes full of pain.

"I could make you happy. I am a good man."

"Oh, Tican, I know that you are a good and wonderful man."

"Then hear what I have to say. This is your home; I understand that. But it is not a happy place for you or for your daughter. If you stay here, you will suffer for the rest of your lives. I know that you do not feel about me as strongly as I feel about you, but I could make you happy. Be my wife. I will take you and Mi-sa far away to a place where no one knows you, a place where Mi-sa will have a chance at happiness."

Miakka looked up at Tican as he brushed her cheek with his fingertips. She started to speak, but he put his finger over her lips.

"Do not answer yet. Weigh what I have said. I

promise not to press you." Tican stood. "Let me take you back to the plaza. We will stay in your village for a few more days and nights."

Miakka reached out and took his hand as they walked.

———

CHEROK STOOD BENEATH an aromatic sweet bay tree, leaning against the smooth gray trunk. He looked up toward its narrow, rounded crown and picked one of its shiny green leaves. He turned the leaf in his fingers, from the glowing green of the topside to the whitish underside.

He brushed a mosquito away from Mi-sa's face. "I would take you as my wife," he said. "I would do anything to spare you. But I do not think we would be granted permission. We are from the same clan. Your father is mine. That is too much taboo. And when the time comes for me to take the responsibility of shaman, you would be alone again. I have thought about it."

"I love you, Cherok," she said, kissing his cheek.

"You would never have to worry about being cared for and provided for. We would not share a bed."

"As you said, we would never be granted permission. It is not a real option. And it would be only a temporary solution. Once you become shaman—"

"Perhaps I should not …"

"You should not what?" she asked, confused by his statement.

"Become the shaman."

"Cherok, what are you talking about?"

"Mi-sa, you know there is something missing. I have told you many times. I am afraid that when the time comes, I will not be able to serve the People. I do not have the Gift—only little pieces of it. I merely come close, sometimes."

"Developing the Gift takes time and training."

"You have heard the stories of Atula when he was a child and the ways he showed signs so early. They are incredible stories, full of power and prophecy."

"Everyone is different," Mi-sa said. "And you do have the Gift. I have seen it."

"I do not sleep sometimes. I have dreams. Terrible dreams. I wake up sweating and breathing hard. I dream that I fail the People. I think my dreams are some kind of visions."

"No, they are not visions. They are your fears. All of us dream about things we are afraid of. Those are nightmares. That is all."

Cherok picked one of the immature cone fruits. "At the change of seasons," he said, "this will turn red, an indication of its maturity, of its readiness. Do you see how simple everything is? Even the plants have signs. I do not have any sign of readiness."

"Atula will know when you are ready. Everyone has faith in you, Cherok. Do not doubt yourself."

Cherok picked a small spidery flower from its long stem. It was fragrant, its green and yellow petals striped with deep purple. "You use this sometimes to scent water and splash yourself with, is that not so?"

"Yes," she answered him, curiosity and bewilderment evident in her voice.

"But did you know that a decoction of the crushed petals and bulb given to a woman who bleeds too heavily after childbirth will slow the blood flow? And this," he said as he pulled a plant from the soil, roots and all, "can be boiled down and added to fat to make a good healing salve. But be careful not to include the fruit or it will be an irritant."

Mi-sa followed him as he walked rapidly toward

another short tree with clusters of white flowers. "And this. Do you want to know all the different ways this can be prepared and what medicine each recipe will yield? And each of those recipes has different words to be said, different songs to sing. None of the medicines are good without the songs."

"Why are you telling me these things, Cherok? I do not understand."

"Because these are things a shaman must know. Atula has taught me. I memorize what he says. I say the words over and over to myself. I spend days and days practicing, committing the lessons to memory. Then I come out here alone, and I see a plant that I should know, and I cannot remember what it is for or how to prepare it or the words that go with it. A shaman knows. He doesn't forget. That is why he has the Gift."

Cherok picked at the thin coppery bark of a gumbo-limbo tree, flaking away pieces of the shiny skin. "And this tree—it has so many uses I cannot remember them all."

"There is still time, Cherok. Atula will continue to teach you. Every day you will become more and more ready. You have heard Atula. He knows that with each generation the Gift grows weaker. He tells the stories of how much more potent was his father, Ochassee. He, too, fears that one day the Gift will be washed over."

Cherok looked at her and smiled. "I took you away from the crowd to ease your troubles, but I have told you mine."

"Have we not always shared with one another our deepest, our most frightening, our most wonderful thoughts? Besides, you did an impressive job of making me forget my small unhappiness."

Mi-sa slapped his shoulder, surprising him. "A

mosquito," she said. They both laughed but knew that the things that ate at each of them were not resolved.

Chapter Twenty-six

MIAKKA LIKED THE FEELING of a man's strong hand holding hers. It made her feel safe, content, able to let down some of her defenses.

It was pleasant to be wanted, needed, and loved. Tican was such a gentle man. She did like him, and he did make some valid points. Yes, she was fond of him, she thought, turning her head to look at him as they walked into the village. Perhaps this feeling would flower if she let it. He had been right. Her eyes had always been for someone else. It was time she let go of those things that never could be.

Tican stopped and took her other hand, turning her to face him. "I would be a good husband. I will not ask anything of you that you are uncomfortable with. It would be enough to be near you, to provide and care for you. Do you understand what I am trying to say?" he asked, hoping she realized he would not insist on taking her to his bed if she did not also feel the desire. He didn't want to seem too bold in raising such a delicate subject.

Miakka rose up on her toes, stretching to reach him, and softly kissed his cheek. "I am envious of the seasons your wife had with you."

Tican looked to the crowd of young people at the center of the village. "Can we spend the day quietly? I am too old for such antics."

"I would like that," she answered.

———

ATULA STOOD NEXT TO WAKULLA and Shakia, watching the gallant warriors and coquettish maidens. Two other figures beyond the crowd caught his attention. His heart lurched when he saw their hands, like lovers' hands, fingers entwined; as they walked together. When had this happened? How? He had not seen Tican for so long. And had he not heard that Tican had a wife?

He watched the couple walk toward Miakka's hearth. Suddenly Atula realized how much time had passed since he had last held her, touched her, smelled her hair and skin. He had always thought their separation was temporary. They were just waiting for the right time. But now he realized the right time had never come and probably never would. Seeing her with Tican stung. That man had so much more to offer her. He—Atula—could not let Miakka go away with Tican.

He looked across the mound and saw Kachumpka standing near his mother. He swayed, his large tongue protruding from his open mouth. Atula waved away a buzzing mosquito and swatted others that landed and stung his legs. He looked back at Kachumpka—gnats seemed to create a cloud near the boy's face. Amakollee had been misled by the child's deficits. As Kachumpka had become an adolescent, the clan only humored Amakollee, smiling and listening to her claims. But they still did not rebuke her. There remained that thread, that possibility, that Kachumpka was the true child with the Gift, or at least some supernatural connection. Amakollee would never let them challenge her claims.

Atula turned to his son, the cacique.

"Wakulla, excuse yourself from your wife and come with me."

Wakulla looked blankly at Atula.

"I must speak to you about a matter of importance," Atula said.

"Is it so urgent? Can it wait until later?"

"No," Atula answered.

Shakia squeezed her husband's hand. She, too, had seen Miakka with Tican, but unlike Atula, she was pleased by the sight.

The cacique and the shaman trod the paths that coiled around the village. Shield ferns banked the depressions that the people had worn in the earth.

"Though you are my son, I wish you to listen with the ears of the cacique, for I do not want you to suffer any anguish over what I am about to say. As Jegatua and I watched you grow to a man, we noticed those things that make you a good leader. As I watched you, I have also watched Cherok. I have already begun his training. I have not yet told him all of the secrets, but I can do so soon. Cherok is anxious to learn. He is a good choice to become shaman."

Wakulla twisted his mouth and eyes, forming quizzical lines across his face. Why was Atula speaking about this now? What was making Atula feel rushed to complete Cherok's training? he wondered. "The heir to the position of shaman is not a choice that men make," he stated.

"Look at those who come from my seed. Cherok is the only one, the only choice. If Micco had been the chosen one, the spirits would not have called him to the Other Side. He would have been allowed to fulfill his destiny."

"I agree with you. I accept Cherok. Why do you present this argumentatively?"

"Because the time is here. It is time for me to pass the responsibility to someone else."

"I do not understand. Why this sudden urgency?"

"I will tell you because you are cacique, but this information is not for the rest of the clan."

"I will keep it to myself," Wakulla responded.

"I want to take Miakka and Mi-sa away from here. Mi-sa is not living a full life. She is dying. The People will never allow her to live as long as she is here." Atula paused. "And I fear that I will lose her mother to another. Tican has come for her. If the People had not misunderstood Mi-sa's sign and listened to Amakollee's vicious talk, Miakka would have been my woman. But our relationship gave credence to all the rumors that the People had heard. For Mi-sa's sake Miakka and I ended our relationship, but..."

"But you never ended it in your heart," Wakulla finished for him.

"She will never sacrifice Mi-sa, and I cannot either. I have seen Miakka today with Tican. He will persuade her to go with him, to be his wife."

"You wish to relinquish the position of shaman to Cherok? I question if your heart leads your head. I understand your emotions, but you are shaman. Like the atala, the beautiful black and orange butterfly that feeds only on coontie, you feed only on spiritual food. That is the way the spirits made you. The Gift is not something you can toss away at the whim of your heart."

———

WHEN THE TWO MEN HAD WALKED AWAY, Shakia followed the path to Miakka's platform. She saw the two sitting in the cool shadow of the shelter. Perhaps she was intruding, but her visit was well intended.

Miakka and Tican looked up as Shakia began to speak. "You two smile with eyes that hold secrets." She waited a moment, hoping that Miakka would confirm her hopes. "It is so good that you have come, Tican," she began again.

"It is good to see you and Miakka once again. And what is this that I notice? You carry a child?"

Shakia relaxed the muscles that girdled her, pushing her belly out even farther.

MI-SA LEFT CHEROK to visit with her mother and Tican. Cherok saw Atula from a distance. He was walking away from Wakulla. Today Cherok was to practice the ritual that would be performed tonight. It was not very complicated, more dramatic and flamboyant than significant and profound, a mirthful ceremony that would launch the night dancing. It would set the mood for the young men and women as the courtships progressed. If only all the shaman's duties were so simple.

"Atula," he called as he got closer. "Is this a good time?"

Atula hesitated and then consented. "Come to my hearth, away from all this activity where we can concentrate."

At the base of Atula's platform, the shaman began to demonstrate the steps of the dance, leaving his arms still and the chant unsung. "One step at a time."

Cherok watched, but his mind drifted. He moved his feet, mimicking the steps of his father.

"Cherok, where are you? Your feet obey, but there is no enthusiasm, no exaggeration in your steps, no amplitude in your posture. Make your movements more clearly defined, like this."

Atula's movements were sharp and clean. The

sculpture of his muscled legs and the precision of his confident steps were magnified when he added the arm movements, great sweeping motions, ruggedly graceful, turning, curling, extending, stretching.

Cherok did not move but watched in awe. He knew that though his execution was accurate, he lacked the charisma of a shaman.

Atula stopped. "It comes from inside. Work, Cherok," he said, sounding a little annoyed.

Again Cherok performed the dance, but as he watched his father, he saw Mi-sa in his imagination. Those easy, fluid, flowing movements were hers.

"Again," Atula said, pushing Cherok with the tone of his voice. "Do it alone. Let me watch."

Cherok started, stepping, hunching, and straightening, gradually adding arm movements.

"Feel the dance, Cherok. Let the ritual overwhelm you," Atula said before breaking into the rhythmic chant that accompanied the dance. He joined Cherok, moving with the warm air as if the wind were the blood that coursed through him.

"Stop," Atula ordered. He could see that there was no improvement. "Why is this so difficult? It is a simple dance. You know all the steps, all the movements, all the words, but you do not perform them, live them, feel them. You have to understand this. You are too old to play games and not take your training seriously. Those days are gone."

Cherok looked confused. Atula had always been patient and encouraging.

"I am trying, Shaman. I will do it again."

Atula tilted his head back, sighing with frustration, and then reached out and touched Cherok's shoulder. "No, not again. Sit and let me talk to you, not as an instructor but as a man."

Cherok lowered himself to the ground, sitting across from his father.

"My father left this world early in his life," Atula said. "I was afraid. Being the shaman is quite a responsibility. I was afraid that I did not know enough. That possibility still worries me. I push you so that you will learn as much as you can."

Cherok's eyebrows dipped, forming a troubled V.

"The time is here for you now, Cherok. It is not too soon for you to assume the responsibility. We have worked hard. You know almost all the secrets, all the magic."

Cherok's stomach tightened. "No, I am not ready. I know too little."

"You know even more than I did when Ochassee died."

Cherok stood up and began to pace. "I know the plants. I know the words. I know the steps to the dances. But the knowledge does not come from inside me, as it does for you. It comes from my head because I practice, practice, practice. You know and remember from somewhere inside. The skills come easily, naturally, as they do to Mi-sa. Those things you want from me, expect from me—"

"Mi-sa?"

Cherok was startled that he had mentioned her name but perhaps the truth had to be told. "Mi-sa has the magic. Your magic. I have always seen the Gift in her. On the night of her naming ceremony, I saw it in her eyes. She takes me with her."

The truth came flooding from Cherok, spilling like dammed water that had at last found its release. "When I am with her, she helps me do the things that you want from me. I cannot do these things without her. I get so close, and once when Mi-sa was little and so sick, I thought I was able to travel outside my body alone, but even then the skill was hers. She was the light in the darkness."

Atula sat, stunned, as Cherok sat down again.

"Why have you not said this to me before?" Atula inquired.

"What would the People have thought if I had told them that Mi-sa has magic? My words would only have confirmed what they had been saying—that she is evil, that she is in touch with evil spirits."

"Perhaps your imagination makes you believe she has the Gift. You and Mi-sa are very close."

Cherok began to list the times that Mi-sa had helped him see things, know things, and the times she had taken him from his body. He spoke of the many events that had made him recognize her magic.

"It is not evil that resides in her. It is goodness," Cherok ended.

"These are powerful things you say."

"I am glad that I have told you at last. So often I have wanted to."

"Mi-sa is special to you, is she not?"

"I cannot explain the connection between us. It is more than friendship."

"Then it is a good thing that you have spoken. If what you say is true, and if the rest of the clan finds out ... well, you understand how terrible that will be. Mi-sa already lives as an outcast. I think you will be glad to hear what I have to say now. It is even more important that you be ready to become the shaman. I want to take Miakka and Mi-sa away from here. That will be best for Mi-sa. You must admit that. And I have spent a lifetime wanting to have Miakka as my woman. That would be impossible here, because of Mi-sa. I am ready to turn the position of shaman over to you."

"But I am not ready."

"You must be ready. I am going to leave, and you must serve the People. They depend on you."

"But I will fail. Something is missing in me. Just as no one can explain what is missing in Kachumpka that would make him a man, I cannot explain what is missing in me that would make me a shaman—a good shaman."

"You are frightened, just as I was. Do not let those doubts govern you. This is a test. Everything is a test. Accept your responsibility. You are the fruit of my seed. Can you deny that?"

Cherok stared at his father. He was right. There was no one else. If his father left, he would have to become shaman. That was his destiny.

"Perhaps it is just too soon. I need more time. As you have said, the Gift becomes weaker with each generation."

"Circumstances indicate that this is the time. I must take Miakka and Mi-sa away now."

Atula stood up. Cherok would make himself accept the situation. That was the kind of man he was. Atula was proud of him. Later he would speak to Miakka, when Tican was not present.

"Practice some more, alone," he told Cherok. "Do not let yourself be inhibited. Let yourself go. Become a part of the dance. You can. I know it. Tonight you will have a chance to show us all."

Cherok's heart skipped a beat as he stood and placed the back of his hand to his forehead in respect for the departing shaman.

"I will be ready," he forced himself to say.

Chapter Twenty-seven

TO THE WEST THE SKY CHURNED, gathering deep gray clouds that sped across the sky, rushing to the sea. The hot wind suddenly became cool and charged with the storm that brewed.

The People kept an eye on the sky as they finished their daily chores. Tican dipped a shell ladle into the pot by the central hearth and then drank from it. It was a good soup made from turtle stock. Always this large pot was accessible to anyone who was hungry. Mealtimes were not set. The clan ate when their stomachs told them to. If a hunter had been unlucky, the community kept him fed by always providing food at the central hearth. But never was a man so lazy that he did not hunt for himself and give a portion of his kill to the clan. Disgrace and dishonor would have resulted from such behavior. The clan always provided something to fill a hungry stomach, and so there was no greed or selfishness when it came to food.

Visitors were also welcome to partake of the food. A few of the young men who had come with Tican also took broth from the pot. They talked in low voices, prattling on about their flirtatious adventures, sometimes laughing and poking at one another in jest.

A sudden gust of wind turned their smiles to worried

frowns. "I hope the storm does not ruin the evening," said a man who held the ladle and scanned the dark sky.

"It may pass us by," another added.

———

CAUTIOUSLY, AS THE SKY DARKENED with the sunset and the looming storm, the people of the village and the visiting men began to gather. Lightning flashed in the distance in fleeting spurts of brilliance that illuminated the pearly gray clouds, outlining them with opalescent silver.

The young maidens lined up, their families behind them. Across from them, the suitors arranged themselves. Between them stood Atula. He wore merry colors—purple feathers of the gallinule, dark blue slashes outlined in white across his chest and arms. In front of him, hanging over his breechclout was the fur of a fox, front legs and head dangling down, dancing their own dance as he began the ritual. Trailing from his wrists were fox tails, swooping through the air as he danced.

At first the tempo was slow, but then Atula picked up his pace. The dance was light and fun, and the shaman smiled, as did the crowd. The chant was cheerful with no plaintive sounds, and it rolled pleasantly from his tongue.

At the end he stopped to catch his breath, but before losing the crowd's attention he motioned Cherok forward.

"I will do the dance again," he announced. "This time Cherok will dance and sing with me. Watch and see what the spirits prepare for our future. Cherok?" he asked. "Are you ready?"

Cherok nodded. He should have smiled, should have been happy that the shaman had invited him to participate. The invitation was an honor, a show of confidence and pride on Atula's part. But he could hot smile. He was afraid, but not of the dance.

The apprentice began taking small steps, moving in precision with Atula.

Cacema was filled with pride, and the rest of the clan felt the excitement that Cherok should have experienced. He was good. He did not hesitate. His eyes were closed, and he remembered the dance and the words without help.

He had worked all afternoon, performing the dance and saying the words over and over. He had said prayers, asked the spirits to help him perform admirably.

When the dance was finished, Atula embraced Cherok proudly, and then made him face the crowd so that he could see their approval.

The clan was smiling, shouting compliments and cries of praise.

"You see," Atula said to his son.

Cherok smiled at him, but it was an empty smile.

Shakia and Miakka called out with the rest, commending the young man. They walked toward Cacema, intending to offer their praise for Cherok.

"You should go. You know that, do you not?" Shakia said to Miakka as they drifted through the crowd.

"Go where?" Miakka asked, turning to look at her friend.

"With Tican."

"And how do you know that he has asked?"

"Of course he has. You are foolish if you deny him again."

Miakka took Shakia by the arm and stopped walking. "He is a good man, but I am uncertain."

"Do you love your daughter? Think of it that way. Tican is offering her a chance for a better life. How fortunate to have that opportunity."

"You are right. For Mi-sa it is the right thing to do. I have not even discussed it with her."

"Do not let her know that you go with Tican for her sake. She will never leave if she thinks you sacrifice for her. You must convince her that Tican, not her father, is the man in your heart."

"Shakia, I do love Tican, in a way, but not like—"

"That was when you were young and full of youth and passion. Tican can give you more than that."

"If I turn him away, he will never come back. I will have to answer him before he leaves."

"Tell him and then tell Mi-sa. Make your plans."

"I will tell him in the morning."

Shakia breathed out a frustrated sigh. "Why wait? You torture the man."

"I must be sure. In the morning I will give him my answer. Then there will be no chance of changing it."

"Nothing will happen between now and the morning to change your mind. I think you are just putting off the decision."

"Maybe," Miakka answered. "But marriage is a commitment for a lifetime. It is worth one night's thought."

"As long as you make the right decision."

"Come. Let us speak to Cacema before she thinks we have bad manners."

They told Cacema what a fine shaman Cherok was going to make, how proud she should be, and how fortunate the clan was to have him.

Amakollee stood in the distance. She had watched the shameless flaunting of Atula's choice. She stroked her son's head as he stood next to her. Kachumpka smiled at all the merriment, the movement, the color.

"You should be the next shaman. Can you not feel the

injustice? Why do the spirits not give you the inclination to argue and claim what is yours?"

Kachumpka rocked sideways, then back and forth, as if he had not heard his mother.

"Kachumpka," she said, touching his chin and directing him to look at her. She gazed into her son's eyes. There was no response. "Never mind. Enjoy watching the festivities," she said and walked away. When would the spirits let themselves be known? She was tiring, and though she tried to contain her emotions, she often felt angry and resentful. Still she helped Kachumpka through his daily activities. She was afraid that one day she would not be able to carry on. Every time she thought of her son as a burden she was overwhelmed with guilt. For days she offered prayers, going through her rituals and routines that she felt made her remorse known to and forgiven by the spirits. Over and over she performed the same meticulous and reverent tasks, sometimes forgetting to eat.

Kachumpka was usually patient, sitting, watching, humming, and mumbling. Tonight he followed her to the platform where she started her rituals again. She lit a small torch to light the inside of the shelter. Usually she did not carry fire into her house. One spark and it would go up in flame. But tonight she needed to be able to see.

Amakollee spread the contents of her medicine bag on the floor in front of her. Her son sat on his mat, watching. She told the story behind each article. She respectfully thanked the spirits. But when she was almost done, Kachumpka grumbled something to her, distracting her.

"Quiet," she blurted. "Now I will have to start over. You have ruined it."

Kachumpka frowned and uttered a strangled

complaint. "The mosquitoes," he mumbled, clawing at his arms and legs. They were covered with welts from mosquito bites. He looked at his mother's sour expression. "I am sorry," he said, pouting. His words were difficult to understand because his mouth and tongue did not cooperate in making clear sounds.

"I know. I know," she told him apologetically. She should not get so short-tempered and angry with him.

Amakollee started over after telling Kachumpka to remain still and quiet until she spoke to him again. He agreed, indicating with a nod of his head that he understood.

The music and noise outside seemed to grow louder and intrude on her quiet private mission. She would never be finished if they continued to be so loud. She couldn't think, couldn't concentrate. Too much distraction. Again she started and soon stumbled over her words. She slammed her hand down on the floor, clenching her teeth and growling.

A moment later Amakollee closed her eyes and breathed in and out, slow and easy, controlling her breath, restraining her anger.

"Later," she said aloud. "When all is quiet and you are sleeping," she said, turning to look at Kachumpka.

She smiled eerily, as if-convincing some invisible audience of her composure. "Now is not a good time." Her voice was nearly a whisper. Kachumpka leaned forward to hear her better, but his mother did not repeat herself. She crawled over to him and began to stroke his back. Kachumpka stretched out on his mat.

MI-SA HAD STAYED AWAY from the festivities. If no one saw her, perhaps she would be out of their minds. She was quite comfortable sitting by the dying embers of the small fire at her hearth, and the smoke helped keep the mosquitoes away. She had heard Atula's song and could feel his dance. It frightened her because something stirred inside her. She felt as though she had done the dance before. Though the shaman was obscured by the crowd and the distance, she imagined each step, each movement. Her arms wanted to move and her lips formed some of the words of the chant. It was good that she was away from the rest so that no one saw her. Surely if she'd been seen she would have caused quite a disturbance.

The music had pleased her. She felt light and happy. The music and the words had set a mood of frivolity and glee. She had the greatest compulsion to dance, to bend and dive, to soar and swing through the air. Certain words beckoned her to stretch, to reach into the night sky, while other phrases made her feel like plunging close to the ground. Moving as Atula did was such a natural state, she thought. But for her to do so would have been outrageous.

Mi-sa was happy to see Cherok approaching. She would enjoy his company.

"I heard your voice with Atula's," she said when he was close enough.

She expected to see him smiling, but as the firelight lit his face she saw lines of strain.

He wished that he could talk to her about Atula's decision, but he knew that he could not. Atula had not spoken with Miakka. And Cherok did agree that for Mi-sa it was a very good decision. He could not burden her with his concerns—his fear that he would fail, that the People would have no proper link to the spirits, that they would fall into some black abyss and become people with no spirits. The thoughts made him shudder.

"Why are you not smiling, Cherok? Tonight must have

been exciting for you."

"I am exhausted. I put much effort into the dance and song. Now I need some peace. I need to be with my friend."

Mi-sa could see that he was troubled, that he was keeping things from her. She would not ask. If and when he wished to discuss his problem with her, he would. She would not pry and make him uncomfortable. Perhaps all he did need was peace. Telling old stories and recalling silly events would be a most pleasant way to spend the evening.

———

MIAKKA FACED TICAN. In the last band of firelight, he had found her as she retreated from Cacema, Shakia, and the rest.

"There is some coolness in the air tonight. The season gets ready to change, a small reminder that nothing stays the same," he said to her. "The cool air will put an end to the mosquitoes."

Miakka sniffed, looking for the crispness that usually rode the cooler air. "Too much smoke and too many warm bodies."

"The storm did not come. Such a big threat, full of false pride. It had all the signs of being quite a thunderstorm. I lost track of it when the sun disappeared."

Still in the distance there were broad flashes of flickering light in the sky, but no thunder. The storm had passed them and unleashed its fury somewhere else.

"I have thought about your proposal. I do not want you to think that I have not. I wish to give you my answer in the morning."

The corners of Tican's mouth turned up.

Chapter Twenty-eight

TALASEE BANKED THE FIRE at the central hearth for the last time. It would survive the night. He was usually the last to retire.

Cherok did not sleep. He needed to find a better answer. He wanted to feel things from the inside—like Atula, like Mi-sa. He prayed that the spirits would show him the way and give him the answer. Soon. Very soon.

Atula crossed the mound, surprising his friend Talasee.

"If the fire had been lower, I would not have seen you coming, Atula," he said. "Even in this light, you made me flinch."

"Why do you start at the sight of a friend?" Atula asked, curious about Talasee's nervousness.

"One of our visitors tells of trouble to the north."

"Tell me more," Atula said, sitting and watching Talasee hurl another heavy log into the fire.

"He says a group of young warriors on the way to the Big Water found a man who is one of our tribe—from a clan to the north of us. The warriors saw him lying prone on the bank of the river. They brought their canoe closer and saw that the man was bleeding, near death. They stopped to help, then took him back to their village, postponing their journey. On the way back, he whispered to them, 'A-po-la-chee.' That was all he could say. He slipped into unconsciousness."

"He could have been out of his mind. Anything could have happened to him," Atula said.

"Our visitor said they thought the same, but the man recovered. When he was well enough to speak, he said that the A-po-la-chee were moving south in a great secret arc, coming by surprise, extending their territory farther and farther this way. He had been captured, then managed to escape, but not before being bludgeoned. He said the lances and arrows and knives missed him because the spirits must have willed it. Our visitor says the man believes he was spared to warn us. He still recovers in their village."

"And that is what makes you so cautious," Atula said, understanding.

"A long time has passed since the A-po-la-chee last came here. I fear that the young ones do not know and the old ones forget. I will never put away that horrible memory. But when I watched the younger men hear the tale told by our visitor, they became excited, anxious to fight, boasting of how they would tear an A-po-la-chee limb from limb. Atula, they have no idea what an attack is really like. All they think of is the glory of the battle, and I cannot make them understand the truth."

Talasee had touched a nerve. Atula knew exactly what he was talking about, and it was frightening. "I think that we should do as we used to for a long time after the last attack. We men should gather regularly, discuss responses in case of attack, and practice our battle skills. We have been neglectful and have grown clumsy in our false complacency. If the A-po-la-chee came tonight, we would be most vulnerable. We practice only by hunting animals that cannot respond with weapons. We should post sentinels around the village, lookouts who can give us warning, the way we used to. We have grown lax."

Atula stood as Talasee dusted off his hands, finished with the chores of the fire. And then the shaman touched his friend's shoulder before bidding him to sleep well.

Talasee had given Atula a lot to think about. He would have to take care of many things tomorrow. He proceeded, walking in front of the shelters. The night was so quiet that as he passed some of the platforms, he could hear breathing, snoring, coughing, and clearing of throats. He heard a mat rustling and a throaty sigh from the home of Acopa and Tabisha. It made Atula smile. Acopa still had the fire.

As he stood at the base of Miakka's platform, he said an extra prayer to the spirits, asking them to spare him. He did not want to find her in the arms of Tican, but he had to take this chance.

He did not say anything as he climbed the ladder and went inside, then waited for his eyes to adjust. She was alone.

"Miakka," he whispered.

She turned toward the opening and saw Atula's silhouette. She sat up and pulled a small blanket over her. The air had cooled quite a bit. The season was indeed changing. She could feel her heart pound as the moonlight outlined his shining body. Her breath rushed from her, and she hoped he had not heard.

"May I come closer?" he asked.

"You may," she said, filling with memories of him whispering urgent pleas as he joined with her. She suddenly realized that he was speaking again and she had not heard his words.

"You cannot," he said.

Miakka shook her head. "Cannot?" She had missed what he had said.

"You cannot go with Tican. I will make you my woman, and our lives will be as they always should have been."

Atula knelt and leaned forward, touching nothing but her lips with his. The kiss was supposed to be brief, but his mouth was hot and wet, and he consumed her, beginning with short hungry kisses and proceeding until he could not tear his mouth from hers.

Miakka reached for him to balance herself, afraid that she would fall forward from the awkwardness of her position and the weakness that he caused in her. She wrapped her hands around his neck and buried her fingers in the thickness of his hair.

Atula tossed the coverlet away and laid her back on her mat. The texture of his masculine skin against the softness of hers was like breath to the flame. She knew him, even from so long ago—every crevice, every curve and cord of muscle, the taste of his skin, the warmth of his breath, the measure of his heartbeat.

His hands sought all those places that brought her ecstasy, and he delighted in her response. The firmness of her breasts, the silkiness of her long hair as it tangled between them, the secret indentation where her thigh joined the soft petals of her womanhood, were as he had remembered. Nothing had changed. Had he not lain against her just yesterday? Had it really been so long since he had heard her soft moans answering the touch of his hands and mouth?

He entered her, hearing her breath catch, and dared not move. He reached beneath her, lifting her to him, holding her still until his surge of urgency retreated.

"Atula," she whispered, wanting him, calling him to crush her, overpower her, let her melt away and flow into him. She loved the sound of his name as it gushed out of her when he filled her.

He answered her with his body, lowering some of his weight onto her, rocking her to the song their bodies sang until the music of their love and passion rose to crescendo.

This time he whispered her name as he fell against her.

Miakka wondered what had brought him to her tonight, but she let her curiosity go, pushed it away, at least for the moment. Right now she wanted to think of nothing but how welcome his weight was upon her, how complete she was with him.

She was afraid to speak, afraid that the magic would disappear if she broke the spell with the sound of her voice. And so she let her fingers draw delicate lines across his back until her arms finally felt too heavy to move.

They slept.

———

WHEN THE PALE SPRINKLES of early light washed through the thatch, Miakka stirred. She had never awakened to the warmth of Atula's sleepy body before. In the night he must have covered her as the air grew cooler. A blanket of fur rested over them. She stared at his sleeping face. Easy lines of confidence, wisdom, and gentleness carved his features. She snuggled closer, moving slowly and carefully, not wanting to wake him, because when he awoke she was sure he would have to leave her.

Perhaps the song of the birds or the rustling of the dry thatch in the morning breeze awakened him. He opened his eyes for a moment and then closed them, reaching out to pull her even closer. She turned as she moved so that her back lay flush against him, her body warmly seeping into all the curves of his. His face nestled in her hair, and one hand was filled with the softness of her breast.

"Can your magic make everyone else disappear?" she asked.

"If I knew that magic, it would be done," he answered, feeling the luxuriance of her hair brush his face.

Miakka turned to face him. "I am angry with myself."

Atula propped himself up on one elbow so that he looked down on her. "Perhaps what I have to tell you will take that anger from you."

"All this time I have learned to live without you," she said. "And now the wound is open again. I should have resisted—asked you to leave and hoped that you would honor my request."

"Listen to what I have to say, Miakka. I have a way. We will be together."

Miakka looked up into his eyes. What kind of plan could he possibly have? Had he forgotten Mi-sa?

"I am going to take you away. You and Mi-sa. We will go far. We will keep searching until we find a clan in which no one will turn from Mi-sa."

"But you cannot," she said. "You are the shaman. You cannot leave the People and turn your back."

"Cherok is ready to become the shaman. I can take you as my woman, my wife. We will not stay here. We will be free. We have waited long enough."

Miakka could not speak. Could this really happen? As the sun grew brighter, would this dream evaporate?

"You cannot go with Tican," he said. "I know he wants you. Tell me you will stay. Be mine."

"I have always been yours," she answered.

The loud shrill whooping of many, many voices broke the peace of the morning. Atula jumped to his feet, and Miakka sat up.

"The A-po-la-chee!" he said, stunned, scrambling down the ladder. Miakka followed, tying her skirt as she moved.

Two platforms were already ablaze, roaring with the fierce voice of the flames. Men, suddenly awake, were scuttling down the short ladders, barely touching the rungs as they sprang to the ground, weapons in hand. Frightened children ran across the mound, some screaming, some so scared that they were unable to make any sound. Mothers desperately called their children's names, running zigzag with no direction among the vividly painted A-po-la-chee as they ravaged the village.

"Mi-sa," Miakka screamed, hoping to hear her answer. The burning thatch crackled and spit when it first caught, then built to a roar. Fire-tipped arrows zinged past, some missing their targets, falling to the ground, but others impaling themselves in the platforms and in an instant setting the whole shelter ablaze, pouring smoke and noise into the air.

Amakollee pushed Kachumpka ahead of her. "Out!" she screamed, yelling at him to get down the ladder and out of the platform before it was set afire.

Kachumpka fumbled with a few of his favorite possessions, not recognizing the emergency.

"Leave it," his mother screamed again, pushing him toward the exit. "Hurry!"

Kachumpka made his way down the ladder, moving as he usually did, slowly and cautiously, afraid that he would fall. Amakollee moved right behind him, nearly stepping on his hands. "Hurry, Kachumpka. Hurry," she kept telling him.

She heard arrows stream past her. Two of them stuck in the thatch, immediately setting it ablaze. Her home was going up in flames. She could feel heat so intense it made her grimace.

She dragged Kachumpka across the mound. He

stumbled, his awkward gait slowing them as she tried to run. She pulled on his arm, tugging him, trying to speed him up. When she turned to look at him, she saw an A-po-la-chee running toward them.

Her foot caught on something, and she tumbled to the ground, crashing onto a dead warrior's body sprawled in front of her. His blood splashed on her face. Kachumpka stood over her. She reached for his hand and saw the A-po-la-chee gaining. He was nearly on top of them. He had singled them out and was coming for Kachumpka. With her free hand she grabbed the dead warrior's lance.

Amakollee kicked Kachumpka's feet from under him and pulled him down. The A-po-la-chee swung his club through the air, missing Kachumpka's head as she flung him down. She lifted the lance as the attacker tripped over Kachumpka's body and flailing feet. The attacker fell forward.

His mouth flew open as the tip of the lance broke through the flesh of his chest and forced its way through his ribs, then rammed through him and came out the other side.

The fatally wounded A-po-la-chee landed heavily on top of her. A string of blood and saliva dribbled from his mouth and rolled down Amakollee's face. Her midsection was awash in his blood. She suddenly felt a wave of nausea and was sure she was going to be sick.

Amakollee pushed up on the dead A-po-la-chee, rolling him off her. She still could not stand. Her arm, the one she had used to pull Kachumpka down, was buried beneath her son.

"Get up," she told him.

Kachumpka lifted his face, stared at the blood on his mother and the dead A-po-la-chee. His bottom lip quivered and he began to cry.

"No," she shouted at him. "Help me up, Kachumpka. There is no time to cry."

Kachumpka staggered to his feet, rubbing the tears from his face, sniffing and wiping his nose with his hand.

When he lifted his weight from her arm, she realized she was in more trouble than she suspected. All at once she felt pain and looked at her mangled arm. It rested in a peculiar, unnatural position. As Kachumpka landed, his body had snapped her forearm. The tip of the broken bone seemed to lie just beneath the already bluing skin. She was thankful it had not come through.

"Help me," she told him, raising her healthy arm. Kachumpka pulled on it, helping her to her feet.

"Run," she said, supporting her injured arm with her other. "Keep up with me." Amakollee followed the trail to the cenote. They would hide in the heavy brush around the sinkhole. There was no escape from the mound. If they tried to run through the shallow water, their feet would sink into the mud, and they would have no cover. The cenote was the only place. They would have to wait it out, staying hidden as best as they could.

———

MIAKKA WOULD NOT LEAVE until she found Mi-sa. "Mi-sa," she screamed again, hoping that her daughter could hear over all the other cries.

Suddenly she heard her daughter's voice.

"Here."

She was near, but Miakka couldn't see her. Bodies, men, weapons, all moved in front of and around her.

"Mi-sa," she shouted again, maneuvering her way through the chaos. At last she saw her daughter, stooped over Omo-ko who lay on the ground.

"Mi-sa," she called to her. "Come!"

She was close now, and Mi-sa stood up and turned to face her mother. "Omo-ko is injured."

Miakka tugged at her. "Not now. Get out of the way."

"Help me," Mi-sa insisted as she grabbed Omo-ko's legs and began to drag him out of the center of the battle. Miakka saw that Mi-sa would not be dissuaded. She decided to help her move him so that the task could be done quickly.

When Omo-ko was safely laid down in some brush, Miakka leaned forward, hands on her knees, catching her breath. "Come," she said breathlessly. "We must get away."

Mi-sa's eyes darted back toward the village, and she lifted her head. "Wakulla! Shakia!"

Miakka was confused.

Mi-sa began to trot back toward the village, calling Wakulla and Shakia.

"No, Mi-sa," her mother called. "Stop!"

But Mi-sa continued, running faster, screaming the names louder and louder, terror altering her voice. Miakka ran behind her.

Suddenly she saw Mi-sa stop dead. Miakka ran up next to her and looked where Mi-sa stared. The platform that belonged to Wakulla and Shakia was blazing, billowing smoke into the sky. It must have been one of the first to be set on fire. The A-po-la-chee had easily recognized and targeted the house of the cacique. The roof had fallen in, the once ornately carved supporting posts were burned black, and one had begun to crumble. Mi-sa called Shakia's name again, and then began to run toward the burning platform.

"No," Miakka yelled, grabbing Mi-sa and spinning her around. "There is nothing you can do."

Mi-sa turned to watch the platform burn. "Shakia,"

she cried, eyes welling with tears. Then she turned her head, focusing farther down the line of platforms. Her home was now beginning to burn, orange flames lapping like evil tongues up the side of her shelter.

Mi-sa stood very still and looked up at the sky, following the trail of smoke that billowed from her platform. Her mother looked up also. Miakka raised her eyebrows. Her eyes widened and her mouth dropped open.

Something frighteningly bizarre was happening.

Chapter Twenty-nine

ALTHOUGH IT WAS MORNING, the light was becoming milky and gray, but not from the thick smoke.

Others had also noticed and in the midst of battle looked into the sky. The sun was going out! Only a small crescent of it remained. The People looked away quickly. This was the work of the spirits and not for man to watch. They fell to their knees—even the A-po-la-chee—and began their prayers, eyes to the ground in fear. Some dared to take another glimpse. The sun was gone—only a string of spots of intense light, like a strand of brilliant beads, was left.

The warriors, women, and old men called out to their spirits. The children old enough to understand their parents' fright clutched at their mothers' skirts and legs. The battle had been brutal enough, but the People were terrified as they watched the light of the sun go out. Mothers covered the little ones' eyes. They told their children not to look or the spirits would surely punish them. The shadow of the Darkside covered the daystar. They pleaded with their spirits to protect them and to drive the evil away.

The prayers grew louder and louder, and then complete darkness fell suddenly. Miakka glanced up quickly and then looked away. The sun was a black disk surrounded by a fine rutilant ring and streamers of frosty white against the black sky, which now glittered with stars.

A loud cry rang out from the brush, calling the A-po-la-chee to their feet. Twice now a sign from the spirits had interfered in their battle with these people. The signs were a warning. They would leave this land to the infidels who talked to the Darkside. If they lived, if the earth did not come to an end without the sun, the A-po-la-chee would never return here.

As they withdrew, the sun began to reappear. It was a good omen.

The clan was stunned. Women and children stood, lifting their heads above the brush where they had hidden. The world was hushed, the animals and men in awe. The shadow slowly slid away, giving back the sun to the People.

"Do not look," Atula called out loudly. "This is spirit work."

Though the temptation to look was great, the People kept their eyes on the earth.

Atula came to Miakka, a small trickle of blood running over his forehead and down the side of his face. Miakka reached out and held him. His arms surrounded her as light returned.

"Shakia," she said, tears streaming down her face. "And Wakulla. The baby," she cried, turning her head into his chest.

A loud crash announced the complete collapse of another burned shelter. Other platforms smoldered on the ground. Only a few remained. Even one of the old trees that had shaded part of the village had caught fire. The men took their axes and chopped down the small saplings that stood nearby, clearing the area. Atula prayed that the tree would not topple until it had burned out. They watched as it writhed in the flames, sputtering ash and sparks as it burned. It fought until the end, until the fire had nothing left to consume, and the tree stood like a giant black skeleton against the sky.

Atula attended the injured and the dying. Cherok helped prepare the bodies of the dead. Special songs and prayers needed to be sung. It was the shaman's responsibility to present the departing members of the clan to the spirits. Without the words of the shaman, the song of the holy man, the spirits of the dead would not be recognized, and they would not be allowed to cross over. The shaman introduced the dead and led them across.

Cherok stumbled over the song as he sang it along with Atula. He closed his eyes in frustration and fear. The magnitude and the gravity of the responsibility weighed heavily on him. If he performed the rites without Atula, perhaps the spirits of the dead would not cross to the Other Side.

Cherok paused, opened his eyes, and watched his father. Atula's facial expressions came from deep inside him. He was communicating with the spirits. His voice was filled with emotion. He radiated a special quality that could not be copied or imitated. No matter how hard Cherok tried, no matter how sincere he was, he would never succeed.

Without saying anything to his father, he left.

———

MIAKKA SAT BY HER HEARTH at the base of her platform thankful that she was one of the few who still had a shelter. Miakka had worked hard all day, and her muscles ached. She had helped Mi-sa and others go through what was left of the platforms, looking for anything that could be salvaged. She had tried to help others and nurse some of the injured, but many had turned her away.

She sipped a ladleful of soup and put a few berries in her mouth, though she was not very hungry. She watched as one of the women, supported by two others, walked to the central hearth. Her hair had been cut short with her deceased husband's knife. She was in mourning. Not until her hair reached her shoulders would she look at another man.

Tomorrow the Council of Men would meet to discuss many serious topics.

Miakka pressed her hands to her eyes. They stung as she thought again of Shakia and Wakulla. The pain was so deep. Shakia had been more her sister than her friend. And Wakulla. Who would be the next cacique? Though she was sure the A-po-la-chee would never return, she knew the clan was in grave trouble. The Council would have much to decide.

Tican walked up behind her and placed his hands on her shoulders, kneading them. Miakka closed her eyes and let her head fall back as she enjoyed the massage by his strong hands.

"You are so tense," he said, moving his hands to her neck, working the muscles and tendons.

"Tican—" she started.

"I know," he interrupted. "I saw you embrace Atula. You have always been his, but you were always my dream."

"Oh, Tican, I am sorry," she said, taking one of his hands and leading him in front of her.

"I have been selective in my life. I do not regret it."

"I wish things could be different."

Miakka stood up and kissed his cheek. Tican dropped

her hand, backed away, turned, and left.

Miakka watched him go. He would remain in the village for the night, but all the visitors would leave in the morning. Some would return to continue the courtship or to take a woman back to become a wife. But as Miakka watched Tican walk away from her, she knew she would never see him again. The thought saddened her.

As the sun continued to go down, the air became cool enough to be uncomfortable. Where was Mi-sa? she wondered. Her daughter was going to stay with her.

The wind blew harder. Miakka wrapped some furs around her shoulders and huddled closer to her fire. The wind dried her eyes and chilled the end of her nose. She breathed down into the furs, letting her breath warm her face.

———

BEFORE NIGHTFALL Miakka had another visitor. Cherok sat cross-legged across from her.

"Aside from those we have lost, a few people are injured so badly that we may lose them as well," Cherok said, beginning the conversation.

Miakka squinted, her eyes burning from the cold air. "Should you not be with Atula?"

"No," he answered. "I do not belong there."

"What is the matter?" she asked, hearing the tribulation in his voice.

"I have seen for a long time that I cannot do those things that are expected of me. I have had doubts, but now I am sure."

Miakka started to protest, but Cherok stopped her.

"I am not here to argue the point. I have come to you for a good reason. I know about Atula's plan."

"What plan? What are you talking about?"

"He has told me to be prepared. He is going to leave and take you and Mi-sa with him. I cannot let him go."

"And I cannot let him, either," she said, surprising him. "The People need him now more than ever. I cannot permit him to give up the clan for Mi-sa and me."

"And I cannot assume his responsibilities if he leaves. Miakka, I do not have the Gift. The People would be without a shaman."

"I could not go with Tican. My heart would never be his. That would be unfair."

Cherok moved closer. "Listen to what I suggest. Instead of Atula taking you and Mi-sa away, I will do so. We will go as far as we need to. Perhaps in another place you and Mi-sa will find happiness. I cannot allow Atula to pass his responsibilities on to me. I am not a shaman."

Miakka sat, not saying anything. She had realized during the day how desperately the People needed their shaman. The ill, the grieving, and the well all needed his skills. The clan needed his prayers to the spirits for protection, and through him they needed to give thanks. What if Cherok did not have that special ability? Atula's offer had seemed wonderful just last night, but it was impossible to consider now.

"Yes," she answered. "I will speak with Mi-sa. Give me a day. We will be ready then."

Cherok heaved a sigh of relief. A burdensome weight had just been lifted from his shoulders.

"I will prepare for the journey." He hesitated a moment before speaking again. "I will not reveal this plan to anyone."

"Neither will I. Only to Mi-sa. If we went to Atula, he would not accept this plan. It is better to keep silent."

Cherok's face relaxed. This was the right thing to do.

WHAT WAS LEFT of the daylight was tinged with the pink of the sunset. Miakka wrapped herself in the fur blanket and went to look for Mi-sa. Twilight was quickly approaching, and the air grew even colder. The icy breath of the ancient beasts blew against her back.

Miakka stopped where her daughter's platform had once stood. Nothing but ashes remained among a few blackened timbers that fell apart at the touch. She and Mi-sa had cleared away most of the debris.

The activity of the day had slowed, and the noises were dying down. Fluttering brittle leaves pirouetted and twirled about her feet, and the cold wind blew her hair into her face and brushed the nape of her neck, sending a chill down her spine. Even the birds seemed quiet, huddling in the trees, feathers ruffled and puffed up against the cold. The black earth, usually warm beneath her feet, was now cool and dry.

A noise startled her. Miakka held her breath. She had hoped that the village would remain quiet and still. What had she heard? She cocked her head, listening again.

Somewhere near the stacks of debris the People had collected, she heard a strange voice, high and soft. Miakka stepped closer. Strange words—unfamiliar lilting words—spoken in a fragile voice.

"Mi-sa?" she whispered.

There was no answer. Miakka stepped closer.

"Mi-sa?" she said again, stepping over a burned timber. The light had quickly dimmed to night. The mound was wreathed in eerie shadows. The cloak of fur fell from her shoulders, and a shudder from the sudden chill racked her. She gathered the blanket around her and looked into the night. The voice was still.

"Mi-sa?" she said in the darkness.

Chapter Thirty

A SUDDEN GUST OF WIND howled through the trees, blowing ashes in great dirty swirls. Where green fern once grew thick near Mi-sa's platform, the earth was now brown and black, no more than soot, ashes, and charcoal.

Miakka heard the voice again, a mystic murmur, a euphonic lyric. It was Mi-sa's voice.

"What song do you sing?" she called out, still unable to see her.

The song stopped, and the raw chilling wind that had stung through Miakka's furs dwindled to a biting breeze.

"Mother?" Her voice was faint and fragile.

Miakka moved toward her daughter's voice.

"Where are you, Mi-sa? I cannot see you. It is too dark."

"Here," Mi-sa directed her, her voice stronger.

Mi-sa stood in front of her clutching two sticks. Crudely tied to one end of one stick was the feather of an osprey. A small piece of brown rabbit fur was tightly wrapped around the stick at the other end. The other stick had a few more feathers but no fur at the end. Even in the darkness the girl's mother could see that Mi-sa had cut a swatch from the blanket she had given her.

"What is this?" her mother asked.

Mi-sa stared blankly.

"What are you doing? Where have you been? I was concerned." Miakka paused, moving closer, looking curiously at her daughter. "What is it that you do?"

"I made these," Mi-sa answered, holding out the sticks, looking at them nearly as curiously as her mother. "I needed to thank the spirits."

"We all need to thank them," her mother answered. "But why these? Why here? Are you all right?" she said, stepping even closer to her daughter.

"I am sorry that I worried you," Mi-sa said, her face appearing less strained than it had a moment ago.

Miakka sighed. "But you are fine. That is all that matters. Come," she said, "I have to speak with you about something of importance."

Miakka adjusted the fur wrap around Mi-sa, fingering the raw edge where the girl had cut away the swatch. Her daughter's skin felt cold.

"Let us go and sit close to the fire," Miakka said, gently putting her hand on Mi-sa's back, encouraging her to walk with her. She took the strange sticks from her daughter and tossed them deep into the brush.

Mi-sa shivered and wrapped herself tighter in the fur as she walked with her mother.

Miakka pitched some wood into the fire and watched it catch. Satisfied, she sat next to Mi-sa.

"We are going away," she said.

When she finished explaining the new plan, Mi-sa started to argue about Cherok's abilities, but Miakka eased her doubts. "What matters is that Cherok does not believe he has the Gift. You believe in him, but he must have faith in himself. If indeed you believe in him, then you must trust him and trust his decisions. His plan will be good for all of us."

"You have always loved my father. I cannot let you deny yourself happiness, to leave him forever because of me."

"It is not my happiness that guides my choices. It is my love for the People. I cannot let Atula leave them. He thinks he would be happy someplace else, and he would be for a time. But the day would come when his decision would eat at him. Even before he is a man, he is shaman. I love him enough to leave him. I love the People enough. Do you understand?"

Mi-sa understood and finally agreed when she realized that this decision was not based only on saving her from further disgrace and pain.

Miakka sent her daughter up to sleep while she remained by the fire. She was not ready to sleep.

———

ATULA HOPED MIAKKA was still awake. He had hardly seen her during the day, their time having been so seriously occupied. He was relieved to see that she sat at her hearth. Being with her would soothe him and help him forget the strenuous, draining events of the day. Being near her would help him leave all his troubles in some dark space.

She saw him coming and made herself smile. Across the crest of the mound, his body glistened in the glow of the central hearth. His black hair fell to his shoulders; his gait was proud and confident. She stood as he came close.

Without a word he reached for her and held her. She opened her fur wrap and cloaked him inside with her.

"You are cold," she whispered.

"And you are my hearth," he said, pressing his lips into her hair.

"I do love you," she said, hoping she would not cry.

They had come so close to happiness—twice. But it was not meant to be. The spirits would not allow them to be together, and she would have to accept her fate.

Atula pulled back and lifted her chin with his hand. "There was something different in your voice when you said that—what makes you sound so despondent?"

"This day has made everyone feel disheartened," she answered him. "The A-po-la-chee, the sun going out, Wakulla and Shakia ... all the others."

Atula gently touched his lips to hers and then looked into her eyes. "We will find strength in the strong sign the spirits gave to us. The A-po-la-chee will not come again. The sign of the sun has told us that the spirits smile on the People."

"They smile because we have a worthy shaman."

"When all of this is behind us and the People are quiet and settled, there will be time for us."

"The People need you."

"I will stay until the clan is tranquil. I cannot leave now. But soon. Very soon."

Miakka wanted to tell him Cherok's plan. It seemed more than unkind to keep the secret.

His mouth touched hers lightly, nipping tenderly at her lips. "You leave me weak," he said.

She pulled away and ran a hand from his hairline to his cheek as if she could imprint the feel of his skin, the angle of his jaw, on her memory by touching him. His hand was suddenly on top of hers, and he kissed her palm, holding it to his mouth, looking long into her eyes.

Again the cold wind huffed, blowing her hair into her face.

Atula let go of her hand. "Tomorrow," he said as he walked away.

Miakka thought she had hidden the secret well, but

when Atula turned away from her, he closed his eyes for a moment. He was the shaman, and he heard more than spoken words. But her thoughts were not clear enough for him to understand. He stopped and turned back to her again, but it was too dark now. Her image had been swallowed by the night.

————

ANOTHER DAY OF RECOVERY passed slowly. Miakka, Misa, and Cherok prepared for their journey. They would leave just before dawn. They did not have much time for preparation because they were needed to help with other things. Along with the rest of the People, they rebuilt platforms, cared for the injured, cleared away the destruction, and consoled and comforted the grief-stricken.

Miakka also helped tend to the pot at the central hearth. She gave most of her stored roots, berries, and dried meat to the community. She could not give all of her food away; that would have seemed suspicious. Many other women also brought food from their hearths. This was not a time to eat at one's own fire. It was a time for members of the clan to share and to help one another. The bountiful food at the central hearth was available to those who were too badly injured, too filled with grief, or too busy helping others to hunt or cook for themselves. The tragedy had bonded the clan anew.

Miakka carried some food to Tabisha for Acopa, who had a puncture wound in his leg from the tip of an A-po-la-chee spear. Atula had treated it and insisted that Acopa stay off of it. Acopa wanted to help the rest of the clan by getting up and walking on his bad leg, but Tabisha would not allow it. She argued with him, refused to get him a walking stick, even pushed on his shoulder when he tried to stand. She had lost Shakia; she would not let her husband hurt himself. Acopa finally gave in and rested inside his platform. The last time she tapped him on the shoulder, setting him off balance so that he fell back, he had grabbed her hand and pulled her down with him. The pain in his leg made him grunt. Tabisha was afraid she had hurt him, and she lifted her weight quickly, but Acopa reached behind her neck, drew her to him, and planted a long kiss on her mouth. When the kiss ended, she lay next to him, hiding her face in his chest. Both of them wept, holding each other, almost afraid to let go.

———

As MIAKKA WALKED from the central hearth, she saw Amakollee sitting at Sassacha's hearth. Atula knelt in front of her, examining her arm. Cherok stood behind him, leaning over, watching. Kachumpka was on his feet, mumbling and swaying at Amakollee's side. Miakka scolded herself for feeling whatever the strange emotion was that pumped through her. It wasn't anger or hate or jealousy, but it was close to all three. The day was cold, but she suddenly felt a hot flush that accompanied that emotion.

Miakka called up to Tabisha, who dried her eyes and greeted Miakka from the opening of her platform.

"We thank you," she called down. "Come up and see Acopa. He needs your company."

Miakka had been hoping that Tabisha would ask her up. She and Acopa were her family—the only family she knew except for Mi-sa. She needed to grieve with them. She needed to mourn the death of Shakia with other people who had loved her. She put the food by the fire and went up the ladder.

———

LATER IN THE DAY, Miakka went to visit Kita. The loss of her son, Wakulla, had stabbed Kita with intolerable grief. She lay on her mat, refusing the food that Miakka brought, turning her back to her visitor.

"I am old. Let me go. Let the spirits take me. I am finished here."

Kita's husband had crossed to the Other Side several seasons ago. His death had been hard for her, but she had had Wakulla then. Now it seemed she had nothing, no reason to go on. She was tired. Kita closed her eyes and continued her silent prayer for the spirits to take her, to relieve her of this deep, lonely pain.

"We must all share the anguish of our losses," Miakka said softly. "Let us help. Come to the central hearth tonight. Our wounds begin to heal when we gather. Many shoulders are greater than one."

Kita swallowed but did not answer.

"Think about it. Wakulla would want you to come. He would expect it of his mother."

Miakka left quietly. Tonight after the gathering she would check her basket to be sure that everything she was going to take with her was there. Mi-sa and Cherok would do the same. Before dawn they would leave.

The last of the russet horizon leisurely wilted beneath the black film of night. The darkness came like a cold cloak, wrapping the People in its shivery winds. Was this what it would be like if the sun went out? They wondered silently about that but were afraid to ask the question aloud. How cold could the earth get? Could they still depend on the sun as they always had? Would every sunrise bring with it relief?

Talasee built the fire to a snapping blaze. Fire was both friend and enemy; he had always understood that. Now its crackling flames called the People to gather around.

"Cherok," Atula called, "look at Amakollee's arm. See if she is taking care of it as she should."

Cherok nodded, understanding his father's reluctance to give Amakollee the least bit of attention. She would either misconstrue his intentions or use the time to plague him. But Atula would not let her injury go untended.

The clan gathered around the central hearth; some people collected beneath the canopy of thatch, and others milled about, visiting, finding friends with whom they wished to spend the evening.

Atula disappeared as the villagers collected. He slipped by them, returning to his hearth and platform so that he could dress for the occasion and prepare himself. He called Cherok to help.

"Add this to the mixture," he told his son, handing him some shaved rootstock.

Cherok dropped the ingredients into the bowl of steeping leaves and fungi. "You prepare a strong tea," he commented.

"These are demanding times. I must gather all the power that is available to me."

"But you have taught me that this combination is dangerous because it is so potent."

"It has to be. A shaman does not often use a tea so strong—so extreme. Watch carefully so that when you must do the same, you will know how."

Cherok cracked a thumb knuckle as he clenched his fist. He watched Atula prepare himself, but for the first time he merely observed him; he did not study him.

Atula drank the decoction with confidence. As he waited for it to work, he brought down from his platform a necklace that trickled with graduated cone-shaped alligator teeth. About his shoulders he draped a shawl of deer hide ornamented with raccoon tails. In one hand he held the skin drum he would use to set the rhythm of his call.

Atula reached behind his neck and withdrew the bone pins that held his hair in place, letting his black mane fall to his shoulders.

He had fasted, and the magical medicine was quick to work. The cold night air seemed to disappear as he broke into a sweat. He felt a sudden storm of dizziness and sat down to wait it out. If he had prepared the tea correctly and had ingested the right amount, the dizziness would be transitory. He would know in a few moments. He called upon the spirits to lead him through this narrow and dangerous passage between potency and poison. He asked the spirits to protect the People and to open the doors to the other world for him. He asked them to recognize him and welcome him on this night.

Cherok sat across from him, entranced by the whole process and by Atula's faith and confidence. In his father's place, he would have been frightened, and he knew the spirits would have recognized his weakness and lack of faith. A sense of relief came with these thoughts for the first time. He would never be faced with this situation. He had made the right decision.

For a moment Atula was silent. His head slumped forward, and he listed to one side. Cherok started to move toward him, a streak of foreboding flashing through him. But then Atula raised his head. His eyes were glassy, unnaturally shiny and piercing. He pulled a shock of hair free from the front and center of his head and laced it with rawhide, binding it at the bottom and threading the ends of two hawk feathers into it.

Over his forehead he tied a large circular shell medallion, its luster flickering in the firelight.

"Paint my face," he told Cherok with no emotion in his voice or face.

Cherok knelt at his side and dipped his first finger into the dye. It was slick and greasy. Beneath Atula's eyes he drew diagonal red lines, beginning at the corner of each eye, close to his nose and then slanting out and down across his cheekbones, ending at an imaginary line drawn down from the outside corners of his eyes. Red was an intense color—the color of passion and war.

Cherok stepped back, looking at the holy man who sat so straight and sure, his face showing poise and commitment. He handed his father the medicine rattle and drum. Atula crossed his arms in front of his chest, holding the drum and rattle close.

"I am ready," he told Cherok.

Cherok offered his hand, but Atula stood on his own. Cherok walked in front of his father, feeling the shaman's eyes hot on his back.

"Cherok," Atula called, making his son stop and turn to face him. "The medicine helps me see into men through their own eyes."

"Yes, I know," Cherok answered, turning away to continue toward the central hearth. But something—a voice that controlled him from within—made him turn back. He looked at his father.

Atula had not taken a step. He stood, his arms still crossed in front of his chest, his seriousness evident in the creases of his face. "Is there something you keep from me?" he asked.

Cherok hesitated. "No, Shaman. Nothing."

Atula still did not move.

Cherok finally turned and continued toward the main hearth.

Chapter Thirty-one

EVERYONE WATCHED and listened as the shaman called upon the spirits. His voice echoed, finding a ride on the cold wind gusting through the small village, rushing through the trees, and bending the tall sedge. He gathered the clansmen's spirits in his hands as he reached into the flames. Except for his voice, the pounding of his feet, the beat of his drum, and the roar of the wind, no sound could be heard.

Tamed by his magic, the fire licked the shaman's hands and arms. His hair tumbled across his shoulders, and like black water it reflected the firelight. His power was keen, breathtaking, engulfing, bringing some of the clansmen to their knees, in touch with or overtaken by the spirits.

"Come this way," he called to the stars, the ever-burning hearths above them. "Come this way," he sang, holding hot coals in his hands, lifting them above his head in offering, displaying them before the amazed clan.

Miakka stood back, watching. As the night wore on, the shaman continued his calls and songs. Energy radiated from him to those who let the magic take them. Atula sang into the night until his voice was husky and his body weak. He had taken the People to the spirits. They had ridden on the wings of his magic, gone with him to the sky, to the place of the spirits. From high above they had seen the tiny speck of light that burned in their village. The spirits had touched them. Only a pure shaman, a powerful holy man, could take the souls of the People to that other plane and let them feel the warmth of the spirits.

When the ceremony was over, wonderful sweet exhaustion swept through the villagers. Some had given up their grief to the spirits. Some had relinquished their anger, and others had gathered strength and purpose. The ceremony had served many.

Miakka waited until everyone had gone except the shaman. The ceremony had lifted her sadness, but she felt that she was doing the right thing by planning to leave. Atula was needed here, and she was going to ensure that the People would not be without him.

"Atula," she whispered as she stood on her toes and offered her mouth to him.

With one hand he touched her hair, caressing the thick silken strands. With his other hand he opened her wrap and drew her to him, touching her hips to his, her flesh to his.

He led her away from the fire, along the narrow paths by the cenote. She watched as he removed the ornaments, took off his breechclout and cape, and stepped into the water. He sank beneath the water and then stepped out into the cold air. She shivered for him and lay down on the cool earth, pulling him beside her, folding him into her furs and the warmth of her body. Tonight he was especially tender and gentle, sometimes just holding her close. When the time did come for that exquisite exchange of gifts, that remarkable giving of pleasure to another, it seemed unending.

Miakka kissed his shoulder as he bowed his head over

hers. She wanted to remember how his body felt against her. She wanted to remember forever the sound of his voice, the touch of his hands, the passion of his mouth on hers and on her body. When he lifted his weight to move off her, she held him, discouraging him from moving. Atula rested back on her, kissing her face, her eyes, her neck.

"I love you, woman," he murmured in a husky voice.

Miakka's arms tightened around him. The sudden pain of his wonderful words cut deep. She was glad that he could not see her face as he nuzzled her neck and the softness of her hair.

Atula escorted her back to her platform, stopping to kiss her before she went up. Miakka stood at the top of the ladder and watched him drift into the darkness. She relished the last glimpse of him.

"Mother," Mi-sa called. "Everything is ready."

"Yes," Miakka said, walking into the shelter. "Everything."

————

CHEROK PUSHED OFF and jumped into the canoe. He quickly took the pole and drove it into the peat. The canoe moved along the shallow trail, parting the renegade clumps of saw grass. The cold stung his face as the air moved swiftly past him.

Miakka and Mi-sa huddled together, wrapped in the same blanket. The cold did not usually last too long, and they ached for this blast of frigid air to move away. Miakka heard the sedge sweep against the canoe and now and again a ripple of water. But many of the night sounds—the buzzing of the insects, the chirping of the crickets—had been silenced by the cold weather. At least the chill provided for some relief from the mosquitoes.

Only a few days ago those annoying insects had seemed to feast upon them.

Cherok noticed the sky first. It faded from blinding black to indigo and finally, far away across the big water somewhere, a faint glimmer of lavender and pink. He nudged Mi-sa, waking her so that she could see it also. Together they watched across the savannah as the sun painted coral, pink, lavender, and citrine swatches in the low sky as it rose.

As the sun climbed higher in the sky, the air warmed. Though the temperature was chilly, the sun beat on the deerskin Cherok had wrapped himself in. He could feel the warmth on his back. But he was still cold. He shivered even as Mi-sa and Miakka loosened their wraps.

Miakka took some coontie bread from a basket and shared it with the other two.

"Someone may have noticed by now," she said.

"What?" Mi-sa asked, not understanding her mother's statement.

"That we are gone."

Mi-sa nodded, and Cherok turned to look at her. "Are you regretful?"

"No," Miakka answered quickly.

Cherok said, "Atula will understand why we left. His heart will heal. It belongs to the spirits."

"Yes," Miakka agreed, sitting with her back straight and her eyes forward. But then she turned to her daughter. "Your life begins this day. We will find a place."

Mi-sa smiled at her mother.

The day dragged on, the scene never changing. Soon bright sunlight bounced off the water into their eyes. The world was mostly brown with only a few promises of green. The freeze that had occurred this far inland had stolen the green from just about everything except some of the trees and underbrush that stood on the hammocks. They saw some hammocks where there were villages, but Cherok avoided them. He poled on, and when the water deepened, he paddled and Mi-sa helped him steer by pushing or dragging the paddle through the water from the stern.

Near nightfall they banked the canoe on an uninhabited hammock, then dragged it securely out of the water. Cherok used his knife to cut away the tangle of brush and vines by the water, but once they made their way beneath the mantle of trees, the underbrush thinned out. Miakka and Mi-sa used a fallen palm frond to brush the soil, clearing a spot for them. Cherok carefully removed a burning coal from the pouch he had so carefully packed and tended during the day. With it he began a small fire. The flames were comforting. They provided warmth and discouraged animals from coming close.

They used their stored food to fill their stomachs, sitting closer to the fire as the chill of night set in. Cherok unrolled a hide for his bed and curled up in it. His head ached. He was glad the first day was done.

Miakka fed the fire more wood. She wanted to be sure it burned through the night. It protected them, and besides, they would need a coal to take with them tomorrow. It was so much easier that way.

At first she thought it was her imagination, but when she looked up and could not see the stars, she realized that she had felt a droplet of rain. There was no thunder, no lightning, just a little breeze that quickly died. The rain began to fall in large drops, splattering, leaving tiny craters in the soil. As the drops became smaller, the rain fell harder. The three of them huddled beneath their hides. This was not a vicious windblown rain, but it was steady. The soil began to wash away beneath them.

They tried to protect the fire. Cherok and Mi-sa worked to keep the rain off it, hunkering down on either side of the hearth, holding a canopy of hide over the fire. But the water that stood on the ground crept beneath their feet and beneath the bed of the fire. They coughed and sputtered from the smoke. Slowly the wood was becoming wet. If the rain did not end soon, the fire would go out.

Cherok grabbed the pouch, hoping to salvage a coal, but the sack was soaked inside. The flap was askew, the drawstring loose, and the rain had poured in. He threw it to one side, angrily shouting at himself. He had been neglectful, and now they would pay. He should have thought of that before going to sleep. And he should have awakened to tend to the fire. But his head had hurt so badly—it still ached. The pattering of rain angled at his back. He was so cold. So cold, he thought, shivering.

By morning everything was soaked. The fire was destroyed. The rain had created a soggy curtain of fog. Miakka and Mi-sa rummaged through the baskets. The bread was drenched. They threw it out, settling for some dried venison and a few berries. Cherok was not hungry.

"Perhaps later," he told them, rubbing his temples. He could not think of eating, not with his head hurting like this.

Cherok tipped the canoe sideways, sloshing most of the water out. The rest they would bail. Miakka and Mi-sa climbed in the canoe. Cherok pushed the dugout into the water and hopped inside as it began to glide on the surface. He reached for the pole but lost his balance, nearly stumbling. He wrapped his hand around the pole, lifted it, and dug one end into the shallow water. The pole seemed heavier today, and his best effort was more than strenuous. Too little sleep, too much rain, and too much strain.

Today the air lost its crispness by noon, and hot rays of sunlight soaked up the excess water, dried the furs and skins, and took the chill from the air. The sky was clear blue, softened by white clouds.

"May I use one of your furs?" Cherok asked even as the sun reached down with its hot, bright streams.

"Are you cold?" Mi-sa asked, looking at his pale face, reaching for one of the wraps that lay in the bottom of the canoe. There was no need for them on such a beautiful day.

"Here," she said, handing it to him. "Cherok, what is wrong?"

"I am fine," he told her, but his voice was weak, and she knew him so well that the lie seemed obvious to her. His shoulders slumped, his back curved, and his head drooped as he stood in the canoe.

Mi-sa stood and reached out to touch his shoulder. She closed her eyes for a moment and then looked back at him. "No, you are not fine."

Cherok turned and pushed the pole down into the mush of peat. His arms ached and trembled with the effort. He pulled the borrowed fur around his shoulders.

Miakka tapped Mi-sa on the shoulder and gave her a perplexed look. Mi-sa shook her head, her eyes dark with worry. All was not right with Cherok, and she knew it.

As the day dragged on, Cherok struggled with the pole. He threw the blanket from him only to retrieve it and snuggle inside it again. His stomach churned, and he was lightheaded. He dug the pole into the water, pushing it down into the spongy bottom. Mi-sa stood, wrapped a hand around the pole, and helped him push it. The canoe responded, moving smoothly through the water.

"Let me," she said, taking the pole. "You rest a while."

Cherok wanted to argue, but his body told him not to. Carefully he stepped past Mi-sa and lay down in the bottom of the boat, then covered himself with both of the women's blankets as well as his.

"Just a little while," he said.

Mi-sa and Miakka navigated the canoe through the shallow channels and sloughs, floating over the saw-grass prairie. As Cherok slept, the water deepened and they could see a more noticeable current. They used the depth of the water to guide them, following the slow current. Before long they found themselves being spilled into a river.

Now they could use the paddles. Miakka directed the canoe, sometimes forming swooping arcs with the paddle to make turns, and Mi-sa stroked with the paddle in front. They passed higher ridges and hammocks banked by great oaks, thickets of elderberry and wax myrtle, and luscious green draperies of moonvine.

Cherok lifted his head. "I am going to be sick," he barely whispered.

Mi-sa dropped the paddle and helped him up. Cherok leaned over the side of the canoe and vomited. She helped support him while Miakka fought to keep the canoe balanced.

Mi-sa's hands grew hot from his skin. "He has fire inside him," she told her mother.

Cherok hung limply over the side. Mi-sa held up a handful of water. Cherok rinsed his mouth, and Mi-sa helped him lie back down.

"Mother, we need to stop. Ahead," she said, pointing.

"There."

Just ahead was a spot where the brush along the bank seemed to stand back, leaving space to beach the canoe.

To avoid overturning, they kept their centers of balance low and ducked beneath the hanging branches instead of pushing on them. They pulled the canoe up onto the bank, grounding the bow. Mi-sa and Miakka stepped back into the canoe and helped Cherok to his feet. He mumbled something that did not make sense. Each woman put one of his arms around her shoulders.

"Step out of the canoe," Mi-sa told him, but Cherok was unresponsive.

"Hold him," she told her mother. She got out of the canoe and then reached for him and let him lean against her chest, her arms wrapped under his arms, her hands clasped behind his back. Straining, she dragged him out of the canoe. Miakka helped move his legs over so they did not scrape and bump the edges.

When Cherok was clear of the boat, Miakka stepped out. Mi-sa laid him on the ground. In the shade of a large old live oak, she cleared a space, unrolled a blanket from around Cherok, and laid it on the ground for his bed. Miakka carried his legs, and Mi-sa lifted his shoulders. Together they transported him to the shady bed they had prepared.

Throughout the afternoon, Mi-sa took care of Cherok, supporting him, holding his head, wiping his mouth when he vomited, giving him sips of water. Now she sat, his head cradled in her lap. Miakka cleaned the area, scooping away the fouled soil and disposing of it. She brought fresh water and wiped his body, though he shivered at the coolness. Mi-sa had taken all the wraps off him so that his body could cool.

Every so often he seemed lucid, acknowledging her,

but most of the time he slept, rousing only to begin another bout of vomiting.

"I need to prepare a tea," Mi-sa said. "Something to help him."

"He cannot keep it down," her mother replied.

"No, a medicinal tea made from bark. I know the tree."

"How do you know this?" Miakka asked.

"I just do. I cannot explain. I can feel his sickness when I touch his skin, and I can see the tree and the bark. This is like the time when I helped Choktulee with his head wound. But this is much more grave. I fear that Cherok will die."

"I do not understand, Mi-sa. I never have."

"Mother, if I tell you the tree, will you look for it? Here," she said, taking Cherok's knife from its sheath. "Take this and shave some of the bark away. Then cut away some slivers and shavings of the pulp inside. Would you do that?"

"Tell me what tree it is," Miakka answered.

"The nitchiti."

"I know it," her mother answered. "And you know this tree's bark is medicine for his sickness?"

"Yes," Mi-sa said, and Miakka left in search of the medicinal tree.

Mi-sa stared down at Cherok's pale face. She closed her eyes and began to hum, sinking into herself, centering herself, focusing. In an instant she had shed her body and was calling to Cherok. She waited at the misty portal from which Cherok should have come, but the haze cleared as if blown away by a wind, and there was nothing but darkness. She called again, deepening her concentration, reaching, stretching.

"Help me, Cherok," she said. "Come to me so that I

can help you."

Out of the darkness she heard words. Divine, healing, sacred words. The melody was familiar, old, and comfortable, and in a moment she was singing, the words flowing from her tongue like a warm delicious tea. The chant came easily, like a forgotten song that had been recalled.

"I have it," Miakka called out, breaking the spell as she returned with a handful of bark.

The carol was lost. Mi-sa's eyelids fluttered, and she looked toward her mother. "I need to boil it and steep it," she said.

"Fire," Miakka said. "We need a fire." She looked at Cherok and hoped that Mi-sa really could help him. There were such mysteries about her daughter, but she had long ago ceased trying to understand them. All that was important was that she trusted Mi-sa's intuition and sagacity.

"Here," she said, handing the bark shavings to Mi-sa. Her daughter dropped them into a pouch.

"I am afraid, Mother," she whispered, looking at Cherok.

"We do not need a coal. I can start a fire. I have watched it done before. I just need the right things and patience."

Mi-sa sighed. "What can I do to help?"

"Stay with Cherok. Comfort him. Get some fresh water and sponge down his hot body. Keep the fire cool within him." She paused. "And talk to the spirits, Mi-sa, as you always do. Make sure they hear us and see us," she said as she walked away.

Miakka stepped into the river, leaning out to look down the bank. A clump of willows grew not far from her. She decided to walk along the bank rather than fight her way through the heavy underbrush. If she tried to walk among the trees, she was afraid she would miss the willows.

In the mesh of spreading and drooping branches, she searched for a slender dead limb. If she chose one from the ground, it would be either too brittle or too powdery, or it would have absorbed too much moisture. She would also need a nice green one, but first she wanted to find the dead branch that she could use as a drill. Embedded in the long leaves and hanging branches she found one. It was wedged there, never having made the journey to the ground to rot. Miakka huffed as she wrestled the dead brown branch from the tangle of live growth. Then with Cherok's knife she cut a long green branch that would serve as the bow. Now from the willow she needed only a fire board. She wrenched a wider dead limb from the cluster of small trees. Across her knee she broke it, shortening it. Then she repeated the task until she had a piece as thick as three of her fingers and as long as the space from her wrist to her elbow.

Miakka shoved the tip of the knife into the wide piece of wood, then picked up a piece of limestone. It felt rough in her hands. With a swift stroke she slammed it down on the knife handle, driving the blade into the dead wood, splitting it. She now had a piece of wood as thick as her thumb with a flat surface. She trimmed the bark side so that it would lie flat.

Miakka tucked the three wood pieces under her arm and walked by the river, searching the ground and shallows for a small stone. She lifted one and turned it over in her hands. It was too rough and wouldn't work. Smooth river stones were not easy to find.

It suddenly occurred to her to look in the canoe. Inside was a celt, an adz made from the thick lip of the strombus shell. Perfect. She cut away the rawhide that bound the adz to its handle, being careful to cut it only once so that she could save a long piece of it with which to string the bow.

Satisfied that she had all she needed, Miakka trotted back to Mi-sa. Cherok looked no better. Mi-sa had folded one of the furs and put it under his head. As Miakka approached, she saw Mi-sa swabbing his body with a clump of moss that she had dipped in water.

Miakka squatted, then decided to sit. She stripped the bark from the green willow branch that was about as big around as her first finger and as long as her arm. She trimmed it but left the end with a crotch in it. Around this end she wound and tied the strip of rawhide. At the other end she cut a notch to hold the cord, then flexed the branch into a bow. There was a little rawhide left over. It was too valuable to be cut up. She wound it around the bow a few more times, taking up the excess, and tied it off.

"Do you think you can start a fire?" Mi-sa asked, watching her mother.

Miakka looked up at her but did not answer. Instead she picked up the fire board and put one end under her foot. Yes, there was enough of the board left exposed to work with.

"Has he spoken?" she asked her daughter as she began to shape the drill. She sharpened one end into a point, then tapered the other end but left the tip blunt.

"No," Mi-sa responded. "I cannot find him."

"What does that mean?"

"Cherok and I can ... we can reach each other, talk without speaking."

Miakka pushed her hair from her face. "Where is the power, Mi-sa, if it is not in Cherok?" She paused before speaking again, nearly afraid to ask the question. "Is it in you?" she asked, looking away from her daughter, etching a small indentation into the fire board where the blunt end of the drill would spin.

Mi-sa's eyes welled with tears that formed painful pools. "I can do things—things Cherok has helped me do and things I do alone—that he believes he cannot do. I wish ..." Mi-sa choked on the last words, her voice full of a lifetime of agony. The question her mother asked was opening all the closed doors to her secret. She stared at her mother, waiting for Miakka to look up. When her mother's eyes met hers, she was brave enough to ask the question that had haunted her all her life. It surged out of her, flooded from her, gushed out before she could stop it.

"Am I a spirit from the Darkside, Mother?"

Chapter Thirty-two

MIAKKA DROPPED the nearly finished fire bow. She moved to her daughter, wrapped her arms around her, and held her tightly, then took Mi-sa's shoulders and positioned her so that she looked into her eyes.

"No." Again she hugged her Light. "That was Amakollee's poison talk. Jealous, sick venom."

"Then why do these things happen to me?" asked Mi-sa. "I do not ask for them. Sometimes I am not even aware of them until they are over. And these things I know ... what spirit would tell me such things? One from the Darkside?"

"No, Mi-sa. I do not understand either, but this is not the work of a bad spirit. It is born in you for a good reason. That is the reason the spirits sent the star. You are the daughter of the shaman. Inside you there is something special. If you were a man ..."

"But I am not a man."

"Perhaps when we resettle, the magic will go away. When Cherok is well."

"But what if it does not go away? What if we finally find another village and the clan accepts us? What if I do something strange then?"

"You will not. You will be careful."

Mi-sa stood up. "Still you do not really understand.

349

Neither do I. Sometimes I cannot help it. And those things like knowing medicines—how can I live with myself if I know something and do not use the knowledge to help someone? I speak in strange tongues that come naturally for me. I sing songs and chants to the spirits that only the shaman sings. I know the words even as I hear him. This is never going to end, Mother, no matter where we go."

"Yes, it will, even if the three of us have to keep moving for a lifetime. You will look back on this one day. And you will have a husband and children, and I will be an old grandmother. Cherok will train your son. You will see, Mi-sa. One day you will sit on a ridge overlooking the saw grass, enjoying the way it billows just before the wind dies down at the end of the day, the way it bristles against the painted sky. Standing at your side will be your grandchild. Your nose will fill with the muskiness of the damp muck as you tap the ground for her to sit next to you, and then you will tell her grandmother stories. You will tell her how life was for you and how everything turned out. You will pass on to her your heritage, your proud line. Your grandchild will come to you with all her worries, and you will make them vanish with your stories."

"I hope so, Mother." Mi-sa sat down and touched Cherok's arm and then his forehead. "The fire still burns inside him."

Miakka scraped a well out of the center of the strombus shell. She took the pointed end of the drill and rubbed it in her hair to gather oil for lubrication. "I hope I am doing this right," she said as she wrapped the string of the bow once around the drill, then placed the blunt end of the drill in the depression she had nicked out of the fire board. At the top of the drill she placed the shell, settling the socket over the tip. As she held it, her thumb rested at the end of the bow between the cord and the bow, creating tension. She moved the bow slowly and smoothly in long strokes, watching the drill spin, pressing down into the fire board. She tipped the end of the drill down slightly so that the cord would not work its way up the drill. At first she used very little pressure, adding more and more as the drill worked its way down into the fire board, finally blackening it. She stopped.

Setting the bow down, she picked up Cherok's knife, and the fire board. "Get me a cattail," she directed Mi-sa. While she waited for her return, Miakka cut a notch on the underside of the fire board beneath the black mark. This would allow the ember to fall through. The powder from the friction would form a coal—she hoped.

When Mi-sa returned, Miakka had her tear apart the top of the cattail, compress the down with her hands, and hollow out the center, making a tinder bundle nest to receive the ember. Again she worked the bow, this time with a leathery green leaf beneath it. The process was slow, Miakka moving the bow back and forth, back and forth, faster and faster. Finally she smelled a whiff of smoke. She continued to move the bow, twirling the drill, though her arms felt as if they might fall off. If she stopped too soon, the ember would be too small and would die before she could transfer it to the cattail tinder.

Carefully she removed the spindle and lifted the fire board. A small glowing ember was wedged in the notch. She tapped the board, freeing the tiny ember. It fell onto the leaf tray. Almost afraid to move it, she lifted it and placed it inside the tinder nest. She pressed the cattail more firmly around the ember. Miakka drew in a breath, pursed her lips, ready to blow. Gently she directed her breath toward the fragile ember and tinder. Suddenly it burst into a small flame.

Mi-sa's face lit up as she smiled at her mother. "You did it," she said softly, afraid that her voice might somehow extinguish the tiny new fire.

Gingerly Miakka placed the burning tinder bundle on the ground and slowly added small kindling until at last they had a fire.

Mi-sa had everything else ready. Into the earth she drove two sticks with crotches at the top in which she rested a third horizontal one. She rocked it with her hands, testing for stability. It was secure. She hung a pot of water over the fire, sliding the leather cord over the horizontal stick and carefully replacing the end back into the crotch. She dropped the bark shavings into the water. Soon the water began to bubble, and Mi-sa slid the pot to the side of the fire to reduce the heat.

When the tea had steeped and then cooled, Mi-sa stirred the brew with her finger, bringing the residue to the top so that she could skim it off.

"Lift his head, Mother."

Miakka sat behind Cherok, put his head in her lap, and then raised him up.

"Cherok?" Mi-sa called to him. He did not answer. She wiped his face with cool water and called to him again. His eyelids fluttered.

"Drink this," she said, touching the rim of the pot to his mouth.

Cherok parted his lips and let the liquid dribble into his mouth. He grimaced at the taste and closed his eyes.

"More," Mi-sa told him. "Come on, Cherok, just a little more."

Though his eyes stayed closed, he opened his mouth, accepting the bowl again.

Mi-sa fed the fire as the afternoon faded to dusk and on into night. Miakka unrolled the hide that was her bed and stretched out on it. Mi-sa lay next to Cherok so that she could watch him through the night. She lay on her back, looking at the black night with the small, shimmering, twinkling stars.

———

EARLY IN THE MORNING Miakka walked to the river. In a warmer season, more vegetable food would have been available. She hesitated to use their stored food. They might need it later. Better if they could find fresh food. Cherok would have hunted if he had not gotten sick. They had not counted on this. She scanned the river. Always, it seemed, turtles sat along banks, basking in the warmth of the morning sun. But not today. No turtles.

A thorn scratched her leg. Miakka looked down at the offending plant, and it gave her an idea. She knew how the fishermen made bone and shell hooks, but she also knew that men showed young boys how to catch fish using strong thorns. She finished unloading the canoe, then carried their baskets back to the fire.

"I think we will have fish this morning," Miakka said, fumbling through Cherok's basket. She had hoped to find a hook, but there was none.

"Did you find anything?" Mi-sa asked.

"No. I suppose he thought that if he needed fishing hooks or fish lances, he would make them."

Suddenly Miakka's face brightened. "Then so will I." She held a little piece of dried meat in her hands. "I hope the fish like it." She trekked off toward the river again, stopping to slice off a length of slender vine. When she found the thorny plant again, she removed two of the largest and sharpest thorns. As she sat by the river, she bound the two thorns together, blunt ends touching. She used some palm fiber—fraying strings of palm fronds—to bind them. She wrapped the fiber over and over, making a thick bundle in the center where the two thorns joined. She hoped it would hold. Then she tied the long piece of vine around the center of the united thorns. The meat was tough but not too brittle; it had absorbed some moisture from the recent rain. She worked each of the thorn prongs into the meat, covering as much of the thorns as she could. Miakka turned the makeshift hook over in her hands, looking at it. It looked good, considering.

Finally she tied the free end of the vine to a long, slender branch she had cut from a nearby wax myrtle. She stripped the leaves from the branch and then eyed her creation, hoping it would work.

Miakka swung the stick over her shoulder, pointing behind her, then slung it forward, watching the vine-tethered baited hook fly through the air, out over the water, finally landing with a ripple and slowly sinking beneath the water. She waited.

Mi-sa walked up behind her, reached secretively behind her mother, and tapped the butt end of the stick that stuck out from her mother's grasp.

Miakka jumped, jerking the stick skyward in the hope of sending the thorns into the tissue of a fish's mouth.

Mi-sa giggled, giving away the prank.

Miakka turned around, startled, and began to laugh. "I thought I had a big one," she said and chuckled.

A sudden tug on the vine pulled at the pole in Miakka's hand. She turned sharply, knowing this was not her daughter's mischief. She lifted the pole, feeling weight at the end. She raced hand over hand to the end of the stick until she reached the vine and began to haul it in.

Just as she lifted the bream out of the water, the hook snapped off, and the fish fell back into the water. Miakka stood staring at the ripples of water where the fish had disappeared.

Frustrated, she plopped down on the bank.

"Do it again," Mi-sa encouraged her. "If the water was not so brown we could see the fish and spear them, or scoop them with our hands if we could get close. But that is not our fortune."

Together they made a new hook and baited it. Mi-sa emptied a basket and brought it down to the bank. Miakka tried again. This time she was rewarded. Just as she pulled the fish to the surface, Mi-sa stepped closer, lay on her stomach, reached out, and scooped the fish into the basket, capturing it before it was out of the water.

The two women squealed with success, congratulating each other.

The fish was small, really only enough for one person, but it was especially tasty because they had caught it. Mi-sa tried to get Cherok to eat but could not rouse him. At noon she did manage to get him to sip her medicine. But as the day wore on, he became less and less responsive.

Mi-sa bent over Cherok. "He looks worse." She touched his skin, pulling it together, wrinkling it. When she released it, it was slow to return to its natural state. Cherok's lips were cracked, and dark circles surrounded his sunken eyes.

"The medicine should have helped," she said, shaking her head in puzzlement.

"Perhaps he is too sick, Mi-sa."

"But he should be better, not worse."

"Give him some more. Maybe the medicine does not work very fast."

Mi-sa called to her friend, her half brother. She cooled

his face with water, tapped his cheeks, dripped water into his mouth. "Please, Cherok. Wake up. Get better. Get better."

Cherok did not respond.

By late afternoon Cherok had sunk farther and farther from consciousness. His lips were white, and fissures lined them. His hair had lost its luster, and his skin was sallow.

"We have to go back," Mi-sa said.

"No, Mi-sa. This is your chance to get away. Keep trying to wake him. We will get the medicine into him."

"He needs Atula. He is going to die, Mother. We have to go back."

"But, Mi-sa—"

"I have lived there all my life. I will not die, but Cherok will if we do not go back."

Miakka thought for a moment. Was Mi-sa never to have a happy life? Had she been doomed since the night of her birth? Miakka would handle Atula. She would turn him away, and he would continue as shaman, as he should. If they stayed here, Cherok would surely die. Then they would have no future anyway. What clan would take two extra women with no one to provide for them? The People were not selfish, but they were practical. Everyone had a function. They were like a tightly woven basket, and if a hole was left in the weave, the basket was useless.

Miakka looked down at Cherok. They had to go back. "Will we find the way?" she asked.

"If we leave at night. I know the stars," Mi-sa answered.

———

MI-SA'S LONG HAIR trailed down her back as she tilted her

head to gaze at the heavens. With sure, even strokes she began to paddle. As they made their way up the river, Miakka and Mi-sa dipped their paddles on opposite sides, strategically guiding their craft against the current toward home.

Mi-sa, who sat in the bow, turned to look at Cherok who lay motionless on the bottom of the canoe. She was glad she was not looking at him in the sunlight. Even in the moonlight his skin lacked vitality, and his body seemed smaller than it really was.

"I am taking you home, Cherok," she said, even though she wasn't sure that he could hear.

As they moved silently through the water, they heard the return of the common night sounds. The cold air retreated, and every creature seemed to be celebrating.

Miakka swirled the water into a glimmering eddy that funneled around her wooden paddle. They moved slowly, unable to see fingers of land that sometimes jutted out from the banks, or drifts of sediment deposits that could jar, tip, or ground them.

Miakka looked at the bank, catching a fleeting image of dark overhanging trees that dipped soft curls of spidery smoky gray air plants . Sometimes if the light of the moon was just right, she saw eyes—startled eyes, hungry eyes of possum, bobcat, and panther and, floating in the water, drifting silent and alert, alligator eyes. The sight made her feel vulnerable. The canoe was nothing but a flimsy shell that could easily be swamped, spilling them out among all those eyes.

Mi-sa called to her mother. "There," she said, pointing out a formation of brilliant stars.

———

IN THE DAYTIME they stopped to eat and sleep in the

shade. When they reached the shallows where the water was never more then knee or ankle deep, the world looked the same in all directions. There were no idiosyncrasies or landmarks, just undulating brown saw grass and dense green hammocks. Mi-sa needed the stars.

At night they started again, gently moving Cherok back into the canoe. He mumbled incoherently as they lifted him.

Finally, in the early dawn, though the tree island looked like all the others in the distance, they saw it. The teardrop shape of the hammock was the same shape as the others. The flora it supported was no different from that of any other hammock. It was not especially larger than many. But without hesitation, without the smallest thread of doubt, as soon as it appeared as a dark speck in the distance, they knew it. There was a mystic feeling, a familiar smell, an instinctual sense that ahead of them was home.

It was early, which was why the village seemed so quiet, thought Miakka. Even the trees seemed still, the leaves heavy and drooping. Winter-brown rushes stood still and stiff, as did the grasses and sedge that usually yielded so easily to the caress of the gentle wind.

Miakka stood in the canoe, feeling it bump the land. She stepped out into the shallow water and walked up onto the hammock, tugging at the bow of the canoe. Mi-sa lifted Cherok by the shoulders. She was ready to raise him up to her mother, who would lift him from the canoe. Miakka reached for him, but Mi-sa suddenly signaled for her to be still.

There was something else in the air besides familiarity; a strange unpleasant element that Mi-sa did not recognize, so thick it was almost palpable.

Chapter Thirty-three

THE VILLAGE WAS TOO QUIET. The border shrubs that stood at the edge of the hammock sheltered unusually quiet grackles and other small birds. Silent turtles lazily balanced themselves on rocks and banks, catching the great shafts of sunlight. One of the many trees that dunked its feet in the brown water fluttered beneath the flapping of a wood ibis's wings as it took flight.

Mi-sa paused. What was it that made her apprehensive? What was it that made her skin prickle?

Cautiously she and Miakka removed Cherok from the canoe. He opened his eyes at the jostling, but they were uncommunicative, distant eyes. Before there had been a hint of struggle in them, but now even that was gone.

"Leave him here," Miakka told her, indicating a clear shady spot.

"Let me go into the village alone," Mi-sa said, helping her mother to lower Cherok to the ground. "Something is wrong. Do you not feel it? You stay with Cherok."

"I am going with you, Mi-sa," she answered, walking next to her daughter. "We will stand together."

They walked up one of the less-traveled paths. Miakka was afraid to think of what she might see. What had Mi-sa sensed? The village was still, but she did smell smoke.

Someone's fire burned.

The brush thinned as they approached, moving up the slope of the mound. Miakka had hoped to see the movement of people. Instead the village appeared to be uninhabited. But smoke rose from the central hearth.

Miakka went to Tabisha and Acopa's dwelling and made her way up the ladder. Mi-sa waited before following her mother. She touched the hearthstones. They were cold.

When Miakka's eyes adjusted, she saw that Tabisha and Acopa lay curled up on their mats.

"Tabisha?" she called softly. There was no answer. "Acopa?"

Miakka knelt over Tabisha and Mi-sa came inside and stooped next to Acopa. Miakka extended her hand and nudged Tabisha on the shoulder. The movement was enough to spur a low moan from the woman.

Mi-sa listened for Acopa's breath. "He breathes," she said.

The inside of the shelter reeked with the odors of sickness. The smell was pungent and seemed tangible enough to foul the skin.

Mi-sa touched Acopa, feeling the heat but going deeper, reaching inside him. In an instant she understood. "This is the same sickness that Cherok has."

"Atula," Miakka said, her face filled with dread as she moved toward the ladder. She hurried across the mound. Was everyone dying? Was Atula alive?

As she hurried up the shaman's ladder, she called his name.

"Miakka," she heard him whisper when he saw her.

He lay on his mat with his head propped up on a rolled deerskin. Next to him were several pots of medicine, special elixirs he had prepared. Nearby were baskets of leaves, bark, petals, mosses, lichens, roots, dried berries, and fungi.

"Hand me that one," he said and weakly pointed to a black pot.

Miakka recognized the aroma of the tea as she swirled it under her nose. It was the one that Mi-sa had made for Cherok.

She lifted his head and held the pot to his dry lips. Atula sipped, then drew in a deep breath from the effort. He started a chant—strange, forced, breathless words— but soon gave in to his exhaustion.

"What has happened?" she asked, drawing his head to her breast.

"A sickness has swept the village," someone said behind her.

She turned, lowering Atula's head onto his deerskin.

"Talasee, you are well?"

"Some of us have been spared. We do what we can to help those who are ill. But there are so many, and it seems that every day we lose someone."

"Who has died?"

"Omo-ko, Hamet, Sassacha, Kita—"

"Cherok also has the sickness," she said, interrupting him. "That is why we have returned. He is near the canoe. Will you carry him to the village?"

Talasee nodded and descended the ladder. Atula groaned.

"What is it?" she asked, fearing that he suffered.

"Cherok is also sick?"

"Yes," Miakka answered him, touching his cheek.

"Then we will all perish," he whispered, closing his eyes.

Miakka understood. The People were sick and dying, and there was no shaman to help, no one to ask the spirits to come, no one to prepare the medicines, no one to say the magic and holy words.

———

MIAKKA STOOD in the center of the village. Except for a few people, the village seemed deserted. She had seen Sima and Amakollee. They were both well. They had taken some food from the central hearth, as others had, and then wandered away. A few platforms had been started to replace those that had burned, but they stood unfinished, like skeletons, empty of thatch. No streams of smoke curled into the air; no bustle animated the village. No voices rang out, and the village was littered with debris. Death hung in the air.

Mi-sa stood next to her mother. She felt a tap on her shoulder.

"Where is Cherok?"

Cacema stood behind her, circles around her eyes, her cheeks hollow.

"Talasee brings him," Miakka answered.

Cacema's face contorted with despair. She wobbled, weak and dizzy.

"He is not dead, Cacema," Mi-sa said, taking her arm. "He is sick, but he is alive."

Cacema covered her face with her hands and began to sob when she saw Talasee with Cherok in his arms.

"Come," Miakka said, following Talasee.

———

MI-SA COULD NOT SLEEP. Something crawled inside her. If only she could reach Cherok. He always helped her understand. She had to see him. Had to reach him. Had to try again.

Mi-sa went to Cacema's platform and called up to her.

"May I come up?" she asked.

Only a short time ago, Cacema might have discouraged a visit from Mi-sa. But what did it matter now? She wanted to honor her son's feelings toward this young woman. "Come," she answered.

Mi-sa climbed the ladder into the platform.

"My son is dying. I have seen the disease sweep through the village."

"Cherok is strong," Mi-sa said. "He fights."

"The rest of my family also suffers," she said, looking at the other bodies inside the platform. "But the sickness does not touch me. I have screamed to the spirits to take me, too, but they do not hear me." She started to cry.

"When did you last sleep?" Mi-sa asked.

"Days ago. Nights ago. Before all this. I do not remember."

"Cacema, you need to rest."

"But who will look after them? Who will give them water and wash the heat from their bodies?"

"I will," Mi-sa answered. "Let me. You sleep for a little while."

Cacema was too tired to object. Without further argument she obeyed like a child, letting Mi-sa lead her to the far side of the platform. Mi-sa unfurled a deerskin and placed a grass mat on top of it. Cacema curled her knees up to her chest and closed her eyes.

"Sleep, Cacema."

Quietly Mi-sa knelt beside Cherok and then sat back on her heels. She took Cherok's hand in hers, closed her eyes, and concentrated. She would find him, and he would tell her what to do.

She began to hum, a rhythmic melody, a low and detached sound that came out deeper than her voice. Slowly and completely she emptied her mind, clearing away her thoughts, letting them cascade out from her, seeing them sail on her song. She centered herself in the crown of her head, pulling tighter and tighter until she broke free and flew through dazzling flaxen and vermilion bursts of light.

"I am here, Cherok. No harm will come to you. Show me the way. Help me find you."

Mi-sa saw herself standing alone in the white haze. It was cool and safe, a gentle comforting place to be. "I have come for you, Cherok," she called again.

She focused harder, until her concentration was needle sharp. "Help me find you. The People need you, Cherok." As if made of the haze, she floated forward on the air, whispering her song.

Then there was a trail of sound—a voice in Cherok's mind that answered her.

The corners of her mouth turned slightly upward in a knowing, soothing smile. "Yes, Cherok, I hear you. I feel your strength. Fight hard, Cherok. Help me. Help the People."

Again a whisper, and Mi-sa moved closer. "Reach out for me," she hummed. "Hold out your hand."

Through the fog she began to see a form, weak and fading in and out. "Yes, Cherok. I see you now. Try hard. Reach for me."

Mi-sa extended her hand and stepped deeper into the haze, watching it clear as she moved through it. There, just in front of her, she saw him. Cherok reached out, and Mi-sa grasped his hand.

"You did it, Cherok. You have a strong spirit."

Cherok smiled at her.

"Many suffer from this sickness. Atula is also ill. I want to help them. I thought I knew the medicine. Help me, Cherok. Tell me what to do."

Cherok did not speak, but she heard his voice: "Trust yourself."

Cherok's image began to fade. Soon he had no color, no form; he was just a breeze, a fleeting mist.

"Wait," she called, but he was gone.

She sat by his side, moistening his lips. Through the night she delivered water to Cherok's thirsty throat and dry mouth and swabbed his hot body with cool water. She wished for some of the cold air to return. The platform seemed to fill with the steam of their hot breath. Stifling.

———

ATULA DRIFTED, floating free in his dream. Miakka sat at his side, watching him thrash and then rest. She held some water to his cracked lips, but he refused it, pushing the pot away.

"There," he said hoarsely, pointing to a small basket by the wall.

Miakka went to get it.

"Use it all," he said, trying to lift his head.

Miakka was unfamiliar with the contents. The basket was filled with several plant parts, most of which she had never seen used as food or tea. These were the herbs of the shaman.

"What do you want me to do with these?" she asked. "I do not know how to prepare them."

Atula could not keep his head up any longer. He closed his eyes and leaned back. His lips quivered as he tried to speak, forming sounds too weak to be heard. Miakka leaned closer.

"All of it. In a tea," she heard him whisper.

"Yes," she answered him. "I will prepare a tea."

Below the platform she started a fire from a coal she

took from the central hearth. How easy this was, she thought, remembering how hard it was to make a fire with the fire bow she had made.

It seemed the water would never boil. When at last the bubbles rolled in the water, she emptied the cache of herbs. There seemed so many, but she had never watched the shaman prepare his special brews. As she watched the herbs tumble, she sighed and felt her throat constrict and her eyes burn. There was so much to cry for. So many losses. So many worries. She had to help Atula. After all this time she could not lose him to death now. It would be enough to see him well. How she would treasure seeing him fresh from slumber standing near his fire, still warm with sleep, waiting for his tea. She wanted to see him again, in full costume, strong, compelling, magical. She felt inadequate and helpless.

Miakka moved the tea to the side of the fire and covered the pot. It would take a while to cool.

A noise surprised her, a banging and cracking sound. She stood and looked into the distance. She walked through the village, searching for the source of the noise.

Illuminated by his fire, Talasee swung his shell ax, breaking the wood to just the right size. He threw it on the pile of logs.

"Talasee, why are you chopping wood?" she asked, walking up to him.

"For the dead," he answered.

Miakka looked at the stack of wood. He also had lashing to bind the logs together.

"A crypt," he added without looking up. "To stack the bodies."

Miakka looked sick.

"We have to take care of the dead."

"Not that many have died, Talasee."

"But have you counted the sick? No one has gotten well. They will die also."

"No. No."

"Miakka, I do not want them to die either."

Miakka wandered away. She could not stay and watch Talasee perform his morbid task. She dipped her finger into the tea she had left to cool. It was warm, but not too hot. She took it to Atula.

"The tea is ready," she said, lifting his head.

Atula opened his eyes, noticing the faint light of dawn creeping into his. platform. He wrapped his trembling hand around hers that held the pot, helping her put it to his lips. He opened his mouth and sipped at first, then gulped and coughed.

Miakka moved the bowl away, but Atula urged it closer. He opened his lips again. Miakka stared at him, questioning. He nodded, and she touched the vessel to his mouth. He finished all the tea and closed his eyes, fighting the coughing spasms that followed.

She put the bowl on the floor and took his hand. He squeezed it, saying the things she wanted to hear without speaking a word. Miakka leaned forward and touched her lips to his. "You will be well," she said just before her soft lips touched his once again.

She lowered her head, resting her forehead on his chest. She did not want to cry. She was not going to allow herself to do so.

Miakka suddenly felt Atula's chest rise, hard and full. She looked at him. He was rigid, his eyes staring blankly ahead. Small tremors began to shake him, his legs jumping, his abdomen shuddering. Atula's neck arched, and his eyes rolled back in his head.

"No," she cried, "you cannot die."

Chapter Thirty-four

A SUDDEN BREEZE RUSHED through the platform, stirring the contents of the baskets, blowing some of the leaves and petals across the floor. Miakka thought she heard a soft melodic chant. But Atula lay still, his lips not moving. She touched his chest and then the side of his neck. Life still pulsed within him. But where was that sweet serenade coming from, that mellow song she was sure she could hear?

Atula was soaring through a dark tunnel. He could see the brilliant light at the end. He could feel it pull at him, stretching his spirit thin like a wisp of smoke. The light exploded with colors as he neared it. Suddenly he was thrown through the mouth of the tunnel, and his vision began.

It had been a long time since he had seen these things. He stood near the river as the dark clouds rolled above him and finally burst. The air was cool, and the falling rain chilled him. Lightning ripped a jagged line through the dark sky, and the earth shook with the rumble of thunder. The storm whipped the trees, tearing boughs free and hurling them through the air. The giant rushes, tall sedge, and frail grass buckled.

Atula had seen this same storm before, and as it

roared, he watched carefully. The river flooded, cutting a deep gully, birthing a new river. As the storm cleared, he saw that the old river was dry. This time the men in the canoe did not come. He stood alone at the fork. He saw on one side of him the dry cracked floor of the old riverbed, on the other was sparkling fresh water in the new river. Atula stepped closer.

The face he had seen below the water so long ago was there again. But this time he called it forward, implored it to move to the surface so that he might recognize it.

As the face rose closer and closer, it became clearer. The water glinted, making Atula squint. Suddenly he knew to whom the face belonged. The realization took him by surprise.

This was Mi-sa's face. The revelation was startling. He remembered the old vision and the discussion and quarrel the men had had over which river to follow. Some were afraid of the new river, though the old river could no longer support them. Of course. How clear it seemed now. Mi-sa was the child with the Gift. She was the new river. The People were to trust in her, for she offered all those things that the old river had once offered.

Atula suddenly felt unworthy. How could he have missed the meaning when the spirits had given him such a vision? Mi-sa was a female, and that one fact had kept him from recognizing her as the chosen one. As a man of the spirits he was not supposed to be confused by earthly issues. The old river was no more than the line of shamans who had come before—a male line. Mi-sa was indeed the new river, the inheritor of the Gift.

The spirits were kind, he thought as the vision faded. He knew what he must do.

Miakka watched as Atula's eyelids fluttered. At first he stared blankly, readjusting. Then he looked into her eyes, which had grown dull with weariness and worry.

"Mi-sa," he murmured. "Bring Mi-sa to me."

———

MI-SA FOLLOWED HER MOTHER up the steps to the shaman's platform. She wondered what he wanted with her. She clutched her stomach as it seemed to turn over.

Miakka sat near Atula. "She is here, Atula. I have brought Mi-sa."

Atula opened his eyes and waved Mi-sa closer. She stepped forward and sat next to him.

"Mi-sa," he whispered, touching her hand. "Listen carefully to me." Atula dragged in a breath.

"Yes, Shaman," she answered.

"You are the new river," he told her.

Mi-sa shook her head, and then looked at her mother. "I do not understand."

"You are the chosen one, Mi-sa. Do you not know that?" he asked, lightly squeezing her hand.

"Mother?" she asked, hoping Miakka would explain, but Miakka shook her head.

"You have the Gift, Mi-sa," the shaman said. "Cherok tried to tell me. The spirits tried to tell me. But I have been blind. The People have been blind."

"No," Mi-sa responded, pulling her hand from his, leaning back as if she could keep his words from reaching her.

"It is true," he whispered. "The sickness. The spirits test you—test me."

Mi-sa's hands trembled.

"You know the medicine."

Mi-sa looked hard at him.

"The wisdom comes from inside you. And some of the songs ring in your heart. Is that not so?"

Mi-sa did not answer.

"But you have missed the lifetime of instruction a shaman gives the child who inherits the Gift."

"No," she finally said. "I thought I knew the medicine, but I did not. I made a tea for Cherok, but he has not recovered. I do not know anything. I am guided by a false spirit."

"No, Mi-sa. You touch the stars, the hearths of the spirits and of those who have gone before."

Mi-sa pushed herself back, not wanting to hear any more. But Atula kept on talking.

"It is the prayers and the answer of the spirits that make the medicine work. You have bits and pieces, but the knowledge is buried inside you. Closer," the shaman urged. "Come closer, Mi-sa."

Mi-sa leaned forward, and Miakka moved back. Atula closed his eyes and began to hum. At first she could barely hear him, but then the song rang louder in her ears, in her heart. Before she realized it, she had raised her voice with his and was singing a song so pure and clear that she could not deny its power. The sounds pealed from her.

Miakka's hand went over her mouth as she fought tears. But Mi-sa's face was quickly streaked with tears as she sang with her father, the shaman.

Atula's voice faded, leaving only hers, filling the platform, vibrating in the air.

She knew the song's meaning, and she raised the bowl of medicine above her as she called to the spirits. The air was alive, charged with the energy of her magical voice and the answer of the spirits. She felt their warmth cloak her and blend into her. She held the bowl to Atula's lips, and he drank, afterward resting his head.

"You are a healer," he said. "You bring the spirits. Go

out and meet your destiny. Save the People—your people."

The doubts were gone, and at last she understood. She felt whole and good as she went to Cherok first.

———

As THE DAYS PASSED, she helped those who allowed her to approach them. Mi-sa stood with her mother on Amakollee's platform. She did not call up because she knew that Amakollee would send her away. Inside the dark platform she saw Kachumpka. His frame looked fragile as he lay curled on his mat.

"Get her out," Amakollee screeched at Miakka.

"Let her help, Amakollee. She can help your son."

"She is evil. Get her away."

Amakollee rose to her feet, flailing her arms as she shooed Mi-sa and Miakka to the ladder. "Get out!"

The women moved down the ladder. A half a moon cycle had passed since Atula called her to his side. One other had died, someone who had denied her help, but she had helped many others.

"Kachumpka will die," Mi-sa said to her mother. "He does not have much time left."

"You cannot help him unless Amakollee allows it."

The two women walked to the cenote and collected fresh water to prepare more medicine.

"I will go for more bark," Mi-sa told her.

Mother and daughter parted, Miakka walking to the dwelling of Atula. When she was close, she thought she heard him call to her.

Miakka looked up. He was standing in his platform, looking out. Miakka began in a trot and then a run, leaving the bowl on the ground and scrambling up the ladder.

She flung her arms around him. "You are well!"

Atula stumbled backward. "Woman, you are strong," he said and laughed.

"Oh, I am sorry," Miakka answered. "You are still weak. I did not mean ... I should have thought ..."

Atula put his hand over her mouth. She tried to talk through it, mumbling while he smiled at her attempts.

"I am not going to die," he said, "but I do not think I am ready to hunt." He finally took his hand away from her mouth.

"Of course not. Here," she said, leading him back to his bed. "Rest. Do not exert yourself."

Atula stretched out and enjoyed watching her flutter about.

"Come here, woman," he whispered to her.

Miakka sat at his side.

"Lie with me," he told her.

Miakka reclined, resting her head on his shoulder.

"Now I can rest," he said, closing his eyes.

———

MI-SA LEFT THE BASKET of bark near the central hearth. She went to Cherok's bed. He was sitting up with the others inside his platform. Cacema was beaming.

"Cherok was right," she said when she saw Mi-sa. "All that time. I am sorry, Mi-sa. You have suffered so much pain."

"Shh," Mi-sa urged. "This is the way the spirits wanted it. We are not to question them."

Cherok reached out and took both of her hands in his. He closed his eyes and could hear the wind above the earth. He could feel the coolness of the clouds on his face and the warmth of the sun on his back.

Mi-sa closed her eyes as she joined him. They smiled

at each other, and then she took them back.

"Did I not always tell you that you are special?" he asked.

"Oh, Cherok. If not for you ... if not for you," she said, her eyes brimming with tears.

"I want to see the outside, the sunshine," he said, starting to stand.

Mi-sa and Cacema helped him to his feet, walking him to the opening. Cherok looked outside.

"Go and take care of the others," he told Mi-sa. "I am all right."

Cacema reached out and hugged her.

———

WHEN THE NIGHT CAME, those who had not been stricken gathered at the central hearth. Slowly they straggled in. Though Mi-sa had treated most of their loved ones, they still shied away from her. Some, however, had refused to let her help,

The group stood as they saw a man stride through the darkness. When he was close enough that the firelight could reveal him, they realized it was Atula.

"The shaman is well," one of them said.

"Atula," Miakka scolded, "you should not have left your platform. You are not strong enough yet."

"The People must see what Mi-sa has done. They must not doubt her powers."

"Take him home, Mother," Mi-sa said. "Do not risk your health for me," she told him.

Amakollee tore a piece of dried meat from the strip she held in her hand and threw the rest in the fire, mumbling as she walked away. She needed to get back to Kachumpka and take care of him. She would make him well, not that evil spirit, no matter how she had healed

Atula. She wanted no part of the girl's evil magic.

Kachumpka was curled into a ball. She turned him, thinking he must be stiff from lying in one position for so long. When she shifted him, he did not even groan or open his eyes. He had to recover. The spirits would see to that. They would not desert their favored soul.

Amakollee began to rock back and forth. Her eyes roamed her home. Was something out of place? Did the spirits hear her?

———

MI-SA WAS ALONE in her mother's platform. Miakka stayed at Atula's side. Mi-sa felt the exhaustion claim her as she settled on her side. Nearly as soon as she closed her eyes she slept. No dreams. No nightmares.

In the darkness Amakollee crept through the village. She paused at the foot of Mi-sa's ladder, hesitating. She asked for the spirits to make her strong as she began her ascent.

Chapter Thirty-five

AMAKOLLEE STOOD OVER MI-SA. She wrung her hands and a stream of perspiration rolled down her back.

"Can you help my son?" she whispered.

Mi-sa turned onto her back and looked up. Startled to see Amakollee in the shadows, she sat up.

"Can you help him?" she asked again.

Mi-sa looked at the desperate woman. Suddenly Mi-sa shivered, and then she remembered. She was again inside this platform, but she was a child. Sleeping. She felt someone's hot breath on her back and twisted around to see who it was. The sharp pain. Amakollee.

Mi-sa stared at the woman, remembering that night so long ago. She was not surprised. She had always sensed that the attacker was Amakollee, but for the first time she remembered clearly. The woman's face had looked much as it did tonight, overwrought with fear.

"Please help him," Amakollee pleaded.

Mi-sa stood and gathered her things. They stopped at Mi-sa's hearth. "Carry this," the young woman said, handing a bowl to Amakollee.

———

THIS HAD NOT BEEN an easy thing for Amakollee to ask. The rest of the village remained asleep as she sponged her son and tried to get him to drink. But as the night wore on, he seemed to sink deeper and deeper, ebbing away from her. She had dragged his head and chest into her lap and held him, singing those old lullabies that had comforted him as a child.

Kachumpka's lips had paled to the same gray as the rest of his face. His breathing was labored, and he was making sucking and rattling noises as he struggled for air. But then the labor became-too much, and he had stopped. Amakollee had shaken him, lifted him, and cried out to the spirits not to take her son, the child who had saved her from a lifetime of humiliation and disgrace. She would do anything. Anything!

When Kachumpka pulled in another long-awaited breath, Amakollee had wept. She would do anything to save him.

She would go and get Mi-sa.

———

MI-SA HAD LITTLE HOPE. Kachumpka was sicker than the others she had helped. Even Cherok had not been this close to death. She looked at Amakollee who stood in a corner, afraid to watch what she was about to allow.

"Come and hold his head," Mi-sa directed.

Amakollee moved forward and propped Kachumpka's head in her lap.

"We need to get him to drink, Amakollee. He needs the medicine."

Amakollee nodded understanding.

"Be still and quiet until I am finished. Do you understand?"

Again Amakollee nodded.

Mi-sa closed her eyes, concentrated on slowing her breathing and the rapid thumping in her chest. In a moment she was taking slow, deep, and easy breaths. She began to chant, calling the spirits.

Amakollee sat stunned at the response. Mi-sa's power was overwhelming, maybe even stronger than her father's. The breeze whirled inside the platform, and Mi-sa's hair seemed to be borne on the air, blowing out and away from her face.

Mi-sa held the bowl up, opening her eyes. Her voice reverberated through the small dwelling, bouncing off the thatch, echoing in Amakollee's ears. The song went on and on, growing louder and louder. Strange pulsing words, magic words, filled the night. The platform seemed ready to explode with the sound as the words and the melody resounded across the land.

A shaft of bright light filled the room, but soon it was gone as quickly as it had come.

Mi-sa sat quietly and then opened her eyes. She held the bowl to Kachumpka's lips, tilting it so that the liquid dribbled out. But it spilled down over Kachumpka's chin.

"Call him, Amakollee. Rouse him enough to swallow. He cannot get well if he does not drink the medicine."

Amakollee called her son's name. Her voice was scratchy. She cleared her throat and called to him again. Kachumpka did not respond. "Please, Kachumpka. Please."

Mi-sa wiped his face with cool water. "Try again," she said.

Amakollee heaved her son up higher so that his head wobbled at the height of her aching shoulder. "Drink, Kachumpka," she pleaded, saying it over and over until she was screaming. "Help him," she yelled, looking up toward the roof. "Do not desert him. Please. Please," she begged.

Perhaps the spirits did hear her. Kachumpka lifted his

eyelids to small slits. Amakollee began to sob. "Yes, son. Now open your mouth and drink the medicine."

Mi-sa spilled a little of the liquid into his mouth, letting him drink slowly so that he did not choke. Amakollee continued to cry, her tears falling on her son's hair.

Mi-sa put down the bowl. "Keep making him drink," she said, standing to leave.

Amakollee did not look up. Mi-sa stopped at the head of the ladder and looked back. Amakollee was still crying, holding her son against her, calling his name softly, and rocking him.

Chapter Thirty-six

THE SUN REACHED DOWN and touched the feathers of the red-shouldered hawk as it dipped and pitched, cruising over the marsh. The cypresses had endured the cold air, and speckles of lacy green had begun to emerge on the gray trees now that warmer air embraced the region.

Lizards and crickets skittered through the brush. Snakes lethargically moved under the low growth of wire grass and vines. The warm water flashed with the iridescent colors of the male sailfin mollies, darting, catching the sun as they pursued the females. A sally of shiners glimmered as they churned the water, evading the feeding bass.

Everything was waking, happy at the return of the steady warmth. The recent cold season had been especially mild, eliminating the nuisance of mosquitoes for only a brief time. The swamp was alive with their buzzing, and the water jiggled with wigglers, so many that even after the tiny mosquito fish had filled their bellies with the larvae, there would be swarms left to take wing.

Mi-sa stood at the cenote. Perhaps what her mother had said would actually one day be true. Maybe she would sit on a ridge with her granddaughter. Perhaps she would tell her story. And, yes, she would take her granddaughter on her first spirit flight. She would accompany her so that the child would not be afraid, so that the little one would understand and never have to be frightened, as she had been.

She looked out across the water. Today was special. It was her last day as a simple woman.

———

THE EDGE OF NIGHT slipped uneventfully over the sun. Talasee hurled large branches and logs into the fire. He had gathered many baskets of pine cones and brought them back to the village. They were always exciting to add to the fire. They crackled and quickly flamed, then glowed. He had taken extra care in the preparation of this fire. The heat, so close, made him feel as though he might melt, but the honor attached to his task prevailed, and so he endured the discomfort, actually finding some reward in it.

The clan had fasted in anticipation of the upcoming event. Atula had prepared his medicine, consecrating it with his most compelling and passionate liturgies. When he had effectively purged himself, he sat close to his fire, sometimes boiling special blends of plant parts, creating a steam that he leaned into and breathed. By nightfall he was cleansed, without a trace of impurity.

He colored his face with the deep ruby of red ocher. He daubed small black circles in a waving line across his cheek, over the bridge of his nose and onto the other side of his face, enhancing his cheekbones. With each touch of pitch to his cheeks he recited an incantation, his sonorous voice hastening the advent of the spirits.

On his head he placed a stuffed owl skin, the insignia of his great wisdom and divination. Just below each knee he tied a band of owl feathers and tinkling shells. Atula reached into a small basket. There, wrapped in soft deerskin, rested a piece of yellow-white calcite crystal and a bear claw. He peeled away the wrapping and held the crystal and the claw in the palm of his hand.

From another basket he pulled a small bundle, from which he extracted a piece of lightning-riven pine, four small perforated shells, and a shark tooth the length of his middle finger The tooth had been the prize of a great shaman who had lived during the time of the giant beasts. It was a treasure that had survived the many ensuing generations.

Atula sat on the floor of his platform, spreading all the items onto a square of buckskin that was crisscrossed with crooked red and yellow lines. He took a sip of a special formula, tracing its journey by the warmth that trickled down his throat and into his stomach. He had only heard the words once, when his father taught them to him. Atula had said them himself when he assumed the responsibility and the power of shaman. Now he said them again over the special charms.

When he finished, he drank the rest of the elixir and packaged the talismans. Gently he touched the triangular amulet that dangled from his neck. Ochassee would have been proud. Mi-sa had been a supreme challenge to his perceptiveness and strength. He had proved his honor and merit by his correct interpretation of the long-ago star sign and the new river vision. The new river marked the beginning of change for the People. He was fortunate to be a part of this transition. Yes, his father would have been proud.

Atula stepped out of his platform. From the top of the ladder he could see the flames of the central hearth illuminating the night with their light. As he descended the ladder and walked closer, he heard the crowd hush, then saw the People bend to him, parting to create a path, pressing the backs of their hands to their foreheads. The full moon sent its glow through the trees, mottling their bodies with phantom silver light.

Atula stood before them. The villagers straightened as he held out one hand, palm up, raising it in the signal to assume their normal posture. He surveyed the clan. The People had suffered tremendous losses from the A-po-la-chee and the illness, but they were strong.

Amakollee stood near the back, Kachumpka, as always, lolling and dawdling at her side. Talasee stepped away from the fire. Cacema, filled with pride, stood at the front with her husband, Okapi.

Atula held the bear cloak in one hand and the cacique's staff in the other as he began to dance, swirling the animal skin through the air in great arcs, spinning in slow, exaggerated circles. By flexing his wrist, he made the cloak seem alive, twisting and dancing in the air. Sometimes he prodded it with the stick, then swiftly wrapped himself in it, holding the staff up over his head.

"Cherok," he called, his voice booming.

From out of the darkness Cherok walked through the crowd as it separated for him. When he stood in front of Atula, the shaman tossed a handful of powder at the fire. The hearth sprayed hot white cinders into the air, sizzling and crackling after the first puff of smoke.

Cherok lowered his head in respect as Atula presented him to the spirits. At the end of his prayer, the shaman touched Cherok's head, letting him know that the incantation was finished.

Cherok lifted his face and turned to the People. Atula charged the young man with his new duties and obligations. There were no dissenters in the crowd, their intense faces breaking into smiles. Cherok felt humbled when Atula handed him the staff. He was now the cacique. How proud he was.

Atula felt the same. All those wonderful bright qualities he had seen in Cherok for so long were the signs of a leader, not a shaman. He wished he had understood that earlier, but he was happy that the spirits had finally made it clear.

With Cherok at his side, Atula again began to chant. Then he called Mi-sa's name. The crowd, no longer jubilant, suddenly fell mute.

Mi-sa stood in the opening of her mother's shelter. The villagers turned to see her.

Again Atula called her name. Mi-sa descended the ladder and approached the gathering. She held her breath as she took her first step into the assembly. Sima stepped back, allowing her to pass. The others who stood in Mi-sa's path followed Sima's lead. With each step Mi-sa waited for the next few people to part and let her pass. She stood face to face with one woman, the sister of Sassacha, but then the woman stepped aside.

Standing next to Cherok, Atula told the story of his vision. He told the story as a hunter might have related his adventures. He gathered his people with the way he spoke and moved—charismatic and mystic. The People were soon drawn into his tale, seeing the great thunderstorm that transformed one river into two. They could feel the dust at the bottom of the old river and the delightful, life-giving water of the new river. They understood the dilemma as Atula told them of the fishermen's deliberations over the predicament and how the two rivers had created an impasse. And finally he told them about the face—the identity of the new river.

Atula asked Mi-sa to observe the People she had been chosen to serve. She looked out across the hammock, seeing the eyes of the company watching. He handed her the two bundles that he had guarded since his father's death. Only a shaman touched or looked upon these sacred objects. He placed them in her hands, then began to sing the words that only Mi-sa understood. Her voice, fragile and tremulous at first, joined his in a harmony the People had never heard before. In a few moments the curious chant had become nearly indistinguishable from the sounds of the wind, the leaves, and the insects and the call of the panther. The song enveloped the village, chiming in accord with the swish of the saw-grass sedge as a sudden gust of wind blew over the mound. The music was sweet in their ears.

Miakka watched, her throat feeling tight and constricted. She would not let the People see her cry, not even with happiness and pride.

Atula stripped the bear cloak from his shoulders and put it around Mi-sa. He wrapped his fingers around the triangular amulet that hung around his neck. This was the special gift of Ochassee, and now Atula would hand it over to the next shaman of their pure lineage. He fingered the necklace, and then lifted it over his head. As the people watched, he lowered it over Mi-sa's head. Everything seemed to slow to an unnatural pace; the amulet dangled in front of her eyes and then came to rest on her chest. Silence. Even the sounds of nature paused for this moment.

Atula placed the owl headdress on his daughter's head and then stepped away and made his way to Miakka.

Mi-sa stood quiet, still, and alone. The villagers stared. In some of their eyes, she was afraid she still saw a scant sprinkling of doubt.

From the back of the crowd she heard a commotion. Someone was pushing through the group. As the figure came into the light, she recognized Amakollee.

Miakka's eyes grew wide with fear, and she started to step forward. She would not allow this woman to defile this sacred moment. Amakollee had done enough. As Miakka started to step forward, Atula drew her back.

Mi-sa stood tall, watching the woman approach. She could hear startled gasps as everyone realized what was happening. Kachumpka swayed in the rear of the crowd, watching his mother.

Amakollee stood squarely in front of Mi-sa, and the two women stared at each other.

Amakollee finally looked away, bent forward, and placed the back of her hand against her forehead.

At first the villagers remained still in amazement, but then one by one they followed Amakollee's example, lowering their heads, touching their hands to their foreheads, showing respect for the shaman.

Mi-sa stepped closer to the hearth, then reached into the flames and lifted a coal out of the fire. The moonlight and firelight danced on her face as the People watched her. She was an enchantress. But this demonstration of her power was not enough.

Mi-sa replaced the coal, then began a soft, melodic song.

Atula squeezed Miakka's hand.

Ending her song, Mi-sa turned to Cherok. He smiled at her and nodded. She turned her back to the crowd and raised a hand into the plush black night sky. Above was the moon, surrounded by the glittering stars. She stretched upward, reaching higher. In her mind the words tumbled, the words of the secret songs of those who had come before, the songs that had ached to be sung. For an instant she closed her eyes, hearing only the voices of the spirits.

She lowered her hand and turned to face the assemblage, unfolding her fingers one at a time, revealing a blinding blue-white light. She held the brilliance out—to her people.

About the Author:

LYNN ARMISTEAD MCKEE has worked as a writing trainer for Broward County Schools and Citrus County Schools in Florida. Her interest in archaeology and her work with the Broward County Archaeological Society led her to write historical fiction about the indigenous peoples of South Florida. Writing as Lynn Sholes she also co-writes thrillers with Joe Moore. Lynn is a member of International Thriller Writers, Mystery Writers of America, Florida Writers Association, and The Authors Guild. She writes from her home in the Sunshine State.

Books by Lynn Armistead McKee

WOMAN OF THE MISTS
TOUCHES THE STARS
KEEPER OF DREAMS
WALKS IN STARDUST
SPIRIT OF THE TURTLE WOMAN
DAUGHTER OF THE FIFTH MOON

Books by this author, writing as Lynn Sholes with Joe Moore

THE GRAIL CONPSIRACY
THE LAST SECRET
THE HADES PROJECT
THE PHOENIX APOSTLES
THE 731 LEGACY
THE COTTEN STONE OMNIBUS
THE BLADE
THE SHIELD
THE TOMB
THOR BUNKER, A Short Story
BAM! JUST LIKE THAT (short story)

Sample Chapter

KEEPER OF DREAMS

Chapter One

THE SILENCE WAS BROKEN by the sound of men sucking in their breath in disbelief. The women of the Tegesta village stood still, holding their children against their moss skirts, clutching infants to their breasts. They stopped their tasks, and those who had been seated stood to watch. They stared, dark eyes wide, mouths agape, stricken by what they saw.

Mi-sa approached from behind the crowd. She wished she had a man to stand beside her. Not her father. Not her brother. A man like the one who came to her in her dreams—powerful, faithful, protective, with long flowing hair, dark like the night.

She walked into the gathered Council, moving and weaving her way between the seated men, a silent startling form, until she stood by Cherok, the cacique, the chief. Next to him she sat cross-legged. The air was so dense with mugginess and tension that it could nearly be touched, sculpted between the palms of a man's hands.

She had not entered the Council ever before. No woman had. But she was the new shaman, and it was time. The young woman looked out into the focused black eyes that stared from carved and creased faces. Brows dipped, fissuring their foreheads. Jaw muscles tightened the lines of their mouths, drawing their lips thin with misgivings.

"Is this not the place of the shaman?" she asked, indicating her spot, holding her hands out in front of her, palms up in question.

The eyes still peered at her with incredulity.

Atula stood, quickly drawing the crowd's attention. "It is the correct place, Shaman," he answered in a clear, firm voice, and then sat down.

Cherok nodded. "Yes," he said, agreeing with Atula.

The small village broiled beneath the sun. The air was thick, heavy with gnats, heat, and humidity. Perhaps the heat would inflame tempers. Cherok hoped not.

At first the Council's elders focused on the mundane things about which they always parleyed. But this time the discussions seemed limited, the men intimidated, strained. Mi-sa sat quietly listening, not joining in. She was observing different perspectives, grasping dispositions and personalities.

The air boiled with swarms of pests, tiny insects in flight, spots and specks of annoyance and nuisance. The gathered men swatted and fanned the bugs away from their faces.

At last the Big Water journey was brought into the discourse. Cherok tensed, knowing what was coming. If only Mi-sa could give the People more time, he thought, as with a new food, allowing time for the clan to taste it slowly, time to make sure that it agreed with them. Trails of perspiration dripped down the sides of his face, and he felt another stream trickle down his back. Cherok mopped his forehead with the back of his hand, and then nodded at a man who wished to speak.

"Soon the moon will be right for the Big Water journey," a man in the rear reiterated.

In Council they began to lay out their plans, discuss

responsibilities. Had every man checked his stash of harpoons, spears, nets, weights, shell hooks? Those articles would become communal weapons and tools once they were out to sea. Except for a man's knife, which he kept for himself, all the other gear was shared. Knowing that others would use his tools and weapons, the maker took extra pride in his work. Respect for his craftsmanship, his manhood, was at stake.

"I have no weapons or implements to contribute," Mi-sa said, speaking out, surprising them.

"Women do not touch such things," an irritated man remarked, not waiting for Cherok to call upon him.

"But I wish to contribute," Mi-sa continued. "All of you contribute, and so should I."

"There is no reason," the man argued, hearing rumblings of agreement circulating through the group.

"Is it not true that everyone is expected to contribute and share on a Big Water journey?" she asked. "Perhaps I am too ignorant because this is new to me." Mi-sa lifted an eyebrow. "Perhaps it is acceptable that someone may use the communal weapons and devices without offering some of his own."

The men quickly understood her meaning and fidgeted uncomfortably. She intended to go with them.

"Cherok!" demanded a short man whose round chest glistened with sweat. "What is this, a woman on a Big Water journey—using weapons?"

"I think you should address Mi-sa," Cherok returned.

"I do not recognize a woman in the Council," the short man said, wiping the beads of sweat from his upper lip, and then folding his arms across his chest. Thinking of something else, he leaned forward, squinted, and pursed his lips to emphasize what he had to say. "She may be the shaman because the spirits have recognized her as the seed of Atula, but only men go on Big Water journeys." He sat up straighter, affecting a lofty pose. "Men fashion and use weapons. The spirits have not taken it upon themselves to change her from a woman into a man." The man sat back, pleased with his short oration.

"May I speak?" Mi-sa asked Cherok.

The hammock exhaled in great transpiring huffs of steam. Like the men, the leathery leaves of the strangler fig formed wet beads and rivulets. Everything oozed moisture, the sun drawing the hidden sogginess out of the muck and the flesh, and into the air. The men shifted with aggravation and discomfort. This was not a good time, Cherok thought as he acknowledged Mi-sa with a wave of his hand.

Atula lifted his head with pride. Mi-sa, his daughter, was one to be admired. Nothing could alter her streak of pride. A shaman's pride.

Mi-sa saw her father's expression, and it gave her strength. "I know that it has been difficult for you to accept a woman as your shaman, but that is the decision of the spirits," she began. "The spirits decided that the Gift was to be passed to me through my father. And so I speak to the spirits on your behalf. I have been called by many of you to heal your bodies or the bodies of those you love. When you come with such eloquent requests, you always speak with the respect a man gives his shaman. You have asked me to see into the future, to interpret your dreams, to ask the spirits to bless you. I have done this with eagerness. It is my responsibility and my pleasure to serve the spirits and the People. I fear for you—for all of us. A clan without a shaman is a clan that will die. We all know and understand that. If you allow me to serve you only as a woman, to serve you in such diminished ways, then you have no real shaman. I have power, and my power is not limited because I am a woman. Mine is a great power that comes to me through the Gift. This is my charge. Let me be whole and bring to you the light of the spirits." Mi-sa looked back at Cherok. "I will leave the Council so that every man's voice can be heard without my interference."

Cherok watched her leave. He knew Mi-sa, her substance and determination. She was not afraid of controversy. She had been fearful and uncertain too often as a child when the People did not understand that she was the chosen one. She would not be afraid now.

The rest of the Council also watched Mi-sa leave. Her slim female body, formed of provocative curves, moved gracefully and proudly among them. The men looked at her face—the clean straight lines of her nose and cheeks, the fire that burned beneath the black coals of her eyes. Acknowledging her as the inheritor of the blood gift had caused rifts within the clan. She was indeed an enigma, the essence of a woman, the marrow of a shaman. Mi-sa's body spoke with the suppleness and softness of a woman—heavily lashed dreaming eyes, promising full lips, sensual rounds and arches, smooth tender hollows. But she spoke of such strange notions. She had ideas about taking part in the work and duties of men. She stirred ambiguous, confused emotions as she passed them. She could feel their eyes at her back—eyes that languorously wandered to her narrow waist, the crown of her hip, the length of her shapely legs.

She had joined with no man, although she could choose any male she desired. The spirits had not denied her satisfaction of a primal need. But she would never have a man as a husband. A shaman did not have someone live at his hearth—her hearth—and so Mi-sa had known no man. Unlike other women, she had a choice, and she protected her maidenhood. Because she had the choice, she valued it. She had never met a man extraordinary enough to make her entertain the thought of ending her celibacy. That was something she did not want to think about now, but one day she would need to produce an heir to carry on the line. But what man would want a shaman, a woman within a man's world? The spirits had been asking her to make sacrifices since the night she was born. Dealings with the spirits had never been a matter of choice. She had no power or control over the Gift.

Mi-sa left without looking back. As she passed the women, they returned to their chores, looking away quickly and timidly, ushering their children off to play. They had listened to the discussions. They had heard the men. But they had also heard Mi-sa. They wondered how she could fulfill her obligations as shaman if she was limited to a woman's world. They were glad they did not have to make the decision.

Mi-sa decided that she would wait alone for the men to come to an agreement. She wished to visit with her mother, talk with her about what had happened in Council, but she did not want to burden her. Instead she walked to the *edge* of the village, on the north side.

At night the men hung their medicine bundles near their heads. They slept with their feet pointing to the south and their heads to the north. There, behind the medicine bundles, on the north side, the Trails of Men began, threading out across the vast saw-grass prairie. She stood at the edge, daring herself to step past the invisible line, the boundary that separated the territory of men from that of the women. The men believed that women, especially menstruous ones, would ruin the hunt if they touched those northern grounds.

Mi-sa looked across the tips of the undulating scored blades of the sedge. In her platform she kept two long bones from an animal that she had heard of in legends. Her father had given them to her to use in certain rituals. She thought about that animal, a tall four-legged beast, larger than a deer but built much the same. According to the legends, it had hooves, a long tail, and a shock of hair at mid-forehead in its long face. The creature also had a mane of hair, more like a man's than an animal's, along the ridge of its neck. Sometimes when she was holding those bones she could almost see the world as that animal had seen it. She could almost go there, move back into ancient times. She came so close sometimes.

Now, as she looked across the saw grass, she thought of the animal again. What had this place been like when the legendary animal lived here? What had that creature seen? She wondered if the People would one day suffer the same fate and vanish. Would nothing be left but their old bones?

The wind brushed her face, whipping her hair to her back. Above her the sky began to churn; eerily luminous gray clouds were moving in, gathering together, clustering and brooding. Her small hand captured a maverick strand of hair that crossed in front of her eyes. She swept it back, letting the wind seize it.

Mi-sa breathed in deeply. This was one of those times that overcame her, creeping in on her from another world. She recognized the feeling and concentrated on clearing her mind, relaxing, becoming receptive. The purling wind embraced her as if it might lift her. A voice spoke on the wind, finding its way to her, calling her. Cautiously she raised one foot. She held it up, hesitating. She could feel the land pulling her, drawing her, expecting her to step onto it. And the wind sang her name.

Mi-sa put her foot down, feeling the tooth-edged saw grass swipe at her leg. The storm echoed, rumbling, threatening. Again through the swishing and lashing of the saw grass she distinctly heard the unearthly voice beckon. Words, sounds, spun from her tongue in a quiet song, and in a moment she felt the wind move her. Beneath her feet she could feel the spongy island of peat vibrate with the crack of thunder. Even through her closed eyelids she saw the lightning flash.

After taking a few more steps—or was it many?—she opened her eyes. Slashing rain stippled her with rolling drops until one blended into another. The young woman turned, facing each of the four directions, watching the rain and wind thrash the stubborn swords of sedge. The strong, dank smell of the peat rose to her nose. The voice of the wind summoned her, directed her, and Mi-sa raised her hands to the black sky, lifting her face to the rain. She stood mired in the soggy peat, singing to the clouds.

Miakka had seen her daughter walk toward the north edge of the mound. When she did not return and the storm seemed to grow fierce, Miakka went to see. Still standing within the village, she saw Mi-sa in the distance, her arms raised, not in supplication but in honor.

A loud crack of thunder followed a brilliant jagged bolt of lightning. Miakka shuddered. She didn't like the lightning. "Mi-sa," she called out, a little uncertain as to whether she should interfere. Mi-sa didn't seem to hear her. Miakka wished her daughter would get out of the storm. She worried that someone would see that Mi-sa had entered the territory of men. She didn't want any more altercations or squabbles surrounding her daughter. There had been enough. This was a new beginning, marking the fragile acceptance of Mi-sa, a woman shaman.

"Mi-sa!" she called again, louder this time. Miakka turned, shielding her eyes from the rain, looking back to see if anyone else had heard her call or had seen Mi-sa. She was relieved that she saw no one.

Miakka trotted closer, standing at the edge of the north line of the platforms. She raised one hand to her mouth to help channel her call, but just as her lips formed her daughter's name, she froze.

Above the howl of the wind and the splattering of the rain, she heard a thrumming, a buzzing, a vibration. As the sound filled her ears, she witnessed a bright blue-white light surround Mi-sa. The halo of light fanned out, and flickers of brilliance broke free like sparks from a green-wood fire.

Miakka stood awestruck. She watched as the light faded. Mi-sa looked down as she lowered her arms. Finally the young woman stood still, her body appearing taut and tense. Miakka watched the transformation as Mi-sa's shoulders relaxed and her body slackened.

The rain turned to drizzle, and the wind quieted. Mi-sa turned around and looked at her mother, then took a deep breath and walked closer to Miakka, closer to the invisible border that separated the men's exclusive land from the common land.

Miakka was anxious, fearing that someone still might see. "Come," she said, trying to hurry Mi-sa.

At last Mi-sa was close enough. The mother reached for her daughter's hand. Mi-sa stood on neutral ground, earth that was appropriate for women to occupy.

Miakka looked deep into her daughter's eyes; every time she did so she realized that there was a dimension to her daughter that she would never know. A part of her child belonged only to the spirits. And a part of her daughter would always be a child, the child born beneath the shooting star, the child whose father, the shaman, had named Mi-sa, Light in the Darkness.

Mi-sa's hand was cold. Miakka removed a skin she had wrapped around herself to keep dry and draped it over Mi-sa's shoulders.

"The Council has decided," Mi-sa said.

Connect With Lynn Armistead McKee Online:

Facebook: SholesandMoore.com

Website: www.sholesmoore.com